AN AWAKENING OF CONSCIOUSNESS IN AN EXPLOSION OF LITERATURE

One of the dramatic events in American writing has been the arrival of a galaxy of dazzling new talents with roots in the Mexican-American experience. At long last this rich and vital yet previously generally ignored part of our national life has been given eloquent voice.

In this enthralling anthology are the finest of this new literary generation—such talents as Ron Arias, Francisco Jiminéz, Hugo Martínez-Serros, Estela Portillo, Arturo Islas, Rogelio Gomez, Denise Chávez, and Genaro Gonzalez. They appear here with trail-blazing literary pioneers and Anglo contemporaries who have found the Mexican-American world a fertile terrain.

Complete with biographical notes, historical background, and a comprehensive introduction by Edward Simmen, the result is a major expansion of our vision—as illuminating as it is enjoyable.

Anthologies You'll Want to Read

NORTH OF THE RIO GRANDE

❦ ❦ ❦

The Mexican-American Experience in Short Fiction

Edited and with an Introduction by
Edward Simmen

A MENTOR BOOK

for Carolyn Osborn

MENTOR
Published by the Penguin Group
Penguin Books USA Inc., 375 Hudson Street,
New York, New York 10014, U.S.A.
Penguin Books Ltd, 27 Wrights Lane,
London W8 5TZ, England
Penguin Books Australia Ltd, Ringwood,
Victoria, Australia
Penguin Books Canada Ltd, 10 Alcorn Avenue,
Toronto, Ontario, Canada M4V 3B2
Penguin Books (N.Z.) Ltd, 182–190 Wairau Road,
Auckland 10, New Zealand

Penguin Books Ltd, Registered Offices:
Harmondsworth, Middlesex, England

First published by Mentor, an imprint of New American Library, a division
of Penguin Books USA Inc.

First Printing, January, 1992
10 9 8 7 6 5 4 3 2 1

Copyright © Edward Simmen, 1992
All rights reserved

For permissions to reprint these stories, please turn to pages 429–31.

 REGISTERED TRADEMARK—MARCA REGISTRADA

Library of Congress Cataloging Card Number: 91-62528

CONTENTS

❀ ❀ ❀

PREFACE

In 1967, I began searching for American short stories that revealed something about the Mexican-American experience so that I might include them in an advanced literature course. At the time, I was teaching at what is now the University of Texas at Pan American, located in the Rio Grande Valley in the city of Edinburg, just a few miles from the Texas-Mexico border. Eighty-five percent of my students were of Mexican descent, and it seemed only natural that such stories should be included in a course. At that time, there was no such thing as a Mexican-American Studies program similar to African-American Studies programs that were cropping up in colleges and universities across the nation.

In my search for stories, I first questioned my colleagues at Pan American and other institutions. Each time I got the same answer: "Flight" by John Steinbeck. A fine story it certainly is, but it was obvious that one story would not be enough. The search was on.

I decided to use a historical approach and trace Mexican-American characters as they appeared from the beginnings to the present. It was not easy; it took me three years of searching to gather enough titles for my course.

As I collected, I realized that the stories fell into three distinct categories. First, there were the early stories by Anglo writers such as Hamlin Garland, Bret Harte, and Gertrude Atherton which were typical of the late 1800s. For the most part, these stories were romantic renditions with strokes of local color offering characterizations of Mexicans and Mexican-Americans that were merely stereotypes rather than realistic portrayals. Of these early stories, the most effective was "The Mexican" by Jack London, published in 1911 in the *Saturday Evening Post*.

It is London at his best, railing out at a society which, given the "right" situation, could be vicious in its bigotry. Therein, he presented a very real conflict between Anglos and Mexicans that had never appeared before, a conflict of racial prejudice that exploded when the two cultures clashed.

The next category I defined as "realistic profiles." Included were two stories that appeared during the Depression decade of the thirties: Paul Horgan's "The Surgeon and the Nun" and Steinbeck's "Flight." There was also "With a Hey Nonny, Nonny." Published in 1936, it was one of the first short stories written by William Saroyan, the Armenian-American writer. The story is a minor milestone. As Antonio Marquez, literary critic, editor, and professor at the University of New Mexico, has pointed about, "Saroyan's existential story [about a violent uprising between farm owners and their migrant farm workers in Southern California] is notable because there is no stereotyping, either positive or negative . . . [and it] is free from the cheap sentimentality that often accompanies sympathetic views of the Mexican in twentieth-century fiction."

The last category defined as "From World War II to the Present: Portraits and Self-Portraits of the Awakening Minority," and divided into two parts: "The Anglo-American View" and "The Mexican-American View." The first part included stories which had first appeared in highly regarded quarterlies or magazines published by universities such as *The Southwest Review* at Southern Methodist University, *The Literary Review* at Fairleigh Dickinson University, *The Texas Quarterly* at the University of Texas at Austin, the *New Mexico Quarterly* at the University of New Mexico, and *The University of Kansas City Review*. These included stories by the well-known Ray Bradbury as well as writers who were relatively unknown such as Robert Granat, Richard Brown, George Seale, James Bowman, and Richard Dokey.

Then, I came face-to-face with my grestest problem: finding stories written by Mexican-Americans for the second part. They were the most difficult of all to locate. Most often I discovered them in the most accidental fashion.

One came from a colleague in the political science

department who game me a copy of *The Texas Observer*, a liberal, biweekly publication devoted primarily to Texas politics. The issue contained "The Hammon and the Beans," a story written by Américo Paredes, a professor of literature at the University of Texas at Austin. In addition, another source led me to a series of short sketches written by Mario Suarez that had appeared in a 1947 issue of the *Arizona Quarterly*. I also located a lively story, "Cecilia Rosas," that had been published in 1965 in the *New Mexico Quarterly*. When I wrote to the author, Amado Muro, complimenting him on his fine work, he responded by thanking me and remarking that he was merely a humble railroad worker in El Paso with a high school education who wrote short stories as a pastime.

But beyond those three stories, I found nothing. There were no stories by Mexican-Americans to be found in the national magazines like *Harper's*, *Atlantic*, or *Redbook*. Even the literary magazines and reviews sponsored by colleges and universities were not publishing the short fiction of Mexican-Americans.

Then, late in 1969, one of my Mexican-American students who knew of my research project surprised me by showing me an anthology published earlier that year, *El Espejo/The Mirror*, and several copies of a journal, *El Grito*, begun in 1967 and intended, according to the editors, "to provide a forum for Mexican-American self-definition and expression." Both were handsomely produced by Quinto Sol Publications at the University of California at Berkeley. Of course, both were what could be considered "regional productions" with limited distribution. Nevertheless, it became obvious to me that since the Anglo establishment was doing very little to encourage Mexican-American authors, the Mexican-American community at Berkeley was taking the matter into its own hands. But few people realized at the time how important the anthology and the journal would be nor how much the publishing house would affect the future of Mexican-American literature. From *El Espejo*, I selected Nick Vaca's "The Week in the Life of Manuel Hernández," and from the Spring 1968 number of *El Grito*, I took "The Coming of Zamora" by Philip Ortego, a professor of literature at the University of Texas at El Paso.

Finally, during the spring semester of 1969, I discovered in the student literary magazine at my own university another story: "Un Hijo del Sol." The author, Genaro Gonzalez, a former migrant worker, was a freshman in the school's honors program. Over the next few months, he rewrote and expanded the story.

Together, all of the stories that I had collected became the content for the first literature course taught in the Southwest that was devoted completely to the Mexican-American experience. Likewise, I realized that together they comprised an anthology like no other. I was also aware of the fact that, as a minority, Mexican-American students in colleges and universities throughout the West and Southwest were not only becoming more visible, they were becoming more vocal in their demands to have programs similar to other ethnic studies programs. They wanted a special identity. To the chagrin of many of their more conservative parents, older Mexican-Americans, including university professors, these active young people called themselves "Chicanos," a label which for some at the time had rather dubious and somewhat derogatory connotations.

On that basis, I wrote a critical introduction and, in February of 1970, I sent the manuscript, which I had entitled *The Mexican-American: From Caricature to Self-Portriat*, to be considered for publication, noting that no such anthology existed and the need for one was pressing.

The first fourteen times the manuscript was mailed out, it was returned with the publisher's regrets. The fifteenth publisher showed interest, but he advised me that it would not be published until 1975, the year which their marketing department had advised them would be "the Year of the Chicano." Then, I got a chance to offer my own "regrets" and asked for the return of the manuscript.

Granted, rejection slips or letters are always a great disappointment for any writer. However, what was truly disturbing was the obvious fact that not one publisher I contacted—the vast majority were established houses in the East—had any immediate interest in the Mexican-American experience or in the literature about it.

Persevering, on June 2, 1970, I sent it off for the sixteenth time, this time to New American Library. On August 3, 1970, an editor answered saying that they were all "quite enthusiastic about the proposed book." Few changes had to be made. Then, with a slightly altered title, *The Chicano: From Caricature to Self-Portrait*, the first anthology devoted to the Mexican-American was published in April 1971.

The anthology was reprinted five times, sold 150,000 copies, and stayed in print seventeen years. It became a mainstay of many college courses not only in literature but in sociology, anthropology, and psychology. For many readers, both in the United States and abroad, *The Chicano: From Caricature to Self-Portrait* was their first introduction to the Mexican-American.

When it finally went out of print in 1988, plans were initiated to bring out a new edition. However, it did not take long to realize that in twenty years a great deal had happened to the Mexican-American, especially the Mexican-American in short fiction. A revised edition would not suffice; a completely new collection was warranted. The result is *North of the Rio Grande: An Anthology of Mexican-American Short Fiction*.

As I have done in the past, I would like to mention more than just a few persons and organizations without whose advice and support this anthology would not have been completed. First are the librarians at several institutions, beginning with the excellent Benjamin Franklin Library in Mexico City, a division of the United States Information Service. Invaluable were two of its directors, Jesse Reinburg and Michael Pipkin, and several members of their staff, including Irma C. de Perez Monroy, the assistant librarian, and Berta Velasquez, Jorge Monroy, Rodrigro Rodriguez, Josefat Perez and Edmundo García. The librarians at the Galveston branch of Texas A and M University, where for several years I taught during the summer session, were always ready to hunt for and find whatever I needed, especially the director Natalie Weist and Diane Watson and Ramona Martinez, as well as several "Aggies" in the Learning Resource Center who helped do more than cure my disks of a recurring virus. Stephen Curley and Donald Willett, two members of the faculty, have been invaluable by carefully reviewing with red pen the introduction and biographies preceding each story.

Next, there are the director of the unique Rosenberg Library of Galveston, John Hyatt, and his executive secretary, Judy Young, and the experts at the Texas History Center: Lisa Lambert, Casey Greene, Margaret Schlanky, Julia Dunn, and my long-time companion in search of peanuts Lise Darst. The Rosenberg has always been central in my life since as a child I was taken there on Saturday mornings to listen to Miss Emma Lee, an institution in her own right, as she opened up for generations of children the wonderful world of books.

Important also to this publication are several persons at Texas Tech University who in April of 1989 invited me to deliver remarks on developments in Mexican-American fiction over the last two decades: Donald Haragan, Executive Vice-President, and Professors Wendell Aycock, Gary Elbow, Phil Dennis, and Roy Howard. Those lectures were the seeds that grew into this anthology. That visit also gave me the opportunity to be again with Joaquin Marcos Palacios of Chipas, Mexico, who at that time was completing his doctoral studies in computer science at Texas Tech. As well, I "seized the day" to renew a long overdue "graduate school" friendship with Nellie and Tom Langford, now the Associate Dean of the Graduate School at Tech.

Instrumental also in completing this anthology were several research grants provided me by the Institute for Advanced Studies/Instituto de Estudios Avanzados of the Universidad de las Americas. In particular I would like to thank the Rector of the University, Enrique Cardenas, Vice-Rectors Jorge Welty and Antonio Sanchez, Raul Fonseca, Director of I.D.E.A., and Sergio Diaz Moñtano, a former scholarship student transformed into the Chairman of the Department of Languages. Staff members who so often assisted me include Helia Solis, Juanita Trujillo, Leticia Bermudez, Marina Gonzalez, and Ana Berta Pinales.

I would also like to acknowledge Bruce Baker, a fellow survivor of graduate school currently with the University of Nebraska at Omaha, who aided me with the biography of Willa Cather; Ernestine N. Eger, respected literary critic, bibliographer, and member of the Spanish depart-

ment at Carthage College in Wisconsin, who gave me the
initial details that set me off on the wild chase to discover
María Cristina Mena; and Covelle Newcomb, whose
good memory filled in so many blanks about Mena's
adult life. Others to be thanked are old friends and new:
Aquiles S. Serdan, Joe Osborn, Enrique Rivera (no
longer lost in Central Park), Dee Simpson, Rebecca
Lightsey, Enrique Perez, Jose Luis Sánchez, Barbara and
Darrel Young. And Guadalupe Espinosa, she continues
to inspire. And how could I forget Luis Salinas, Marshall
Cedilot, Valerie Wilson, Carmen Lopez Blumenkron,
and a great friend to so many, the late Fred Weyrich.
Closer to home, I would like to mention two very good
friends who have long been and, I trust, will always be
near: Nancy McDonough and Meme Frankel Mackey.
And finally, three others who have helped to keep so
many memories alive and well, Mary Virginia Hinkley,
Teddie Latimer, and Sue Yeatman.

                                        —Edward Simmen
                                        Universidad de las Américas
                                        Cholula, Puebla, Mexico
                                        February 19, 1991

INTRODUCTION

❦ ❦ ❦

During the last two decades, an explosion has occurred in American literature, an explosion which, for a variety of reasons, has gone virtually unnoticed by the majority of mainstream American readers. However, more than ever before, Americans now have the opportunity to learn about a hitherto ignored but significant contribution to American culture: the Mexican-American experience.

A great deal of this newfound interest in Mexican-Americans—or Chicanos, as many prefer to call Americans of Mexican descent—is due to the fact that the country of Mexico and its people are each day becoming more and more important to the United States, primarily, of course, because of the fact that the two countries share a two-thousand-mile border. Because that border is virtually impossible to monitor, each day increasing numbers of Mexican nationals are crossing it, legally or illegally, to work in the United States at jobs that, for the most part, Americans disdain.

The number of Americans of Mexican descent has increased from 4.2 million in 1970 to over 12 million in 1990. Indeed, some analysts predict that the figure will inflate to 20 million by the year 2000, making Mexican-Americans the nation's largest minority. Along those lines, it may certainly surprise both Mexicans and Americans to learn that the city with the third largest population of Mexicans in the world is not a Mexican city at all, but is Los Angeles, California, ranking after Mexico City and Guadalajara.

Increasingly, Mexican-Americans are influencing American culture, bringing a fresh voice and vision to its literature. More and more Americans of Mexican birth or descent are writing, being published, and even

1

more important, being read. Mexican-American authors like Américo Paredes, Sandra Cisneros, and Arturo Islas are receiving critical praise and winning prestigous literary awards. Their novels, short stories, and poems explore the rich cultural heritage, and examine the everyday lives of Mexican-Americans long neglected by and forcibly excluded from Anglo culture. At the same time, Anglo writers are drawing upon their experiences in Mexican-American communities in their own fiction—something virtually unheard of in the past. Together, these Mexican-American and Anglo-American writers are bringing new themes and a new focus to American literature, offering readers a dual perspective on the Mexican-American experience: the Anglo on the outside looking in and the inside view from the too-seldom-heard Mexican-American.

Anglo Writers on the Mexican-American Experience

Included in this collection are eleven stories by Anglo writers—two of them using Spanish pseudonyms—which have been published over the last century and give a historical picture of the Mexican-American experience as seen from the outside.

In approaching the topic of the Anglo's role in communicating the Mexican-American experience, I asked three of the writers included in this anthology—each one a prize-winning author—to consider the question.

Natalie Petesch replied: "My love for Texas has been expressed many times in my work; it seems a natural extension of that love that I should speak of Mexico as well.

"I have always felt a deep communion of spirit with the Mexican people, not only because historically they were defeated by the cunning Cortes, nor because they were enslaved by the Spaniards, but also because their Indian past recalls for me some Jungian memory, perhaps, of the Russian steppes, where my own roots began.

" 'Ramón el Conejo' was inspired by an item which appeared in the Austin *Statesman* in 1964, describing what seemed to me the heroic attempt of a young boy who had tried—without anyone to help him—to reach the United States, where (he believed) if he worked like a man he would be paid like a man: a land where he believed he might prosper and send for his mother and little brother. It is a tale which has been repeated again and again in America, the dream of The Promised Land: the same dream that brought my own mother to Ellis Island. Ramón's story spoke to me all the more poignantly because my mother too—an illiterate immigrant—had crossed first the ocean, then half a continent, alone. And perhaps that is the mysterious and scared alembic of my love for Mexican children: in their longing to read and learn and be truly free. Perhaps it is my mother of whom I am writing; perhaps it is her ordeal which I am describing.

"It has now been over a quarter of a century since I wrote 'Ramón el Conejo.' At the time, I had not lived very long in Texas; I did not yet know any Spanish, and except for my sister-in-law, I did not know any Mexicans. Since then—I suppose in the wistful hope of becoming part of a large loving family, something unknown to me—I've written many Spanish stories. I've just finished a new collection of stories in which all the characters are Hispanic. But throughout these stories, I seem to see the image of an important woman following me, a woman who died before she could fulfill her dream of learning to read and write, a woman following me everywhere, with her passion, her yearning in the New World, her hand outstretched, her voice murmuring: *Una caridad, por amor de Dios.*"

Mary Gray Hughes, author of the award-winning story "The Judge," responded: "Every subject is fair game for every writer. Men write about women and women about men, even men in wars. The young write about the old and the old the young. Should Crane not have written about the Civil War, or Tolstoy about Anna?

"Mexican-Americans were a part of my life, like the Anglos around me, like the landscape of south Texas, where I was born. If I reflect on your question and step back from writing fiction, I can imagine one might say that the presence of two cultures, mixing slightly and holding apart more, shows up sharp differences between people. And, because I grew up close to both groups and knew both well, I was also aware of bone-marrow common traits in human nature. Out of that, with luck, fiction can be made."

Carolyn Osborn's comments started with a reference

to her short story included in this collection: "I did not begin 'Overlappings' in an effort to illustrate conflicts between Mexican-Americans and Anglos. I began it, instead, in a particular place, one I know well, an isolated small ranch in Central Texas.

"As in much of my work, the process was accretive. The isolation of the land, of the people, remained primary. Gradually, I began to use other conflicts. The one between Mexican-Americans and Anglos I had first witnessed when I came to Texas from Nashville, Tennessee, in 1946. In the south, one grew up conscious of Black versus White, but until I was twelve, I had never seen a Mexican-American.

"The degree of racial conflict seemed less severe. At school in a small Central Texas town, there were few. I can remember only one who graduated. People did speak of 'Meskins.'

"In the middle of this vast new place, English was sprinkled with "*Sí!*" and "*Buenos días*" and "*Adíos.*" Spanish was in the air. We studied it. Out of the decorous mouth of our teacher came, "*Soy, eres, es, somos, sois, son.*" We conjugated the present tense of irregular verbs on the blackboard. Although our streets were named Bridge and Main, the name of the river was Leon. We ate enchiladas, tacos, frijoles.

"We went to Uvalde to see an uncle, crossed the river to a border town. Wind-blown, dusty, poor, these towns still are the part of Mexico best known to many Texans. At thirteen, it was my first foreign country, exotic yet somehow familiar like the parrot a cousin smuggled home. Mexicans, of course, crossed the Rio Grande to us. I met some working at spring round-up at another uncle's ranch. A few of those men came from distances as great as Guanajuato. All of them were *mojados* (wetbacks or illegals) and they, as far as I knew, returned to Mexico.

"The Mexican-Americans who lived near our own ranch were shearers. A crew arrived every spring and fall to shear the goats. They were a part, I suppose, of a pastoral tradition which existed after the region was settled by Anglos long after the wars were won and lost. The shearers are still working.

"Nowadays, in most all rural lives in Texas, cities impinge, but how is one to escape provinciality—a state of mind that often leads to racism—if one wants to escape? My character Bernardo, the intelligent son of a shearer, returns to Mexico to live with a land-owning uncle. Here he receives a university education. At the same time, he becomes a member of a new class. The racial conflict apparent in the story, however, is not necessarily solved. For the younger generation, it was never especially great since they have known each other most of their lives. It simply ceased to exist for them. They have other problems now."

Racial conflict between Anglos and the Mexican-Americans is a common theme in the stories in this collection. Tension between Anglos and Mexican-Americans is the very foundation of Stephen Crane's "A Man and Some Others," the story that opens the collection, and the first short story to introduce Mexican-American characters into American literature.

Laden with offensive sterotypes, this story of an American sheepherder killed by Mexican *vaqueros* provoked an interesting reaction when it appeared in *The Century Magazine* in 1897. Crane sent a copy of the story to the police commissioner of New York City—he knew that the commissioner was familiar with his work because he had written Crane about *The Red Badge of Courage.* "For as much as I like your other books, I think I like that book the best," he said. However, the police commissioner found certain aspects of "A Man and Some Others" most disturbing, especially the death of the Anglo sheepherder. He urged Crane to write "another story of the frontiersman and the Mexican Greaser in which the frontiersman shall come out on top." The police commissioner felt that "it was more normal that way"! Crane's critical commissioner was none other than the Rough-Rider-to-be, Teddy Roosevelt. To his mind, no "Mexican Greaser" could get the best of an American adventurer, no matter how disreputable and unworthy the man. Nearly one hundred years later, the tension between Anglos and Mexican-Americans continues to be the subject of some of this country's most important writing.

Mexican-American Writers: A New Voice Emerges

The view from the inside is offered by seventeen writers, beginning with three stories set in Mexico by María

Cristina Mena, which appeared in two important monthly magazines in 1913. A brief summary of the history of the Mexican-American writer in American literature from Mena's early success to the present day is most revealing. Thirty-four years pass before another Mexican-American writer appears: Mario Suarez. His stories first appeared in 1947, not in a national magazine but rather in a scholarly journal, the respected *Arizona Quarterly* published by the University of Arizona, where Suarez was a student. Next is Américo Paredes, whose "Over the Waves Is Out" appeared in a 1953 issue of the *New Mexico Quarterly*, from the University of New Mexico, another important but scholarly publication with a limited reading public. Nine years later, in 1962, *Harper's Magazine* published Daniel Garza's "Saturday Belongs to the Palomía" after the *Altantic Monthly* rejected the story as being inappropriate. Apparently, the editors felt that their readers would not be interested in the lyrically told story of a young Mexican-American boy's first experiences with prejudice and guilt.

The works of Suarez, Paredes, and Garza are set, for the most part, in Mexican-American barrios and deal with typical Mexican-American themes and conflicts, whether they be conflicts which erupt within the family or barrio or conflicts which grow out of situations where Anglos and Mexican-Americans come into contact, conflicts that all too frequently result in a violent cultural clash.

During late fifties and early sixties, a few Mexican-American authors experienced limited success, such as Jose Antonio Villerreal, whose major work, *Pocho*, was published in 1959. John Rechy is perhaps the best-selling of Mexican-American authors, but he is an anomaly because since he did not write about the Mexican-Americans, he is not generally thought of as a Mexican-American writer. His first novel, *City of the Night*, was published in 1963, followed in 1967 by *Numbers*. Both attracted national attention. Several other novels followed and remain in print.

Until the mid-1960s, those writers who were able to publish fiction exploring the Mexican-American experience were merely isolated successes. Then in 1967 a major change took place with the appearance in California of a new publication that focused directly on the Mexican-American people and culture: *El Grito*, a quarterly journal published by Quinto Sol Publications at the University of California at Berkeley "to provide a forum for Mexican-American self-definition and expression." In 1969 that press made another major contribution by publishing *El Espejo/The Mirror*, the first anthology of literature written by Mexican-Americans, or Chicanos as the editors chose to refer to themselves. The literature included in these publications was not always critically praiseworthy, but Quinto Sol was breaking ground by providing an opportunity for Mexican-Americans, who were routinely ignored elsewhere, to publish.

The need for, as well as the value of, this type of magazine is made evident when one considers the experiences of Américo Paredes trying to publish his own short stories. Paredes recently commented on his writing and his effort to publish: "What fiction I have written was done in the thirties, forties, and fifties. Most of it remained unpublished because it did not appeal to the tastes of the times."

What Paredes means, of course, by "the taste of the times" is that during this period, the national magazines were not interested in publishing fiction about minority cultures. Only the university journals would take a chance and occasionally publish a story with a Mexican-American theme.

Much of Américo Paredes's fiction "is now lost or thrown away." Remarkably, one manuscript survived, the first draft of a novel, *George Washington Gomez*, that was begun in 1936 and finished four years later. Set during the Depression in a Texas city located at the mouth of the Rio Grande, it is the story of young Mexican-American child growing up in a barrio and suffering the often devastating effects of racial prejudice and internal familial conflicts. It is unfortunate that Paredes had to wait fifty years to see *George Washington Gomez* in print—Arte Publico Press published the novel in 1990 with a grant from the National Endowment for the Arts.

As one who had disappointing experiences in trying to find a reading public, Paredes comments on how different the cultural climate is today: "The emergence of a Chicano literature (and outlets for its publication) has been an important step in the recognition of the Mexican-American as a creative force in the varied fabric of North American culture." This literature could not have emerged without the pioneering efforts of Quinto Sol Publications, with its quarterly journal, *El Grito*, and anthology, *El Espejo/The Mirror*.

More than a few writers whose works are well-known today first appeared in these publications, including Tomás Rivera, Rolando Hinojosa-Smith, Estela Portillo, and Rudolfo Anaya.

The California publishing house took another important step forward when, in 1970, it awarded the first Quinto Sol Prize for literature to Tomas Rivera for his novel *. . . no se trago tierra/ . . . and the earth did not part*. The following year the award went to Rudolfo Anaya's *Bless Me Ultima*. The novel has sold over 200,000 copies, earning it the distinction of being the best-selling of recent fiction written by a Mexican-American. In 1972, the third Premio Quinto Sol was presented to Rolando Hinojo-sa-Smith for *Estampas del valle y ostras obras/Sketches of the Valley and Other Works*. All three prize-winning books were first novels. Also, in 1972, a special Quinto Sol award for literature was presented to Estela Portillo for an early version of *The Day of the Swallows*, a drama in three acts, which was first published by Quinto Sol in 1971. Portillo had edited the first issue of *El Grito* dedicated solely to the writing of Mexican-American women.

The seventies gave rise to a variety of Chicano literary prizes and small presses and magazines. The First Chicano Literary Contest was established in 1971, sponsored by the Spanish and Portuguese Department at the University of California at Irvine. The winner of the first award was Ron Arias for "The Wetback"—included in this collection. That story became a chapter in his brilliant first novel, *The Road to Tamazuchale*, which critic Peter Beagle praised as a "marvelous and auspicious debut!" and Tomas Rivera remarked that it gave "a most creative dimension" to Chicano literature. Finding a publisher was not easy. When the novel finally did appear in 1975, this praiseworthy effort came out as an issue of the literary magazine *West Coast Poetry Review* and was paid for in part by the Coordinating Council of Little

Magazines and the National Endowment for the Arts. If publishers were indifferent to Arias's novel, critics were not—*The Road to Tamazunchale* was nominated for the National Book Award. (The novel has recently been brought back into print by the Bilingual Review/Press with a scholarly introduction by Eliud Martinez and a bibliography of work by and about Ron Arias by Ernestine N. Eger.)

Unlike the Quinto Sol Prize, which disappeared in the mid-1970s along with *El Grito* and Quinto Sol Publications, the Chicano Literary Contest at the University of California at Irvine has flourished, with the sixteenth annual award going to Carlos Nicolas Flores in 1990, represented here with his story "Smeltertown."

Another journal destined to become of great importance to Hispanic writers appeared in 1972 at the University of Indiana: *Revista Chicano-Riquena*. Seven years later, the publishers of *Revista* founded the Arte Publico Press, and a year later moved to the University of Houston. In 1986, the quarterly changed its name to *The Americas Review* in order to reflect more accurately the widening scope of the journal. Arte Publico Press has published works by Tomás Rivera and Rudolfo Anaya, and also by a number of writers included in this collection: Denise Chávez, Lionel García, Rolando Hinojosa-Smith, Sandra Cisneros, Hugo Martínez-Serros, Genaro Gonzalez, and Estela Portillo.

Regional presses and little magazines will always have an essential and prominent place in publishing the works of new as well as established authors. But ultimately what Mexican-American writers want is what any other writer wants: to be recognized and read by the general public. Toward that end, they want most to have access to the more prestigious publishing houses whose books are widely distributed and reviewed in major newspapers, magazines, and journals. As Mexican-American writers break out of the confines of regional presses and into the literary mainstream, they are winning a wider and more diverse audience. For example, Sandra Cisneros's collection of lyrical sketches *The House on Mango Street*, which was originally published by Arte Publico Press in 1984, was reissued in 1991 by Random House to great acclaim. Arturo Islas's award-winning novel, *The Rain*

God, was published by Alexandrian Press in 1984, but the second volume of the trilogy about the Angel family, *Migrant Souls*, was published by William Morrow.

In addition, national magazines such as *Redbook, The New York Times Magazine, The New Yorker, Rolling Stone, Harper's, The Threepenny Review,* and *Alantic,* are now publishing literature by Mexican-Americans such as Sandra Cisneros, Rogelio Gomez, and Dagoberto Gilb as well as stories by Anglos who write about the Mexican-American experience, Mary Gray Hughes, Natalie Petesch, Carolyn Osborn, and Alice Marriott, among them.

However, the best evidence that the Mexican-American writer has, indeed, "arrived" appears in the form of Volume 82 of the *Dictionary of Literary Biography,* entitled: *Chicano Writers, First Series.* Published in 1989, the work was edited by two respected scholars of Mexican-American literature, Francisco Lomeli and Carl Shirley, who note in their preface that the work "marks an important step in the evolution of literature and criticism. Although much research has been published in the field over the last few years, this volume gathers for the first time fifty-two biographical/critical essays representing a broad cross section of authors who have contributed to the growing body of Chicano literature." Included are fifty-two biographies of poets, playwrights, novelists, and writers of short fiction written by scholars who, as Luis Leal notes in the foreword to the volume, have presented objective, accurate, and balanced portraits that "demonstrate that Chicano literary criticism has established a solid foundation."

So much has happened during the last two decades. The infrequent appearances of stories by Mexican-American authors in the forties, fifties, and sixties have been followed by an outpouring of literary works from Mexican-Americans in the seventies, eighties, and nineties. The Mexican-American has now been recognized as, in the words of Américo Paredes, "a creative force in the varied fabric of North American culture." The short stories included in *North of the Rio Grande,* indeed, confirm the idea that the Mexican-American experience—seen from both inside and out—fits comfortably into American literature and adds one more dimension to the ever-increasing complexity of the American character and culture.

STEPHEN CRANE

❦ ❦ ❦

Stephen Crane (1871–1900) was one of the first American writers to use Mexican characters in a short story. The author of The Red Badge of Courage *was, in fact, the first American writer to visit Mexico, which he did in March 1895, and he drew upon his experiences south of the border in several stories and essays. "A Man and Some Others" is one of those stories. Set in the desolate range of Southwestern Texas, the story actually has its origins in Mexico. Crane's biographer, R.W. Stallman, writes that Crane, twenty-four years old at the time, had purchased "some expensive equipment and headed for the badlands with a servant and a horse. In some Mexican lodging house, a Bowery fellow turned sheepherder told him that a band of Mexicans had tried to run him off his land and that he had shot them down." This situation gave Crane the idea for "A Man and Some Others" but, as Stallman points out, "he reverses it by having the former Bowery saloon-bouncer shot down by the Mexicans." The story is classic Crane: Tension increases as two irreconcilable forces move closer and closer to the inevitable collision. "A Man and Some Others" depicts the conflict that arises when the Mexicans—whose ancestors had settled the region two centuries before—find their existence being threatened by Anglo-American settlers. These American migrants were well-armed not only with guns but also with an uncompromising belief in their "manifest destiny." These were American pioneers who had since the mid-nineteenth century been migrating westward in great numbers, seizing land at will, displacing whoever was there, be it native American Indians or Mexican-American landowners.*

In "A Man and Some Others" we get the first taste in American literature of what happens when Mexican- and Anglo-Americans meet in a head-on confrontation. Crane describes a clash between Mexican settlers and an American migrant. Later the roles would be reversed, the American being the settler and the Mexican the migrant. Times and situations might change, but the clash of the two cultures—Mexican and Anglo—has for the most part been an explosive one.

A Man and Some Others

I

Dark mesquite spread from horizon to horizon. There was no house or horsemen from which a mind could evolve a city or a crowd. The world was declared to be a desert and unpeopled. Sometimes, however, on days when no heat mist arose, a blue shape, dim, of the substance of a specter's veil, appeared in the southwest, and a pondering sheepherder might remember that there were mountains.

In the silence of these plains the sudden and childish banging of a tin pan could have made an iron-nerved man leap into the air. The sky was ever flawless; the maneuvering of clouds was an unknown pageant; but at times a sheepherder could see, miles away, the long white streamers of dust rising from the feet of another's flock, and the interest became intense.

Bill was arduously cooking his dinner, bending over the fire and toiling like a blacksmith. A movement, a flash of strange color perhaps, off in the bushes, caused him to suddenly turn his head. Presently he arose, and, shading his eyes with his hand, stood motionless and gazing. He perceived at last a Mexican sheepherder winding through the brush toward his camp.

"Hello!" shouted Bill.

The Mexican made no answer, but came steadily forward until he was within some twenty yards. There he paused and, folding his arms, drew himself up in the manner affected by the villain in the play. His serape muffled the lower part of his face, and his great sombrero shaded his brow. Being unexpected and also silent, he had something of the quality of an apparition; moreover, it was clearly his intention to be mystic and sinister.

The American's pipe, sticking carelessly in the corner of his mouth, was twisted until the wrong side was uppermost, and he held his frying pan poised in the air. He surveyed with evident surprise this apparition in the mesquite. "Hello, José!" he said. "What's the matter?"

The Mexican spoke with the solemnity of funeral tollings: "Beel, you mus' geet off range. We want you geet off range. We no like. Un'erstan'? We no like."

"What you talking about?" said Bill. "No like what?"

"We no like you here. Un'erstan? Too mooch. You mus' geet out. We no like. Un'erstan'?"

"Understand? No; I don't know what the blazes you're gittin' at." Bill's eyes wavered in bewilderment, and his jaw fell. "I must git out? I must git off the range? What you givin' us?"

The Mexican unfolded his serape with his small yellow hand. Upon his face was then to be seen a smile that was gently, almost caressingly murderous. "Beel," he said, "git out!"

Bill's arm dropped until the frying pan was at his knee. Finally he turned again toward the fire. "Go on, you doggone little yaller rat!" he said over his shoulder. "You fellers can't chase me off this range. I got as much right here as anybody."

"Beel," answered the other in a vibrant tone, thrusting his head forward and moving one foot, "you geet out or we keel you."

"Who will?" said Bill.

"I—and the others." The Mexican tapped his breast gracefully.

Bill reflected for a time, and then he said: "You ain't got no manner of licence to warn me off'n this range, and I won't move a rod. Understand? I've got rights, and I suppose if I don't see 'em through, no one is likely to give me a good hand and help me lick you fellers, since I'm the only white man in half a day's ride. Now, look; if you fellers try to rush this camp, I'm goin' to plug about fifty per cent of the gentlemen present, sure. I'm goin' in for trouble, an' I'll git a lot of you. 'Nuther thing: if I was a fine valuable cabballero like you, I'd stay in the rear till the shootin' was done, because I'm goin' to make a particular p'int of shootin' you through the chest." He grinned affably, and made a gesture of dismissal.

As for the Mexican, he waved his hands in a consummate expression of indifference. "Oh, all right," he said. Then, in a tone of deep menace and glee, he added: "We will keel you eef you no geet. They have decide'."

"They have, have they?" said Bill. "Well, you tell them to go to the devil!"

II

Bill had been a mine owner in Wyoming, a great man, an aristocrat, one who possessed unlimited credit in the saloons down the gulch. He had the social weight that could interrupt a lynching or advise a bad man of the particular merits of a remote geographical point. However, the fates exploded the toy balloon with which they had amused Bill, and on the evening of the same day he was a professional gambler with ill fortune dealing him unspeakable irritation in the shape of three big cards whenever another fellow stood pat. It is well here to inform the world that Bill considered his calamities of life all dwarfs in comparison with the excitement of one particular evening when three kings came to him with criminal regularity against a man who always filled a straight. Later he became a cowboy, more weirdly abandoned than if he had never been an aristocrat. By this time all that remained of his former splendor was his pride, or his vanity, which was one thing which need not have remained. He killed the foreman of the ranch over an inconsequent matter as to which of them was a liar, and the midnight train carried him eastward. He became a brakeman on the Union Pacific, and really gained high honors in the hobo war that for many years has devastated the beautiful railroads of our country. A creature of ill fortune himself, he practised all the ordinary cruelties upon these other creatures of ill fortune. He was of so fierce a mien that tramps usually surrendered at once whatever coin or tobacco they had in their possession; and if afterward he kicked them from the train, it was only because this was recognized treachery of the war upon the hoboes. In a famous battle fought in Nebraska in 1879, he would have achieved a lasting distinction if it had not been for a deserter from the United States army. He was at the head of a heroic and sweeping charge which really broke the power of the hoboes in that county for three months; he had already worsted four tramps with his own coupling stick, when a stone thrown by the ex-third-baseman of F Troop's nine laid him flat on the prairie, and later enforced a stay in the hospital in Omaha. After his recovery he engaged with other railroads, and shuffled cars in countless yards. An order to strike came upon him in Michigan, and afterward the vengeance of the railroad pursued him until he assumed a name. This mask is like the darkness in which the burglar chooses to move. It destroys many of the healthy fears. It is a small thing, but it eats that which we call our conscience. The conductor of No. 419 stood in the caboose within two feet of Bill's nose and called him a liar. Bill requested him to use a milder term. He had not bored the foreman of Tin Can Ranch with any such request, but had killed him with expedition. The conductor seemed to insist, and so Bill let the matter drop.

He became the bouncer of a saloon on the Bowery in New York. Here most of his fights were as successful as had been his brushes with the hoboes in the West. He gained the complete admiration of the four clean bartenders who stood behind the great and glittering bar. He was an honored man. He nearly killed Bad Hennessy, who, as a matter of fact, had more reputation than ability, and his fame moved up the Bowery and down the Bowery.

But let a man adopt fighting as his business, and the thought grows constantly within him that it is his business to fight. These phrases became mixed in Bill's mind precisely as they are here mixed; and let a man get this idea in his mind, and defeat begins to move toward him over the unknown ways of circumstance. One summer night three sailors from the U.S.S. *Seattle* sat in the saloon drinking and attending to other people's affairs in an amiable fashion. Bill was a proud man since he had thrashed so many citizens, and it suddenly occurred to him that the loud talk of the sailors was very offensive. So he swaggered upon their attention and warned them that the saloon was the flowery abode of peace and gentle silence. They glanced at him in surprise, and without a moment's pause consigned him to a worse place than any stoker of them knew. Whereupon he flung one of them through the side door before the others could prevent it. On the sidewalk there was a short struggle, with many hoarse epithets in the air, and then Bill slid into the saloon again. A frown of false rage was upon his brow, and he strutted like a savage king. He took a long yellow night stick from behind the lunch counter and started importantly toward the main doors to see that the incensed seamen did not again enter.

The ways of sailormen are without speech, and, together in the street, the three sailors exchanged no word, but they moved at once. Landsmen would have required three years of discussion to gain such unanimity. In silence, and immediately, they seized a long piece of scantling that lay handy. With one forward to guide the battering ram and with two behind him to furnish the power, they made a beautiful curve and came down like the Assyrians on the front door of that saloon.

Strange and still strange are the laws of fate. Bill, with his kingly frown and his long night stick, appeared at precisely that moment in the doorway. He stood like a statue of victory; his pride was at its zenith; and in the same second this atrocious piece of scantling punched him in the bulwarks of his stomach, and he vanished like a mist. Opinions differed as to where the end of the scantling landed him, but it was ultimately clear that it landed him in southwestern Texas, where he became a sheepherder.

The sailors charged three times upon the plate glass front of the saloon, and when they had finished, it looked as if it had been the victim of a rural fire company's success in saving it from the flames. As the proprietor of the place surveyed the ruins, he remarked that Bill was a very zealous guardian of property. As the ambulance surgeon surveyed Bill, he remarked that the wound was really an excavation.

III

As his Mexican friend tripped blithely away, Bill turned with a thoughtful face to his frying pan and his fire. After dinner he drew his revolver from its scarred old holster and examined every part of it. It was the revolver that had dealt death to the foreman, and it had also been in free fights in which it had dealt death to several or none. Bill loved it because its allegiance was more than that of man, horse, or dog. It questioned neither social nor moral position; it obeyed alike the saint and the assassin. It was the claw of the eagle, the tooth of the lion, the poison of the snake; and when he swept it from its holster, this minion smote where he listed, even to the battering of a far penny. Wherefore it was his dearest possession, and was not to be exchanged in southwestern Texas for a handful of rubies, nor even the shame and homage of the conductor of No. 419.

During the afternoon he moved through his monotony of work and leisure with the same air of deep meditation. The smoke of his suppertime fire was curling across the shadowy sea of mesquite when the instinct of the plainsman warned him that the stillness, the desolation, was again invaded. He saw a motionless horseman in black outline against the pallid sky. The silhouette displayed serape and sombrero, and even the Mexican spurs as large as pies. When this black figure began to move toward the camp, Bill's hand dropped to his revolver.

The horseman approached until Bill was enabled to see pronounced American features and a skin too red to grow on a Mexican face. Bill released his grip on his revolver.

"Hello!" called the horseman.

"Hello!" answered Bill.

The horseman cantered forward. "Good evening," he said, as he again drew rein.

"Good evinin'," answered Bill, without committing himself by too much courtesy.

For a moment the two men scanned each other in a way that is not ill-mannered on the plains, where one is in danger of meeting horsethieves or tourists.

Bill saw a type which did not belong in the mesquite. The young fellow had invested in some Mexican trappings of an expensive kind. Bill's eyes searched the outfit for some sign of craft, but there was none. Even with his local regalia, it was clear that the young man was of a far, black Northern city. He had discarded the enormous stirrups of his Mexican saddle; he used the small English stirrup, and his feet were thrust forward until the steel tightly gripped his ankles. As Bill's eyes traveled over the stranger, they lighted suddenly upon the stirrups and the thrust feet, and immediately he smiled in a friendly way. No dark purpose could dwell in the innocent heart of a man who rode thus on the plains.

As for the stranger, he saw a tattered individual with a tangle of hair and beard, and with a complexion turned brick-color from the sun and whiskey. He saw a pair of eyes that at first looked at him as the wolf looks at the wolf, and then became childlike, almost timid, in their glance. Here was evidently a man who had often stormed the iron walls of the city of success, and who now sometimes valued himself as the rabbit values his prowess.

The stranger smiled genially and sprang from his horse. "Well, sir, I suppose you will let me camp here with you tonight?"

"Eh?" said Bill.

"I suppose you will let me camp here with you tonight?"

Bill for a time seemed too astonished for words. "Well," he answered, scowling in inhospitable annoyance, "well, I don't believe this here is a good place to camp tonight, mister."

The stranger turned quickly from his saddle girth.

"What?" he said in surprise. "You don't want me here? You don't want me to camp here?"

Bill's feet scuffled awkwardly, and he looked steadily at a cactus plant. "Well, you see, mister," he said, "I'd like your company well enough, but—you see, some of these here greasers are goin' to chase me off the range tonight; and while I might like a man's company all right, I couldn't let him in for no such game when he ain't got nothin' to do with the trouble."

"Going to chase you off the range?" cried the stranger.

"Well, they said they were goin' to do it," said Bill.

"And—great heavens!—will they kill you, do you think?"

"Don't know. Can't tell till afterwards. You see, they take some feller that's alone like me, and then they rush his camp when he ain't quite ready for 'em, and ginerally plug 'im with a sawed-off shotgun load before he has a chance to git at 'em. They lay around and wait for their

chance, and it comes soon enough. Of course a feller
alone like me has got to let up watching some time.
Maybe they ketch 'im asleep. Maybe the feller gits tired
waiting, and goes out in broad day, and kills two or three
just to make the whole crowd pile on him and settle the
thing. I heard of a case like that once. It's awful hard on
a man's mind—to git a gang after him."

"And so they're going to rush your camp tonight?"
cried the stranger. "How do you know? Who told you?"

"Feller come and told me."

"And what are you going to do? Fight?"

"Don't see nothin' else to do," answered Bill, gloom-
ily, still staring at the cactus plant.

There was a silence. Finally the stranger burst out in
an amazed cry. "Well, I never heard of such a thing in
my life! How many of them are there?"

"Eight," answered Bill. "And now look-a here: you
ain't got no manner of business foolin' around here just
now, and you might better lope off before dark. I don't
ask no help in this here row. I know your happening
along here just now don't give me no call on you, and
you'd better hit the trail."

"Well, why in the name of wonder don't you go get
the sheriff?" cried the stranger.

"Oh, hell!" said Bill.

IV

Long, smoldering clouds spread in the western sky,
and to the east silver mists lay on the purple gloom of
the wilderness.

Finally, when the great moon climbed the heavens and
cast its ghastly radiance upon the bushes, it made a new
and more brilliant crimson of the campfire, where the
flames capered merrily through its mesquite branches,
filling the silence with the five chorus, an ancient melody
which surely bears a message of the inconsequence of
individual tragedy—a message that is in the boom of the
sea, the silver of the wind through the grass-blades, the
silken clash of hemlock boughs.

No figures moved in the rosy space of the camp, and
the search of the moonbeams failed to disclose a living
thing in the bushes. There was no owl-faced clock to

chant the weariness of the long silence that brooded upon the plain.

The dew gave the darkness under the mesquite a velvet quality that made air seem nearer to water, and no eye could have seen through it the black things that moved like monster lizards toward the camp. The branches, the leaves, that are fain to cry out when death approaches in the wilds, were frustrated by these mystic bodies gliding with the finesse of the escaping serpent. They crept forward to the last point where assuredly no frantic attempt of the fire could discover them, and there they paused to locate the prey. A romance relates the tale of the black cell hidden deep in the earth, where, upon entering, one sees only the little eyes of snakes fixing him in menaces. If a man could have approached a certain spot in the bushes, he would not have found it romantically necessary to have his hair rise. There would have been a sufficient expression of horror in the feeling of the death-hand at the nape of his neck and in his rubber knee joints.

Two of these bodies finally moved toward each other until for each there grew out of the darkness a face placidly smiling with tender dreams of assassination. "The fool is alseep by the fire, God be praised!" The lips of the other widened in a grin of affectionate appreciation of the fool and his plight. There was some signaling in the gloom, and then began a series of subtle rustlings, interjected often with pauses during which no sound arose but the sound of faint breathing.

A bush stood like a rock in the stream of firelight, sending its long shadow backward. With painful caution the little company traveled along this shadow, and finally arrived at the rear of the bush. Through its branches they surveyed for a moment of comfortable satisfaction a form in a gray blanket extended on the ground near the fire. The smile of joyful anticipation fled quickly, to give place to a quiet air of business. Two men lifted shotguns with much of the barrels gone, and, sighting these weapons through the branches, pulled trigger together.

The noise of the explosions roared over the lonely mesquite as if these guns wished to inform the entire world; and as the gray smoke fled, the dodging company in back of the bush saw the blanketed form twitching.

Whereupon they burst out in chorus in a laugh, and arose as merry as a lot of banqueters. They gleefully gestured congratulations, and strode bravely into the light of the fire.

Then suddenly a new laugh rang from some unknown spot in the darkness. It was a fearsome laugh of ridicule, hatred, ferocity. It might have been demoniac. It smote them motionless in their gleeful prowl, as the stern voice from the sky smites the legendary malefactor. They might have been a weird group in wax, the light of the dying fire on their yellow faces and shining athwart their eyes turned toward the darkness whence might come the unknown and the terrible.

The thing in the gray blanket no longer twitched; but if the knives in their hands had been thrust toward it, each knife was now drawn back, and its owner's elbow was thrown upward, as if he expected death from the clouds.

This laugh had so chained their reason that for a moment they had no wit to flee. They were prisoners to their terror. Then suddenly the belated decision arrived, and with bubbling cries they turned to run; but at that instant there was a long flash of red in the darkness, and with the report one of the men shouted a bitter shout, spun once, and tumbled headlong. The thick bushes failed to impede the rout of the others.

The silence returned to the wilderness. The tired flames faintly illumined the blanketed thing and the flung corpse of the marauder, and sang the fire chorus, the ancient melody which bears the message of the inconsequence of human tragedy.

V

"Now you are worse off than ever," said the young man, dry-voiced and awed.

"No, I ain't," said Bill, rebelliously. "I'm one ahead."

After reflection, the stranger remarked, "Well, there's seven more."

They were cautiously and slowly approaching the camp. The sun was flaring its first warming rays over the gray wilderness. Upreared twigs, prominent branches, shone with golden light, while the shadows under the mesquite were heavily blue.

Suddenly the stranger uttered a frightened cry. He had arrived at a point whence he had, through openings in the thicket, a clear view of a dead face.

"Gosh!" said Bill, who at the next instant had seen the thing; "I thought at first it was that there José. That would have been queer, after what I told 'im yesterday."

They continued their way, the stranger wincing in his walk, and Bill exhibiting considerable curiosity.

The yellow beams of the new sun were touching the grim hues of the dead Mexcian's face, and creating there an inhuman effect which made his countenance more like a mask of dulled brass. One hand, grown curiously thinner, had been flung out regardlessly to a cactus bush.

Bill walked forward and stood looking respectfully at the body. "I know that feller; his name is Miguel. He—"

The stranger's nerves might have been in that condition when there is no backbone to the body, only a long groove. "Good heavens!" he exclaimed, much agitate; "don't speak that way!"

"What way?" said Bill. "I only said his name was Miguel."

After a pause the stranger said: "Oh, I know; but—" He waved his hand. "Lower your voice, or something. I don't know. This part of the business rattles me, don't you see?"

"Oh, all right," replied Bill, bowing to the other's mysterious mood. But in a moment he burst out violently and loud in the most extraordinary profanity, the oaths winging from him as the sparks go from the funnel.

He had been examining the contents of the bundled gray blanket, and he had brought forth, among other things, his frying pan. It was now only a rim with a handle; the Mexican volley had centered upon it. A Mexican shotgun of the abbreviated description is ordinarily loaded with flatirons, stove-lids, lead pipe, old horseshoes, sections of chain, window weights, railroad sleepers and spikes, dumbbells, and any other junk which may be at hand. When one of these loads encounters a man vitally, it is likely to make an impression upon him, and a cooking utensil may be supposed to subside before such an assault of curiosities.

Bill held high his desecrated frying pan, turning it this way and that way. He swore until he happened to note the absence of the stranger. A moment later he saw him leading his horse from the bushes. In silence and sullenly the young man went about saddling the animal. Bill said, "Well, goin' to pull out?"

The stranger's hands fumbled uncertainly at the throat-latch. Once he exclaimed irritably, blaming the buckle for the trembling of his fingers. Once he turned to look at the dead face with the light of the morning sun upon it. At last he cried, "Oh, I know the whole thing was all square enough—couldn't be squarer—but—somehow or other, that man there takes the heart out of me." He turned his troubled face for another look. "He seems to be all the time calling me a—he makes me feel like a murderer."

"But," said Bill, puzzling, "you didn't shoot him, mister; I shot him."

"I know; but I feel that way, somehow. I can't get rid of it."

Bill considered for a time; then he said diffidently, "Mister, you're an eddycated man, ain't you?"

"What?"

"You're what they call a—a eddycated man, ain't you?"

The young man, perplexed, evidently had a question upon his lips, when there was a roar of guns, bright flashes, and in the air such hooting and whistling as would come from a swift flock of steam boilers. The stranger's horse gave a mighty, convulsive spring, snorting wildly in its sudden anguish, fell upon its knees, scrambled afoot again, and was away in the uncanny death-run known to men who have seen the finish of brave horses.

"This comes from discussin' things," cried Bill, angrily. He had thrown himself flat on the ground facing the thicket whence had come the firing. He could see the smoke winding over the bush tops. He lifted his revolver, and the weapon came slowly up from the ground and poised like the glittering crest of a snake. Somewhere on his face there was a kind of a smile, cynical, wicked, deadly, of a ferocity which at the same time had brought a deep flush to his face, and had caused two upright lines to glow in his eyes.

"Hello, José!" he called, amiable for satire's sake. "Got your old blunderbusses loaded up again yet?"

The stillness had returned to the plain. The sun's brilliant rays swept over the sea of mesquite, painting the far mists of the west with faint rosy light, and high in the air some great bird fled toward the south.

"You come out here," called Bill, again addressing the landscape, "and I'll give you some shootin' lessons. That ain't the way to shoot." Receiving no reply, he began to invent epithets and yell them at the thicket. He was something of a master of insult, and, moreover, he dived into his memory to bring forth imprecations tarnished with age, unused since fluent Bowery days. The occupation amused him, and sometimes he laughed so that it was uncomfortable for his chest to be against the ground.

Finally the stranger, prostrate near him, said wearily, "Oh, they've gone."

"Don't you believe it," replied Bill, sobering swiftly. "They're there yet—every man of 'em."

"How do you know?"

"Because I do. They won't shake us so soon. Don't put your head up, or they'll get you, sure."

Bill's eyes, meanwhile, had not wavered from their scrutiny of the thicket in front. "They're there, all right; don't forget it. Now you listen." So he called out: "José! Ojo, José! Speak up, *hombre*! I want have talk. Speak up, you yaller cuss, you!"

Whereupon a mocking voice from off in the bushes said, "Señor?"

"There," said Bill to his ally; "didn't I tell you? The whole batch." Again he lifted his voice. "José—look— ain't you gittin' kinder tired? You better go home, you fellers, and git some rest."

The answer was a sudden furious chatter of Spanish, eloquent with hatred, calling down upon Bill all the calamities which life holds. It was as if some one had suddenly enraged a cageful of wildcats. The spirits of all the revenges which they had imagined were loosened at this time, and filled the air.

"They're in a holler," said Bill, chuckling, "or there'd be shootin'."

Presently he began to grow angry. His hidden enemies called him nine kinds of coward, a man who could fight only in the dark, a baby who would run from the shadows of such noble Mexican gentlemen, a dog that sneaked. They described the affair of the previous night, and informed him of the base advantage he had taken of their friend. In fact, they in all sincerity endowed him with every quality which he no less earnestly believed them to possess. One could have seen the phrases bite him as he lay there on the ground fingering his revolver.

VI

It is sometimes taught that men do the furious and desperate thing from an emotion that is as even and placid as the thoughts of a village clergyman on Sunday afternoon. Usually, however, it is to be believed that a panther is at the time born in the heart, and that the subject does not resemble a man picking mulberries.

"B' Gawd!" said Bill, speaking as from a throat filled with dust, "I'll go after 'em in a minute."

"Don't you budge an inch!" cried the stranger, sternly. "Don't you budge!"

"Well," said Bill, glaring at the bushes—"well—"

"Put your head down!" suddenly screamed the stranger, in white alarm. As the guns roared, Bill uttered a loud grunt, and for a moment leaned panting on his elbow, while his arm shook like a twig. Then he upreared like a great and bloody spirit of vengeance, his face lighted with the blaze of his last passion. The Mexicans came swiftly and in silence.

The lightning action of the next few moments was of the fabric of dreams to the stranger. The muscular struggle may not be real to the drowning man. His mind may be fixed on the far, straight shadows in back of the stars, and the terror of them. And so the fight, and his part in it, had to the stranger only the quality of a picture half drawn. The rush of feet, the spatter of shots, the cries, the swollen faces seen like masks on the smoke, resembled a happening of the night.

And yet afterward certain lines, forms, lived out so strongly from the incoherence that they were always in his memory.

He killed a man, and the thought went swiftly by him, like the feather on the gale, that it was easy to kill a man.

Moreover, he suddenly felt for Bill, this grimy sheep-herder, some deep form of idolatry. Bill was dying, and the dignity of last defeat, the superiority of him who stands in his grave, was in the pose of the lost sheepherder.

The stranger sat on the ground idly mopping the sweat and powder stain from his brow. He wore the gentle idiot smile of an aged beggar as he watched three Mexicans limping and staggering in the distance. He noted at this time that one who still possessed a serape had from it none of the grandeur of the cloaked Spaniard, but that against the sky the silhouette resembled a cornucopia of childhood's Christmas.

They turned to look at him, and he lifted his weary arm to menace them with his revolver. They stood for a moment banded together, and hooted curses at him.

Finally he arose and, walking some paces, stooped to loosen Bill's gray hands from a throat. Swaying as if slightly drunk, he stood looking down into the still face.

Struck suddenly with a thought, he went about with dulled eyes on the ground, until he plucked his gaudy blanket from where it lay, dirty from trampling feet. He dusted it carefully, and then returned and laid it over Bill's form. There he again stood motionless, his mouth just agape and the same stupid glance in his eyes, when all at once he made a gesture of fright and looked wildly about him.

He had almost reached the thicket when he stopped, smitten with alarm. A body contorted, with one arm stiff in the air, lay in his path. Slowly and warily he moved around it, and in a moment the bushes, nodding and whispering, their leaf-faces turned toward the scene behind him, swung and swung again into stillness and the peace of the wilderness.

WILLA CATHER

❀ ❀ ❀

Willa Cather (1873–1947) was born in Virginia, but her family soon moved to a ranch near Red Cloud, Nebraska, and Cather lived much of her life in the Midwest. Her understanding of the Midwest, its farms and ranches and the pioneering spirit of the immigrant settlers—Swedes, Norwegians, French-Canadians, Czeches, Germans and the occasional Mexican ranch hand—forms the substance of most of her fiction.

"The Dance at the Chaveliers," which was published under the pseudonym "Henry Nicklemann" in the April 28, 1900, issue of The Library, *is one of her first short stories and a real potboiler. The time is the late 1900s; the place is a ranch in Oklahoma owned by a wealthy French-Canadian immigrant named Chevalier, a widower who lives with his daughter, Severine. The story opens on the day that a dance is to be given. Against this festive background, the central conflict unfolds, a traditional lovers' triangle. Severine is the object of affection of two ranch hands: Denis, a "big choleric Irishman," and Signor, "a little Mexican who had strayed up into the cattle country." Cather's characterizations of her protagonists are blatant clichés, reflecting the racial attitudes and prejudices of that period—particularly where Mexicans are concerned. As the third side of the triangle, the Mexican is regarded by others in the story as insignificant. Neither his name nor his nationality are important: "What his real name was, heaven only knows, but we called him 'The Signor,' as if he had been Italian instead of Mexican." He has one admirable quality: He is "a first rate man with the cattle." Beyond that, he is presented as a most despicable individual. For example, in a card game, Denis catches him cheating and exclaims: "Stop pulling cards out of yor sleeve, you confounded Mexican cheat!" Another ranch*

27

*hand warns Denis: "They are a nasty lot, these Greasers.
I've known them down in Old Mexico. They'll knife you
in the dark, any one of them. It's the only country I could
never feel comfortable in. Everything is dangerous—the
climate, the sun, the men, and most of all the women.
The very flowers are poisonous." Denis concludes: "I
don't like Greasers, they're all sneaks."*

It should be remembered that at the time of the story's
publication, Cather was in an apprenticeship stage as a
writer, and it would be quite unfair not to mention Cather's later fiction, where Mexican characters are fully realized and free of the clichés in "The Dance at the
Chevalier's." Of special note is her highly regarded novel
Death Comes for the Archbishop (1927), in which she
introduces a variety of Mexicans, clergymen as well as
laymen and women from different social backgrounds,
from the very poor to the very wealthy. Here her characters reveal a catalog of human traits—vanity, humility,
greed, compassion, understanding, cowardice, and courage—and are treated with precision and sensitivity. "The
Dance at the Chevaliers," however, must, in the end, be
read as a document that gives the modern reader an inci-
sive glimpse of the harsh, prejudicial Anglo attitudes
toward Mexican migrants at the turn of the century.

The Dance at Chevalier's

It was a dance that was a dance, that dance at Chevalier's, and it will be long remembered in our country.

But first as to what happened in the afternoon. Denis
and Signor had put the cattle in the corral and come in
early to rest before the dance. The Signor was a little
Mexican who had strayed up into the cattle country.
What his real name was, heaven only knows, but we
called him "The Signor," as if he had been Italian instead
of Mexican. After they had put the horses away, they
went into the feed room, which was a sort of stable salon,
where old Chevalier received his friends and where his
hands amused themselves on Sundays. The Signor sug-

gested a game of cards, and placed a board across the top of a millet barrel for a table. Denis lit his pipe and began to mix the cards.

Little Harry Burns sat on the tool box sketching. Burns was an eastern newspaper man, who had come to live in Oklahoma because of his lungs. He found a good deal that was interesting besides the air. As the game went on, he kept busily filling in his picture, which was really a picture of Denis, the Mexican being merely indicated by a few careless strokes. Burns had a decided weakness for Denis. It was his business to be interested in people, and practice had made his eye quick to pick out a man from whom unusual things might be expected. Then he admired Denis for his great physical proportions. Indeed, even with his pipe in his mouth and the fresh soil of the spring ploughing on his boots, Denis made a striking figure. He was a remarkably attractive man, that Denis, as all the girls in the neighborhood knew to their sorrow. For Denis was a ladies' man and had heady impulses that were hard to resist. What we call sentiment in cultured men is called by a coarser name in the pure animal products of nature and is a dangerous force to encounter. Burns used to say to himself that this big choleric Irishman was an erotic poet undeveloped and untamed by the processes of thought; a pure creature of emotional impulses who went about seeking rhymes and harmonies in the flesh, the original Adam. Burns wondered if he would not revel in the fervid verses of his great countryman Tom Moore—if he should ever see them. But Denis never read anything but the Sunday New York papers—a week old, always, when he got them—and he was totally untrammelled by anything of a reflective nature. So he remained merely a smiling giant, who had the knack of saying pretty things to girls. After all, he was just as happy that way, and very much more irresistible, and Harry Burns knew it, for all his theories.

Just as he was finishing his picture, Burns was startled by a loud exclamation.

"Stop pulling cards out of your sleeve, you confounded Mexican cheat!"

"You lie! You lie!" shouted the Signor, throwing a card on the table and attempting to rise. But Denis was too quick for him. He caught the back of the Mexican's greasy hand with the point of his belt knife and, regardless of the blood that trickled through his fingers, proceeded to search his sleeve.

"There, Signor, chuck a whole deck up, why don't you? Now the next time you try that game on me I'll run my knife clean through your dirty paw, and leave a mark that men will know."

"I'll kill you for this, you dog of an Irishman! Wait and see how I will kill you," snarled the Mexican, livid with rage and pain, as he shot out of the door. Denis laughed and lay down on a pile of corn.

"Better look out for that man, Denis," said little Burns, as he lit a cigarette.

"Oh, if I was looking for a man to be afraid of I wouldn't pick the Signor."

"Look out for him, all the same. They are a nasty lot, these Greasers. I've known them down in Old Mexico. They'll knife you in the dark, any one of them. It's the only country I could never feel comfortable in. Everything is dangerous—the climate, the sun, the men, and most of all the women. The very flowers are poisonous. Why does old Chevalier keep this fellow?"

"Oh, he's a good hand enough, and a first-rate man with the cattle. I don't like Greasers myself, they're all sneaks. Not many of 'em ever come up in this country, and they've always got into some sort of trouble and had to light out. The Signor has kept pretty straight around the place, though, and as long as he behaves himself he can hold his job."

"You don't think Chevalier's daughter has anything to do with his staying?"

"If I did I'd trample him like a snake!"

When the Signor left the barn he shook the blood from his wounded hand and went up to the house and straight into the sitting room, where Severine Chevalier was shaving a tallow candle on the floor for the dance. The Signor's scowl vanished, and he approached her with an exaggerated smile.

"Come, Severine. I've cut my hand; tie it up for me, like the sweet one that you are."

"How came you to cut your hand on the day of the dance? And how on the back, too? I believe you did it on purpose."

"And so I did, to have you tie it up for me. I would cut myself all over for that." And as Severine bent over to twist the bandage he kissed her on the cheek.

"Begone, you sneak; you can tie up your own cuts, if that's the way you treat me."

"*Dios mio!* That is treating you very well, my sweet. If that is not good what is there in this world that is? I saw that hulking Irishman kiss you last night, and you seemed to like it well enough."

"That depends on the person, Monsieur Signor," said Severine, tartly, as she slid over the tallow shavings. But she blushed hotly, all the same.

"See here, Severine, you have played with both of us long enough. If you kiss him again I will kill you. I like to kill the things I love, do you understand?"

"*Merci, monsieur!* I compliment you. You have great tact. You know how to coax a sweetheart. You know all about love-making."

"You baby! women have gone mad after me before now. You see how I love you, and it does not move you. That is because you are a baby and do not know how to love. A girl who doesn't know how to love is stupid, tasteless, like—like so much water. Baby!"

The girl's eyes were hot with anger as she drew herself up and faced him.

"You fool! you think you know all about love, and yet you cannot see that I am in love all the time, that I burn up with love, that I am tortured by it, that my pillows are hot with it all night, and my hands are wet with it in the day. You fool! But it is not with you, Monsieur Signor, *grace á Dieu,* it is not with you."

The swarthy little Signor looked at her admiringly a moment, and then spoke in a low voice that whistled in the air like a knife—

"Is it the Irishman? It is the Irishman!"

"Yes, stupid beast, it is. But that is my own affair."

Frightened at her own rashness, she fell to shaving the candle with trembling hands, while the Mexican watched her with a smile that showed all his white teeth. Severine had time to repent her rashness, and a sickening fear of the consequences arose within her.

"You'll keep that to yourself, Signor? You won't tell father?"

"That is my affair, Mademoiselle."

She dropped the wax and touched his arm.

"Play fair, Signor, and keep it, please."

"It is I who make terms now, Mademoiselle. Well, yes, I will keep it, and I will ask a very little price for my silence. You must come out and kiss me tonight when I ask you."

"Yes, yes, I will if you will only keep your word."

He caught her in his slender, sinewy arms.

"You said once!" she cried, in angry protest, as she broke away from him.

"This was only to show you how, my sweet," he laughed.

As he left the room he looked back over his shoulder and saw that she was still rubbing her lips with her hand, and all the way up stairs to his own room he laughed, and when he packed his belongings away in his canvas saddlebags he was still smiling. When he had finished and strapped his bags he stood looking about him. He heard a snatch of an old French song through the window and saw Severine working out in her flower bed.

He hesitated a moment, then shook his head and patted his bandaged hand. "Ah, love is sweet, but sweeter is revenge. It is the saying of my people."

And now for the dance at Chevalier's, which was a dance, indeed. It was the last before the hot season came on and everybody was there—all the French for miles around. Some came in road wagons, some in buggies, some on horseback, and not a few on foot. Girls with pretty faces and rough hands, and men in creaking boots, with broad throats tanned by the sun, reeking with violent perfumes and the odors of the soil.

At nine o'clock the dance began, the dance that was to have lasted all night. Harry Burns played an old bass viol, and Alplosen de Mar played the organ, but the chief musician was the old Bohemian, Peter Sadelack, who played the violin. Peter had seen better days, and had played in a theatre in Prague until he had paralysis and was discharged because his bowing was uncertain. Then in some way, God knows how, he and his slatternly wife and countless progeny had crossed the ocean and drifted out into the cattle country. The three of them made right merry music, though the two violinists were considerably the more skilful, and poor Alplosen quite lost her breath in keeping up with them. Waltzes, quadrilles and polkas they played until the perspiration streamed down their faces, and for the square dances little Burns "called off." Occasionally he got down and took a waltz himself, giving some young Frenchman his instrument. All those Frenchmen could play a fiddle from the time they were old enough to hold one. But dancing was bad for his lungs, and with the exception of Severine and Marie Generaux there were very few girls he cared to dance with. It was more amusing to saw away on the squeaky old bass viol and watch those gleeful young Frenchmen seize a girl and whirl her away with a dexterity and grace really quite remarkable, considering the crowd and the roughness of the floor, and the affectionate positions in which they insisted upon holding their partners. They were not of pure French blood, of course; most of them had been crossed and recrossed with Canadians and Indians, and they spoke a vile patois which no Christian man could understand. Almost the only traces they retained of their original nationality were their names, and their old French songs, and their grace in the dance. Deep down in the heart of every one of them, uncrushed by labor, undulled by enforced abstinence, there was a mad, insatiable love of pleasure that continually warred with the blood of dull submission they drew from their red squaw ancestors. Tonight it broke out like a devouring flame, it flashed in dark eyes and glowed in red cheeks. Ah that old hot, imperious blood of the Latins! It is never quite lost. These women had long since forgotten the wit of their motherland, they were dull of mind and slow of tongue; but in the eyes, on the lips, in the temperament was the old, ineffaceable stamp. The Latin blood was there.

The most animated and by far the most beautiful among them was Severine Chevalier. At those dances little attempt was made at evening dress, but Severine was in white, with her gown cut low, showing the curves of her neck and shoulders. For she was different from the other French girls, she had more taste and more ambition, and more money. She had been sent two years to a convent school in Toronto, and when she came back the other girls could never quite get used to her ways, though they admired and envied her from afar. She could speak the French of France, could Severine, and sometimes when it was dull and too rainy to gallop across the prairies after the cattle, or to town for the mail, and when there was nothing better to do, she used to read books. She talked with little Burns about books sometimes. But, on the whole, she preferred her pony, and the wild flowers, and the wind and the sun, and romping with her boys. She was a very human young woman, and not wise enough to disguise or to affect anything. She knew what the good things of life were, and was quite frank about them. Tonight she seemed glowing with some unspoken joy, and many a French lad felt his heart thump faster as he clutched her hand with an iron grasp and guided her over the rough floor and among the swaying couples; many a lad cast timid glances at old Jean Chevalier as he sat complacently by his brandy bottle, proudly watching his daughter. For old Chevalier was a king in the cattle country, and they knew that none might aspire to his daughter's hand who had not wider acres and more cattle than any of them possessed.

And for every glance that Severine drew from the men, Denis drew a sigh from the women. Though he was only Jean Chevalier's herdman, and an Irishman at that, Denis was the lion of the French dances. He danced hard, and drank hard, and made love hardest of all. But tonight he was chary of his favors, and when he could not dance with Severine he was careless of his other partners. After a long waltz he took Severine out to the windmill in the grove. It was refreshingly cool out there, the moonlight was clear and pale, and the tall lombard poplars were rustling their cool leaves. The moon was just up and was still reflected in the long lagoon on the eastern horizon. Denis put his arms about the girl and drew her up to him. The Signor saw them so, as he slipped down to the barn to saddle his horse, and he whispered to himself, "It is high time." But what the great Irishman whispered in her ear, the Signor never knew.

As Denis led her back to the house, he felt a dizzy sensation of tenderness and awe come over him, such as he had sometimes felt when he was riding alone across the moonlit lagoons under the eyes of countless stars, or when he was driving his cattle out in the purple lights of springtide dawns.

As they entered the house, the Mexican slipped in behind them and tried to edge his way through the crowd unseen. But Marie Generaux caught him by the arm.

"This is our dance, Signor, come along."

"Make it the next, my girl," he whispered, and escaped upstairs into his own room.

His saddlebags were already on his horse, but in his chest there lay one article which belonged to him, a pint whisky flask. He took it out and unscrewed the top, and smelt it, and held it up to the light, shaking it gently and gazing on it with real affection in his narrow, snaky eyes. For it was not ordinary liquor. An old, withered Negro from the gold coast of Guinea had told him how to make it, down in Mexico. He himself had gathered rank, noxious plants and poured their distilled juices into that whisky, and had killed the little lizards that sun themselves on the crumbling stones of the old ruined missions, and dried their bodies and boiled them in the contents of that flask. For five years that bright liquor had lain sparkling in his chest, waiting for such a time as this.

When the Signor went downstairs a quadrille was just over, and the room was echoing with loud laughter. He beckoned Severine into a corner, and whispered with a meaning glance:

"Send your Irishman upstairs to me. I must see him. And save the next dance for me. There he is. Hurry."

Reluctantly she approached Denis, blushing furiously as she accosted him.

"Go upstairs and see the Signor, please, Denis."

"What can he want with me?"

"I don't know. I wish you'd go, though."

"Well, Signor, what is it?" he asked as he reached the top of the stairs.

"I must tell you something. Take a drink to brace you, and then I'll talk. It will not be pleasant news."

Denis laughed and drank, never noticing how the hand that held out the glass to him was shaking.

"I can't say much for your whisky," he remarked, as he sat down the empty glass.

The Mexican came up to him, his eyes glittering with suppressed excitement.

"I want to tell you that we have both been fools. That French girl has played with us both. We have let her cuff us about like schoolboys, and coax us with sugar like children. Today she promised to marry me, tonight she promises to marry you. We are decidedly fools, my friend."

"You liar! You say that again—"

"Tut, tut, my friend, not so fast. You are a big man, and I am a little one. I cannot fight you. I try to do you a service, and you abuse me. That is not unusual. But you wait here by the window through the next dance and watch the windmill, and if I don't prove what I say, then you may kill me at your pleasure. Is not that fair enough?"

"Prove it, prove it!" said Denis from a dry throat.

In a moment he was alone, and stood watching out of the window, scarcely knowing why he was there. "It's all a lie; I felt the truth in her," he kept saying to himself while he waited. The music struck up downstairs, the squeak of the cracked organ and the screech of the violins, and with it the sound of the heavy feet. His first impulse was to go down and join them, but he waited. In a few minutes, perhaps two, perhaps three, before the waltz was half over, he saw the Signor stroll down towards the windmill. Beside him was Severine. They went straight to that moonlit bit of ground under the poplars, the spot where twenty minutes before he had been seized and mastered and borne away by that flood-tide of tenderness which we can know but once in our lives, and then seek, hunger for all the rest of our sunless days. There, in that spot, which even to his careless mind was holy ground, he saw Severine stop and lift her little flowerlike face to another man's. Long, long he held her. God knows how long it must have seemed to the man who watched and held his breath until his veins seemed bursting. Then they were gone, and only the quivering poplar leaves cast their shadows over that moonlit spot.

He felt a deadly sickness come over him. He caught the flask on the table and drank again. Presently the door opened, and the Signor entered. He should have been gone indeed, but he could not resist one more long look at the man who sat limply on the bed, with his face buried in his hands.

"I am glad you take it patiently; it is better," he remarked, soothingly.

Then over the big Irishman, who sat with his head bowed and his eyes darkened and the hand of death already heavy upon him, there came a flood of remembrances and of remorse.

"Yes," he groaned. "I can be patient. I can take torture with my mouth shut—women have taught he how." Then suddenly starting to his feet he shouted, "Begone, you Satan, or I'll strangle ye!"

When Denis stumbled downstairs his face was burning, but not with anger. Severine had been hunting for him and came up to him eagerly. "I've been looking for you everywhere. Where have you been so long? Let's dance this; it's the one you like."

He followed her passively. Even his resentment was half dead. He felt an awful sense of weakness and isolation; he wanted to touch something warm and living. In a few minutes something would happen—something. He caught her roughly, half loving her, half loathing her, and weak, trembling, with his head on fire and his breast bursting with pain, he began to dance. Over and over again the fiddles scraped their trite measures, while Severine wondered why the hand that gripped hers grew so cold. He lost the time and then swayed back and forth. A sharp cry of alarm rang from the end of the room, and little Burns bounded from the table, and reached him just as he fell.

"What is it, Denis, my boy, what is it?"

Severine knelt on the other side, still holding one of his hands.

The man's face was drawn in horrible agony, his blue eyes were distended and shot with blood, his hair hung wet over his face, and his lips were dashed with froth. He gasped heavily from his laboring breast.

"Poison—they—she and the Mexican—they have done me.—Damn—damn—women!"

He struck at Severine, but she caught his hand and kissed it.

But all the protestations, all the words of love, imperious as a whirlwind, that she poured out there on her

knees fell upon deaf ears. Not even those words, winged
with flame, could break the silences for him. If the lips
of the living could give warmth to those of the dead,
death would be often robbed, and the grave cheated of
its victory.

Harry Burns sprang to his feet. "It's that damned Mexican. Where is he?"

But no one answered. The Signor had been in his saddle half an hour, speeding across the plains, on the swiftest horse in the cattle country.

MARÍA CRISTINA MENA

❦ ❦ ❦

*María Cristina Mena holds a unique place in American
literature: She is the first naturalized American from Mexico to write in English and publish in prestigious American
magazines. Born in Mexico City on April 3, 1893, Mena
was the daughter of a Spanish mother and Yucatecan
father of European blood. Politically powerful and socially
prominent, Mena's father was a partner with several
Americans in a variety of businesses during the last two
decades of the rule of Porfirio Diaz, renown general and
president of Mexico. She lived the life of a privileged
young lady, educated at an elite convent school in the
Mexican capital, Hijas de María (Daughters of Mary),
and later at an English boarding school. An unusually
intelligent, sensitive, and perceptive child, she began to
write poetry when she was ten years old.*

*As the result of the political turmoil in Mexico during
the first decade of the twentieth century, Mena was sent at
the age of fourteen to live with family friends in New York
City. There she continued her studies and began to write
in earnest. She was twenty when her first two short stories
were published in November of 1913: "John of God, the
Water-Carrier" in* The Century Magazine *and "The Gold
Vanity Set" in* The American Magazine. *By 1916, Mena
had published a total of eight stories and one biographical
essay. "John of God" was reprinted in the October 1927
issue of* The Monthly Criterion, *a literary journal published in London and edited by T.S. Eliot. Edward
O'Brien selected the work for his volume of* Best Short
Stories of 1928. *In 1916, she was married to the Australian
playwright and journalist Henry Kellett Chambers, a
divorced man twenty-six years her senior. The couple traveled in literary circles and counted D.H. Lawrence and
Aldous Huxley among their friends. Chambers died in*

39

1935 and with the death of her husband, Doña María, as she now preferred to be called, became a virtual shut-in. When she did venture out, it was to attend the regular meetings of the Catholic Library Association and the Authors Guild of New York, where she was able to continue her friendships with editors, librarians, educators, and other writers such as Clare Booth Luce, Theodore Maynard, and Wilfred Sheed and where she made new friends such as Covelle Newcomb, a promising young writer from San Antonio. Mena continued to write children's novels, publishing five books between 1942 and 1953. She died in Brooklyn on August 3, 1965.

For the most part, Mena's children's books are reworkings of the stories she published as a young girl. But it is for those early stories that María Cristina Mena will be remembered. In them, she touches on the lives of the religious and the sacrilegious, the faithful and the hypocritical, the industrious and the lazy, the wise and the gullible. The reader is given a meticulous study of the complex social structure of Mexico. At the top is the foreigner or foreign-born Mexican. Next is the criollo, *a Mexican born to foreign parents. Beneath the* criollo *is the* mestizo, *a Mexican with a mixture of foreign and Indian blood. Finally, there is the Indian, the lowest on the Mexican ladder. The period between 1900 and 1930 saw a great influx of Mexicans into the United States, many of them, like Mena, fleeing the turmoil of the Mexican revolution that began in 1910. Mena dedicated herself to giving American readers vivid and true portraits of the many faces of the many Mexicos. As T.S. Eliot noted when he published "John of God" in 1927, María Cristina Mena had "written perhaps the most comprehensive series of stories of Mexican life published in English."*

John of God,
The Water-Carrier

Most of the inhabitants were still on their knees in the middle of the street, praying that there might be no repetition of the trembler. Others were searching anxiously for divine symbolism in the earthquake's handwriting of crossed and zigzagged crackings in adobe walls. It had come without warning. Through the ground had passed a series of shudders, like those of a dying animal, with a twitching of houses, a spilling of fountains, and a quick sickness to people's brains.

Several horses from a burning stable were running wild through the streets. An Indian boy who had just risen from his knees unslung his lazo and tried to catch one that galloped past him, but it swerved from the flung noose and charged through an open cabin, striking down a kneeling woman in the doorway. The boy ran to her and lifted her head, then lowered it quickly and crossed himself. Beneath the wetted hair, where a hoof had struck, he had felt the grate of a fractured edge of bone.

Suddenly he was driven at one bound into the street by a thin cry inside the hut.

"Mamá!" said the voice, and then, "Mamacita!" with a drawling petulance on the diminutive.

The boy moved a little nearer, calling:

"Come out, muchachita!"

But the unseen raised her voice and replied that she could not come out without her mamá, being a little bad with fever. Also, her name was Dolores and she did not desire to be called "muchachita," and she was thirsty, and where was her mamá?

"I will come to thee, Dolores," the boy replied in a shaking voice.

As he stepped past the dead woman he turned his head aside with a prayer. There in a corner was the child, swaddled in coarse cloth, lying on a straw mat. Her head was tied up with fresh leaves of rosemary and mallow,

41

which are sovereign for fever if allowed to wither on the skin. He gave her drink from a water-jug and then she sucked her lips and looked at him searchingly from eyes like balls of black onyx.

"Who art thou?" she demanded.

"I am Juan de Dios, son of Pancho, the aguador."

Baptismal names of sacred meaning are in high favour with the Inditos, and in "John of God" there was nothing uncommon except the solemnity of the youth's tone as he announced himself to the wondering child.

"And thou," he added, "what age hast thou?"

"Five Aprils," she replied impatiently. "Where is my mamá?"

"Perhaps with thy papá."

"That cannot be. My papá is dead." And then raising herself on one elbow to see him better, "Why dost thou weep?"

"There is dust in my eyes," said Juan de Dios. "Tell me—thou hast brothers and sisters?"

"I have none."

"Grandparents?"

"*Quién sabe?*"

"How '*quién sabe*?' Hast thou no one?"

"Foolish one! My mamá is enough. Where is my mamá?"

"Perhaps at the church. We have had a trembler."

"*Santa Bárbara bendita!* Then it woke me!"

"It was a very strong trembler, and if we should have another—"

"Take me out, Juan de Dios!" she cried, holding out her arms to be lifted.

He wrapped her in a blanket, covering her face so that she might not see her mother, and carried her out. An unnoticed figure in that agitated hour, he walked, he stopped, he ran a few steps, he looked around wildly. At last, discerning a closed carriage approaching soberly, he dropped to his knees, uncovering the child's head and his own. The black curtains over the carriage windows were partly drawn, but not sufficiently to hide from view the gold chalice covered with an embroidered cloth which an acolyte in red and white held steadily before a black-robed ecclesiastic. Poor and rich, old and young, kneeled in the dust as it passed, for this was the carriage of Our

Master—"Nuestro Amo"—and the whole pueblo felt blessed, comforted and protected by the divine mystery which it bore among the people. The boy, after its passing, rose with a light heart and continued on his way, uplifted by what seemed to him a personal message of pardon and peace. The little girl, who a few moments earlier had said, "Why dost thou weep, Juan de Dios?" now said, "Why dost thou smile, Juan de Dios?" He only replied, "Nuestro Amo has passed." And she fell asleep, and the warmth of her little body filled him with a troubled tenderness.

His parents ran to meet him, thanking the saints for having preserved their first-born.

"But what thing bringest thou?" said his father, looking at the bundle in his arms.

"A little sick one," said Juan de Dios, displaying the green herbs that crowned his protégée and permitting her sleeping face to make its own appeal. It was the face of a toast-coloured cherub.

"*Qué bonita!*" exclaimed his mother, admiringly. "But of whom is she, son of mine?"

And he told them in a whisper how the child's mother had been killed, not mentioning the unluckily thrown lazo and his own blood-remorse, but adding simply that Nuestro Amo had sent him the thought to take care of that little orphan.

"Be it so, son of ours!" exclaimed the water-carrier and his wife in one voice; and Juan de Dios, who still looked at the face of the sleeping child, added:

"The chiquita will grow fat and strong for helping, and when she has taken her first communion I will marry her."

And so it was settled. No one else claimed the orphan, and the priest saw no reason why Pancho, the water-carrier, should not add a ninth young mouth to the eight that already busied themselves at feeding-time beneath the flat roof of his abode cabin. After Juan de Dios, who was twelve, came Tiburcio, two years younger, and then a mixed rabble of bare-footed infancy, in which the newcomer took a middle place and proved able to hold her own. The new home was a counterpart of the old one, except that it was more populous and amusing. The tortillas were just as warm and as grateful to little stomachs;

there wasn't a pin to choose between the niceness of the
beans, black and red, or of the sauces that would sometimes bite little tongues; and as for the *chilitos verdes*—
little green peppers just the size of her fingers—Juan de
Dios would bring them to her in handfuls, knowing that
she adored to crunch them between her sharp little teeth.
She developed a strong affection for the household altar
which stood in one corner and was touched by no one
but Juan de Dios. It consisted of an image of the Virgin
of Guadalupe stamped on a large piece of leather and
decorated with delicate white plumes, at its feet an
earthen dish of oil in which a butterfly was always burning—not a real butterfly, of course, but one of those little
contrivances of a short wick stuck in a float called by the
same name, *mariposa*.

A month after his adoption of Dolores, Juan de Dios
was a different person. By parting with certain property,
to wit, one carved leather belt, one knife, one lazo, fash-
ioned in a superior manner with fancy knots and stained
in bright colours, one flute, which he had made from a
piece of sugar-cane, and one veteran fighting-cock with
a bamboo leg, he had raised enough money to buy an
income-earning equipment consisting of two water-jugs
suspended at either end of a long pole which he balanced
on his shoulder. So burdened, he embarked in business
in a small way, delivering water to households of the
humbler sort, and earning about three reales a week.
And he was soon rich enough to buy Dolores three white
shirts, three skirts of gaily striped and figured baize,
much green cotton ribbon for her hair, a medal of their
Mother the Virgin of Guadalupe, and scapularies of
Santa Barbara, who protects from thunder, the Virgin of
the Conception, who defends chastity, and the Archangel
Gabriel, who watches over little children.

When his day's work was over Dolores would beg for
a story; and sitting cross-legged, with their backs against
the sun-warmed cabin wall, he would tell her stories of
the miracles and apparitions of saints, and she would
catch her breath and stretch the rims of her eyes at the
exciting parts, just as children of the northern land do
over the deeds of giants and fairies.

And she would tell him the events of her day. She had
spread the clothes on the rocks to dry for the mamacita

washing at the brook; she had fetched holy water from the church; she had gathered wild jasmine, pink and white, and made a basket of posies which she had taken to the station with Tiburcio and some of the sisters, and the passengers in the trains had given her many centavos, which she had tied in a corner of her rebozo to keep them from Tiburcio, who was as full of tricks as a monkey.

Sometimes Juan de Dios would remonstrate with Tiburcio for teasing the little motherless one; and then Tiburcio, taking the scolding in good part, would make Dolores laugh with his comical grimaces. He had bright, impudent eyes and a mole under his mouth which gave him a laughing look and earned him many gracious glances from the señores on the trains when they bought his pomegranates or purple passion-fruit.

Juan de Dios saved enough money in the course of a year to discard his long pole, which caused the *portcros* of the better residences to exclude him from their patios, and provide himself with a mature aguador's outfit like his father's. Thenceforward he bore a very large jug on his back, balanced by a smaller one on his breast, and his knees bent more than ever, and he was very proud. No other Indito was so alert in undertaking small errands or so faithful in performing them. And at last it fell out that some of the oldest families in the pueblo, lifelong patrons of the deliberate Pancho, would ask him in emergencies for the services of his son. Now, Pancho loved his son, but he also had his proper pride, and one day he said to Juan de Dios:

"Son of my life, comfort of my soul, thou art now a man and mayest choose thine occupation."

"Choose my occupation?" stammered the astonished youth. "But your honour knows that I have chosen it these four years."

"Not so," replied Pancho positively. "Of aguador, sufficient with thy father. Better that thou be a donkey-driver. It is my wish, thou consolation of my miseries; and the day of thy saint I will give thee a burro—and may God accompany thee!"

Juan de Dios was silent. The thought of changing his occupation filled his heart with anguish. Was he not sixteen, and long settled in life? Did not all the world know him as Juan de Dios, the aguador?

That evening at twilight, as he and Dolores squatted against the wall, he said to her:

"To-morrow we will go to early mass, and after we will speak to the padre about thy confirmation. I have to leave thee, Dolores."

"To leave me!" Incredulity and indignant protest struggled with a very lively curiosity.

"Even as I say. I have a weight in my heart, Dolores, but all is for the best. I am going to work for thee a few years in the capital."

She looked at him with mingled terror and admiration, for in the imagination of the Indian of the pueblos, the City of Mexico is enveloped in formidable and sinister mystery. With the same feeling in his heart, and a sudden surge of loneliness, Juan de Dios wept. She tried to comfort him, begging him not to go, but he stammered:

"The road of the glory is sown with thorns. I will go. Resign thyself, little daughter. When I return we shall receive the benediction of the padre, and thou shalt be my little wife."

"Yes, yes, Juan de Dios!" she joined her bronze hands flatly as in prayer, bowed her forehead on the fingertips, and then threw back her head with a heavenward glance of mild ecstasy. "Yes, yes! I shall be very big when thou comest back, and thou wilt take me to my own little cabin—oh, what enchantment!"

She kissed his hand reverentially, and her heart was filled with the great calm that assurance of protection gives to the weak and ignorant.

And so a morning arrived when Juan de Dios departed from his birthplace, accompanying a party of donkey-drivers who were taking various wares to sell in the capital. It was a morning of farewells, promises, benedictions, and tears. The capital was only two days' easy march distant, but it seemed to all that Juan de Dios, the confidant and comforter, whole daily blessing of the hut had carried an unnamable gentle charm, was embarking into dark distances full of dangers.

The capital, as sensitive of its reputation as an elegant woman, has a code of manners for Inditos and enforces it in times of peace, peremptorily though kindly. Juan de Dios learned that in the City of Mexico one may no longer enjoy the comfort of going barefoot, and dutifully he taught his feet to endure the encumbrance of leather sandals. He learned that the city aguador may not blow his whistle to halt the traffic while he gravely crosses the street, but must wait for the passing of many vehicles, some with horses and some outlandishly without. From early morn to the fall of the afternoon he would go from fountain to fountain and from portal to portal, his lean body so accustomed to bending that he never thought of straightening it, his head bowed as if in prayer.

On the first day of each month he visited a little shop in the street of San Felipe Neri, where a good old widow sold tobacco and snuff, candles for the poor, for the rich, and for the church; flags of silver and gold paper stuck in dry oranges to adorn altars; toys, candies, lottery tickets, and many other necessaries. With her Juan de Dios understood himself very well. She would change his mountain of centavos into silver pesos, and from her he would buy his meagre supplies for the month, including his lottery-ticket, with which he never won a prize although he never neglected to have it blessed by holding it up in church at the moment of the benediction. Very happy, he would jog home, the heavy silver pieces in his leather pockets making a discreet and dulcet *trink-trak* between his jugs and his body. He lived with a charcoal-seller in one room at the back of a bodega, where the odours of dry fish and vats of wine mingled with the dust of the charcoal nightly swept into the farthest corner of the soft earth floor to make place for his sleeping-mat.

When his first jugs had worn out—the sweet-scented, porous red clay becomes perforated in time—he had buried them to their necks in the corner where he slept, and they were now his treasury. On returning home from the widow's he would uncover them and drop his coins one by one into their depths, receiving a separate thrill of satisfaction at the piquant echo of each one from the hollow of its prison.

Once in a year or so he received word from his family by the mouth of some donkey-driver or pilgrim. They were well. They sent him benedictions. And he, as opportunity offered, sent them gifts for their saint-days.

* * *

It was the month of June, which always makes the heart restless. During his five years in the capital, Juan de Dios had treated himself to fewer holidays than most peons—not celebrating the days of more than ten or a dozen favourite saints each year—and now his spirit rebelled at many things. The rainy season was, as usual, depriving him of the centavos which at other times accrued from the sprinkling of the streets in front of his customers' houses, as ordained by law. And then there was a new and mischievous spirit in the air, a spirit named "modern improvement," and it now possessed and agitated one of the houses on his route, a three-patio building inhabited by fifteen families of the middle class. The plumber—worker of evil and oppressor of God's poor—had been exercising his malign spells. Was it the will of God that water should run upstairs, except in jugs sustained by the proper legs of a man? Was the roof of a building a fit place for a large and unsightly tank? Was it reasonable to suppose that a man could fill such a reservoir with water by see-sawing laboriously an erect stake of painted iron, as tall as his breast, which had sprouted diabolically in a patio at the margin of the fountain? Or that the tenants could supply themselves with water by no more than turning a stick of brass not as large as an honest man's finger? Was it for him, Juan de Dios, to become a confederate in these mysteries by hauling and thrusting that painted stake, instead of making many sociable trips between the fountain and the kitchens of his customers? No! He would not so endanger his soul. With firmness he had refused to serve the strange gods of the plumber. And the owner and tenants of the building, liking well their patient and apostolic-looking aguador, and understanding perfectly his prejudices, had murmured "*Mañana!*" and allowed the highly painted and patented American force-pumps in the three patios to rust in unlovely idleness.

But the incident had given Juan de Dios a shock and turned his heart toward the simplicity and piety of the pueblo. His Dolores was fourteen now, and ready for marriage. He had saved enough money. He could build a little hut and buy a burro, and lead an easy and blessed existence with his chattering little squirrel of a wife, and the babies that would crawl in the sunshine at their cabin door.

Meanwhile the excellent business which he had built up in the capital should not be lost to the family, for Tiburcio should succeed to it. That part of it had already been arranged; it only remained to send him word that the time had come.

Then came many days of patient waiting and of serious preparation—days, too, of fasting and prayer—until one afternoon there dawned upon his vision at the public fountain which he had appointed as their meeting place, a radiant young spark whom he would not have identified as the weeping boy he had left in the road, except for the eloquent mole under the still-laughing mouth. He wore leather trousers, wondrously tight-fitting, and laced up the sides from foot to hip between double rows of brass buttons; a white shirt, without a collar, but with a large, flowing scarlet bow sewed to the middle of the bosom; a leather belt hung with a fancy knife, a plain knife, and other decorative items; from his neck a religious medal which clashed cheerfully against the metal of the knife; on his feet, heavy shoes of wine-coloured leather, much overlaid and ornamented in punctured designs; on his head a cheap sombrero heavily bound to its very apex with silver rope, richly knotted.

· Tiburcio saw his brother trotting along with head bended as of old, and moved to meet him; and with many simple ejaculations of joy and affection they placed each his hands on the other's shoulders, with smiles and graceful bendings of heads, and strokings and pattings, like a pair of friendly ants. Thus they remained regardless of the disorganized traffic, until a gendarme, himself an Indito, ran to them and in a friendly fashion, moved them on. And at length Juan de Dios permitted himself to take cognizance of Tiburcio's elegance.

"But, brother of my soul," he protested, "thou appearest a Judas!"

Tiburcio hung his head in shame at this allusion to the garishly bedizened effigies of Judas which are hanged in the streets and plazas on Saturday of Glory and burned amid festive mockery and the sputtering of fire-crackers. Fortunately he had working garments tied up in the blanket, and the portero of a neighbouring house where Juan

de Dios was known allowed him to change there and
emerge in the simple habit that God had undoubtedly
ordained for water-carriers. And not until then did he
remember to impart to his brother a piece of important
news. Laughing, he said:

"Brother, with all thy scoldings thou didst put it away
from my memory to tell thee that Lola is here."

"Lola?" repeated Juan de Dios, not understanding.

"Dolores—she came with me."

"Protect me, Saint of my name! Dolores here—but for
what? And where is she?"

"While I found thee I left her at the cathedral."

"Well chosen the place. But I beat my brains to comprehend. Did I not tell her to wait for me in the pueblo?
And now—Ay! Ay! What sinful impatience that she must
come to meet me here! What sad fortune that I could
not have embraced her as I always wished, in the cabin
where I left her!" He wagged his bended head with a
heavy sigh at this upsetting of his plans. Tiburcio looked
uncomfortable and opened his mouth to speak, but Juan
de Dios, having erased himself of his pique, began to
rejoice: "But since God wishes it to come sooner, the
pleasure, so much better. She is here, my young woman!
What little moments we will pass! Uy, újule!"

And with that liquid cry of joy he unharnessed himself,
pulling over his head the shoulder-straps, with the leather
breast-and-back plates and head-piece, and the heavy
jugs, and proceeded to harness his brother, saying:

"Do me this service, Tiburcio. Carry on this street five
journeys to number fourteen, six to number eighteen,
three to number twenty, and eight to the principal patio
in number twenty-two. Take care not to touch the pots
of flowers in the corridors, and where the cages of birds
hang be sure to bend lest thou knock them down. If the
parrots speak to thee, answer them not, for the señoras
like them not to learn our manner of expressing ourselves. If thou seest a melon or a bunch of flowers swimming in a patron's water-jar, touch them not, for after
thou hast poured the water, they will but dance a little
and come up again. Here are my colourines." He passed
over a leather bag filled with scarlet beans.

"With these count thy journeys, leaving one each a
time with the servant of the house. Conduct thyself well,

and that God may accompany thee. I go to the cathedral
to find my Dolores. Adiós! Adiós!"

The new aguador attracted the attention of a lady and
gentleman sitting in the principal patio, and they asked
him about Juan de Dios. Tiburcio explained everything
with great care, and added in a confident and winning
manner that he expected to give just as good service as
his brother, if not a little bit better. And the lady in
some excitement whispered to her husband:

"Perhaps this youth will agitate the pump, and by the
grace of God we can utilize at last our porcelain bath!"

The lady's husband, who was the owner of the house,
jumped at the idea, and Tiburcio was conducted to the
pump. He rolled his eyes at it distrustfully, and seemed
to regard the señor's explanation of its raison-d'etre as a
rather lame one; but when the señor himself grasped the
lever and moved it sturdily back and forth without suffering any other penalty than a shortness of breath—for he
was a fat and not young señor—the youth recovered his
courage.

"Lend here, Patrón," he said; and getting free of his
jugs and rolling up his trousers; he attacked the business
with confidence. The proprietor and his wife put heart
into him at intervals by remarking what a strong fellow
he was and how the capital was the proper place for him;
and although Tiburcio's muscles were not hardened to
such labour he kept at it, his spirit swimming in the ether
of pride and praise, for half an hour. Meanwhile the
news that an aguador who would pump was on the prem-
ises had spread to the second and third patios, and so
flattering were the overtures made to him that Tiburcio,
concealing his fatigue, addressed himself with zeal to the
other two force-pumps. When his arms failed him he continued by employing the weight of his body, the forward
plunge pulling a quart of water from the fountain and
the backward fall projecting it toward the roof—for it is
the ungracious nature of a force-pump to work equally
hard both ways. On abandoning the third pump, Tiburcio
felt a weight in his chest, and his legs bent under him
like green twigs; but he was wonderfully happy as he
took the silver pieces that he had earned by the sweat of
his body, and with them made the sign of the cross on
his brow, his eyes, his mouth, and his breast. After which

he rolled himself in a straw mat in a shady corner, and abandoned himself like a tired child to his well-earned siesta.

Juan de Dios and Dolores met under the trees of the plaza in front of the cathedral—a new Dolores, almost as tall as himself, with dove's eyes and a sad little voice, very desirable—and they embraced just as he and Tiburcio had embraced, hands on shoulders, with the same little glances and bendings and ejaculations. And she called him "Padrino" as of old, at which he protested playfully, *"Qué padrino ni que calabazas?"*

"What godfather nor what pumpkins? Not thy padrino, but thy husband, who forgives thee for coming to him."

At that she was troubled, and abruptly withdrew her hands from his shoulders, averting her face. That gesture smote him with the knowledge that an evil had come between them. Trembling with anger, he exclaimed:

"What thing is this I see? What thing? What thing?"

His voice pitched higher and higher. Her hands flew to her downcast face. He seized her wrists and shook them, making her whole body reel like a palm in a hurricane.

"Don't beat me, don't beat me!" she sobbed. "Where is Bucho?"

The endearing diminutive of his brother's name, or the tone of instinct in which it was uttered, told him all. He fetched a great sobbing breath and struck her in the face with the back of his hand, and then again with the palm, and then rained blows on her head and shoulders; and she, being a woman and born of blood impressed with the proverb, "Who well loves thee will make thee weep," snuggled against him, whimpering. While beating her he swore many oaths, such as "Lightnings and chains of fire!" and spoke bitter reproaches of ingratitude and perfidy, weeping all the while. They were near the central terminus of trolley-lines, and a crowd gathered about them, and there were calls for a gendarme. Hearing that, Juan de Dios turned her about and gave her a push to make her walk in front of him.

Tiburcio had not been seen at number fourteen, nor eighteen, nor twenty, but in the principal patio of twenty-two Dolores heard snores which she recognized, and they found Tiburcio curled in slumber.

Deeply curled, for it required several kicks from his brother to awaken him, and even then his fatigue pressed upon him so heavily that he stared up at them with a vague smile, unconscious of the fury in one face and the fear in the other. Soon, however, it dawned on his sluggish senses that Juan de Dios was declaiming angrily, then that Lola was weeping, then that her love and his own was the cause of the outburst, and then that the girl had thrown herself between them with upraised arms, crying to Juan de Dios:

"Don't curse him! Don't curse Bucho! Bucho, speak to him!"

"Lightnings!" shouted Juan de Dios, his voice muffled with foam. "For his sorceries with which he hath bewitched thee, that God may cripple him!"

Dolores gave a gasp of horror. Tiburcio, his face suddenly bleaching to a waxen yellow, tried to rise to his knees for prayer, but at the first movement an intense pain shot through his back between the shoulders and he tumbled over on his face, howling:

"Crippled! God favour me, miserable sinner that I am! Brother, brother, thy words have fallen over me! I am crippled truly! I cannot move! *Ay-ay-ay!*"

In a series of shrieks he described the progress of his affliction, which extended to all the muscles that he had brought into unwonted action during his intemperate exertions with the force-pumps. Dolores screamed for help, sputtered incoherencies at the portero and ran round the patio like a wild animal, kneeling at intervals to pray but not daring to go near Tiburcio for fear of the demon that possessed him. Shudder after shudder convulsed him as he sprawled with his forehead on the pavement, the poison of terror augmenting that of fatigue. From the house emerged many servants, male and female, asking questions, offering advice, chattering and crossing themselves, afraid to approach.

It was important to get Tiburcio away. Juan de Dios lifted him to his feet at last, despite his piteous moans. It appeared that he could use his legs but from loins to neck he seemed paralyzed. Supported by his brother and Dolores, and uttering cries at each step, he traversed the

streets to the charcoal-seller's and was laid on a mat.
Juan de Dios rubbed his body with holy water, sprinkling
what was left of it all over the room to frighten away
evil spirits.

Night fell over the anguish of the three, but without
abating it. Toward Juan de Dios and his prayers the other
two deferred in a spirit of humility and anxious expec-
tancy, while he performed such prodigies of spiritual con-
centration that he shook as with an ague, and his tears
lost their identity among the drops of sweat that rolled
down his contorted visage. They would not believe that
he could pray in vain—he, the blessed one, he at whose
curse the punishment had fallen! And yet, soon after the
great clock of the palace had boomed out eleven, Tiburcio reported to Dolores in a whisper that he seemed to
be breaking into two pieces. She wailed loudly, and in
desperation, demanded of Juan de Dios what thing she
could do, or he and she together, that would incline the
good God to show mercy to Bucho. Since he was angry
at the broken troth, might it not appease Him if she
renounced her love of Tiburcio and became the little wife
of Juan de Dios? Tiburcio from his mat begged that the
efficacy of that method of cure might be tested. Juan de
Dios said nothing, but his eyes burned as he looked at
Dolores, and shortly afterward he abruptly went out into
the rain. From the door she could see him dimly, by the
light of a distant street lamp, sitting motionless under the
sky with his knees to his breast, his face upturned in
submission and inquiry.

Hours passed before he returned, and then he was
alight with resolve. Making a sign to Delores that she
should help him, he uncovered the buried jugs and
removed by handfuls all his savings, which they packed
in two leather bags. Soon afterward the three set forth
into the dark and rain-swept night, Tiburcio travelling as
a passenger on his brother's back, partly sustained by a
leather band which passed across the other's forehead,
and inadequately counterpoised by the two bags of silver
pesos which alternately patted Juan de Dios's chest as he
trotted. They traversed unfrequented streets until they
reached the outskirts, and then struck the road along
which a trolley-line runs to the Villa de Guadalupe, the
Mecca of the Mexicans. Tiburcio suffered severely from

the jolting and straining of sore muscles; but the knowledge of his destination so filled him with hope that he suppressed his groans.

The sun was rising when they reached the Villa de Guadalupe. Juan de Dios stretched his brother on one of the heavy iron benches in the plaza at the foot of the hill. Tiburcio seemed a little easier, which was not to be wondered at, for many miracles had been known to follow the mere arrival of the sufferer within the precincts of the sacred pueblo. To Juan de Dios the very air was sanctity and he breathed it with rapture. Faint incense instilled it, bells trembled in it, some as remote voices imploring faith, others strong and impatient mandates to repentance. Padres in long black cassocks flitted hither and thither from church to church and from chapel to chapel. Their houses loomed sombrely above gardens which seemed thronging congregations of flowers. Even the rag awnings fluttering here and there under the old trees of the plaza played their part in the enchantment, for beneath them were exposed for sale every imaginable aid to devotion—rosaries, images, ribbons of saints, and many other objects, even to little dark papers of blessed earth, the virtue of which is notorious all over Mexico. Juan de Dios bought some of the earth and all three devoured it, as is the way of the faithful, Tiburcio receiving the largest share. It was a natural transition to blessed water. This they obtained from the sacred well at the foot of the hill in the centre of a little ancient domed temple, by casting into its rocky depths, a heavy, conical cup of iron attached to a chain. Tiburcio drank of the water as much as he could, its abominable flavour strengthening his faith in its miraculous powers. Also his brother poured a cup of it over him.

And now Juan de Dios was ready for the pilgrimage proper. Shading his eyes with his hand, he traced the course of the stone stairway mounting heavenward from his feet, flight after flight, at first shaded by great trees and at last almost lost amid wild creepers as it aspired in curves like those of a snail's shell to the lofty summit, with its coronet of churches and chapels now ethereal with the golden light of the young morning. With an eagle glance which seemed to perceive in that radiance

an authentic sign from the Virgin of Guadalupe whom
he had adored from childhood, he exclaimed:

"If yonder thou art, Mother of mine, unto thee I bear
a sinner. He is my brother. Make thee the road hard,
dangerous. Put me obstacles; all that may be necessary
to make merit for my presentation before thee with
Tiburcio—that is his name."

He wiped the sweat from his forehead with one finger,
and continued in a tone of exaltation which thrilled the
others.

"I will carry him to thee on my knees, over all those
steps, unto thine altar! This act of devotion, I offer it to
thee for the health of my sinner brother, that thou wilt
permit him to move the body again, if thou thinkest he
merits it."

And having signed himself, he dropped to his knees
and with much difficulty, Dolores assisting, hoisted
Tiburcio to his shoulders with feet hanging down in front
and hands clasping his brother's brow. Juan de Dios held
his body upright, balancing carefully, as he felt his way
upward, one knee after another, slowly—always slowly.
Dolores followed, marvelling at his sanctity. It being the
rainy season, there was no great throng of pilgrims, but
the few who were ascending to the shrine—some women
carrying wax candles decorated with gold paper, others
with plates of sprouting wheat of a delicate pallor from
having been grown in the dark, and a few Inditos with
bamboo cages containing fighting-cocks to be blessed in
church that they might have fortune in battle—these
remarked the superior zeal of Juan de Dios, and regarded
him respectfully as a holy person, one whom it was fortunate to have seen. The same spirit was manifested by the
sellers of blessed articles on the landings of the stair.
While he rested, Juan de Dios caused Dolores to buy the
largest and most beautiful candle obtainable, and there-
after she carried it, unlighted, in front of them. Also,
for refreshment and edification of them all, they bought
blessed fruit, blessed tortillas fried in chili sauce, and
tortillas of the Virgin, which are made sweet and very
small and dyed in different colours.

As he climbed, Juan de Dios prayed, and the more he
suffered the more he thanked God. His wide cotton trousers gave but the scantiest protection to his knees, and

that not for long, yet he did not look for smooth places, and Tiburcio groaned more than he. Once he slipped on a rolling pebble, and after that he mounted every step with the same knee, lifting the hurt one after it. The time came when even his strength of aguador wore out, and he clawed the stone balustrade to raise himself and stopped on each step, his breath hissing between his locked teeth from which the lips were stiffly peeled; and still his eyes pleaded for martyrdom. Dolores at every opportunity would wipe Tiburcio's face where the thorns had scratched it.

When Juan de Dios reached the top he signed to Dolores to light the candle, and he held it at arm's-length as he continued his march into the ancient church of the hill, his knees leaving prints of red on the white marble pavement. Into the depth of the church, straight to the blazing shrine he went, and Dolores saw his face working frightfully as he unlocked his teeth to proclaim that he had kept his word; but no sound came from his throat, and he suddenly fell forward in a swoon, spilling Tiburcio, who executed a series of instinctive movements, too quick for eye to follow, which landed him on his feet, supple and free from pain; and he and Dolores threw themselves on their knees beside the unconscious one at the shrine, to recite a multitude of "gracias" for the miracle.

Dolores fully expected to become the little wife of Juan de Dios. He had come from the confessional when he said to them:

"I now comprehend that I do not serve for this world. The love of woman confounds me too much. God will free me from committing more barbarities. I will remain in this saintly place, for which it seemeth to me I was ordained before my mother bore me. Thou, Dolores, and thou, Tiburcio, serve for this earth. Go, and may the good God accompany you always. Take this bag of money, that it may help you to marry and live justly as good Christians. The other bag I have given to the good padre, who will manage it so that I shall have enough prayers and masses said for the guidance of my steps while I live."

They left him, and he continued to be an aguador,

carrying water from the sacred well to the top of the sacred hill with which to refresh pilgrims, especially the sick and crippled, after the ascent. He himself was crippled, never recovering from a stiffness of one knee, which remained bent. And in this manner Juan de Dios became veritably John of God.

The Gold Vanity Set

When Petra was too big to be carried on her mother's back she was put on the ground, and soon taught herself to walk. In time she learned to fetch water from the public fountain and to grind the boiled corn for the tortillas which her mother made every day, and later to carry her father his dinner—a task which required great intelligence, for her father was a donkey-driver and one never knew at what corner he might be lolling in the shade while awaiting a whistle from someone who might require a service of himself and his little animal.

She grew tall and slender, as strong as wire, with a small head and extremely delicate features, and her skin was the color of new leather. Her eyes were wonderful, even in a land of wonderful eyes. They were large and mysterious, heavily shaded with lashes which had a trick of quivering nervously, half lowered in an evasive, fixed, sidelong look when anyone spoke to her. The irises were amber-colored, but always looked darker. Her voice was like a ghost, distant, dying away at the ends of sentences as if in fear, yet with all its tenderness holding a hint of barbaric roughness. The dissimulation lurking in that low voice and those melting eyes was characteristic of a race among whom the frankness of the Spaniard is criticized as unpolished.

At the age of fourteen Petra married, and married well. Her bridegroom was no barefooted donkey-driver in white trousers and shirt, with riata coiled over his shoulder. No, indeed! Manuelo wore shoes—dazzling yellow shoes which creaked—and colored clothes, and he had a profession, most adorable of professions, playing the miniature guitar made by the Mexican Indians, and singing lively and tender airs in drinkshops and public places wherever a few coins were to be gathered by a handsome fellow with music in his fingers. Most Mexicans, to be sure, have music in their fingers, but Manuelo was enabled to follow the career artistic by the good fortune of his father's being the owner of a prosperous inn for peons.

Petra's attractions made her useful to her father-in-law, who was a widower. At the sight of her coming in from the well, as straight as a palm, carrying a large earthen pot of water on her head, the peons who were killing time there would suddenly find themselves hungry or thirsty and would call for pulque or something to eat. And so she began to wait on customers, and soon she would awake in the morning with no other thought than to twist her long, black hair into a pair of braids which, interwoven with narrow green ribbons, looked like children's toy whips, then to take her husband his *aguadiente*, the little jug of brandy that begins the day, and then to seat herself at the door of the inn, watching for customers beneath trembling lashes, while bending over the coarse cloth whose threads she was drawing.

In six months she had formed the habit of all that surrounded her life. The oaths no longer sounded so disagreeable to her, the occasional fights so terrifying. Manuelo might lose his temper and strike her, but a few minutes later he would be dancing with her. Her last memory going to sleep was sometimes a blow, "Because he is my husband," as she explained it to herself, and sometimes a kiss, "Because he loves me." Only one thing disturbed her: she did not like to see her handsome Manuelo made inflamed and foolish by the milk-white pulque, and she burned many candles to the Virgin of Guadalupe that she might be granted the "beneficio" of a more frequently sober husband.

One afternoon the pueblo resounded with foreign phrases and foreign laughter in foreign voices. As a flock of birds the visitors kept together, and as a flock of birds appeared their chatter and their vivacity to the astonished inhabitants. American fashion, they were led by a woman. She was young, decisive, and carried a camera and guide book. Catching sight of Petra at the door she exclaimed:

"Oh, what a beautiful girl! I must get her picture."

But when Petra saw the little black instrument pointing at her she started like a frightened rabbit and ran inside. The American girl uttered a cry of chargrin, at which Don Ramon came forward. Don Ramon, the planter, had undertaken to escort these, his guests, through the pueblo, but had found himself patiently bringing up the rear of the procession.

"These are tenants of mine," he said with an indifferent gesture. "The house is yours, Miss Young."

"Girls, do you hear that?" she cried. "This is my house—and I invite you all in."

Immediately the inn was invaded, the men following the women. Manuelo, his father, and the peons in the place formed two welcoming ranks, and the Patrón's entrance was hailed with a respectful:

"Viva Don Ramon!"

Manuelo's father looked a little resentful at these inquisitive strangers occupying the benches of his regular customers, who obsequiously folded up their limbs on straw mats along the walls. To be sure, much silver would accrue to the establishment from the invasion, but business in the Mexican mind is dominated by sentiment.

Don Ramon, reading his mind, tapped him on the shoulder with a sharp:

"Quick, to serve the señores!"

Then he clapped his hands for Petra, who came in from the back with oblique looks, and soon the guests were taking experimental sips of strange liquors, especially aguamiel, the sweet unfermented juice of the maguey plant. Manuelo tuned up his instrument and launched into an elaborate and apparently endless improvisation in honor of the Patrón, standing on one foot with the other toe poised, and swaying his body quite alarmingly—for he had drunk much pulque that day. As for Petra, she was followed by the admiring looks of women and men as she moved back and forth, her naked feet plashing softly on the red brick floor.

"I positively must have her picture!" exclaimed Miss Young.

"Of course—at your disposition," murmured Don Ramon.

But the matter was not so simple. Petra rebelled—rebelled with the dumb obstinacy of the Indian, even to weeping and sitting on the floor. Manuelo, scandalized at such contumacy before the Patrón, pulled her to her feet and gave her a push which sent her against the wall. A shiver and murmur passed through the American ranks, and Don Ramon addressed to the young peon a vibrant speech in which the words *"bruto"* and *"imbécil"* were refreshingly distinguishable. Miss Young, closing her camera with a snap, gave her companions the signal for departure, and they obeyed her as always. Don Ramon gave the innkeeper a careless handful of coins and followed his guests, while the innkeeper and his customers ceremoniously pursued him for some distance down the street, with repeated bows and voluble *"Gracias"* and *"Bendiciónes"* over the Patrón, his wife, his children, his house, his crops and all his goods. But Manuelo threw himself upon a mat and fell asleep.

Miss Young had left her guide book on the table, and Petra pounced upon it as a kitten upon a leaf. Some object in the midst of its pages held it partly open. It was a beautiful thing of gold, a trinity of delicate caskets depending by chains from a ring of a size of one's finger. With one quick glance at the unconscious Manuelo she stuck it into the green sash that tightly encompassed her little waist. The book, in which she had lost interest, she put in a drawer of the table. Then she ran outside and climbed the ladder by which one reached the flat stone roof.

Wiping the palms of her hands on her skirt, she extracted the treasure. Of the three pendants she examined the largest first. It opened and a mirror shone softly from its golden nest. A mirror! Novelty of novelties to Petra! Two things startled her—the largeness of her eyes, the paleness of her cheeks. She had always imagined that she had red cheeks, like the girls in Manuelo's songs, some of whom even had cheeks like poppies. Feeling saddened, she opened one of the smaller caskets. It contained a little powder of ivory tint and a puff which delighted her with its unheard-of delicacy. She caressed the back of her hand with it, perceived an esthetic improvement, and ended by carefully powdering the backs of both hands, even to the finger nails.

And the the third box. A red paste. It reddened the tip of her nose when she sniffed its delicate perfume. She rubbed the spot off with her finger and transferred it to one cheek, then roughed a large patch on that cheek, then one on the other, with a nice discretion partly influenced by her memory of the brilliant cheeks of the American señorita of the brave looks, the black box, and the golden treasure.

Thus did Petra discover the secret of the vanity set. But her concept of it was not simple, like Miss Young's. Its practical idea became a mere nucleus in her mind for a fantasy dimly symbolic and religious.

Her eyes—how much larger they were, and how much brighter! She looked into them, laughed into them, broke off to leap and dance, looked again in many ways, sidelong, droopingly, coquettishly, as she would look at Manuelo. Truly the gold treasure was blessed and the red paste was as holy as its smell, which reminded her of church.

Where should she hide it, the treasure? She would bury it in the earth. But no; Manuelo had the habit of burying things—foolish, Indian things—and in his digging he might find her talisman. Better to leave it on the roof. And she did, wrapped in a dry corn husk, covered with a stone.

The afternoon was falling when she went down from the roof. Manuelo slept noisily on the same mat, his father peacefully on an adjacent one. Wild to be looked at, Petra lifted her husband's arm by the sleeve and shook it, but he jerked it free with childish petulance and cuddled into a deeper sleep. She laughed and, inspired with a thought of further embellishment, ran out of the house, too excited even to notice the distant approach of a storm, which at any other time would have kept her indoors praying her rosary. When she returned she was crowned with yellow jonquils, their stems wet from the brook, and in her hand was a long stalk of spikenard with which to awaken Manuelo. But first she would make light, for it was already dusk in the inn. So

she lit the antique iron lanterns which hung by chains
from wooden arms at the front and back doors, and two
candles, one of which she placed on a window ledge and
the other on the floor near Manuelo's face, and she
squatted in front of the second one and held the spikenard beneath his nose, mystically tracing with it in the
air the sign of the cross, until its intoxicating incense
pierced his consciousness and he opened his eyes.

He blinked at the light, then blindly caught her hand
and smiled with a flash of white teeth as he inhaled luxu-
riously with the flower against his nostrils. Then, as he
was thirsty, she fetched him a jug of water, and at last
he saw the jonquil wreath, and the eyes beneath them,
and those cheeks of flame.

He did not speak, but looked at her for a moment,
and then, with the abrupt and graceful movement that
she knew so well slung forward his guitar—it never left
his shoulder by day—and the words he sang to her in
passionate Spanish softened by Indian melancholy were
these:

> "Whether thou lovest me I know not;
>   Thou knowest it.
> I only know that I die
>   Where thou art not."

He had not sung her that since the nights of his sere-
nades outside her father's adobe hut, and even then his
tones had not pulsed with the magic tenderness that was
in them now as he stared at her in the candle light. She
crept along the floor to him and he caught her under his
arm, pulling his poncho over her head, and cuddled her
to him with protecting caresses which she received with
the trembling joy of a spaniel too seldom petted. They
were startled by a voice exclaiming:

"That our sainted Mother of Guadalupe might permit
that you should always be like this, my children!"

It was the old man, whom the music had awakened.
Manuelo quickly kissed the medal that hung at his waist,
stamped with the image of the patron saint of Mexico.
No other saint so intimately rules the hearts and lives of
a people nor rewards their love with so many miracles
and apparitions, and the falling of her name at that

instant of love tinged with a half-felt remorse, produced
a powerful effect upon the young husband. He scrambled
to his feet, lifting Petra with him, and cried:

"Yes, yes, yes, my father, that the blessed Mother of
our Country may hear thee!"

As he looked upward, a murmur of thunder made
them all jump. They crossed themselves, and their voices
mingled in a tremulous chorus of fear and piety. Manuelo, pale as a ghost, seized Petra's hand and led her with
bended body before the old man.

"Thy benediction—give us thy benediction, Father
mine, while I make a vow." He shook with sobs as he
and the girl knelt beneath the father's benediction, and a
louder rumble sounded in the sky. "I promise our blessed
Mother, the Virgin of Guadalupe, that I will never again
maltreat my Petrita, and if I keep not this promise may
she send a thunder to fall on me!"

Petra uttered a wail of terror, and just then a withering
light flashed on the world and a deafening blast of thunder shook the building and sent the three on their faces,
where they remained in an ecstasy of devotion until long
after the storm god had rolled the last of his chariots
across the reverberating platform of the sky.

And it was by the miracle of Manuelo's vow and its
answer from the heavens that Petra's mind grasped the
unalterable faith that the golden treasure was a blessed
thing, most pleasing to the Mother of Guadalupe.

Next morning the planter was driving his guests
through the pueblo, and they were talking of many
things, including the loss of Miss Young's vanity set,
when they saw Petra coming toward them in the direction
of her home, her great eyes looking out like an Egyp-
tian's from between the folds of her scarf. The joy of her
heart shone in her face and her native shyness almost
vanished as she pulled the scarf down from her chin to
give them her graceful *"Buenos dias!"* which they
acknowledged with smiles. And Petra ran on singing like
a bird—singing of the exceeding richness of American
señoritas who can lose golden treasures of miracle-
producing potency and still smile.

"One thing I'm convinced of," said Miss Young to the

planter as they drove on. "That girl hasn't got my vanity set. She looked me straight in the face."

"You don't know my people, Miss Young," returned the Patrón with a heavy sigh—he was anguished because of his guest's loss. "The girl has an innocent heart—yes; but that proves nothing. These are children of the youth of the world, before the limits of 'mine' and 'thine' had been fixed. When an Indito finds lost treasure he believes that he receives a gift from God."

"It's a mighty comfortable belief, and not confined to Mexico," declared the American. "Well, if those cheeks of hers weren't their own natural color this morning, I must say that her complexion makes a stunning blend with my rouge."

Don Ramon trembled at her frankness. Not for worlds would he have smiled, or mentioned her vanity set by name. "How original!" he reflected, epitomizing the thought of all his people when they meet the people of the North.

"But why not have put the question to her right straight out?" pursued Miss Young.

"It was wiser to put her off her guard," he replied. "If these people have your—your ornament, it is probably buried in the earth. Now it is likely to be brought to light, and when I got to the inn—"

"You will take me with you?"

"I beg you not to trouble yourself. It may be painful. I—"

But she insisted, and when dinner was over at the hacienda, Don Ramon sacrificed his siesta to drive with her to Petra's home. Taking a leaf from Mexican tactics, Miss Young allowed the Patrón to precede her, and received with dignified apathy the greetings of the natives who, like marionettes pulled by one string, scrambled into rank as a reception committee. Don Ramon ushered her through the house to the courtyard and seated her there, assigning Petra to defend her from mosquitos with feather fan. That was part of his plan. With Inditos one must employ maneuvers. Reëntering the inn, he caused it to be cleared of strangers. The innkeeper and his son, questioned concerning the missing gold, professed profoundest surprise and ignorance. Without ceremony the Patrón searched them. Feeling a foreign object beneath

Manuelo's sash he drew forth Miss Young's guide book, which Manuelo had found in the drawer—a thing of no apparent utility, but a treasure of a sort, possibly of occult virtue.

This discovery, while unexpected, fell in with the Patrón's plan, which was to stir Petra's fears through her husband—his instinct telling him that she was the key to the problem. And Petra's feather fan fluttered to the earth when she heard the Patrón's stern voice raised in the ringing command to accompany him to the prefecture.

In a flash she was inside, crying in Manuelo's arms. Her Manuelo—to be led as a sacrifice into the ominous precincts of justice, there to be interrogated amid terrors unknown! No, no!

"No, no, Don Ramon! My Manuelo did not find the gold! It was I—I found it!"

She sobbed, almost choking with grief. The Patrón allowed a few minutes for her emotion to spend itself before commanding her to restore to the American señorita her property. With a piteous look she shook her head. *Caramba!* What did she mean? Her answer was a fresh outbrust, so violent, protracted and crescendo that Miss Young, disturbed by visions of medieval torture, ran in to protest against further inhumanity in her name. And Petra groveled at the American's feet, wetting the bricks with her tears for a long time. At last a resolve came to her and with face swollen but calm she picked herself up, turned to Manuelo and his father and motioned them toward the courtyard.

When they had gone out she shut the door. Then with bent head, speaking to the Patrón but looking beneath fluttering eyelids at a button on Miss Young's duster, she told the story of the miracle—of how the golden treasure had yielded that which had made her lovely in the eyes of her beloved, of how the blessed Virgin of Guadulupe had inspired him to vow that he would never again maltreat her as yesterday he had before the eyes of the Americanos, of how the saint had acknowledged his vow with much thunder, as the señorita must have heard for herself, and of how Manuelo was so impressed with the peril of breaking a vow thus formidably recognized that he had drunk no pulque that day and had resolved earnestly to become temperate in his use of that beverage for the rest of his life.

All of which Don Ramon translated to Miss Young, who looked puzzled and remarked:

"Well, I just love the temperance cause, but does she want to keep my danglums to make sure of this Manuelo staying on the water wagon?"

"Certainly not!" declared the Patrón, and turned to Petra abruptly demanded the production of the gold.

She turned pale—so pale that the rouge stood out in islands streaked with rivercourses of tears, and Miss Young looked away with a shuddering prayer that she herself might never turn pale except in the privacy of her chamber. And now Petra spoke. The gold was not in the house. She would conduct the Patrón and the señorita to where it was.

So it was that a pilgrimage in quest of the vanity set sallied forth, Petra leading the way on the back of the burro, the surrey following slowly with Miss Young and her escort. Manuelo and his guitar formed a distant and inquisitive rearguard. It passed, the pilgrimage, into the populous heart of the pueblo.

"Have you any idea where we're going?" inquired Miss Young.

"No," returned the planter. "The ways of the Indito are past conjecture, except that he is always governed by emotion."

He was nervous, sensitively anxious about the impressions of his guest from the North.

"You may observe that we always speak of them as *Inditos*, never as *Indios*," he said. "We use the diminutive because we love them. They are our blood. With their passion, their melancholy, their music and their superstitution they have passed without transition from the feudalism of the Aztecs into the world of to-day, which ignores them; but we never forget that it was their valor and love of country which won our independence."

"They certainly are picturesque," pronounced Miss Young judicially, "and it's great fun to run into the twelfth or some other old century one day out from Austin."

Petra halted at the dark, ancient front of the Chapel of

the Virgin of Guadalupe, where was inscribed in choice
Spanish the history of how the saint had made an apparition to her people stamped upon a cactus plant, together
with other miraculous matters. Dismounting from the
burro the girl passed among the beggars and sellers of
"miracles" and entered the church, uncovering her head.
Don Ramon and Miss Young followed her. She knelt
before a shrine at which stood the benignant figure of the
national saint, almost hidden by the girls of the faithful—
"miracles" of silver, of wax, of feather, of silk—and
among these, its opened mirror reflecting the blaze of
innumerable candles, the gold vanity set shone at her
breast, most splendid of her ornaments. The gold vanity
set, imposing respect, asking for prayers, testifying the
gratitude of an Indian girl for the kindness of her
beloved.

Don Ramon fell on his knees. Miss Young, unused to
the observances of such a place, bowed her head and
choked a little, fumbling for her handkerchief.

"Well, if it saves that nice girl from ever getting
another beating, the saint is perfectly welcome to my
vanity set," she assured herself as she left the chapel.
And Manuelo, leaning against the burro, perceiving by
her expression that all was well, cuddled his guitar and
sang:

> "Into the sea, because it is deep
> I always throw
> The sorrows that this life
> So often gives me."

The Education of Popo

Governor Fernando Arriola and his amiable señora
were confronted with a critical problem in hospitality;
it was nothing less than the entertaining of American
ladies, who by all means must be given the most favor-
able impressions of Mexican civilization.

Hence some unusual preparations. On the backs of men and beasts were arriving magnificent quantities, requisitioned from afar, of American canned soups, fish, meats, sweets, hors-d'œuvres, and nondescripts; ready-to-serve cereals, ready-to-drink cocktails, a great variety of pickles, and much other cheer of American manufacture. Even an assortment of can-openers had not been forgotten. Above all, an imperial call had gone out for ice, and precious consignments of that exotic commodity were now being delivered in various stages of dissolution, to be installed with solicitude in cool places, and kept refreshed with a continual agitation of fans in the hands of superfluous servants. By such amiable extremities it was designed to insure the ladies Cherry against all danger of going hungry or thirsty for lack of conformable ailment or sufficiently frigid liquids.

The wife and daughter of that admirable Señor Montague Cherry of the United States, who was manipulating the extension of certain important concessions in the State of which Don Fernando was governor, and with whose operations his Excellency found his own private interests to be pleasantly involved, their visit was well-timed in a social way, for they would be present on the occasion of a great ball to be given by the governor. For other entertainment the Arriola family would provide as God might permit. Leonor, the only unmarried daughter, was practising several new selections on the harp, her mama sagaciously conceiving that an abundance of music might ease the strain of conversation in the event of the visitors having no Spanish. And now Próspero, the only son, aged fourteen, generally known as Popo, blossomed suddenly as the man of the hour; for, thanks to divine Providence, he had been studying English, and could say prettily, although slowly, "What o'clock it is?" and "Please you this," and "Please you that," and doubtless much more if he were put to it.

Separately and in council the rest of the family impressed upon Popo that the honor of the house of Arriola, not to mention that of his native land, reposed in his hands, and he was conjured to comport himself as a true-born caballero. With a heavy sense of responsibility upon him, he bought some very high collars, burned much midnight oil over his English "method," and became sud-

denly censorious of his stockinged legs, which, accomm-
panying him everywhere, decoyed his down-sweeping
eyes and defied concealment or palliation. After anxious
consideration, he put the case to his mama.

"Thou amiable comparison of all my anguishes," he
said tenderly, "thou knowest my anxiety to comport
myself with credit in the view of the honored Meesees
Cherry. Much English I have already, with immobile
delivery the most authentic and distinguished. So far I
feel myself modestly secure. But these legs, Mama—
these legs of my nightmares—"

"*Chist, chist!* Thou hadst ever a symmetrical leg, Popo
mine," expostulated Doña Elvira, whose soul of a young
matron dreaded her boy's final plunge into manhood.

"But consider, little Mama," he cried, "that very soon
I shall have fifteen years. Since the last day of my saint
I have shaved the face scrupulously on alternate mornings; but that no longer suffices, for my maturing beard
now asks for the razor every day, laughing to scorn these
legs, which continue to lack the investment of dignity.
Mother of my soul, for the honor of our family in the
eyes of the foreign ladies, I supplicate thy consent that I
should be of long pantaloons!"

Touched on the side of her obligations as an international hostess, Doña Elvira pondered deeply, and at
length confessed with a sigh:

"It is unfortunately true, thou repose of my fatigues,
that in long pantaloons thou wouldst represent more."

And it followed, as a crowning graciousness toward
Mrs. Montague Cherry and her daughter, that Popo was
promoted to trousers.

When the visitors arrived, he essayed gallantly to dedi-
cate himself to the service of the elder lady, in accor-
dance with Mexican theories of propriety, but found his
well-meaning efforts frustrated by the younger one, who,
seeing no other young man thereabout, proceeded
methodically to attach the governor's handsome little son
to herself.

Popo found it almost impossible to believe that they
were mother and daugther. By some magic peculiar to
the highly original country of the *Yanquis*, their relation
appeared to be that of an indifferent sisterliness, with a

balance of authority in favor of the younger. That revolutionary arrangement would have scandalized Popo had he not perceived from the first that Alicia Cherry was entitled to extraordinary consideration. Never before had he seen a living woman with hair like daffodils, eyes like violets, and a complexion of coral and porcelain. It seemed to him that some precious image of the Virgin had been changed into a creature of sweet flesh and capricious impulses, animate with a fearless urbanity far beyond the dreams of the dark-eyed, demure, and now despised damsels of his own race. His delicious bewilderment was completed with Miss Cherry, after staring him in the face with a frank and inviting smile, turned to her mother, and drawled laconically:

"He just simply talks with those eyes!"

There was a moon on the night of the day that the Cherrys arrived. There was also music, the bi-weekly *serenata* in the plaza fronting the governor's residence. The band swept sweetly into its opening number at the moment when Don Fernando, with Mrs. Cherry on his arm, stepped out upon his long balcony, and all the town began to move down there among the palms. Miss Cherry, who followed with Popo, exclaimed at the romantic strangeness of the scene, and you may be sure that a stir and buzzing passed through the crowd as it gazed up at the glittering coiffure and snowy shoulders of that angelic señorita from the the United States.

Popo got her seated advantageously, and leaned with somewhat exaggerated gallantry over her chair, answering her vivacious questions, and feeling at one translated to another and far superior planet. He explained as well as he could the social conventions of the *serenata* as unfolded before their eyes in a concerted coil of languid movement—how the ladies, when the music begins, rise and promenade slowly around the kiosk of the band, and how the gentlemen form an outer wheel revolving in the reverse direction, with constant interplay of salutations, compliments, seekings, avoidings, coquetries, intrigues, and a thousand other manifestations of the mysterious forces of attraction and repulsion.

Miss Cherry conceived a strong desire to go down and become merged in that moving coil. No, she would not dream of dragging Doña Elvira or Leonor or mama from the dignified repose of the balcony; but she did beg the privilege, however unprecedented, of promenading with a young gentleman at her side, and showing the inhabitants how such things were managed in America—beg pardon, the United States.

So they walked together under the palms, Alicia Cherry and Próspero Arriola, and although the youth's hat was in the air most of the time in acknowledgment of salutes, he did not really recognize those familiar and astonished faces, for his head was up somewhere near the moon, while his legs, in the proud shelter of their first trousers, were pleasantly afflicted with pins and needles as he moved on tiptoe beside the blonde Americana, a page beside a princess.

Miss Cherry was captivated by the native courtliness of his manners. She thought of a certain junior brother of her own, to whom the business of "tipping his hat," as he called it, to a lady occasioned such extreme anguish of mind that he would resort to the most laborious manœuvers to avoid occasions when the performance of that rite would be expected of him. As for Próspero, he had held the tips of her fingers lightly as they had descended the marble steps of his father's house, and then with a charming little bow had offered her his arm, which she with laughing independence had declined. And now she perused with sidelong glances the infantile curve of his chin, the April fluctuations of his lips, the occasional quiver of this thick lashes, and decided that he was an amazingly cute little cavalier.

With a deep breath she expelled everything disagreeable from her mind, and gave up her spirit to the enjoyment of finding herself for a little while among a warmer, wilder people, with gallant gestures and languorous smiles. And the aromatic air, the tantalizing music, the watchful fire that glanced from under the sombreros of the peons squatting in colorful lines between the benches—all the ardor and mystery of that unknown life caused a sudden fluttering in her breast, and almost unconsciously she took her escort's arm, pressing it impulsively to her side. His dark eyes flashed to hers, and for the first time failed to flutter and droop at the encounter: this time it was her own that lost courage and hastily veiled themselves.

"That waltz," she stammered, "isn't it delicious?"

He told her the name of the composer, and begged her to promise him the privilege of dancing that waltz with her at the ball, in two weeks time. As she gave the promise, she perceived with amusement, and not without delight, that he trembled exceedingly.

Mrs. Cherry was a little rebellious when she and Alicia had retired to their rooms that night.

"Yes, I suppose it's all very beautiful and romantic," she responded fretfully to her daughter's panegyrics, "but I'm bound to confess that I could do with a little less moonlight for the sake of a few words of intelligible speech."

"One always feels that way at first in a foreign country," said Alica, soothingly, "and it certainly is a splendid incentive to learn the language. You ought to adopt my plan, which is to study Spanish very hard every moment we're here."

"If you continue studying the language," her mother retorted, "as industriously as you have been doing to-night, my dear, you will soon be speaking it like a native."

Alica was impervious to irony. Critically inspecting her own pink-and-gold effulgence in the mirror, she went on:

"Of course this is also a splendid opportunity for Próspero to learn some real English, which will please the family very much, as they've decided to send him to an American college. I do hope it won't spoil him. Isn't he a perfect darling?"

"I don't know, not having been given a chance to exchange three words with—Sh-h! Did you hear a noise?"

It had sounded like a sigh, followed by a stealthy shuffle. Alicia went to the door, which had been left ajar, and looked out upon the moonlit gallery just in time to catch a glimpse of a fleeting figure, as Próspero raced for his English dictionary, to look up the strange word "darling."

"The little rascal!" she murmured to herself. "What a baby, after all!" But to her mother she only said, as she closed the door, "It was nothing, dear; just one of those biblical-looking servants covering a parrot's cage."

"Even the parrots here speak nothing but Spanish,"

Mrs. Cherry pursued fretfully. "Of course I am glad to sacrifice my own comfort to any extent to help your dear father in his schemes, although I do think the syndicate might make some graceful little acknowledgment of my social services, but I'm sure that papa never dreamed of your monopolizing the only member of this household to whom it is possible to communicate the most primitive idea without screaming one's head off. I am too old to learn to gesticulate, and I refuse to dislodge to my hairpins in the attempt. And as for your studies in Spanish," she continued warmly, as Alicia laughed, "I'd like to know how you reconcile that pretext with the fact that I distinctly heard you and that infant Lord Chesterfield chattering away together in French."

"French does come in handy at times," Alicia purred, "and if you were not so shy about your accent, Mama dear, you could have a really good time with Doña Elvira. I must ask her to encourage you."

"Don't do anything of the kind!" Mrs. Cherry exclaimed. "You know perfectly well that my French is not fit for foreign ears. And I do think, Alicia, that you might try to make things as easy as possible for me, after my giving way to you in everything, even introducing you here under false pretenses, so to speak."

"It isn't a case of false pretenses, Mama. I've decided to resume my maiden name, and there was no necessity to enter into long explanations to these dear people, who, living as they do in a Catholic country, naturally know nothing about the blessings of divorce."

"So much the better for them!" retorted Mrs. Cherry. "However much of a blessing divorce may be, I've noticed that since you got your decree your face has not had one atom of real enjoyment in it until to-night."

"Until to-night!" Alicia echoed with a stoical smile. "And to-night, because you see a spark of reviving interest in my face, you try to extinguish it with reproaches!"

"No, no, my darling. Forgive me, I'm a little tired and nervous. And I can't help being anxious about you. It's a very trying position for a woman to be in at your age. It's trying for your mother, too. I could box that wretched Edward's ears."

"Not very hard, I'm thinking. You wanted me to forgive him."

"No, my dear, only to take him back on probation. We can punish men for their favorite sins much more effectually by not giving them their freedom."

"I couldn't be guilty of that meanness, and I shall never regret having shown some dignity. And I think that closes the subject, doesn't it, dearest?" Alicia yawned.

"Poor Edward!" her mother persisted. "How he would have enjoyed this picturesque atmosphere with you!"

Alicia calmly creamed her face.

Próspero spent a great part of the night over his English dictionary. Again and again he conned the Spanish equivalents listed against the word "darling." A significant word, it seemed, heart-agitating, sky-transporting. He had not dreamed that the harsh, baffling English language could contain in seven letters a treasure so rare. *Predilecto, querido, favorito, amando*— which translation should he accept as defining his relation to Mees Cherry, avowed by her own lips? The patient compiler of that useful book could never have forseen the ecstasy it would one day bring to a Mexican boy's heart.

He was living in a realm of enchantment. To think that already, on the very day of their meeting, he and his blonde Venus should have arrived at intimacies far transcending any that are possible in Mexico except between the wedded or the wicked! In stark freedom, miraculously unchaperoned, they had talked together, walked together, boldly linked their very arms! In his ribs he still treasured the warmth of her; in his fingers throbbed the memory that for one electric instant their hands had fluttered, dove-like, each to each. Small enough, those tender contacts; yet by such is the life force unchained; Popo found himself looking into a seething volcano, which was his own manhood. That discovery, conflicting as it did with the religious quality of his love, disturbed him mightily. Sublimely he invoked all his spiritual strength to subdue the volcano. And his travail was richly rewarded. The volcano became transformed magically into a fount of pellucid purity in which, bathing his exhausted soul, young Popo became a saint.

In that interesting but arduous capacity he labored for many days, during which Miss Cherry created no further

occasion for their being alone together, but seemed to
throw him in the way of her mama, a trial which he
endured with fiery fortitude. He was living the spiritual
life with rigorous intensity, a victim of the eternal man-
date that those fountains of purity into which idealism
has power to transform the most troublesome of volcanoes should be of a temperature little short of the
boiling-point.

His dark eyes kept his divinity faithfully informed of
his anguish and his worship, and her blue ones discreetly
accepted the offering. Once or twice their hands met
lightly, and it seemed that the shock might have given
birth to flaming worlds. When alone with her mama, Alicia showed signs of an irritable ardor which Mrs. Cherry,
with secret complacency, set down to regrets for the too
hastily renounced blessings of matrimony.

"Poor old Ned!" the mother sighed one night. "Your
father has seen him, and tells me that he looks dreadful."

On the morning of the night of the ball the entire
party, to escape from the majordomo and his gang of
hammering decorators, motored into the country on a
visit to Popo's grandmother, whose house sheltered three
priests and a score of orphan girls, and was noted for its
florid magnificence of the Maximilian period.

Popo hoped that some mention might be made in Alicia's hearing of his grandmother's oft-expressed intention
to bequeath the place to him, and he was much gratified
when the saintly old lady, who wore a mustache à la
española, brought up the subject, and dilated upon it at
some length, telling Popo that he must continue to make
the house blessed by the presence of the three padres,
but that she would make provision for the orphans to be
taken elsewhere, out of his way, a precaution she mentioned to an accompaniment of winks and innuendos
which greatly amused all the company, including the
padres, only Alicia and Popo showing signs of distress.

After dinner, which occurred early in the afternoon,
Popo manœuvered Alicia apart from the others in the
garden. His eyes telegraphed a desperate plea, to which
hers consented, and he took her by the hand, and they
ran through a green archway into a terraced Italian garden peopled with marble nymphs and fauns, from which

they escaped by a little side gate into an avenue of orange-blossoms. Presently they were laboring over rougher ground, where their feet crushed the fat stems of lilies, and then they turned and descended a roughly cut path winding down the scarred, dripping face of a cliff into the green depth of a little canon, at the upper end of which a cascade resembling a scarf flung over a wall sang a song of eternity, and baptized the tall tree-ferns that climbed in disorderly rivalry for its kisses.

Alicia breathed deeply the cool, moss-scented air. The trembling boy, suddenly appalled at the bounty of life in presenting him with this sovereign concatenation of the hour, the place, and the woman, could only stammer irrelevantly, as he switched at the leaves with his cane:

"There is a cave in there behind the waterfall. One looks through the moving water as through a thick window, but one gets wet. Sometimes I come here alone, all alone, without going to the house, and *mamagrande* never knows. The road we came by passes just below, crossing this little stream, where thou didst remark the tall bambous before we saw the porter's lodge. The mud wall is low, and I tie my horse in the bamboo thicket."

"Why do you come here?" she asked, her eyes tracing the Indian character in the clear line of his profile and the dusky undertone of his cheek.

"It is my caprice to mediate here. From my childhood I have loved the *cañoncito* in a peculiar way. Thou wilt laugh at me—no? Well, I have always felt a presence here, unseen, a very quiet spirit that seemed to speak to me of—*quién sabe*? I never knew—never until now."

His voice thrilled, and his eyes lifted themselves to hers, as if for permission, before he continued in ringing exaltation:

"Now that thou hast come, now that thou appearest here in all thy lovely splendor, now I know that the spirit I once felt and loved in secret was a prophecy of thee. Yes, Alicia mine, for thee this place has waited long— for thee, thou adored image of all beauty, queen of my heart, object of my prayers, whose purity has sanctified my life."

Alicia, a confirmed matinée girl, wished that all her woman friends might have seen her at that moment (she had on a sweet frock and a perfectly darling hat), and that they might have heard the speech that had just been addressed to her by the leading man. He was a thoughtful juvenile, to be sure, but he had lovely, adoring eyes and delightfully passionate tones in his voice; and, anyhow, it was simply delicious to be made love to in a foreign language.

She was extremely pleased, too, to note that her own heart was going pitapat in a fashion quite uncomfortable and sweet and girly. She wouldn't have missed that sensation for a good deal. What a comfort to a bruised heart to be loved like this! He was calling her his saint. If that Edward could only hear him! Perhaps, after all, she *was* a saint. Yes, she felt that she certainly was, or could be if she tried. Now he was repeating some verses that he had made to her in Spanish. Such musical words! One had to come to the hot countries to discover what emotion was; and as for love-making! How the child had suffered!

As he bowed his bared head before her she laid her hands, as in benediction, where a bronze light glanced upon the glossy, black waves of his hair; and that touch, so tender, felled Popo to the earth, where he groveled with tears and broken words and kisses for her little shoes, damp from the spongy soil. And she suddenly dropped her posings and her parasol, and forgot her complexion and her whalebones and huddled down beside him in the bracken, hushing his sobs and wiping his face, with sweet epithets and sweeter assurances, finding a strange, wild comfort in mothering him recklessly, straight from the soul. At the height of which really promising situation she was startled by a familiar falsetto hail from her mama as the rest of the party descended into the *cañoncito,* whither it had been surmised that Popo had conducted Miss Cherry.

After flinging an artless yodel in response to the maternal signal, and while composing Popo and herself into lifelike attitudes suggestive of a mild absorption in the beauties of nature, she whispered in his ear:

"The next time you come here you shall have two horses to tie in the bamboos."

"*Ay Dios!* All blessings on thee! But when?" he pleaded. "Tell me when!"

"Well, to-morrow," she replied after quick thought;

"as you would say, my dear, *mañana*. Yes, I'll manage it. I'm dying for a horseback ride, and I've had such a lovely time to-day."

To be the only blonde at a Mexican ball is to be reconciled for a few hours to the fate of being a woman. Alicia, her full-blown figure habited in the palest of pink, which seemed of the living texture of her skin, with a generous measure of diamonds winking in effective constellations upon her golden head and dazzling bosom, absorbed through every pore the enravished admiration of the beholders, and beneficently poured it forth again in magnetic waves of the happiness with which triumph enhances beauty. Popo almost swooned with rapture at this apotheosis of the being who, a few hours earlier, had actually hugged him in the arms now revealed as those of a goddess. And to-morrow! With swimming brain he repeated over and over, as if to convince himself of the incredible, *"Mañana!"*

Almost as acute as the emotions of Popo, in a different way, were those of a foreign gentleman who had just been presented to the governor by the newly arrived Mr. Montague Cherry. So palpably moved was the stranger at the sight of Alicia that Mrs. Cherry laid a soothing hand on his arm and whispered a conspirator's caution. Presently he and Alicia stood face to face. Had they been Mexican, there would have ensued an emotional and edifying scene. But all that Alicia said, after one sharp inspiration of surprise, was, with an equivocal half-smile:

"Why, Edward! Of all people!"

And the gentleman addressed as Edward, finding his voice with difficulty, blurted out hoarsely:

"How are you, Alicia?"

At which Alicia turned smilingly to compliment Doña Elvira on the decorations.

Mr. Edward P. Winterbottom was one of those fortunate persons who seem to prefigure the ideal toward which their race is striving. A thousand conscientious draftsmen, with the national ideal in their subconsciousness, were always hard at work portraying his particular type in various romantic capacities, as those of foot-ball hero, triumphant engineer, "well-known clubman," and pleased patron of the latest collar, cigarette, sauce, or

mineral water. Hence he would give you the impression
of having seen him before somewhere under very admirable auspices. Extremely good-looking, with long legs, a
magnificent chin, and an expression of concentrated
manhood, he had every claim to be classed as "whole-
some," cherishing a set of opinions suitable to his excellent station in life, a proper reverence for the female of
the species, and an adequate working assortment of simple emotions easily predicable by a reasonably clever
woman. On the weaknesses common to humanity he had
fewer than the majority, and in the prostration of
remorse and desire in which he now presented himself
to Alicia he seemed to offer timber capable of being
made over into a prince of lifelong protectors.

Alicia had come to feel that she needed a protector,
chiefly from herself. Presently, without committing herself, however, she favored him with a waltz. As they
started off, she saw the agonized face of Popo, who had
been trying to reach her. She threw him a smile, which
he lamentably failed to return. Not until then did she
identify the music as that of the waltz she had promised
him on the night of that first *serenata*. After it was over
she good-naturedly missed a dance or two in search of
him, meaning to make amends; but he was nowhere to
be found.

With many apologies, Doña Elvira mentioned to Alicia, when she appeared the following morning, that the
household was somewhat perturbed over the disappearance of Próspero. No one could remember having seen
him since early in the progress of the ball. He had not
slept in his bed, and his favorite horse was missing from
the stable. Don Fernando had set the police in motion.
Moreover, *la mamagrande*, informed by telephone, was
causing masses to be said for the safety of her favorite.
God would undoubtedly protect him, and meanwhile the
honored señorita and her mama would be so very gracious as to attribute any apparent neglect of the canons
of hospitality to the anxieties of an unduly affectionate
mother.

Alicia opened her mouth to reply to that tremulous
speech, but, finding no voice, turned and bolted to her
room, trying to shut out a vision of a slender boy lying

self-slain among the ferns where he had received caresses and whispers of love from a goddess of light fancy and lighter faith. She had no doubt that he was there in his *cañoncito*. But perhaps he yet lived, waiting for her! She would go at once. Old Ned should escort her as far as the bamboos, to be within call in case of the worst.

Old Ned was so grateful for the privilege of riding into the blossoming country with his Alicia that she rewarded him with a full narration of the Popo episode; and he received the confidence with discreet respect, swallowing any qualms of jealousy, and extolling her for the high-minded sense of responsibility which now possessed her to the point of tears.

"It's all your fault, anyway," she declared as they walked their horse up a long hill.

He accepted the blame with alacrity as a breath of the dear connubial days.

"One thing I've demonstrated," she continued fretfully, "and that is that the summer flirtation of our happy land simply cannot be acclimated south of the Rio Grande. These people lack the necessary imperturbability of mind, which may be one good reason why they're not permitted to hold hands before the marriage ceremony. To complicate matters, it seems that I'm the first blonde with the slightest claim to respectability that ever invaded this part of Mexico, and although the inhabitants have a deluded idea that blue eyes are intensely spiritual, they get exactly the same Adam-and-Eve palpitations from them that we do from the lustrous black orbs of the languishing tropics."

"Did you—ah—did you get as far as—um—kissing?" Mr. Winterbottom inquired, with an admirable air of detachment.

"Not quite. Edward; that was where the rest of the folks came tagging along. But I promise you this: if I find that Popo alive, I'm going to kiss him for all I'm worth. The unfortunate child is entitled to nothing less."

'But wouldn't that—hum—add fuel to the flame?" he asked anxiously.

"It would give him back his self-respect," she declared. "It isn't healthy for a high-spirited boy to feel like a worm."

*   *   *

Mr. Winterbottom, while waiting among the bamboos in company with three sociable horses—Popo's was in possession when they arrived—smoked one very long cigar and chewed another into pulpy remains. Alicia not having yodeled, he understood that she had found the boy alive, and he tried to derive comfort from that reflection. He had promised to preserve patience and silence, and such was his anxiety to propitiate Alicia that he managed to subjugate his native energy, although the process involved the kicking up of a good deal of soil. She reflected, when she noted on her return his carefully cheerful expression, that a long course of such discipline would go far toward regenerating him as a man and a husband.

"Well, how is our little patient today?" he inquired with gentle jocosity as he held the stirrup for her.

"I believe he'll pull through now," Alicia responded gravely. "I've sent him up to his grandmother's to be fed, and he's going to telephone his mother right away."

"That's bully," Mr. Winterbottom pronounced heartily; and for some moments, as they gained the road, nothing more was said. Alicia seemed thoughtful. Mr. Winterbottom was the first to speak.

"Poor little beggar must have been hungry," he hazarded.

"He had eaten a few bananas, but as they're not recognized as food here, they only increased his humiliation. You know, banana-trees are just grown to shade the coffee-plants, which are delicate."

Mr. Winterbottom signified a proper interest in that phase of coffee culture, and Alicia took advantage of a level stretch of road to put her horse to the gallop. When he regained her side, half a mile farther on, he was agitated.

"Alicia, would you mind enlightening me on one point?" he asked. "Did you—give him back his self-respect?"

"Perhaps I'd better tell you all that happened, Edward."

"By Jove! I wish you would!" he cried earnestly.

"Well, Popo wasn't a bit surprised to see me. In fact, he was expecting me."

"Indeed? Hadn't lost his assurance, then."

"He had simply worked out my probable actions, just as I had worked out his. Of course he looked like a wild thing, hair on end, eyes like a panther, regular young bandit. Well, I rag-timed up in my best tra-la-la style, but he halted me with a splendid gesture, and started a speech. You know what a command of language foreigners have, even the babies. He never fumbled for a word, and all his nouns had verbs waiting, and the climaxes just rolled over one another like waves. It was beautiful."

"But what was it about?"

"Me, of course: my iniquity, the treacherous falseness residing as ashes in the Dead Sea fruit of my beauty, with a lurid picture of the ruin I had made of his belief in woman, his capacity for happiness, and all that. And he wound up with a burst of denunciation in which he called me by a name which ought not to be applied to any lady in any language."

"Alicia!"

"Oh, I deserved it, Edward, and I told him so. I didn't care how badly he thought of me if I could only give him back his faith in love. It's such a wonderful thing to get *that* back! So I sang pretty small about myself; and when I revealed my exact status as an ex-wife in process of being courted by her divorced husband, his eyes nearly dropped out of his head. You see, they don't play 'Tag! You're it!' with marriage down here. That boy actually began to hand me out a line of missionary talk. He thinks I ought to remarry you, Ned."

"He must have splendid instincts, after all. So of course you didn't kiss him?"

"Wait a minute. After mentioning that I was eleven years older than he, and that my hair had been an elegant mouse-drab before I started touching it up—"

"Not at all. I liked its color—a very pretty shade of—"

"After that, I told him that he could thank his stars for the education I had given him, in view of the fact that he's going to be sent to college in the U.S.A., and I gave him a few first-rate pointers on the college widow breed. And finally, Ned, I put it to him that I was anxious to do the square thing, and if he considered himself entitled to a few kisses while you were waiting, he could help himself."

"And he?" Mr. Winterbottom inquired with a pinched look.

"He looked so cute that I could have hugged him. But he nobly declined."

"That young fellow," said Mr. Winterbottom, taking off his hat and wiping his brow, "is worthy of being an American."

"Why, that was his Indian revenge, the little monkey! But he was tempted, Ned."

"Of course he was. If you'd only tempt *me*! O Alicia, you're a saint!"

"That's what Popo called me yesterday, and it was neither more nor less true than what he called me today. I suppose we're all mixtures of one kind and another. And I've discovered, Ned, that it's the healthiest kind of fun to be perfectly frank with—with an old pal. Let's try it that way next time, shall we dear?"

She offered her lips for the second time that day, and—

GRACE HODGSON FLANDRAU

❦ ❦ ❦

Grace Hodgson Flandrau (1889–1971) was born in St. Paul, Minnesota. Educated in private schools in St. Paul and Paris, she was married in 1909 to W. Blair Flandrau, the son of a wealthy jurist and author. Flandrau and his bride left immediately for Mexico where he had been operating a coffee plantation for several years, with the occasional assistance of his younger brother, Charles (Charles Flandrau was the author of Viva Mexico!, *a work published in 1909 that many critics regard as the finest account of travel in Mexico written in the twentieth century.) The coffee* finca *was located in the remote Indian village of Mislanta, north of the colonial city of Jalapa in the tropical state of Veracruz, and while there Grace Flandrau began to write and publish stories about the Mexican Indians who lived and worked on the place. "Fiesta in St. Paul" reveals just how much Flandrau learned about Mexico and its people in the time she spent there. The Flandraus lived in Mislanta until 1914, when the Mexican revolution—which exploded in full force in 1910—made it dangerous to remain in that part of Mexico. The young couple returned to Minnesota. Grace Flandrau continued to write as she traveled with her husband throughout the world, publishing numerous books based on her adventures:* Being Respectable *(1923),* Great Northern Railway *(1925),* Indeed the Flesh *(1934),* Under the Sun *(1936), and* Then I Saw the Congo *(1929).*

"Fiesta in St. Paul"—first published in 1943 in The Yale Review—*takes place on September 16th, Mexican Independence Day, and involves Mexicans and their American-born children who make up the Mexican community of that midwestern city. In this story, Flandrau displays rare and sensitive feelings for these transplanted Mexicans.*

Fiesta in St. Paul

The celebration in honor of Mexico's Independence Day was to take place in the city's public picnic grounds. We arrived an hour or so after the exercises were supposed to begin, but nothing, of course, had started. In front of the fine new brick pavilion were one or two delivery trucks got up as floats and draped with Mexican and American colors. They were to have been in a parade, which, owing partly to threatened rain, partly to the fact that the paraders couldn't possibly assemble on time, didn't come off. A number of people, all Mexicans and mostly in native costume, had, however, arrived at the pavilion, and it was odd to see them there. An American city on the upper Mississippi does not seem quite the background for Mexicans—especially these full-blooded Mexican Indians who, for the most part, make up St. Paul's Mexican population.

Inside the pavilion, the noise was already satisfactorily loud. The huge, stone-floored hall re-echoed deafeningly to the shrieks of the children, the loud music of a juke box, and the boom of a drum left standing on a bench and pounded unceasingly by a small boy.

Below the platform—alluded to in the program as *"el Altar Patrio"*—were rows of chairs, still empty. There was only a young Indian woman, suckling a three-year-old boy dressed in the uniform of a naval officer, his white navy cap pushed back from the fat face as he fed.

On a bench near the door a group of very dark, very neatly dressed men were sitting. In spite of their American clothes, they might have been any of the Indians who used to come down from their high villages to work on our Mexican plantation in the coffee-picking season.

"Do you know," I asked one of them, chiefly to hear again the clipped Mexican Spanish, "when the program will begin?"

He rose and politely removed his sky-blue felt hat. "Well—who knows, Señora?" His small, studying eyes, liquid-bright and set deep behind high cheekbones, were fastened intently on my face. And he had the alert, upright carriage of those Totonaco Indians in our state of Vera Cruz who carry such incredible loads for such incredible distances over the mountain trails. But he was darker in color; his features were very small; his head, thatched with stiff black hair, was very flat behind.

"May I ask," I said, "from what part of Mexico you come?"

"From Guanajuato, Señora." He gave me a soft, quick smile. "But not from Guanajuato itself. My earth—*mi tierra*—is more beyond, in the hills."

There has always been a good sound of those words, "my earth." And I've often wondered how these people, who are so much a part and product of their earth, can endure the separation. But one remembers, too, those villages in the hills: the remoteness, the poverty, the slow tempo, the utter monotony, eventlessness, stagnation— for all that the romanticists have written to the contrary.

"Do you like it better here, Señor?"

"Well—" he considered carefully, "flowers. Over there are always flowers. Very beautiful. Also fruits—" his pace accelerated—"every class of fruits. One fruit finishes, another begins. Also, no snow and ice. And always flowers." He lingered on the pleasant syllables, *flo-res*. "But here the work is better. In the beet fields it is good for work."

One of his companions who had not taken his eyes off our faces, now stepped forward and inquired in a loud tone, "Franceeschmeet?"

"I beg your pardon?"

"Mees—" slowly, then all in a breath—"Franceeschmeet? Office of Eemeegration? You know?"

No, I did not know Miss Francis Smith. He bowed and stepping back, resumed his intense scrutiny of our persons. He was different in type from Number One, and had that biblical profile—big hooked nose, big lips and teeth—that is characteristic of certain Indian races.

Number One now had something to say. Might it be, he had been asking himself, that the Señora had lived in Mexico?

I said I had, and also in the hills. Beyond Jalapa. "We had plantations of coffee."

"Ah—coffee." As he took this information inside himself to reflect upon it carefully, Number Two came up with another inspiration.

"El Paso, Texas? Meestairereebraoun? You know?"

Unfortunately, I know neither El Paso nor Mr. R. E. Brown. The smile vanished from his face, and it was plain that he regarded this as not only a melancholy but also a somewhat suspicious circumstance.

Unwilling, however, to close on so negative a note, he suddenly stated: "My Mama"—he pointed to the floor—"here in this same city lives my Mama. Also my sisters. Two." He held up two fingers. "And there you behold them."

Not far off stood the sisters, very dark, very stout, dressed in black with red roses in their hair, and, under the thick paint and powder, their skins showed a faintly bluish tinge. Identical, in every detail, with the young girls who used to walk round and round the park in Jalapa when the moon was shining and the band played bullfight tunes.

They returned our glances with shy and, I thought, expectant curiosity, waiting for him to give them the signal to approach. He did not give it. And I knew that if this were Mexico, he would be riding the donkey, and they trudging dutifully behind in the dust.

The conversation having come to a standstill, we parted with many bows. A refreshment tent had been set up outside under the trees, and we joined the small crowd that was gathering about it. The menu included tamales, and the two varieties of flat corn-cakes—dressed with sauces in which red pepper and garlic annihilate all other flavors—known as *enchiladas* and *tacos*. We chose *tacos*.

But the young girl who was serving shook her head. "I feel it very much, but the *tacos* have not yet arrived."

"*Enchiladas*, then?"

"As little, disgracefully, has the sauce for these come."

"Will it be long?"

"Who knows?" And her smile, notwithstanding many bright gold teeth flecked with carmine lipstick, was rather lovely.

"Excuse me, please," a voice spoke, startlingly, in my ear, "is this not the Señora who owns the rich, the large, the magnificent *fincas* of coffee in Mexico?"

It was a twinkling, skull-like face covered with fine

wrinkles that traced a pattern of sly, amiable insignificance. I replied that I thought it was the *agraristas*, now, owned the plantation—anyhow, not I. And that it had never been especially rich or magnificent.

But this he would not accept. "No, no, very large, very rich, that is certain." Then, unfolding the program, a large sheet of paper in the red and green Mexican colors, he pointed to various items with a dark forefinger narrow as a claw. Patriotic Poem, recited by *el Señor* Refugio Gil. "Myself," he said. Patriotic Poem, recited by the youth, Alessandro Gil. "My son." *Las Chiapanecas*, danced by a group of boys and girls. "My children," he declared with a modest smile.

A truck, in the meantime, had drawn up, and out of the back descended a small man, closely buttoned into an immaculate blue serge suit and carrying a walking stick. Immense steaming kettles were handed down to him, and he dragged them to the tent without once letting go of his cane or removing his pearl-gray derby hat. Following the kettles, out came a stout, pock-marked matron and two young girls in evening dress. Then the head of a small shaggy dog. The dog barked, leaped nimbly to the ground, and scampered off with the air of one accustomed to fiestas.

The *tacos* had come, but no sauce; so we decided not to wait. Through loudspeakers outside the pavilion, records of Mexican songs blared gaily and raucously in the twilight. We left Señor Gil at work with all ten fingers and formidable teeth upon a small mountain of tamales, and went back to the pavilion.

Crowds were pouring in. All the seats were taken, and the floor space was a surging mass of men, women, and especially children. Young men in the uniform of the United States Army, old men in slouch hats and fierce mustachios, crowded about the bar. Young girls strolled in pairs, cracking their gum. And the small naval officer slept soundly, stretched across the laps of his parents.

The non-Mexicans present were few. They were, chiefly, the City Councilmen invited as special guests; the orchestra—and an odd one at that; an unpleasing young man in fancy Western costume, down on the program as "*el Señor* Bert (Sunshine) Kahn," a singer of cowboy songs; and ourselves.

With no diminution of the uproar in the hall, the program got under way. The orchestra leader stepped forward. She was an elderly lady, in spectacles, girlish evening dress, and false curls that nodded coquettishly under one ear. Except for two unconvincing young men, the musicans were female and not young. The banjo-player was a tired blonde in white satin; the pianist a crippled person with a bunch of red roses nodding on top of her pompadour. Why the orchestra should have had to be American I don't know, except that it probably cost more—even this one—and was, therefore, more worthy of so distinguished an occasion.

A dark gentleman in a pink satin blouse stepped to the microphone; a chorus of dark, very plain little children came on the stage. Then to the rousing accompaniment of the ochestra—the schoolmarmish leader alternately playing the violin and conducting with her bow, her foot, her bare shoulders, and her false curls—the Mexican and American national hymns were sung by all.

The reading of the Mexican Act of Independence, in Spanish, and the speeches, in English, of the City Councilmen, were only an incomprehensible booming in the loudspeaker. But when Señor Gil began his recitation, fright diminished his voice to a point where the instrument could pick it up. The poem, however, was a long one, and in the middle of it Señor Gil faltered, stopped, stood with a smile of pure agony rending his face. It was touch and go for a moment; then, alas, memory revived, and he went on for another fifty verses.

More recitations followed. Then came the dances, *jarabes, jotas, zapateadas*. They were danced mostly by children, but the gestures, the music, the costumes, and especially the drumming of feet on the boards were startlingly familiar.

In the old days on our plantation, when the picking season was over and the last of the sacks of coffee had been tied on the mules, and the last of the long caravans had started on its three or four days' journey over the mountain to the nearest railway, the coffee warehouse would be empty and free for more frivolous uses. Often then, on a Saturday, our plantation people would give a dance. All afternoon the rockets would go up, inviting the neighbors to the ball; and the sound of these rockets exploding languidly, without fire or color in the lovely stillness of that remote place, was sad, somehow, and futile—like a pistol fired at nothing.

Far and near, however, they would be heard and heeded. And, as night fell, lights would twinkle along all the jungle-covered slopes and through the groves of coffee. Sometimes it would be a young blood alone on horseback, his gun and knife in his belt, his machete at his side. Oftener it would be a family of Indians, on foot, or with a burro among them. Classic and unchanging their outlines in the dusk—the big hat, the loose white pyjama suit of the man; the woman's head swathed and nun-like, her full ruffled skirts swinging as she walked. The *rebozo* would bind the baby to her back; the children would march sturdily beside her.

Vendors of food came, and of drink; gamblers with their monte tables; the orchestra with harp and the stringed instruments locally called *jaranas*. Torches flared in the darkness under the warehouse porch. And all night there would come to us, distantly, the rhythmic pounding of feet on the wooden floor, stomping out the *zapateadas*.

The dawn is red-gold and sudden in those latitudes, the morning air wonderfully sweet and pure. But this beauty was in no way compatible with the procession that staggered across the patio to our house. The survivors of the dance could not bring themselves to leave without saluting the *patrones*; or the orchestra without offering us a serenade. And, gaily, drunkenly, excruciatingly out of tune, it would play under our window something that could almost be identified as "After the Ball."

Tonight on this Minnesota picnic ground were the same dark, naïve faces, the same feeling of zest, amenity, and good manners that did not in the least preclude the ever-present hint of sleeping violence. And just as on the plantation there had seldom been a ball without its stabbing or shooting, so this St. Paul fiesta produced at least one minor knifing.

"You like, Señora? The fiesta is beautiful, truly?" It would be Señor Gil, his face thrust suddenly into mine. And each time he came back, he would smell increasingly of strong drink. "Poetry, music, the dance! In a word, *el ideal*. Ah!" Then, turning, he would totter off through the dense crowd, in the direction of the bar.

The heat now, the smells, the noise; the children racing about, crowding past you, dripping ice-cream pies down your neck; the stone floor sticky with Cracker Jack, dampened by the indiscretions of the very young; the state of suffocation and general frenzy—whatever they had to do with the ideal, at least indicated a fiest that was a complete success.

It had also reached its climax. Her Majesty the Queen was to be crowned by His Honor the Mayor of the city. His Honor arrived on the dot, but, needless to say, Her Majesty did not. During the interminable wait, a space was cleared and the audience danced. A rather large contingent of Syrians had turned up from their adajacent quarter, and there were a number of Negroes. Also, the lady standing next to me stated that she was an American Indian, half Sioux and half Potawatami. And when at last the pretty Mexican girl arrived, she was crowned Queen by an Irish Mayor in a State that boasts the biggest—or is it second biggest?—Scandinavian city in the world.

So it all seemed very American and heart-warming, the times being what they are. And the presence, too, of the Mexican boys in the uniform of the United States Army gave an authentic accent to his small pageant of international good will.

Outside, my new acquaintances waited to say goodbye. There was the man who knew Franceeschmeet; there was Señor Gil, smelling to high heaven of assorted liquors; and there was the little, very dark Indian from "more beyond" Guanajuato, whose studying look now gave way to one of sudden illumination.

"Your husband, Señora,"—he nodded towards the friend who was with me—"he is the Governor of the State, truly?" But he took it quite well when he learned that he was neither my husband nor the Governor of Minnesota.

And then, with expressions of mutual regret, we said good-bye. The night had already taken their dark faces into itself, but the flash of their white teeth was very friendly under the lights.

MARIO SUAREZ

❧ ❧ ❧

Mario Suarez was born in Tucson, Arizona, in 1925, the child of Mexican parents who, like so many others, had fled to the United States to escape from the Mexican revolution. He grew up in one of Tucson's Mexican-American barrios and attended public schools. Following the Japanese attack on Pearl Harbor, he joined the United States Navy—he had not yet turned seventeen—and served aboard several different vessels in the North Atlantic. Following his discharge, he returned to Tucson and entered the Universtiy of Arizona in 1947, where he began to write a series of vignettes—"cuentos del corozon"—about the Tucson barrio. These stories, which very accurately capture life in a typical Mexican-American barrio in any southwestern city during the 1930s and 40s, also reflect the attitudes of the period—the necessity of regarding assimilation and acculturation of Mexicans and Mexican-Americans into an Anglo society. Suarez's works, which first began appearing in the Arizona Quarterly *in 1947, hold a unique place in contemporary American literature. They are the first literary efforts of an American of Mexican descent, writing in English, to appear in a prestigious U.S. journal. Indeed, they are the first works that offer a predominantly Anglo audience a compelling and realistic portrait of life of the Mexican-American who, at the time, was not only misunderstood, mistreated, and maligned by the Anglo majority, but also for the most part ignored. Suarez was a pioneer in the attempt to change those attitudes. With those stories, Suarez stopped writing. He married, moved to Southern California, raised a family and, of course, went to work. Life and its distractions left him no time or energy for more literary efforts. However, in 1990, after being with Pomona College for twenty-two years, Mario Suarez retired. He says now, "Finally, I have time to return to fiction."*

El Hoyo

From the center of downtown Tucson the ground slopes gently away to Main Street, drops a few feet, and then rolls to the banks of the Santa Cruz River. Here lies the sprawling section of the city known as El Hoyo. Why it is called El Hoyo is not clear. It is not a hole as its name would imply; it is simply the river's immediate valley. Its inhabitants are *chicanos* who raise hell on Saturday night, listen to Padre Estanislao on Sunday morning, and then raise more hell on Sunday night. While the term *chicano* is the short way of saying *Mexicano*, it is the long way of referring to everybody. Pablo Gutierrez married the Chinese grocer's daughter and acquired a store; his sons are *chicanos*. So are the sons of Killer Jones who threw a fight in Harlem and fled to El Hoyo to marry Cristina Mendez. And so are all of them—the assortment of harlequins, bandits, oppressors, oppressed, gentlemen, and bums who came from Old Mexico to work for the Southern Pacific, pick cotton, clerk, labor, sing, and go on relief. It is doubtful that all of these spiritual sons of Mexico live in El Hoyo because they love each other— many fight and bicker constantly. It is doubtful that the *chicanos* live in El Hoyo because of its scenic beauty— it is everything but beautiful. Its houses are built of unplastered adobe, wood, license plates, and abandoned car parts. Its narrow streets are mostly clearings which have, in time, acquired names. Except for the tall trees which nobody has ever cared to identify, nurse, or destroy, the main things known to grow in the general area are weeds, garbage piles, dogs, and kids. And it is doubtful that the *chicanos* live in El Hoyo because it is safe—many times the Santa Cruz River has risen and inundated the area.

In other respects living in El Hoyo has its advantages. If one is born with the habit of acquiring bills, El Hoyo is where the bill collectors are less likely to find you. If one has acquired the habit of listening to Señor Perea's Mexican Hour in the wee hours of the morning with the

radio on at full blast, El Hoyo is where you are less likely
to be reported to the authorities. Besides, Perea is very
popular and to everybody sooner or later is dedicated
The Mexican Hat Dance. If one has inherited a bad taste
for work but inherited also the habit of eating, where, if
not in El Hoyo, are the neighbors more willing to lend
you a cup of flour or beans? When Señora García's house
burned to the ground with all her belongings and two
kids, a benevolent gentleman conceived the gesture that
put her on the road to solvency. He took five hundred
names and solicited from each a dollar. At the end of
the week he turned over to the heartbroken but grateful
señora three hundred and fifty dollars in cold cash and
pocketed his recompense. When the new manager of a
local business decided that no more Mexican girls were
to work behind his counters, it was the *chicanos* of El
Hoyo who acted as pickets and, on taking their individu-
ally small but collectively great buying power elsewhere,
drove the manager out and the girls returned to their
jobs. When the Mexican Army was enroute to Baja California and the *chicanos* found out that the enlisted men
ate only at infrequent intervals they crusaded across town
with pots of beans, trays of tortillas, boxes of candy, and
bottles of wine to meet the train. When someone gets
married celebrating is not restricted to the immediate
families and friends of the couple. The public is invited.
Anything calls for a celebration and in turn a celebration
calls for anything. On Armistice Day there are no fewer
than half a dozen fights at the Tira-Chancla Dance Hall.
On Mexican Independence Day more than one flag is
sworn allegiance to and toasted with gallon after gallon
of Tumba Yaqui.

And El Hoyo is something more. It is this something
more which brought Felipe Ternero back from the wars
after having killed a score of Germans with his body
resembling a patch-work quilt. It helped him to marry a
fine girl named Julia. It brought Joe Zepeda back without a leg from Luzon and helps him hold more liquor
than most men can hold with two. It brought Jorge Casil-
las, a gunner flying B-24's over Germany, back to com-
pose boleros. Perhaps El Hoyo is the proof that those
people exist who, while not being against anything, have
as yet failed to observe the more popular modes of

human conduct. Perhaps the humble appearance of El Hoyo justifies the discerning shrugs of more than a few people only vaguely aware of its existence. Perhaps El Hoyo's simplicity motivates many a *chicano* to move far away from its intoxicating *frenesi*, its dark narrow streets, and its shrieking children, to deny the bloodwell from which he springs, to claim the blood of a conquistador while his hair is straight and his face beardless. Yet El Hoyo is not the desperate outpost of a few families against the world. It fights for no causes except those which soothe its immediate angers. It laughs and cries with the same amount of passion in times of plenty and of want.

Perhaps El Hoyo, its inhabitants, and its essence can best be explained by telling you a little bit about a dish called *capirotada*. Its origin is uncertain. But it is made of old, new, stale, and hard bread. It is sprinkled with water and then it is cooked with raisins, olives, onions, tomatoes, peanuts, cheese, and general leftovers of that which is good and bad. It is seasoned with salt, sugar, pepper, and sometimes chili or tomato sauce. It is fired with tequila or sherry wine. It is served hot, cold, or just "on the weather" as they say in El Hoyo. The Garcias like it one way, the Quevedos another, the Trilos another, and the Ortegas still another. While in general appearance it does not differ much from one home to another it tastes different everywhere. Nevertheless it is still *capirotada*. And so it is with El Hoyo's *chicanos*. While many seem to the undiscerning eye to be alike it is only because collectively they are referred to as *chicanos*. But like *capirotada*, fixed in a thousand ways and served on a thousand tables, which can only be evaluated by individaul taste, the *chicanos* must be so distinguished.

Señor Garza

Many consider Garza's Barber Shop as not truly in El Hoyo because it is on Congress Street and therefore downtown. Señor Garza, its proprietor, cashier, janitor, and Saint Francis, philosophizes that since it is situated

in that part of the street where the land decidely slopes,
it is in El Hoyo. Who would question it? Who contributes
to every cause for which a solicitor comes in with a long
face and a longer relation of sadness? Who is the easiest
touch for all the drunks who have to buy their daily
cures? For loafers who go to look for jobs and never find
them? For bullfighters on the wrong side of the border?
For boxers still amateurs though punchy? For barbers
without barber shops? And for the endless line of moochers who drop in to borrow anything from two bits to two
dollars? Naturally, Garza.

Garza's Barber Shop is more than razors, scissors, and
hair. It is where men, disgruntled at the vice of the rest
of the world, come to air their views. It is where they
come to get things off their chests along with the hair off
their heads and beard off their faces. Garza's Barber
Shop is where everybody sooner or later goes or should.
This does not mean that there are no other barber shops
in El Hoyo. There are. But none of them seem quite to
capture the atmosphere that Garza's does. If it were not
downtown it would probably have a little fighting rooster
tied to a stake by the front door. If it were not rented
to Señor Garza only it would perhaps smell of sherry
wine all day. To Garza's Barber Shop goes all that is
good and bad. The lawbreakers come in to rub elbows
with the sheriff's deputies. And toward all Garza is the
same. When zoot suiters come in for a very slight trim,
Garza who is very versatile, puts on a bit of zoot talk
and hep-cats with the zootiest of them. When the boys
that are not zoot suiters come in, he becomes, for the
purpose of accommodating his clientele, just as big a
snob as their individual personalities require. When
necessity calls for a change in his character Garza can
assume the proportions of a Greek, a Chinaman, a gypsy,
a republican, a democrat, or if only his close friends are
in the shop, plain Garza.

Perhaps Garza's pet philosophy is that a man should
not work too hard. Garza tries not to. His day begins
according to the humor of his wife. When Garza drives
up late, conditions are perhaps good. When Garza drives
up early, all is perhaps not well. Garza's Barber Shop
has been known, accordingly, to stay closed for a week.
It has also been known to open before the sun comes up

and to remain open for three consecutive days. But on normal days and with conditions so-so, Garza comes about eight in the morning. After opening, he pulls up the green venetian blinds. He brings out two green ash cans containing the hair cut the preceding day and puts them on the back edge of the sidewalk. After this he goes to a little back room in the back of the shop, brings out a long crank, and lowers the red awning that keeps out the morning sun. Lily-boy, the fat barber who through time and diligence occupies chair number two, is usually late. This does not mean that Lily-boy is lazy, but he is married and there are rumors, which he promptly denies, that state he is henpecked. Rodriguez, barber number three, usually fails to show up for five out of six workdays.

On ordinary mornings Garza sits in the shoeshine stand because it is closest to the window and nods at the pretty girls going to work and to the ugly ones, too. He works on an occasional customer. He goes to Sally and Sam's for a cup of coffee, and on returning continues to sit. At noon Garza takes off his small apron, folds it, hands it on the arm of his chair, and after combing his hair goes to La Estrella to eat and flirt with the waitresses who, for reasons that even they cannot understand, have taken him into their confidence. They are well aware of his marital standing; but Garza has black wavy hair and a picaresque charm that sends then to the kitchen giggling. After eating his usual meal of beans, rice, tortilla, and coffee, he bids all the girls good-bye and goes back to his barber shop. The afternoons are spent in much the same manner as the mornings except that on such days as Saturday, there is such a rush of business that Garza very often seeks some excuse to go away from his own business and goes for the afternoon to Nogales in Mexico or downstairs to the Tecolote Club to drink beer.

On most days, by five-thirty everybody has usually been in the shop for friendly reasons, commercial reasons, and even spiritual reasons. Loco-Chu, whose lack of brains everybody understands, has gone by and insulted the customers. Take-It-Easy, whose liquor-saturated brain everybody respects, has either made nasty signs of everybody or has come in to quote the words and poems of the immortal Antonio Plaza. Cuco has come from his job at Feldman's Furniture Store to converse of the beauty of Mexico and the comfort of the United States. Procuna has come in, and being a university student with more absences than the rest of his class put together, has very politely explained his need for two dollars until the check comes in. Chonito has shined shoes and danced a dozen or so boogie pieces. There have been arguments. Fortunes made and lost. Women loved. The great Cuate Cuete has come in to talk of the glory and grandeur of zoot suitism in Los Angeles. Old customers due about that day have come. Also new ones who had to be told that all the loafers who seemingly live in Garza's Barber Shop were waiting for haircuts. Then the venetian blinds are let down. The red awning is cranked up. The door is latched on the inside although it is continually opened on request for friends, and the remaining customers are attended to and let out.

Inside Garza opens his little National Cash Register, counts the day's money, and puts it away. He opens his small writing desk and adds and subtracts for a little while in his green record book. Meanwhile Chonito grudgingly sweeps and says very nasty words. Lily-boy phones his wife to tell her that he is about to start home and that he will not be waylaid by friends and that he will not arrive drunk. Rodriguez relates to everybody in the shop that when he was a young man getting tired was not like him. The friends who have already dropped in wait until the beer is spoken for and then Chonito is sent for it. When it is brought in and distributed everything is talked about. Lastly, women are thoroughly insulted although their necessity is emphasized. Garza, being a man of experience and one known to say what he feels when he feels it, recalls the ditty he heard while still in the cradle and says, "To women neither all your love nor all your money." The friends, drinking Garza's beer, agree.

Not always has Señor Garza enjoyed the place of distinction if not of material achievement that he enjoys among his friends today. In his thirty-five years his life has gone through transition after transition, conquest after conquest, setback after setback. But now Señor Garza is one of those to whom most refer, whether for reasons of friendship, indebtedness, or of having never

read Plato and Aristotle, as an oracle pouring out his
worldly knowledge during and between the course of his
haircuts.

Garza was born in El Hoyo, the second of seven Gar-
zas. He was born with so much hair that perhaps this is
what later prompted him to be a barber. At five he
almost burned the house down while playing with matches.
At ten he was still waiting for his older brother to out-
grow his clothes so that they could be handed down to
him. Garza had the desire to learn, but even before he
found out about school Garza had already attained a fair
knowledge of everything. Especially the knowledge of
want. Finally, his older brother got a new pair of overalls
and Garza got his clothes. On going to school he immediately claimed having gone to school in Mexico so Garza
was tried out in the 3B. In the 4A his long legs fitted
under the desk, so he had to begin his education there.
In the 5B he fell in love with the teacher and was
promptly promoted to avert a scandal. When Garza was
sixteen and had managed to get to the eighth grade,
school suddenly became a mass of equations, blocks,
lines, angles, foreign names, and headaches. At seventeen it might have driven him to insanity so Garza wisely
cut his schooling short at sixteen.

On leaving school Garza tried various enterprises. He
became a delivery boy for a drug store. He became a
stock room clerk for a shoe store. But of all enterprises
the one he found most profitable was that of shearing
dogs. He advertised his business and it flourished until it
became very obvious that his house and brothers were
getting quite flea ridden. Garza had to give it up. The
following year he was overcome with the tales of vast
riches in California. Not that there was gold, but there
were grapes to be picked. He went to California. But of
that trip he has more than once said that the tallness of
the Californian garbage cans made him come back
twenty pounds lighter and without hair under his armpits.
Garza then tried the CCC camp. But it turned out that
there were too many bosses with muscles that looked like
golf balls whom Garza thought it best not to have much
to do with. Garza was already one that could keep everybody laughing all day long, but this prevented almost
everybody from working. At night when most boys at

camp were either listening to the juke box in the canteen, or listening to the playing of sad guitars, Garza trimmed heads at fifteen cents. After three months of piling rocks, carrying lots, and of getting fed up with his bosses' perpetual desires of making him work, Garza came back to the city with the money he had saved cutting hair and through a series of deals was allowed a barber's chair in a going-establishment.

In a few years Garza came to be a barber of prominence. He had grown to love the idle conversation that is typical of barber shops, the mere idle gossip that often speaks of broken homes and foresaken women in need of friends. These Garza has always sought and in his way has done his best to put in higher spirits. Even after his marriage he continued to receive anonymous after anonymous phone call. He came to know the bigtime operators and their brand of filthy doings. He came to know the bootleggers, thieves, love merchants, and rustlers. He came to know also the smalltime operators with the bigtime complex and their shallowness of human understanding. He came to know false friends that came to him and said, "We're throwing a dance. We've got a good crowd. The tickets are two dollars." And on feeling superior, once the two dollars had fattened their wallets and inflated their conceit, remarked upon seeing him at the dance, "Damn, even the barber came." But in time Garza has seen many of these grow fat. He has seen their women go unfaithful. He has seen them get spiritually lost in trying to keep up materially with the people next door. He has seen them go bankrupt buying gabardine to make up for their lack of style. Their hair had cooties but smelled of aqua-rosa. The edges of their underwear were frilled even though they wore new suits. They gave breakfasts for half of the city to prove that "they had" and only ended up with piles of dirty dishes. Garza watched, philosophized, cut more hair, and of this has more than once said in the course of a beer or idle conversation among friends, "Damned fools, when you go, how in the hell are you going to take it with you? You are buried in your socks. Your suit is slit in the back and placed on top of you."

So in time Garza became the owner of his own barber shop. Garza's Barber Shop with its three Koken barber chairs, its reception sofas, its shoeshine stand, wash bowls, glass kits, pictures, objects to be sold and raffled, and juke box. Second to none in its colorful array of true friends and false, of drunks, loafers, bullfighters, boxers, other barbers, moochers, and occasional customers. Perfumed with the poetry of the immortal Antonio Plaza, and seasoned with naughty jokes told at random.

Soon the night becomes old and empty beer bottles are collected and put in the little back room. Chonito, who has swept the floor while Garza and his friends have consumed beer, asks for a fifty-cent advance or swears with the power of his fourteen years that he will never sweep the shop again, and gets it. Lily-boy phones his wife again and tells her that he is about to start home and that he is sober. Rodriguez, if he worked that day, says he has a bad cold which he must go home to cure, but asks for an advance to buy his tonic at Tom's Liquor Store. Then the lights are switched off and Garza, his barbers, his friends, and Chinito, file out. Garza, not forgetting the words he heard while in the cradle, "To women neither all your love nor all your money," either goes up the street to the Royal Inn for a glass of beer or to the All States Pool Hall. Then he goes home. Garza, a philospher. Owner of Garza's Barber Shop. But the shop will never own Garza.

Cuco Goes to a Party

One night Cuco Martinez decided not to go home right away. Every night he hurried home from work because his two brothers-in-law did it and thought it right. The brothers-in-law believed that if a man got up very early in the morning and cooked his breakfast, it was right. The brothers-in-law believed that if a man came straight home from work, it was right. The brothers-in-law also believed that if a man worried about the price of household needs and discussed them with the wife, it was right. Maybe it was right. But only to his two brothers-in-law. To Cuco it was very boring. So

tonight he would not go home right away. If his brothers-
in-law wanted to be henpecked and do so, it was all right
with him. Where he came from men did as they pleased,
and here, as long as his name was Cuco Martinez he
would do the same thing. When Cuco walked out of
Feldman's Furniture Store at six o'clock he did not direct
his steps toward his home in El Hoyo as he usually did.
He walked up the street to Garza's Barber Shop. It was
already closed but Garza and his friends were inside.
When Cuco was let in, Garza, who was shaving, said,
"Happy are the eyes that greet you, Cuco."

"The feeling is mutual, Garza. And what is new with
you?" asked Cuco as he sat down with two of Garza's
friends on the long reception sofa and began thumbing
through a magazine.

"Cuco," said Garza, "today is Lily-boy's birthday and
I hope you will join Procuna, Lolo, and myself in hon-
oring him."

"I will be glad to," said Cuco.

So when Garza was through shaving, when the lights
were put out, and when the door was locked, Lily-boy,
who was to be the honored one, Garza, Procuna, Lolo,
and Cuco walked up the street to the Royal Inn. When
they got there it was not yet very full of customers
because it was at the time when most men were at home
eating supper. The bartender was wiping glasses in anticipation of a good night. The juke box was still silent.
Lolo, who walked in ahead of everybody, promptly
found a good table and the five friends sat down and
ordered beer. Cuco went to the juke box and soon the
gay rhythm of *El Fandango* was filling the air. Garza
ordered more beer and Lolo, who is sometimes very
poetic, toasted to Lily-boy. Lily-boy was wished eternal
happiness. Whether he deserved that kind of happiness
was questionable. He was also wished a thousand happy
years. Whether Lily-boy really wanted that many was
also questionable. "Bottoms up," said Garza. The
friends drank. And drank. After a few hours the table
was so littered with bottles that Lolo began to wonder
how much he could get for them should he decide to go
into the bottle-collecting business. Lily-boy went to the
phone booth to tell his wife that he would soon be home
and that he would arrive sober. Lolo, who was the king

of the jitterbugs and an up-and-coming prize fighter as well, was thinking of challenging everybody. He looked across the table to see which one of his companions would make a good match. When Lolo realized that these were no fighters, he looked at a little group of drunks, and on seeing that they did not look like good potential foes, he shouted a few obscenities at them and continued drinking his beer. Garza was trying to brush off a little drunk who was sure that he had seen him somewhere and Garza was trying to convince him that it had probably been at Garza's Barber shop. Cuco was saying to Procuna, "I think that if I had my way about most things I would go to Mexico City and see a full season of bullfights. I sure like them. I truthfully believe that there is nothing as full of emotion as a good bullfight. I remember having been at bullfights from the time I was about eight years old. I used to go with my father. But what I remember best is when I saw Silverio Perez make such a beautiful kill that that supreme moment has lived with me ever since."

"Why, Cuco?" asked Procuna.

"Well," continued Cuco, "Perez is not a good killer. He is a good bullfighter but he is not a good killer. But this bull, which was as big as a house, knocked him down. When Perez was on the ground the bull almost gored him but luckily, when he got up, only his pants were torn. Silverio was so mad that he picked up the *estoque* with which he would soon kill the bull and, in his rage, slapped the bull across his face. Silverio Perez was mad. Then he lined himself up with the left horn. He sighted the bull. The two met. Collided. For a second there was but a mass of enraged animal and embroidered silk. But in the end Silverio Perez was alive, though shaken, and the bull was dead. Yes, Procuna, Silverio Perez is great."

"How about Armillita, Cuco, is he any good?" asked Procuna.

"Is he any good? You ask me. Is he any good? Why—, he is the *maestro* or *maestros*. He is the teacher or teachers. When Armillita wants to be good he can do the impossible. He is great. I saw him perform in the Mexico City arena. He was magnificent. Each time the bull passed by his body it seemed that the great Armillita would end up on the horns of the bull. Yet he was as much at ease in the midst of it all as we are here, drinking beer. There is no doubt. Like Armillita there are not two."

Soon Cuco got up to demonstrate, with the aid of his coat, how the bulls were passed. Procuna acted as a bull, and Cuco told his friends how the different passes were executed. He explained how in the art of bullfighting things must be done with delicacy and finesse. Cuco waved the coat and Procuna, the bull, charged. He charged true and straight and Cuco passed him with grace and charm. He charged again. And again. Each time Cuco passed him with all the known passes in the art of bullfighting. Each time Procuna, the bull, charged he came so close to Cuco that he almost bumped him. But he didn't. After a fine exhibition of cape work Cuco drank some more beer. Then he stood in front of the table of the companions and to Lily-Boy, who was the guest of honor, dedicated as the *matadores* do in Mexico City, the death of the bull. Once again Cuco took the coat and Procuna, the bull, charged. The bull was getting tired. Soon Cuco realized this and went through the motions of killing him. By this time half of the people in the Royal Inn were crowded around Cuco. Procuna, who had been a good bull, got off the floor, dusted himself, and drank some more beer. Garza was proud of them. He hugged both of them. Lolo, who was very anxious for a bit of excitement, challenged Lily-boy to a fight. Lily-boy was very drunk. He, too, was willing to fight. He feared no man so he was willing. So Lolo and Lily-boy went out into the alley followed by a big crowd to fight it out. After a while Lily-boy and Lolo, who had shaken hands after their fight, came back to drink more beer. Lily-boy had merely sat on top of poor little Lolo. But still it had been a great fight. By this time, Garza, who has always been a good barber and better philosopher, was thinking of turning into an impresario. He was thinking of organizing a bullfight at the edge of the Santa Cruz River. He was also thinking of promoting a few boxing matches. Lily-boy once again went to the phone booth to tell his wife that he was about to start for home. Lolo was challenging Garza. Lolo was bribed into silence with another beer. Cuco was telling Procuna more about fighting bulls. Every now and then one of them would get up to execute a pass. Lily-boy was getting so drunk that he was looking for the phone booth in the men's room. After he came back to the table and had another beer he was looking for the men's room in the phone booth. Garza, in truth, was having a hell of a time keeping his friends on their feet. Lolo was insistent about fighting Lily-boy again. He wanted a re-match. Mike, the bartender, gave them a red drink on the house. After all, they had been very good customers. They had broken no chairs and upset no tables. Very soon Mike decided that they deserved another drink on the house. When the second drink went down the throats of the friends they began to drop. Soon the only ones left standing were Procuna, who was executing passes, and Garza. Garza realized that it was late so he bought Procuna another bottle of beer and told him to keep an eye on things while he went for the car to take the friends home. He well realized that if the authorities saw them in their present condition it would be taken for granted that they had been drinking. Garza went for the car and Procuna, who was left in charge, fell asleep on the shoulder of Lily-boy. When Garza came in for his friends he first woke Procuna. Together they carried Lolo, the king of the jitterbugs, feet first to the car. Then they carried out Cuco, a very nice young man, and put him in the car. Last but not least, they tried to awaken Lily-boy, who was very fat, and who had to hurry home to cut his birthday cake. Finally he had to be carried to the car, too. After the three friends were piled into the back seat and the doors closed, Procuna jumped into the front seat with Garza and the car started toward each of their respective homes. Lolo, the king of the jitterbugs, woke up long enough to say that he was hungry. Garza, who cannot stand anybody being hungry as long as they are with him, told Lolo to shut up and go to sleep. Garza turned toward the Hacienda Cafe. When they got there the only ones that were able to get out to eat were Procuna and Garza. Lolo did not wake up so Garza thought it best for him to sleep. After a hot meal and a singeing cup of coffee Garza and Procuna decided that they were still too sober so they went across the street to the Gato Blanco Cafe. They drank a few beers. They shook hands with a few friends and then went back to the car. When they got going again Lolo was taken home first and put to bed because he was training for his next fight and needed rest. Cuco then decided that he did not want to go home right away. He wanted to get out of the car for a certain universal necessity. So Garza patiently stopped the car and Cuco remedied his need. Then he was taken home. Lily-boy was taken home. He was a little bit late to cut his birthday cake but at least he was home. After Procuna, who had to go to school the next day, was dropped off at his house, Garza started for his own. After all, it had been a gay party. Lolo had fought Lily-boy. Cuco had fought many bulls. Procuna had executed passes and had consumed a lot of beer. Garza was happy that his friends had been happy and with a smile on his lips and very glass, tired eyes, drove home. Tomorrow he had to go to work.

The next day, in the early afternoon, Procuna dropped around to Garza's Barber Shop with his schoolbooks under his arm. Garza was putting the finishing touches on a customer when he came in. When he saw him, he said, "My great Procuna, how are you?"

"Fine, Garza, and you?" asked Procuna with a tired voice. "I thought I was going to go to sleep in class today. But wow, I sure had a wonderful time last night."

"Yes. I guess we all did. When you and Cuco started you were fighting little bulls. By the time you got the free drink from the bartender you were fighting bulls from La Punta about five years old," said Garza.

"How about Cuco, has he been in?" inquried Procuna.

"Well, Procuna, I am going to tell you," aid Garza.

"Tell me what," said Procuna.

"Well, Cuco was in here a little while ago and just went out to eat with Lily-boy. He is sad. In fact, he is very sad," said Garza.

"Why in the hell should he be sad today? He was very happy yesterday," said Procuna.

"Well, last night he lost his underwear," said Garza.

"And—?" inquired Procuna.

"Just that poor Cuco has been at odds with his in-laws and they found this as an excuse to turn his wife against him. Poor Emilia," said Garza, "but I think the damned in-laws are talking her into getting a divorce from Cuco."

Garza brushed off the customer's neck and took off the linen apron. He rang up seventy-five cents in the cash register and continued, "Yes, that is the way it is. Cuco really loves his wife too. It is only that his in-laws do not give him a minute of peace."

At that moment Lily-boy and Cuco walked into the barber shop. Lily-boy put on his barber's apron and Cuco sat down in the reception sofa. He looked very sad. He did not want to talk about anything. He picked up a magazine and began to thumb through it. Looking up, Cuco said, "Yes, Garza, I guess it was all a mistake for me to get married in the first place. The only thing that worries me is that Emilia is going to have a child. I really planned to stay married to her. But I guess I will just wait until it is born and then go back to Mexico."

"And her?" asked Garza.

"She will keep the child and I will go back by myself."

Then Cuco once again began to look through the magazine for a little longer and then, without saying anything, got up and walked out of the barber shop. The friends, Procuna, Lily-boy, and Garza, felt sorry for him. He was a good young man. They felt somewhat guilty for having got him so drunk that he had to go and lose his underwear.

Cuco Martinez was not very gay after that. Every day he went home to hear the nagging ways of his in-laws. Cuco was not understood. At first he had been something new but now nobody seemed to like him any longer. The brothers-in-law told him that he was a no-good fancy storyteller that should have stayed working for the railroad. They told him that he would always be but a rest room cleaner at Feldman's Furniture Store. That he was so stupid that he should not expect to ever make over thirty dollars a week. That he was nothing but a no-good drunk and that they did not see how Emilia had ever fallen in love and consented to marry him. Every day the same thing happened. Cuco got mad and said nothing. He knew that conditions would change. As soon as the child was born he would leave. Because he loved Emilia very much, he realized he could not stay long enough for her to dislike him for the same things his brothers-in-law did. He would return to Mexico. That is the way he would have it.

Loco-Chu

Every morning Loco-Chu is on Congress Street asking for nickels. Truthfully, a nickel is not much to give anybody, much less to Loco-Chu. But almost everybody is very tired of giving them to him. Loco-Chu will accept dimes and even pennies but his passion is nickels. When people see him coming, walking as if in a daze with his battered hat pulled well over his eyes, with his shredded tie, his old coat and very patched trousers, they cross the street to avoid him. To be seen close to him is an excuse for someone to say, "I saw you with your relative." So most people try to avoid poor Chu. If one chooses to remain on the same sidewalk until he passes, he is sure to say to him, "Go away, Chu. Go away." Sometimes he does. But sometimes he does not and will follow, pointing, grunting, and cursing. This, most people find very annoying, so Chu almost always gets the nickel he demands. then he smiles. Music is on his mind. He pulls his hat farther down over his eyes and throws back his shoulders. He pulls up his trousers. He walks very happily, puffing on a snipe of a cigarette, into the Canton Cafe because it seems that it is the only restaurant that will accept his small trade. "Coffee," he said. The saliva begins to drip from the corners of his mouth. "Coffee. I have money. I have money. Coffee." In order to avoid difficulties within his establishment, Lin Lew brings him coffee and gives him old doughnuts and pieces of cake or pie. Lin Lew never charges Chu. After eating the pastries and drinking some of the coffee, spilling the rest on his vest and part on the fly of his trousers, Chu gets up and walks out. He wanders up and down Congress Street some more. He goes by Garza's Barber Shop and makes faces at the customers. He makes dirty signs with his hands. He grunts and shouts nasty words. Garza, the barber, then leaves his customer, goes to the door with any old newspaper and a nickel and says to Chu, "Extra, Chu. Go sell it." And Chu happily takes the nickel and the paper and goes up and down the street hollering, "Extra! Extra! Paper! Five cents. Extra paper!"

By noon Chu sometimes has as many as a dozen nickels. He tinkles them and he is happy. He has music on his mind. He then defies everybody. He will insult even without provocation. Once again he goes to the Canton Cafe and sits down. "Food," he shouts, "I want food!" And Lin Lew goes to the kitchen and brings him a dish of rice or a bowl of soup. As Chu eats, leaving food all over the floor and all over the counter, he smiles. He bares his teeth and says with words coming from his heart, "*Buena comida.* Good food." Lin Lew nods and is happy that Chu is content. After eating, Chu automatically gets up and goes to the back room. He emerges with a bucket of hot water and a mop and goes to work. He hums as he glides the mop over the floor and underneath the tables. When he is through he puts the mop away, empties the dirty water, and leaves. Lin Lew smiles, breathes freely, and feels more than paid.

In the afternoon Chu walks past Garza's Barber Shop again, puffing his snipe, and repeats his nasty signs. He goes by the Pastime Penny Arcade and cusses at the top of his voice at the zoot suiters seated along the window sill like crows on a telephone wire. He tells them of their canine ancestry, but they know him and shrug him off saying, "Poor damned nitwit." When of this he gets his fill Chu walks into the Plaza Theater. He never bothers to pay. New ushers there only try throwing him out the first time. He sits in the front row and spreading his arms and feet he hums with the music in the picture. He is happy. Music is on his mind. After the movie, even if he has seen it for three days straight, he is very content. Chu stands in front of the theater and tries to show people the announcements as they continuously try to scare him away. Then he walks up and down the street. He will stop at busy corners and direct traffic. When he tires of this he goes for the last time to the Canton Cafe. He sits down at the counter and orders coffee. He refuses anything else even if it is given him by some stranger who wants to do a good deed when he sees how thin Chu is. It is here that Chu's tired eyes shine like those of a young boy. He takes a new snipe from his pocket, and after lighting it, he smiles and shows the decaying bits of food hanging between his decaying teeth and purplish gums. Chu is happiest at the Canton Cafe. It is here that he sips hot coffee until the wee hours of the night when Lin Lew, with Oriental delicacy pushes him out.

Chu dislikes having to leave because he is happy and with music on his mind. It is at the Canton that Chu spends all the nickels that people give him. He puts them, one by one, into the fancily lighted juke box. As the records mechanically come up, begin revolving, and are touched by the needle, the music, of whatever kind it may be, is singularly Loco-Chu's. If anybody else comes close to the juke box he growls and says, "Mine. Get out. You son of a b—ch. Get out. Mine." And it is rightly Chu's music. It is all he has.

Kid Zopilote

When Pepe García came back from a summer in Los Angeles everybody began to call him Kid Zopilote. He did not know why he did not like the sound of it, but in trying to keep others from calling him that he got into many fights and scrapes. Still everybody he associated with persisted in calling him Kid Zopilote. When he dated a girl with spit curls and dresses so short that they almost bared her garters, everybody more than ever called him Kid Zopilote. It annoyed him very much. But everybody kept saying, "Kid Zopilote. Kid Zopilote." When he reasoned that it was a name given him because he dated this particular girl, he began to go with another one who wore very shiny red slacks and a very high pompadour. But to his dismay he found that he was still Kid Zopilote. All the girls who were seen with him were quickly dubbed Kiddas Zopilotas. This hurt their pride. Soon even the worst girls began to shun poor Kid Zopilote. None of the girls wanted to be seen with him. When he went to the Tira-Chancla Dance Hall very few of the girls consented to dance with him. When they did, it was out of compassion. But when the piece ended the girls never invited Kid Zopilote to the table. They thanked him on the run and began talking to someone else. Anybody else. Somehow all of this made Kid Zopilote very sad. He blamed everything on his cursed nickname. He could dance as well as anybody else and even better. Still he was an outcast. He could not understand what his nickname had to do with his personality. It sounded very ugly.

When he came back from Los Angeles he had been very happy until he went out to see his friends. He had come back with an even greater desire to dance. To him everything was in rhythm. Everywhere he went, even if it was only inside the house, he snapped his fingers and swung his body. His every motion and action was, as they say, in beat. His language had changed quite a bit, too. Every time he left the house he said to his mother, "Ma, I will *returniar* in a little while." When he returned he said, "Ma, I was *watchiando* a good movie, that is why I am a little bit late." And Señora García found it very hard to break him of saying things like that. But that was not the half of it. It was his clothes that she found very odd. When he opened a box he brought from Los Angeles and took from it a suit and put it on Señora García was horrified.

"Why, Pepe, what kind of a suit is that?" asked Señora García.

"Ma, this is the *styleacho* in Los Angeles, *Califo*."

"Well, I certainly do not like it, Pepe."

"Ah, mama, but I like it. And I will tell you why. When I first got to California I was very lonely. I got a job picking fruit in no time at all and I was making very good money. But I also wanted to have a good time. So—one day I was down there in a place called Olvera Street in Los Angeles and I noticed that many of the boys who were Mexicans like me had suits like this one. They were very happy and very gay. They all had girls. There were many others, but they were not having any fun. They were squares. Well, I tried to talk to them, but it seemed as though they thought they were too good for me. Then I talked to the ones that were wearing drapes and they were more friendly. But even with them I could not go too far in making friends. So I bought this suit. Soon I went down to Olvera Street again and I got invited to parties and everything. I was introduced to many girls."

"But I do not like the suit, Pepe. It does not become you. I know now that you came back from California a cursed *pachuco*. A no-good zoot suiter. I am very sorry I ever let you go in the first place. I am only thanking Jesus Christ that your father is dead so that he would not see you with the sadness that I see you now."

"Well, ma, I will tell you something else right now if that is the way you feel about it. I am not the same as I used to be. I used to think that I would never want to wear a suit like this one. But now I like it. If the squares in Tucson do not wear a suit like this one is that my fault or is it for me to question? No. And I do not care. But if I like it and want to wear it I will. Leave me alone, ma, and let me wear what I please."

"You will not leave this house with that suit on, Pepe," said his mother, as she stood before the door, obstructing his path. "I will not have the neighbors see you in it."

"The neighbors do not buy my clothes, ma, so if they do not like my taste they can go to hell," said Kid Zopilote, as he gently moved his mother from the door and went out.

After that Señora García said nothing. Whenever Kid Zopilote went about the house with his pleated pants doing the shimmy to the radio, she merely sighed. When he clomped his thick-soled shoes in rhythm, she left the room in complete disappointment. When Kid Zopilote put on his long finger-tip coat, his plumed hat, dangled his knife on a thick watch chain, and went out of the house, Señora García cried.

Every day Kid Zopilote walked past the Chinese stores, the shoeshine parlors, barber shops, bars, and flop houses on Meyer Street. Sometimes he spent the entire day at Kaiser's Shoeshine Parlor. This was where, through time, a few lonely zoot suiters had been attracted by the boogie woogie music of the juke box. All day they put nickel after nickel into it to snap their fingers and sway their bodies with the beat. On other days Kid Zopilote went uptown to the Pastime Penny Arcade. Here again, the zoot suiters came in hour after hour to try their luck with the pinball machines. They walked by the scales a few dozen times a day and instead of stopping to weigh, they took out a very long comb and ran it through their hair to make sure that it met in back of the head in the shape of a duck's tail. Then they went outside to lean on the window. They sat on the sill and conversed until very late at night. Here they followed the every action of the girls that passed. They shouted from one side of the street to the other when they saw a friend or enemy, their only other action being that of bringing up cigarettes to the lips, letting the smoke out through the nose, and spitting on the sidewalk through the side of the mouth, leaving big yellow-green splotches on the cement.

One morning Kid Zopilote got up very early and went to visit his uncle who was from Mexico. When he got to the house, Kid Zopilote walked in the front door and found his *tío* was still asleep in street clothes. But it was very important to Kid Zopilote to find out the true implication of his nickname. So he woke his uncle. After the two started a fire, made and ate breakfast, with an inquisitive look on his face Kid Zopilote began, "*Tío*, you are a *relativo* of mine because you are a brother of my mother. But I know and you know that my mother does not like for me to visit you because you are a *wino*. But today I came to ask you something very important."

"What is on your mind?" asked the uncle.

"Well, before I went to Los Angeles everybody I knew used to call me Pepe. But since I came back everybody now calls me Kid Zopilote. Why? What is the true meaning of Kid Zopilote?"

"The zopilote is a bird," said his uncle.

"*Sí—?*"

"Yes, the zopilote is a bird . . ." said his uncle, repeating himself.

"What more, *tío?*" asked Kid Zopilote.

"Well—in truth, it is a very funny bird. His appearance is like that of a buzzard. I remember the zopilotes very well. There are many in Mazatlán because the weather there is very hot. The damned zopilotes are as black as midnight. They have big beaks and they also have a lot of feathers on their ugly heads. I used to kill them with rocks. They come down to earth like giant airplanes, feeling out a landing, touching the earth. When they hit the earth they keep sliding forward until their speed is gone. Then they walk like punks walk into a bar. When the damned zopilotes eat, they only eat what has previously been eaten. Sometimes they almost choke and consequently they puke. But always there is another zopilote who comes up from behind and eats the puke of the first. Then they look for a tree. When they ease themselves on the poor tree, the tree dies. After they eat more puke and kill a few more trees, they once again start running into the wind. They get air speed. They become airborne. Then they fly away."

"So you mean that they call me Kid Zopilote because they think I eat puke?" asked Kid Zopilote as his eyes became narrow with anger. "Tell me, is that why?"

"Not necessarily, Pepe, perhaps there are other reasons," said his uncle.

"The guys can go to hell then. If they can't call me Pepe they do not have to call me anything."

"But I would not worry about it anymore, Pepe. If once they began to call you Kid Zopilote they will never stop. It is said that a zopilote can never be a peacock," said his uncle, "and you probably brought it on to yourself." So Kid Zopilote went away from the house of his uncle very angry.

One night there was a stranger at Kaiser's Shoeshine Parlor. While he was not a zoot suiter he had the appearance of one of those slick felines that can never begin to look like a human being even if he should have on a suit of English tweed and custom-made shirts. He was leaning against the wall, quietly smoking a cigarette, when Kid Zopilote arrived. As usual Kid Zopilote saluted the zoot suiters with their universal greeting, "*Esos* guys, how goes it?"

"*Pos ai nomas.* Oh, just so-so," said another *pachuco*.

"Well, put in a good jitter piece," said Kid Zopilote. Before the *pachuco* could slip the nickel into the slot, the stranger slipped in a coin and the juke box began to fill Kaiser's with beat.

Kid Zopilote and the other *pachuco* were thankful. After the stranger sized up Kid Zopilote he said, "Have a cigarette, won't you?"

"Thank you," said Kid Zopilote. And from that day Kid Zopilote smoked the man's cigarettes. In time he was being charged extravagant prices for them but Kid

Zopilote always managed to get the price. He walked into the Western Cleaning Company and walked out with pressing irons. He went into business establishments and always came out with something. He stole fixtures off parked automobiles. Anything. Kid Zopilote needed the cigarettes at any price.

One day the man said to him, "You know, Kid, I can no longer sell you cigarettes."

"I always pay you for them," said Kid Zopilote.

"Yes, I know you always pay for them. But from now on you can only have them when you bring your friends here. For every friend you bring me I will give you a cigarette. Is that fair?"

"Fair enough," said Kid Zopilote. So in time many young *pachucos* with zoot suits began hanging around Kaiser's. Every day new boys came and asked for the stranger and the Kaiser directed them up a little stairway to the man with the free cigarettes. In time he no longer gave them. He sold them. And the guys who bought them were affected in many ways. Tálaro Fernandez crept on the floor like a dog. Chico Sanchez went up and down Meyer Street challenging everybody. Gaston Fuentes opened the fly of his pants and wet the sidewalk. Kid Zopilote panted like a dog and then passed out in a little back room at Kaiser's. Even Kid Zopilote was not getting the cigarettes for nothing because in no time at all he brought in all the potential customers. He had to pay for his smokes as did everybody else. In order to get the money he went to work hustling trade for Cetrina who gave him a small percentage from her every amorous transaction. In the morning when trade was not buzzing Kid Zopilote stayed in her room and listened to dance records. When he tired of that he headed uptown to the Pastime or Kaiser's. Sometimes he walked into Robert's Cafe for a cup of coffee. There, when any of the squares that knew Kid Zopilote from the cradle asked him why he did not go to work, he got mad.

"Me go to work? Are you crazy? I do not want to work. Besides, I have money. I sell kick smokes and I can get you fixed up for five dollars with a *vata* that is really good looking," he said.

"That is not good. You will get into a lot of trouble eventually," they said to him.

"No, I won't. Anyway, I haven't got a damned education. I haven't got no damned nothing. But I'll make out." Then Kid Zopilote got up and snapped his fingers in beat and swayed his body as he walked out.

One day Kid Zopilote was caught in a riot involving the *pachucos* and the Mexicans from the high school whose dignities were being insulted by the fact that a few illogical people were beginning to see a zoot suit on every Mexican and every Mexican in a zoot suit. It ended up with the police intervening. The Mexicans from the high school were sent home and the *pachucos* were herded off to jail. The next day they were given free haircuts. Their drapes and pleated pants were cut with scissors. They crept home along alleys, like shorn dogs with their tails between their legs, lest people should see them.

"I am glad it happened to you, Pepe," said Señora García, "I am glad." But Kid Zopilote did not say a word. His head was as shiny as a billiard ball. His zoot suit was no more. All day he stayed at home and played his guitar. It was strange that he should like it so much but now there was nowhere he could go without people pointing at him should he as much as go past the front door.

"Pepito," said his mother, "you play so beautifully that it makes me want to cry. You have such a musical touch, Pepe, yet you have never done anything to develop it. But you do play wonderfully, Pepe."

One day as Kid Zopilote strummed his guitar, a boy looked over the fence and said to him, "*Tocas bien.* You play very well." But Kid Zopilote said nothing. This boy looked like many of the other American boys he knew that never had anything to do with him. "I play, too," continued the boy, "so I hope you will not mind if I come into your yard and play with you. I will bring my guitar and perhaps we can play together. I learned from my Mexican friends in Colorado. I am attending school here."

"You can come if you wish," said Kid Zopilote. So the boy did and in time they were good friends.

One night the boy said to Kid Zopilote, "You were not meant to be a damned *pachuco*."

"Look, I like to play the guitar in your company but I do not want you or anybody else to tell me what I

should be and what I should not be," said Kid Zopilote
in an angry tone.

"I am sorry. We will just let it go at that," said the
boy.

So, while Kid Zopilote's hair did not grow, he spent
hour after hour with his friend who was thoroughly overcome with the beauty with which Kid Zopilote executed
and with the feeling he gave his music. When Kid Zopilote's hair began to respond to the comb the friend took
Kid Zopilote to visit friends. They went from party to
party. They played at women's luncheons. They played
on radio programs. Both were summoned for any event
which demanded music. —

"Pepe will be the finest guitar player in the whole
Southwest," said Kid Zopilote's friend.

But when Kid Zopilote's hair grew long and met in
the back of his head in the shape of a duck's tail he no
longer played the guitar. Anyway, most zopilotes eat
puke even when better things are available a little farther
away from their beaten runways and dead trees. As Kid
Zopilote's uncle had said, "A zopilote can never be a
peacock." So it was. Because even if he can, he does not
want to.

WILLARD "SPUD" JOHNSON

❦ ❦ ❦

Willard "Spud" Johnson (1897–1968) was a journalist. Although he was at one time on the staff of The New Yorker, *he is best remembered for the work he produced after he moved, with his friend, the poet Witter Bynner, to New Mexico. For a time, Johnson was secretary to Mable Dodge Luhan, patroness of the arts who was responsible for attracting D. H. Lawrence and his wife, Frieda, to Taos, and he became an intimate friend of the Lawrences, accompanying them on Lawrence's first trip to Mexico in 1923 and living with them for several months in Oaxaca. For a time, he was editor of* El Crepusculo *and* The Laughing Horse, *which published a number of important essays by Lawrence. Johnson's story "Almost a Song" appeared in a 1947 issue of the* Southwest Review. *He had a deep love of New Mexico, but as "Almost a Song" demonstrates, he was not always comfortable with the provincial prejudicial attitudes of "the so-called American, English-speaking minority in the community, toward the older inhabitants; who were darker, perhaps, as to complexion, and who had been subjects of Spain, then of Mexico, but who were certainly white, American and now even English-speaking, but who were seldom given credit for any of these attributes."*

Almost a Song

I. EVENING

A lantern quivered in the field beside the road where a man was irrigating corn. Juan Cortez, walking along in the dust of the old street that wound among low houses and occasionally between tiny, garden-sized fields of corn or alfalfa, could see the man outlined sharply against the light of the lantern as it swayed. He watched the great leg-shadows crisscrossing the parallel rows of low, waving corn, and found himself unconsciously keeping step with the shadow and with the sway of the lantern as the man hurried to the far end of the small plot, his shovel over one shoulder.

Juan carried a guitar under his arm and was bound for no place in particular. It was a warm evening, a segment of moon hung in the trees off by the river: he couldn't stay at home on such a night, even though he had no place to go.

He walked on down the road moodily, turned the corner where the houses were more thickly clustered, and paused outside a long, low building with wide open doors and windows from which yellow strips of light fell onto the wooden floor of a portal along the front. An idle hand inside thumbed the strings of a violin, and a click of billiard balls punctuated the soft hum of conversation that floated out of the windows with the lamplight.

Outside, two boys in overalls, who leaned on opposite sides of one of the pillars of the portal, like living buttresses, began to scuffle as Juan hesitated, some feet away, trying to decide whether he would enter the pool-hall or continue on down the road. It was a friendly scuffle, with gentle Spanish curses and soft laughs scattered in the summer night along with the sparks from their cigarettes, which were spilled in the dark like firecrackers that sputter and fail to explode.

No, he didn't feel like playing pool or joking and wrestling with the other fellows tonight, he wanted to be alone—and so he walked on down the road.

A screeching phonograph in a room whose garish, pink wallpaper showed even pinker in its frame of dark window shattered the stillness as he passed, and farther on the gentler sound of a girl's voice, singing *Mi Viejo Amor*, wafted across the hill from another street. He felt as though he were half asleep as he walked along in the half-dark. He was conscious of a deep serenity and of something intangible beneath the calm, as though he could hear or feel the village breathing in its sleep.

Presently he stopped again, this time beside a white latticed gate in an adobe wall. Again it was music that caught his ear—the alien sound of a piano in a mud house which was much like all the others that had lined the road, but whose lighted windows revealed an interior even more alien than the music. Books and a Chinese vase, exactly so upon a mahogany table, showed in the square of one window. A parchment shade, throwing a brilliant flood of electric light across an etching, delicate as lace, upon one of the walls, caught his eye in another. He could not see who was playing the piano, but he thought he knew, and he imagined the agile white fingers of the girl he met on the hillside almost every day on his way home from work, and whom he had followed one night, secretly, to this house. The music was strange to him—as unlike the yearning folk songs he knew, as the electric light was unlike the soft kerosene flame which burned in his own home.

But somehow, foreign as it was, the music harmonized the discrepancy between the ancient world outside and the brittle, fresh interior. The young, girlish fingers he imagined, wove a pattern on the keys and a pattern of discontent in his mind as he lingered at the gate.

He moved on, reluctantly, but paused once more a few feet down the road, and sat on the low wall where it dipped and curved beneath a tree. Putting his guitar across his knees, he leaned his elbows on it and stared into the night as he listened to the music in the house behind him. The polished edge of the guitar gleamed in a ray of moonlight that filtered down through the overhanging branches, but his eyes were dark pools of

thought from which all light had fled. He was a shadow.
He had escaped completely into dream.

A man shuffled past and murmured, *"Buenos noches,"*
as he saw Juan on the wall; then he paused and turned
back. *"Dame un fosforo, amigo,"* he said, and offered a
cigarette. Juan shifted his guitar without a word to reach
into his trousers for a match, accepted the proffered cigarette, but said no word of thanks or cordiality, only a
murmured *"Adíos,"* soft and distant as a whisper. And
he was alone again.

The music ceased inside the house, his cigarette
burned down and he tossed it into the dust of the road;
later the lights in the room behind him were switched
off: but still he sat there, leaning on his mute guitar,
after the moon had set.

II. AFTERNOON

There was a flaming sunset which had spread from the
western skyline over the entire landscape. The desert was
washed in its golden and crimson flood, the town below
the hill dwarfed by its magnificence. Heaven had usurped
the world for a moment, and as Juan stood on the hilltop,
surveying the extravagant spectacle, he marveled that an
earthly creature, without even the advantage of wings,
could see so much sky and so little land—could see both
at the same time in what was to some extent their proper
relationship. He stood, exalted, as he occasionally found
himself looking at the new moon—as though he had
never seen it before, as though it were, in fact, new.

He was so completely absorbed that he did not at first
observe the approach of Ruby Cole as she walked toward
him over the curly, close-cropped, dry grass of the slope.
But once he had caught sight of her, he did not again
look at the sunset. He looked only at her, with his slow,
serious gaze which had so often, in the past few days of
their acquaintance, disconcerted her. She blushed suddenly, but quickly recovered herself and smiled a greeting as she came up to him.

'This is the nicest one yet, isn't it?" she said, with a
gesture toward the glowing west.

"Yes," he answered, and they stood side by side looking across the slowly darkening desert.

It was not the first time they had stood thus together, but on the other hand their friendship was not yet old. Ruby had chosen the perfect hour of the late afternoon, naturally enough, for her daily walk and had come, after her first discovery of it, to this particular hill almost every day. And Juan, skirting the knoll on his way home from work to the little group of houses on the sheltered side of the ridge where his mother kept house for him, had encountered her several times before his friendly eyes had caught an answering smile in hers and they had exchanged a reserved "Hello."

But once their shyness had allowed it, their friendly encounters had increased in intimacy daily, and now it seemed almost as though they were old friends. They talked about themselves, getting acquainted, and she knew of his ambitions and of the bitterness with which he combated the generally accepted attitude of the so-called American, English-speaking minority in the community, toward the older inhabitants; who were darker, perhaps, as to complexion, and who had been subjects of Spain, then of Mexico, but who were certainly white, American, and now even English-speaking, but who were seldom given credit for any of these attributes. She talked to him sometimes about this at length, resenting it with him and feeling that she was helping him to elude the danger of an inferiority complex on the subject by her frank and friendly association with him, as indeed she was.

Not that that was her reason for continuing the relationship. Her liking for him was both genuine and spontaneous. He was a fine-looking boy with broad, straight shoulders and a lean, athletic body as well as keen eyes and a handsome face. His mind was active, if a trifle slow, and she knew quite well that it was only opportunity which he lacked in order to become the man he intrinsically was. She was interested.

Undoubtedly she was also very definitely attracted to him in a purely physical way—but this she had not even admitted to herself. Here was a fine, upstanding fellow with strong arms and a proud manner—to say nothing of his romantic blood—of whom she would have promptly said, had he been of her own set, that she had "a crush" on him. But he did not belong to her world; he was a new kind of animal, a new experience: and therefore, for the moment at least, he was that and nothing more.

This was true with him also, in a way. He was intrigued by this new kind of girl who belonged to a world he had looked at but not known. He was pleased with their friendship. And he, too, was interested in her life and her problems, but scarcely in her body, though he knew well enough that it was good to look at. The point was that he had not allowed himself to think of her as a woman he could possess.

He knew she had come to San Cypriano for her health, but that she was not seriously ill. The doctors had found a "spot" on her lung which might mean nothing, but which had to be considered, and so here she was, apparently free, but in one way a prisoner; apparently blooming with health, but with a feminine fragility that was alluring and also touching. He felt protective toward her—just as she felt toward him, in quite a different way. His protective instinct was physical, hers mental.

And so they stood, unself-conscious, intimate, yet distant, side by side upon the hill looking, like eager lovers, into the west, as though "their purpose held, to sail beyond the sunset"—together!

Presently he turned to her and smiled.

"It will be dark very soon, and you know you promised to walk with me over to the other side of the hill today and see where I live."

"Of course," she said, quickly, awakened out of her dream. "Of course. I *want* to." And they started off together around the knoll to the eastern slope of the ridge that lifted slowly to the main range of mountains behind the town.

"Maybe someday I'll build a little house for myself here," she said; and then added, almost plaintively, "if I find I have to stay in this country. And if I do," she continued, "I hope you'll help me plan it. I want it to look as though it just grew out of the ground like the old ones do. And I want a little well in the front yard— and a yellow rosebush beside it."

"Then you want a house just like mine," he said. "So now you must see it." And they laughed happily as they strode along together in the twilight. A silence fell between them, but not a strained, unnatural silence—

rather one of understanding. It was broken abruptly by
Juan, who said suddenly:

"Did you know that I had been to your house?"

She was somewhat startled by this sudden admission,
not quite comprehending what it meant.

"Why—no," she said, wondering, half-embarrassed, if
he had called on her when she had been out. He too was
slightly constrained after having made the confession, but
explained hurriedly.

"It was one day after I had met you several times, but
before you had spoken to me. I followed you, at a distance, and saw where you lived." He looked at her
quickly to see whether she was annoyed at his impu-
dence, but his look was so naïve and honest that she
could only smile her pleasure at his interest and put aside
at once any suspicion of rudeness on his part.

"Then, one night," he said, "when I was passing your
house, I heard you playing the piano and I sat outside
on the wall for a long time. I hope you don't mind."
Again he looked at her appealingly.

"Why, of course not," she said. But she did not add
what was on the tip of her tongue: "You should have
come in." Instead, there was another silence, and Juan
did not say what was in his mind, either, voicing the
further confession that he had *almost* played his guitar
under her window and sung a song to her, after she had
turned off the lights. But he wished that he had said it,
for he wanted very much to know whether she would be
pleased or not; perhaps there would come another night
under another moon when he would wish to sing to her:
would he dare? But the opportunity to speak again was
gone, now. They were approaching a barbed-wire fence,
and Ruby exclaimed, impulsively:

"Gracious! Must I crawl through that dreadful wire? I
know I'll tear my dress: I always do, no matter how
careful I am."

"I'll lift you over," he said, looking down at her as
they faced each other beside the fence. "I don't think
you weigh over a hundred, do you?" He grinned.

"N-no," she hesitated.

"Well." And stooping quickly, he lifted her lightly in
his arms and across the rusty, barbed fence to the ground
on the opposite side.

But something had happened: he had touched her. Not only that: he had held her. His blood had leaped, unaccountably, in his veins, and for a moment he stood amazed at his own reaction, and simply looked at her. Suddenly his face and hands were hot, and he saw a pink wave of color suffuse her face and neck. He had stopped thinking, or even acting—consciously. He scarcely knew that he moved, but his hands reached instinctively out to her again and drew her body against his. His lips inevitably lowered to hers, and for a moment the barbed-wire fence between them did not exist.

It was not the next moment that the girl choked with sudden, panic terror, it was the same moment: it was almost the prophetic second before. But it was not until after he had kissed her that her hands could reach his face and carve into the brown, firm cheek those long, red, unmistakable lines that only a woman's fingernails can make.

Something quite as instinctive had happened to her as had happened to him; and as she tore herself away from him, turned, and fled down the remaining slope of the hill in a flight as unreasoning as his own simpler gesture, he simply stood and watched her, both hands clasping the top wire of the fence.

He lowered his eyes. Those three strands of taut, twisted metal were all that had separated them.

On one of the sharp prongs of the wire hung a tiny piece of brown tweed from her coat. He jerked it off, irritably, and whispered to the evening star, which blinked sleepily above the last band of yellow that hung along the western horizon:

"Holy Mother!"

III. Morning

Brilliant sunlight poured through the high window behind him. It was like a warm hand on his neck and it threw a great hunched lump of a shadow on the dirty cement floor at his feet. When he lifted his eyes, he saw that the barred entrance to the cell made a checkerboard of shadow on the corridor outside.

These minute physical details absorbed him; he followed their outlines abstractedly as though their reality was all that was left to him. He looked at his hands on his knees in the same way: heavy, brown, stained with toil, yet still young and strong; in spite of their heaviness, still able to make a guitar ring with song. Or were they? Perhaps he would never know. There seemed something so fatal about what had happened. He noted the blunt, stubborn thumb, closing the fist like a hasp.

"Stubborn—and stupid," he thought, bitterly. Vaguely, and without putting his thoughts into words, he yet realized that those hands had reached, unthinking, for what they wanted, without the controlled intelligence to relate the need to the consequences; and he resented his own need, the circumstances, his stupidity and the consequences with a single dulled abhorrence.

Yesterday—could it have been only the evening before?—when the girl who had been his friend had literally torn herself from his innocent unpremeditated embrace, he had lingered in a kind of blurred trance, holding onto the wire of the fence as though for support, and had watched her mad flight down the hillside. Even then he had known that he was a fool, but he certainly had not realized—could hardly now imagine—the widening circle of hysteria that her flight had spread.

He had finally crawled over the fatal fence and walked slowly home; he had troubled his mother by his sullen silence and his refusal to explain the scratch upon his face. He had scarcely eaten a bite of his supper, and had sat, afterward, on the *banco* outside the front door, staring straight ahead of him into the deepening dusk.

And into that slow absorption of dreamlike remorse had come, suddenly and without any kind of warning, first a low baying of hounds, to which he paid no attention; and then a rush of men and dogs, a rattle of chain leashes, of handcuffs, of rough voices.

He had said nothing and they had taken him off in a daze, pushing and clouting him, as his mother wept in the doorway.

The ensuing hours of darkness in the jail had been a nightmare of muddled thought, which he had slowly put together like a difficult jigsaw puzzle, into some semblance of a picture. And the morning newspaper, which the man brought with his coffee, had supplied the remaining fragments. The paper lay in a crumpled heap at the end of his cot where he had thown it.

From the lurid sheet, under flaming headlines, he learned that Ruby Cole had rushed to the Jacobs' house a little way down the road and, still hysterical, had told them that she had been attacked by a Mexican.

Attacked! He reflected bitterly for the hundredth time. So that was what those Americans called an attack! He'd like to show them, sometime, what *he*, a "Mexican," would consider an attack. He picked up the newspaper from the floor and read again the lines: ". . . attacked in an arroyo by a Mexican who accosted her as she was returning home at dusk."

Besides the news-article, blazoning the distorted facts on the front page, there was an editorial on another page, containing such high-sounding phrases as "This sort of thing must stop" . . . "Are our daugthers and sisters and wives to be subjected to such ignominy and danger on the very streets in front of their homes?" . . . "The men of the community, if indeed there are any, must act!"

His anger flared again as he reread these words, and he fumed at the image which came into his mind of self-righteous, ignorant, and completely unimaginative men sitting indignantly in front of typewriters with aggressive cigars stuck between their teeth, allowing the trite clichés to flow easily and vindictively, as they had flowed many a time before in many another newspaper office.

Or was this simply a memory from the movies? He didn't, after all, know what a newspaper office was like, or the men who wrote them. But now, at least, he did know how utterly wrong they could be, how completely they could misrepresent facts, and how unjustly they could persecute.

He heard a door open, somewhere down the corridor, and footsteps approach. He stood up, suddenly remembering another piece of information which he had read in the newspaper: Ruby Cole was to come to the jail this morning to "identify" him.

This plan had seemed somewhat unnecessary to him—merely a matter of form—and he had almost forgotten it. The bloodhounds had led the posse directly to his door, and not only was he the only man who lived in that house, but on his cheek was the obviously incriminating brand made by Ruby's fingernails. Still, here they were.

They stopped in front of his cell and Juan, his dark face darker with mingled anger and humiliation, stood straighter than usual from defiance and sheer nervous tension. His fists were clenched; but beneath the challenge in his eyes there was also an appeal which was not lost on the girl, even though, facing the sunlight which still flooded in from the high window in the opposite wall, she could barely see the swarthy outlines of his features in the shadow, and would have been almost unable to recognize them, had it not been a face which she would probably never forget.

She looked straight at him for a moment, and flushed deeply; then she lowered her eyes to the checkered pattern of bar-shadows on the floor at her feet.

"I'm sorry," she said, "but I never saw this man before."

And then she turned and walked away down the corridor, the others following, puzzled and considerably annoyed.

Juan still stood facing the barred door and listening to the retreating footsteps. Almost as a whisper, he heard the girl's faltering, yet firm words, before the door at the end of the corridor opened and swallowed them:

"I think I would prefer that the case be dropped," he heard her say. "And I hope that poor fellow in there will be released at once. I feel very guilty that an innocent man should have been imprisoned falsely on my account." The men did not answer her and the door clanged shut.

She had said that she felt guilty, and she had certainly blushed with embarrassment when she faced him a moment ago. But there was something else in her face, he thought, standing where they had left him. Something of his own bitter oppression lifted as his thoughts at last left their buzzard-circling around his own carcass and flew toward the girl.

Yes, he decided, he had seen something else in her; and a wave of pity swept him. Behind her troubled, tear-swept eyes, he had caught a glimpse of a deeper emotion than embarrassment or a sense of guilt—it was shame.

ALICE MARRIOTT

❦ ❦ ❦

Alice Marriott was born in Wilmette, Illinois, on January 8, 1910. At the age of seven, she moved with her family to Oklahoma City, where she attended public schools. Upon graduation, she enrolled in Oklahoma City University and in 1930 earned a BA in English and French. After working as a librarian for "three grim years," Alice Marriott realized that most of the books in the library that employed her were about Indians. That led her to earn another bachelor's degree, this time in anthropology. She found employment as a field representative for the Indian Arts and Crafts Board of the United States Department of the Interior and became associated with Native American communities all over the United States. Later, she worked for the Red Cross in communities in Southwest Texas and Western New Mexico, giving her the opportunity to become familiar with the culture and customs of Americans of Mexican descent. During her field work, Marriott began to write—first short sketches for magazines and later, books. Her first book, The Ten Grandmothers, *completed in 1945, was about the ten spiritual guardians of the Kiowas, the first Indian tribe she had worked with as a graduate student. Of the twenty books Marriott has written, three in particular have, as she notes, "a Spanish-American slant":* The Valley Below *(1947),* Hell on Horses and Women, *and* Greener Fields *(1962), several chapters of which appeared in short story form in* The New Yorker. *"El Zopilote" is one of her more poignant works. Of it, she has written: "I have always been rather proud of that one."*

El Zopilote

The boy stood in the deserted Plaza, directing nonexistent traffic with free, swinging waves of his arms. At one end of the street was the Cathedral; at the other end the theater; and between them was the dime store, its window filled with holy statues of St. Francis, skull in hand. It was before this window that the boy had taken up his position.

In the dull, uncertain light of the moon, the boy's face itself might have been a skull. The great hollows below the cheekbones gave only a suggestion of flesh; the high bulge of the forehead had the white bareness of bone. Clothes hung on his body as if only bones supported them; there was no roundness of flesh beneath the rags that flapped in the wind made by their own waving.

So Father Riley first saw the boy, and so he always remembered him. The priest came from his quarters and crossed the street for the earliest mass. He had a dim awareness of the black-draped old women who were always regular communicants at this hour, but he had come in two months to accept those figures as a part of early winter mornings in a Spanish-American town. The boy was a new feature of the landscape, and in some odd way a frightening one.

Later in the day Father Riley saw the boy again. There had been a funeral; an old man, a member of one of the leading Spanish families, had been buried. As he left the Cathedral in the procession to the cemetery, Father Riley saw from the tail of his eye a skeleton figure of grotesque, ragged movement. With a swirl of arms and coat-tails, the boy swooped upon the funeral procession, establishing himself in a place just behind the bier and the eight men who carried it. There could be no doubt that he took, of deliberate intention, the place usually reserved for the chief mourner. Nor was there anyone in the family of the deceased who was disposed to dispute his possession of that place. Simply, the man's widow and daughters stepped back, and allowed the boy to precede them.

131

Because the dead man had been both famous and wealthy, the state police had sent an escort to head the procession to the *campo santo*. As a courtesy, they guided the priests' car back to the Cathedral. Father Riley, now without his robes, and with the gilt discharge button showing on the shoulder of his cassock, found himself saluted by one of the motorcycle officers as he stepped out of the car.

"Where was you, Father?"

"Bataan. At first."

"Yeah. And later?"

"In the Philippines, Camp Sixty-Eight."

"My oldest brother was on Bataan. He died in the hospital there."

The Father nodded.

"Couple of years ago, I'd have said he was the lucky one."

"I miss him yet, though. Just cousins left now, mainly. Good to be back, Father?"

"Yes. Where were you?"

"E.T.O. We had it easy compared to you guys. Name's Garcia, Father. Sergeant Garcia, both places; here, too."

"Is this your home state? You don't speak like most of the people—" Hard to say tactfully, you look Spanish but you don't talk like one.

"I come from Las Cruces, down in the south part of the state. I got cousins up here, though. I went to Agriculture College down there."

"That's why you speak differently."

"Yeah, I guess so. They had a regular police college there, for a while. And I was with the MPs, overseas. We had a lot of northern boys in our outfit; Brooklyn, Boston, all them places. So I guess I learned to talk like them, some. Where you from, Father?"

"Boston, myself. Lots of the boys on Bataan were from New Mexico, though. So I got to know them, and it seems like home, here. They were all right."

"You ought to know, Father. You was with them long enough."

"Yes." An idea came to Father Riley. This man would not laugh at his question. He would accept curiosity as normal, in a fellow veteran. "Wonder if you can tell me something?"

"Try to." The policeman brought a pack of cigarettes from his pocket; hesitated a moment, and then offered them. Father Riley took one; waited for a match, and drew on the tobacco. "What's on your mind, Father?"

"A boy I wondered about. I saw him on the Plaza, this morning—"

"Directing traffic, like?"

"That's the one."

"Yeah." The policeman knocked the ash off his cigarette, carefully careless. "He come to the funeral, too."

"I thought I saw him there."

"Yeah. Well. He's a Spanish boy. Ain't got no father, and his mother died when he was born. His old grandmother brought him up, and then she died a year or so ago. He's got relatives, but he don't have much to do with them. He's kind of not right in the head, and he acts like he's all alone, since his grandma died. Thinks he's got no one to look out for him. He sort of lives on funerals."

"Lives on funerals?"

"Sure. I guess you don't know. A lot of these old-timey Spanish families, when they have a funeral, they have a big feast, too. So everybody comes. Even if the family's poor, and they got to owe the grocer for the next four months, they have a big funeral feast. *Velario*, they call it, like sitting up and watching with the corpse. So this boy, he goes around to the feast and eats, eats. Fills himself up. Seems like he knows, ahead of time. Sometimes even before the person dies, maybe."

"Like a buzzard."

"That's what we say. We call him that. *El Zopilote*, we say. That means buzzard in Spanish."

"But this morning he seemed to be directing traffic."

"Well, he does that, too. Seems to think he's the policeman in charge of the funeral. He's kind of crazy, Father."

"Couldn't he be taken care of? There must be institutions—there are in every state."

The policeman seemed embarrassed.

"He ain't hurting no one, see, Father? He's harmless. And he gets along, with the funerals, and what little help he takes from his people. There's enough funerals in this town to keep him going. And he's kind of a home-town

boy, like. He don't bother nobody. What's the good of
shutting him up? We keep an eye on him, so he don't
get into no trouble, see?"

The priest nodded.

"Yes, I see that. But even if he hurts nobody, maybe
it would be better for him to be taken care of."

"He makes out all right. Well, so long, Father. Got to
get back on the job. Be seeing you." The man swung his
leg over the bar of his motorcycle, kicked backward at
the starter, and was gone with a roar and a rush. Father
Riley turned indoors.

Being conscious of a man's existence makes you see
him, Father Riley thought a week later. First he had
become aware of the boy called *El Zopilote*; then of the
young policeman. Now it seemed to him that he saw
one or the other, or both of them, almost every day.
Occasionally he saw them together. Once it was at the
funeral of a state official. Garcia was directing traffic,
briskly and efficiently, near the Cathedral, and *El Zopilote* stood behind him, following every move that the
officer made. Even the blasts of Garcia's whistle brought
corresponding puckers of the lips, and shrill toots, from
the feeble-minded boy.

Once or twice Garcia came to the Chapter House, asking for Father Riley. The first time he seemed a little
embarrassed.

"There's an old lady up on Goat Road, Father. My
cousin's wife's been sort of looking after her. Seems like
she's dying. Can you come?"

And the policeman was visibly relieved when the priest
said, quietly, "Of course. That's my job."

They rode in a police car, formally, that time. But
when Garcia came again, to take Father Riley to the
scene of an automobile accident, they went on the motorcycle, with the siren screaming.

"He was pinned under when the gas tank blew up. We
can't move him." That was all Garcia said then, but later
he added, "Thanks, Father. I guess you're used to worse
things than that."

Coming back from the wreck, they passed *El Zopilote*,
standing at the entrance of the Plaza, swinging his arms.
When the boy saw Garcia, he burst into a series of shrill,

surprisingly metallic toots, made with his throat and tongue. For a minute Father Riley thought he actually was hearing a police whistle.

After a dozen calls made together, Father Riley began to feel that he knew Garcia's family. The policeman mentioned them occasionally: his cousin, the cousin's wife; their little girl, who seemed to be the center of the whole family. The policeman quoted her; Barbarita had said this or done that; when the child grew up she wanted to teach school and have a big dog; Barbarita had gone wading in the *acequia* behind the house, but had not caught cold. She was a healthy little girl, who didn't seem to get sick easily.

Once, coming back from a sick call, Garcia said,

"My cousin lives right down the street here. Why don't we stop by and drink coffee with them, Father?"

"Will it be all right?" the priest asked. "Won't it put your cousin's wife to too much trouble?"

"Sure not," Garcia said. "She always has the coffee on."

The cousin's wife greeted them with a smile, and a gesture into the room where she stood. She was a young woman, and very pretty; neat and clean as her spotless house. She seated them in a room that seemed to have been furnished from a women's magazine, except for the row of highly-colored plaster saints on the mantel.

"Where's Barbarita?" the policeman asked.

"Out playing in the yard," her mother answered. She stepped to the door and called to the child, who came running in. She was flushed from play; laughing at the sight of her cousin, and solemn when she saw the stranger with him.

"Say howdy to the Father," Garcia said, and the child put out her small hand, and said, "Howdy, Father," in an almost inaudible voice.

"How old is she?" Father Riley asked.

"Almost four," the mother told him.

"She's a big girl. My niece, my brother's child, is a year older, almost five, and she isn't much bigger."

The mother smiled.

"She drinks lots of milk. That's what makes her grow. She goes to the neighbor's every day, when they're milking, with her tin cup, and they fill it for her right from the cow, as many times as she can drink it."

"Some days she drinks five, six cups," Garcia put in.

"My," said Father Riley, impressed, "that's a lot of milk for a little girl."

"Sure it is," said the woman, "but it makes her grow big, like you see."

As summer came on, the priest found himself thinking often of Barbarita. The children of the Spanish seemed to die fast and easily. He was doing a good deal of parochial work; such tasks were often turned over to the younger men of the Chapter by the older fathers, and so it came about that Father Riley was often in families where there were sick or dying children. Sometimes there was a doctor in attendance; sometimes the family had decided against calling a physician, and had enlisted the help of some old neighbor woman who "knew about herbs."

As the weather warmed and the calls to sick children increased in number, Father Riley saw more and more of *El Zopilote*. Sometimes the boy would be hurrying toward a house the priest had just left; sometimes he would appear at a funeral. Often the scarecrow figure stood for hours in the Plaza, directing the summer's influx of out-of-state cars. Sometimes the strange drivers cursed the boy, when they confused his vocal blasts with a real police whistle, but their cursing made no difference to *El Zopilote*. He carried on his self-imposed task with complete seriousness; never stopping, and never speaking to anyone.

One can not feel fear or horror for an indefinite period. Sooner or later its own continuance destroys the emotion. So it was with the priest. The horror he had felt when he first saw *El Zopilote* merged with pity at the sight of the boy's tatters and the bones protruding through them. Father Riley could see the half-wit direct traffic without a shudder; finally without even notice. Only when he met the walking skeleton hurrying to a house he had himself just left, was Father Riley again aware of his first emotion.

Garcia, too, was busy with the out-of-state traffic. He always had time for a nod and a word when Father Riley passed near him, but these days he was always hurried with his greeting.

"Got to keep these damned *turistas* moving," he said once. "Excuse me, Father. But seems like I forget you're

a priest sometimes, since I got to know you. Say, thanks
for stopping to see old lady Vigil the other day. She sure
appreciated it."

"That's all right," said Father Riley. "About the
swearing, I mean. The Army makes that sound natural.
And I like old lady Vigil. Anyway, I told you before,
that's my job. How's Barbarita?"

"Not so good, these last two days," said Garcia. "Hey,
you with the Ohio license, get over there! She's been
kind of tired, or sick, or something. Didn't want to get
up this morning."

"I'd better go by and see her," the priest said.

"Say," said Garcia, his face changing a little, "that'd
sure be swell of you. My cousin's wife would appreciate
that, all right. You do that if you can make it, Father."

It was late afternoon before Father Riley could. Then
he turned in at the gate in the wall that surrounded the
house, and knocked on the front door. The cousin's wife
opened it, her own face tired and worried.

"Come in, Father," she said. "Barbarita will be glad
to see you."

There could be no question that the child was ill. She
lay in a crib, moved into the family living room for coolness. Her face was flushed, and her breath came short
and quick.

"Have you had a doctor?" Father Riley asked, looking
at her.

"Not yet," said the mother. "Do you think we ought
to, Father? I've been giving her my grandmother's herb
tea. She knew about herbs, my grandmother. She was a
good one with them."

"I'd call a doctor," the priest advised her.

"My grandmother was good with herbs," the woman
insisted. "I know all her prayers, too, Father. I been
saying them at just the right times, when I was mixing
and cooking and stirring and all. The herb tea seems to
bring her fever down for a while, but then it goes right
up again."

"Any hot drink will bring the fever down for a while,"
said Father Riley. "Hot water would do the same thing,
and be better for her. Do you know how she got sick?"

"I don't know," said the woman helplessly. "There's
been a lot of sickness around lately. Even the cow died

the other day. Barbarita sure does miss her milk. Even as sick as she is, she cries for it when she wakes up. I got her milk from the store, but she don't like it. It don't taste the same. They cook it, someway."

"Pasteurize it," Father Riley said, automatically. "I'll stop by and send the doctor up on my way to the Chapter House, if you like."

"That's sure good of you, Father. We'd appreciate it. And, Father," the woman's fingers held the corner of her apron tightly, "will you pray for her, please, Father?"

"I've been doing that ever since I came in," said Father Riley sternly, and he left. Halfway down the hill he met *El Zopilote*, moving upward with jerky flutters of his rags. The Father walked faster. He wanted to catch the doctor before he left his office.

"Sure, I'll go," said the doctor, when the priest spoke to him. "But from what you tell me, it won't do much good. If the child's been sick from milk from a sick cow for about three days, you know as well as I do that it's more your case than mine, Father. These Spanish are all alike. They're ignorant, and they don't want to be any other way. But I'll go."

"Call me back about her, will you?" Father Riley asked, and the surprised doctor said, "Sure, if you want me to. You a friend of the family?"

"Yes," said Father Riley, slowly, "I guess that's it. A personal friend."

The doctor's call, when it came, was noncommittal.

"She may make it," he said. "Then again, she may not. It's hard to tell, right now. I've given her sulfa, and left more for the mother to give her. She may make it."

"That's good," answered Father Riley. He hesitated, then inquired, as easily as possible, "That half-wit boy, you know the one, was he there?"

"El Zopilote?" asked the doctor. "Sure he was. Sitting right outside on the wall, beside the gate. That's why I say she may not make it, too. He knows what's going to happen as often as I do."

It was one-thirty when the laybrother from the door awakened Father Riley.

"There's a policeman downstairs asking for you, Father," he said.

"I'm coming," Father Riley told him. He was already feeling for his shoes.

Garcia's big, high-colored face was pale under the unshaded electric light.

"She's sick, Father," was all he said. The motorcyle was waiting.

El Zopilote sat patiently on the wall in the moonlight. Garcia shivered and crossed himself as they passed the boy, and Father Riley nodded and repeated the gesture.

Inside, the house was a blaze of light. Women sat on the floor, still muffled in their shawls against the night and its sorrows. Every door and window was tightly closed; and in addition to the brightly-glowing chandelier, watchlights burned on the mantel shelf before the row of plaster saints. The crib was gone from the room, replaced by a big bed of curly maple. A man sat on the bed, holding the child in his arms, his legs straight out before him.

"That's my cousin," whispered Garcia.

Beside the bed, the door into the kitchen stood open. There were movements, there, of a dim crowd of men; the sound of their voices; heavier sighings than those of the women; and the clink of bottles against glasses. No one spoke above the murmuring of rosaries, as Father Riley stepped to the bed and bent over the sick child.

"She needs fresh air," he said. "Open the windows."

There was a wordless, protesting cry from the women. No one moved in either room.

"Sergeant!" Father Riley's voice cracked like a whistle cutting through the noise of traffic. "Open the window!"

"Yes, Captain," said Garcia, saluting, and he threw the window wide.

"Now, lay her down on the bed," said the priest, taking the child from her father's arms. Again came the wordless, protesting cry, as he stretched Barbarita on the bed.

"Bring warm water and bathe her," he ordered the mother.

"But she's so hot," the woman argued. "Cold water would cool her."

"Bathe her with warm water," said Father Riley.

"Aren't you going to pray, Father?" a man's voice asked from the kitchen doorway. Father Riley turned to face it.

"Prayer without works is dead," he said. "I'll pray, but someone must care for the child!"

Outside there was the long note of a police whistle, shrilling against the moon.

"Go and send that boy away," said Father Riley to Garcia, and without a word the policeman left the room.

"Now," said the priest to the mother, "you take care of Barbarita. Everybody who wants to pray, come outside with me."

Wordlessly, the crowd followed him out into the moonlight, and knelt as he did facing the open door of the house. Beyond the wall, *El Zopilote* leaped and fluttered in the street, shrilling his policeman's cry, in defiance of Garcia, who spoke fiercely to him.

"Go away," Garcia was saying, in Spanish. "Go away. Never come here again. We don't want you."

The boy drew off to the other side of the street, staring at the group kneeling in the yard. Father Riley began the Rosary of the Sorrows, and the people responded. As their voices rose higher and stronger, the skeleton figure withdrew to the shadows of the houses across the street. Then it melted into the darkness and quite vanished. The mother's figure appeared in the lighted doorway.

"She's alive, Father!" the woman cried. "She's alive, and the fever's gone, and she's sleeping!"

And it was true. Barbarita had turned on her side, tucked her fist under her cheek, and fallen into the honest sleep of any tired child.

Going back to the Chapter House on the motorcycle, neither Garcia nor Father Riley spoke. When they stopped, the priest found words.

"That boy must be sent away," he said. "He can't stay here any longer. He must go to the State Hospital."

"I guess so," Garcia agreed. "I sure hate to see him shut up, though. It's hard on them, and he's harmless."

"He isn't harmless if the sight of him scares people to death," said the priest. "He must go, Sergeant."

"Yes, sir," answered Garcia. "He's got to go. I hate to see him shut up, but I love Barbarita more. You see, Father, he's my little brother."

AMÉRICO PAREDES

❦ ❦ ❦

Américo Paredes, professor emeritus of literature and anthropology at the University of Texas at Austin and one of the nation's preeminent folklorists, was born in 1915 and grew up in Brownsville, at the southernmost tip of Texas on the Texas-Mexican border, where his ancestors had settled in the eighteenth century. As a boy, Paredes studied piano and guitar, and at the age of fifteen, began writing poetry, composing his verses first in English and then changing to his native Spanish. In 1934, one of his poems won first place in a statewide contest sponsored by Trinity College in San Antonio. That year, he also began publishing poems regularly in the Spanish-language newspaper La Prensa *of San Antonio. From 1936 until 1943, Paredes worked as a journalist for both the Spanish and English editions of the Brownsville* Herald. *In addition, he contributed feature articles once a month on the folklore of the Rio Grande Valley, concentrating on the* corrido, *or Mexican folk ballad, as it was composed and sung on the border. At this time, he also had a weekly radio program where he played his guitar and sang not only his own compositions but also the popular* corridos, *such as "El Corrido de Gregorio Cortes." Then, in 1943, he entered the United States Army and was sent to Japan at the end of the war where he served as an editor for* Stars and Stripes.*

   In 1952, a collection of six of Paredes's short stories entitled* Border Country *won first prize in a contest sponsored by the Dallas* Times Herald. *The following year, one of those stories—"Over the Waves Is Out"—was published in the* New Mexico Quarterly. *During this time, Paredes was doing graduate work in folklore and Spanish at the University of Texas at Austin and in 1956 he was awarded a doctorate and joined the faculty as a full-time* *member. In 1958, the University of Texas Press published his dissertation,* With a Pistol in His Hand: A Border Ballad and Its Hero, *which became one of the most successful books ever published by that press and which in 1982 was made into the PBS film "The Ballad of Gregorio Cortez," starring Edward James Olmos in the role of the border hero.*

Paredes has written and published widely and received numerous prestigious awards, including the Charles Frankel Prize, which the National Endowment for the Humanities presented to him in 1989. In 1990, he received the Aztec Eagle award, the highest honor that Mexico can bestow upon a foreigner in recognition of services rendered by that individual to Mexico and to humanity. In addition to his lifetime accomplishments and dedication to preserving Mexican culture, Paredes was praised for having "given his best efforts in the defense of the human rights of Mexican nationals in the United States."

Over the Waves Is Out

He had always wanted to be a musician, but his father would not let him, because his father had once known the man who composed "Over the Waves." They had gone to school together in Monterrey, to a real gentleman's school. And then the man who composed "Over the Waves" succumbed to drink and women, which led him to a tragic end.

His father knew about the evils of drink and women, having investigated them in his youth. It was dangerous, besides being unnecessary, for the boy to do any exploring of his own. Besides, he was a delicate boy. That girl face of his wouldn't go well in a brothel. And that was the place of musicians, his father said.

But the boy did not want to play in a brothel. He would often lie on the grass of afternoons and dream he was a minstrel in the court of El Cid Campeador. Except that instead of a harp he played a piano, a shiny three-legged piano with a tail. But his father never could understand, because he had once known the man who composed "Over the Waves."

And there was another thing. In his youth, before he lost a finger somewhere, the boy's father had liked the guitar. Once, as he told himself, he was playing at a funeral. His father, the boy's grandfather, happened by and broke the guitar on his head. The boy's father never played again. He ran away to Tampico, and when he came back he had learned to play cards. It was then that the grandfather stopped speaking to him.

It made it hard on the boy, because he wanted to be a musician. He would sidle up to his father whenever he found him seated close to a window on his days off, reading *The Life and Times of Pancho Villa* or *God, Grand Architect of the Universe*. His father would sit there reading in his shirt sleeves, the cowboy hat and the heavy pistol in the cartridge belt lying on a table beside him, the linen coat hanging on the back of a chair.

"Papa," the boy would say, "why don't you buy a piano?"

His father would jab a thick, freckled forefinger at the page to mark his last word and look at him over his glasses. "Eh? A piano? You've got a phonograph."

"But I just got to have a piano."

"That again." His father would shake his head. "So many things in the world, and you want to be a musician. Why not a carpenter? Or a mason? Or a merchant? Or a barber even; there's a clean, gentlemenly profession for you."

"No," the boy would say firmly, "I want to be a musician."

"Look," his father would say, "what does a musician make?"

"But I'm going to write music."

"Merciful God! Have you ever heard of the man who composed 'Over the Waves'?"

"Yes," the boy would say. "Many times."

So his father would steer the conversation into the technical aspects of music, the different instruments like the clavichord, the clarinet, the drums, and the trumpet. Then he would talk about bugle calls and drift into a story of the Revolution. Soon the boy was listening to a

colorful account of how his father and Villa took Chihuahua City.

And suddenly his father would say severely, "Now run
along and play. I'm busy."

And the boy would go. He was outsmarted every time.

All he could do was dream; so he dreamed of the
piano. At night, in his little recess of a room with its one
window framing a patch of sky, he would lie awake in
the dark, imagining he was a pianist with wild hair and
evening clothes, and that he was playing the piano, playing, playing.

And one night it happened. Softly, so softly he could
barely hear it, there came a sound of piano music. He
sat up in bed. The house and the street were silent, still
the piano sounds ran faintly on. The music was coming
from inside him! He lay back, breathless, and closed his
eyes. His hands ran over an imaginary keyboard. Now
he could distinguish the tripping runs, the trills, and the
beautiful, anxious chords.

He wanted to shout, to sob; he didn't know which.
But he did neither. He just lay quiet, very quiet. Something inside him grew and grew. He was lifted up in a
sea of piano music which continued to pour out of him,
churning and eddying about him in glowing spirals,
slowly burying him in a glittering shower until he fell
asleep.

Next morning he awoke with a feeling that the day
was a holiday. Then he remembered and he smiled
secretly. He tried to put away the memory in a corner
of his mind, tuck it away where no one else might get at
it. But as he dressed he kept trying to remember the
music. It was there, in some cranny of his mind, where
he could just barely touch it. It seemed that if he tried
hard enough, reached down far enough, he could grasp
it, a whole handful of it, and bring it shimmering into
the light. But when he tried to do so it would slip away,
just out of reach. He went in to breakfast, full of his rich
warm secret.

"I'm talking to you," his father said.

"Wha—yessir?" he said.

"No humming at the table."

"Humming, sir?"

"It's bad manners. Eat your breakfast."

He looked down at his plate again and gulped down a few more mouthfuls.

"What if he did hum a little?" his mother said. "You've made him miserable now."

"He will not hum at my table," his father said.

"Your table," his mother said.

"My table," his father said.

"Fine table," his mother said.

"Agh!" his father said.

"I think you like to see him look miserable," his mother said.

"He looks miserable all the time," said his sister.

"You hush," his mother said. "Keep your spoon in your own porridge."

He kept his eyes on his plate. The food he had already eaten lay cold and heavy on his stomach. As soon as he could he excused himself and left the table. He went out, dragging his feet. In the yard he hesitated, looking about him dismally. Then he smiled. He hummed tentatively and smiled again.

Night came at last, and he lay in bed waiting for the house to be dark and still so the music would come again. And finally it came, faintly at first, then more distinctly, though never loud, splashing and whirling about, twisting in intricate eddies of chords and bright waterfalls of melody, or falling in separate notes into the night like drops of quicksilver, rolling, glimmering.

His father left early the next morning, and he, his mother and his sister ate breakfast together. In his father's absence, he could not keep the question to himself any longer.

"Did you hear music last night?" he asked.

"No," his mother said. "Where?"

"A serenade?" his sister asked. "Someone with a serenade?"

He frowned. "Not that kind of music."

"When?" his mother asked.

"Last night."

"I was awake long after you went to bed," his mother said. "There was no music."

He smiled. He looked at his mother and smiled.

"Don't you feel well?" his mother said.

"You didn't hear it at all," he said.

"What was it like?" his mother asked.

He got up from the table, the secret look on his face. "It was heavenly," he said.

"Child!" said his mother.

"He's in love," his sister said.

He included his sister in his rapt smile and walked slowly out.

"Heaven?" his mother said, crossing herself.

His father called him into the living room. The boy came in and stood before his father. His father closed his book and put it down, took off his spectacles and put them in their case.

Then he said, "Your mother asked me to speak to you."

The boy looked at him.

"You're playing a sort of game with yourself every night, I hear," his father said. "You make believe you hear music."

The boy's face brightened. "I do," he said eagerly. "I do hear it."

His father looked at him sharply. "Don't lie to me now," he said.

The boy looked at his father, sitting in judgment in his soggy shirt and day-old beard, with his memories of Pancho Villa and the man who had composed "Over the Waves." And he knew he could never make him understand about the music, how it came from inside him, how beautiful it was, and how it made everything else beautiful.

"A game is a game," his father said.

The boy looked at the floor.

"Your mother's worried something may happen to you."

"Nothing's going to happen," the boy said.

"Not unless you keep worrying your mother," his father said.

"I won't talk about it anymore," the boy said. "Never."

"You go talk to her. Tell her you really don't hear anything."

"But I do hear!" the boy said.

His father gave him a hostile, suspicious look. "Don't lie!" he said.

"I'm not lying."

"You're lying this very minute!"

The boy directed his angry gaze at his own feet.

"You really don't hear anything," his father said, his voice becoming persuasive. "You just play at hearing it, don't you?"

The boy did not answer.

There was a short silence, and then his father said, "What does it sound like?"

The boy looked up quickly. His father was watching him intently, almost eagerly.

"Oh, I don't know," the boy said. "I couldn't tell just how it sounds."

"I once thought I heard music in my head," his father said. "I was in bed in Monterrey when I heard this piano. But it was only a friend out with music. He had a piano in a cart, so we went out and serenaded the girls. And then the mule bolted and—"

He stopped and looked at the boy.

"I told you I had a musician friend," he added.

"Yes," the boy said.

His father became dignified again.

"You mustn't do things like that," he said. "Think of your mother."

The boy hung his head. His father drummed his fingers on the table beside him.

"I'll talk to her myself," his father said. "I'll tell her the truth, and that you're sorry."

The boy was silent.

"Well, go out and play," his father said.

He was lying in bed, looking out his window at the sky, and listening to the music. He was hovering between sleep and wakefulness, floating about on the beautiful sounds, when all of a sudden he was wide-awake. There had been a dull, thudding noise, as though a distant door had been slammed shut.

He sat up in bed. There was a hubbub of voices in the street. He jumped into his overalls and ran out; people were runing towards a light. He ran towards the light too, and caught up with his father, who was hurrying along, buckling on his cartridge belt about his shirtless middle, beneath his flapping coat.

"At the bakery!" his father said to a man leaning out of a window. "Trouble for sure!"

There was anything but trouble in his voice; it was brisk and eager, strangely unlike his father's voice. The boy stayed just behind him, somewhat awed.

It was a bakery where the bakers worked all night making the next day's bread. As his father reached the place, a police car came squealing to a halt in the street.

An excited man in apron and cap shouted above the din, "He ran down the alley there! He's got a shotgun!"

A couple of deputies ran into the dark mouth of the alley, their cowboy boots clomping awkwardly on the pebbles, their pistols drawn. His father started to run after them, but then he saw the sheriff stepping out of the car and he stopped.

The sheriff smiled at his father.

"Stick around, de la Garza," the sheriff said.

The boy's father had his gun in his hand.

"Let me go too, sheriff," he said.

"No, de la Garza," the sheriff said. "I'll need you here."

The boy's father put his gun away very slowly. Then he said to the nearest man in the crowd. "All right, you! Move on!"

He pushed the crowd back.

"Go home to bed!" he said. "Move on! Move on!"

The crowd shifted, parted, and the boy, who had stayed beside his father, almost underfoot, could now look inside into the long shelves of unbaked dough and the glowing ovens. He came closer, trying to see the terrible thing he knew must be inside.

Close to the door he became aware of the piano music. It was bouncing within the bakery's thick walls in a roar of echoes, escaping into the street only as a deep mutter which blended with the mutter of the crowd.

The sheriff walked inside and yelled, "Shut that damned thing off!"

One of the bakers answered in a high, complaining voice.

"We can't," he said. "He shot off the whole face of it."

"Well, pull the string off the wall," the sheriff shouted. The music was cut off abruptly.

The crowd had now retired a respectful distance, and the boy's father followed the sheriff inside. The boy edged closer to the door. He could see it now, a small brown box. It was pitted and broken by the shotgun blast.

"We was here, minding our own business," a big fat baker was saying, "when he walks in, and bang!"

"Maybe he thought there was a man inside," the sheriff said.

The other two deputies came crunching in as the sheriff spoke.

"Is there?" one of them asked.

"Don't be a cow, Davila," the sheriff said. "How could he make himself that small?"

"It cost me a lot of money," the fat baker said, "and I want to see him pay for it."

"Where is he?" the sheriff said.

"He got away, sheriff," said Davila.

The boy's father opened his mouth to say something, then shut it again.

"That's fine," the fat baker said. "That's just fine! A fine bunch of policemen!"

"Let's not get excited," the sheriff said. "You seem to be an excitable man. What were you two fighting about?"

"Fighting?" the baker said.

"Why did he shoot your place up?"

"How would I know?" the baker said. "Ungrateful dog!"

"He used to come here," a younger baker said. "He'd have coffee with us, and we'd always give him bread to take home."

"He'd play his accordion for us and we'd feed him," a third baker said. "And now this."

"So out of a blue sky he shoots your place up," the sheriff said. "I ought to take all of you in for questioning."

The fat baker pursed his lips angrily, but he did not say anything.

The sheriff yawned. "But I think I'll forget it this

time," he said. He yawned again. "Let's go," he said. He smiled. "He's across the river by now."

At the door the sheriff stopped and looked at the boy.

"Yours, de la Garza?" he asked.

The boy's father nodded.

"Fine young man," the sheriff said, and yawned.

"I guess so," his father answered, "except for him thinking he's got a piano inside his head."

"A what?" the sheriff said, almost waking up completely.

"A piano," the father said. His face glowed with revelation, and he turned to his son. "The music!" he said. "That radio thing. That's your music!"

"It isn't!" the boy said. "My music never came out of a box!"

"Now, now," his father said. "You know it did."

"Stop saying that!" the boy cried. "I'll—I'll run away if you don't stop!"

His father took his arm and shook it playfully.

"Temper," his father said, in high spirits. "Temper."

"It's all your fault," the boy said, shaking loose. "It's all your fault if I never hear it again."

"Best thing that could happen to you," his father said.

"But I don't want to stop hearing it," the boy said. "And now you've made it happen. It won't come back again, I know."

"Let's go home," his father said. "Your mother will be worried."

"Wait a while," said the sheriff. He looked thoughtful. "I see," he said, with the air of one who discovers a vital clue. "He thinks he hears music, is that it?"

"That's about it, sheriff," his father said.

"Why don't you get him a piano?"

"Well, I don't see how I—ha-ha, you're joking, sheriff," his father said.

"Tell you what," the sheriff said. "I'll see he gets a piano. We've got one at home, and the kids just play the damn—well, I think I should get them something different. One of them radios, for instance."

His father looked as if he had suddenly swallowed something unpleasant."

"Sheriff," he said, "we just couldn't impose on you like that."

"No trouble at all," the sheriff said. "Fact is. Well, I think I should get the kids something else. It's one of them player pianos, you know. You pump it with your feet and the music comes out."

When the sheriff said it was a player piano, the boy's father lost some of his sickish look. But he said nevertheless, "I just couldn't allow it, sheriff. It's just a silly idea of his."

"Stop being polite with me, de la Garza," the sheriff said. "I'll have that piano at your house tomorrow, and you'd better not refuse it."

"But sheriff," his father said.

"Let's ask the boy," the sheriff said. "Do you want the piano, sonny?"

"Does it play 'Over the Waves'?" the boy asked.

"No," the sheriff said.

"I'll take it," the boy said.

His father pursed his lips and sighed.

"Where's your breeding?" he said. "Say thank you, at least."

After the sheriff left, they went down the dark street, leaving the lights behind them. His father took out his gun as he walked, cocked it and uncocked it, sighted along the barrel, twirled it around and put it back in its holster.

"That Davila," he said. "He couldn't catch the scabies." He laughed. "If the sheriff had let me go, I would have caught the man. I remember once when I was young I ran down a Carrancista officer. We both lost our horses—"

"It was a Federalist officer," the boy said.

"Was it?" his father said.

"It was the last time," the boy said.

"Ah well," his father said. "Maybe it was, at that. It's hard to remember at times, it's been so long ago. So long, long ago."

He sighed, and for a few moments they walked together in silence.

After a while the boy said, "Papa, will you give me a dollar?"

"A dollar?" his father said. "What for?"

"To buy a book."

"A book? A whole dollar for a book?"

"A piano book. Now that we'll have a piano I think I should practice."

His father made a strange noise in the dark.

They walked a few paces in silence.

Then his father said, "You don't have to practice with that kind of piano. You just pump the pedals. Fact is—" His voice brightened. "Fact is, I think I'll try it myself."

The boy jerked his head toward him.

His father smote one hand against the other.

"By God!" he said. "You know what?"

"What," the boy said.

"I'll get me 'Over the Waves' in one of those rolls!"

The boy stopped in his tracks.

His father did not notice. He kept right on walking, saying, "I'll get it tomorrow. By God, I will!"

The boy watched his father disappear into the night. He felt very sad and very old and very much alone. Somewhere in the dark, ahead of him, his father was whistling in a very ornate tremolo.

> *"In the*
> *Immensity*
> *Of the waves, of the waves of the sea . . ."*

DANIEL L. GARZA

❦ ❦ ❦

Daniel L. Garza was born in 1938 in Hillsboro, Texas, the youngest of three sons of Mexican parents from Huala-huises and Linares, villages near the city of Monterrey in the border state of Nuevo Leon. Fleeing from the revolution which in 1916 continued to rage throughout the northern states of Mexico, José Garza crossed the border with his wife, Constancia, at Laredo, taking with them, like most other immigrants to the United States, only their talents and their determination to succeed. The Garza family finally settled in the farming community of Hillsboro, where Jose Garza opened a tailor shop. After graduating from high school in 1956, Daniel Garza worked his way through Texas Christian University, where he had the good fortune to take a creative writing course with the distinguished, award-winning writer John Graves. Graves was the first to encourage Garza not only to write in Spanish, Garza's first language, but to write, Garza recalls, "about my experiences, about how I feel, about going to school and not being able to speak English, about being a Mexican-American in a gringo society. So I wrote about my mother and father and my other relatives. About the people in Hillsboro. About the Mexican migrant workers who came every fall up from South Texas and Mexico to pick cotton." It was in Graves's courses at TCU that Garza wrote "Saturday Belongs to the Palomía," first in Spanish and then, for extra credit, in English. Eventually, in July 1962, "Saturday Belongs to the Palomía" appeared in Harper's *magazine. Garza has since served in the army and worked in public relations, but he continues to write stories, frequently returning to the theme of a young Mexican-American boy growing up in Gringo Town in North-central Texas.*

153

Saturday Belongs to the Palomía

Every year, in the month of September, the cotton pickers come up from the Valley, and the *braceros* come from Mexico itself. They come to the town in Texas where I live, all of them, the whole *palomía*. "*Palomía*" is what we say; it is slang among my people, and I do not know how to translate it exactly. It means maybe gang. It means a bunch of people. It means . . . the cotton pickers when they come. You call the whole bunch of them the *palomía*, but one by one they are cotton pickers, *pizcadores*.

Not many of them have traveled so far north before, and for the ones who have not it is a great experience. And it is an opportunity to know other kinds of people, for the young ones. For the older ones it is only a chance to make some money picking cotton. Some years the cotton around my town is not so good, and then the *pizcadores* have to go farther north, and we see them less.

But when they come, they come in full force to my little town that is full of gringos. Only a few of us live there who speak Spanish among ourselves, and whose parents maybe came up like the *pizcadores* a long time ago. It is not like the border country where there are many of both kinds of people; it is gringo country mostly, and most of the time we and the gringos live there together without worrying much about such matters.

In September and October in my town, Saturdays belong to the *pizcadores*. During the week they are in the fields moving up and down the long cotton rows with big sacks and sweating frightfully, but making *centavitos* to spend on Saturday at the movie, or on clothes, or on food. The gringos come to town during the week to buy their merchandise and groceries, but finally Saturday arrives, and the *pizcadores* climb aboard their trucks on the cotton farms, and the trucks all come to town. It is

154

the day of the *palomía*, and most of the gringos stay at home.

"Ay, qué gringos!" the *pizcadores* say. "What a people to hide themselves like that. But such is life. . . ."

For Saturday the *pizcadores* dress themselves in a special and classy style. The girls comb their black hair, put on new bright dresses and low-heeled shoes, and the color they wear on their lips is, the way we say it, enough. The boys dress up in black pants and shoes with taps on the heels and toes. They open their shirts two or three buttons to show their chests and their Saint Christophers; then at the last they put a great deal of grease on their long hair and comb it with care. The old men, the *viejos*, shave and put on clean plain clothes, and the old women put on a tunic and comb their hair and make sure the little ones are clean, and all of them come to town.

They come early, and they arrive with a frightful hunger. The town, being small, has only a few restaurants. The *pizcadores*—the young ones and the ones who have not been up from Mexico before—go into one of the restaurants, and the owner looks at them.

One who speaks a little English says they want some *desayuno*, some breakfast.

He looks at them still. He says: "Sorry. We don't serve Meskins."

Maybe then one of the *panchuco* types with the long hair and the Saint Christopher says something ugly to him in Spanish, maybe not. Anyhow, the others do not, but leave sadly, and outside the old men who did not go in nod among themselves, because they knew already. Then maybe, standing on the sidewalk, they see a gringo go into the restaurant. He needs a shave and is dirty and smells of sweat, and before the doors closes they hear the owner say: "What say, Blacky? What'll it be this morning?"

The little ones who have understood nothing begin to holler about the way their stomachs feel, and the papás go to the market to buy some food there.

I am in the grocery store, me and a few gringos and many of the *palomía*. I have come to buy flour for my mother. I pass a *pizcador*, a father who is busy keeping his little ones from knocking cans down out of the big piles, and he smiles to me and says: *"Qué tal, amigo?"*

"Pues, así no más," I answer.

He looks at me again. He asks in a quick voice. "You are a Chicano?"

"Sí."

"How is it that you have missed the sun in your face, muschacho?" he says. "A big hat, maybe?"

"No, señor," I answer. "I live here."

"You have luck."

And I think to myself, yes. I have luck; it is good to live in one place. And all of a sudden the *pizcador* and I have less to say to each other, and he says *adiós* and gathers up his flow of little ones and goes out to the square where the boys and girls of the *palomía* are walking together.

On the square too there is usually a little lady selling hot tamales. She is dressed simply, and her white hair is in a bun, and she has a table with a big can of tamales on it which the *palomía* buy while they are still hot from the stove at the little lady's home.

"Mamacita, mamacita," the little ones shout at their mothers. "Doña Petra is here. Will you buy me some tamalitos?"

Doña Petra lives there in the town, and the mothers in the *palomía* are her friends because of her delicious tamales and because they go to her house to talk of the cotton picking, of children, and maybe of the fact that in the north of Texas it takes somebody like Doña Petra to find good masa for tamales and tortillas. Away from home as the *pizcadores* are, it is good to find persons of the race in a gringo town.

On the street walk three *pachucos*, seventeen or eighteen years old. They talk *pachuco* talk. One says: "Listen, *chabos*, let's go to the good movie."

"O. K." another one answers. "Let's go flutter the good eyelids."

They go to the movie house. Inside, on a Saturday, there are no gringos, only the *palomía*. The *pachucos* find three girls, and sit down with them. The movie is in English, and they do not understand much of it, but they laugh with the girls and make the *viejos* angry, and anyhow the cartoon—the *mono*, they call it—is funny by itself, without the need for English.

Other *pachucos* walk in gangs through the streets of the town, looking for something to do. One of them looks into the window of Mr. Jones's barber shop and tells the others that he thinks he will get a haircut. They laugh, because haircuts are something that *pachucos* do not get, but one of them dares him. "It will be like the restaurant," he says. "Gringo scissors do not cut Chicano hair."

So he has to go in, and Mr. Jones looks at him as the restaurant man looked at the others in the morning. But he is a nicer man than the restaurant man, and what he says is that he has to go to lunch when he has finished with the customers who are waiting. "There is a Mexican barber across the square," he says. "On Walnut Street. You go there."

The *pachuco* tells him a very ugly thing to do and then combs his long hair in the mirror and then goes outside again, and on the sidewalk he and his friends say bad things about Mr. Jones for a while until they get tired of it, and move on. The gringo customers in the barber shop rattle the magazines they are holding in their laps, and one of them says a thing about cotton pickers, and later in the day it is something that the town talks about, gringos and *pizcadores* and those of my people who live there, all of them. I hear about it, but forget, because September in my town is full of such things, and in the afternoon I go to the barber shop for a haircut the way I do on Saturdays all year long.

Mr. Jones is embarrassed when he sees me. "You hear about that?" he says. "That kid this morning?"

I remember then, and I say yes, I heard.

"I'm sorry, Johnny," he says. "Doggone it. You know I'm not . . ."

"I know," I say.

"The trouble is, if they start coming, they start bringing the whole damn family, and then your regular customers get mad," he says.

"I know," I say, and I do. There is no use in saying that I don't, because I live in the town for the other ten or eleven months of the year when the *palomía* is not here but in Mexico and the Valley. I know the gringos of the town and what they are like, and they are many different ways. So I tell Mr. Jones that I know what he means.

"Get in the chair," he says. "You want it short or medium this time?"

And I think about the *pizcador* in the grocery store and what he said about my having luck, and I think again it is good to live in one place and not to have to travel in trucks to where the cotton is.

At about six in the afternoon all the families begin to congregate at what they call the *campo*. *Campo* means camp or country, and this *campo* is an area with a big tin shed that the state Unemployment Commission puts up where the farmers who have cotton to be picked can come and find the *pizcadores* who have not yet found a place to work. But on Saturday nights in September the *campo* does not have anything to do with work. The families come, bringing tacos to eat and maybe a little beer if they have it. After it is dark, two or three of the men bring out guitars, and some others have concertinas. They play the fast, twisty mariachi music of the places they come from, and someone always sings. The songs are about women and love and sometimes about a town that the song says is a fine town, even if there is no work there for *pizcadores*. All the young people begin to dance, and the old people sit around making certain that the *pachucos* do not get off into the dark with their daughters. They talk, and they eat, and they drink a little beer, and then at twelve o'clock it is all over.

The end of Saturday has come. The old men gather up their sons and daughters, and the mothers carry the sleeping little ones like small sacks of cotton to the trucks, and the whole *palomía* returns to the country to work for another week, and to earn more *centavitos* with which, the Saturday that comes after the week, to go to the movies, and buy groceries, and pay for *tamalitos* of Doña Petra and maybe a little beer for the dance at the *campo*. And the mothers will visit with Doña Petra, and the *pachucos* will walk the streets, and the other things will happen, all through September and October, each Saturday the same, until finally, early in November, the cotton harvest is over, and the *pizcadores* go back to their homes in the Valley or in Mexico.

The streets of my town are empty then, on Saturdays. It does not have many people, most of the year. On Saturday mornings you see a few gringo children waiting for the movie to open, and not much else. The streets are empty, and the gringos sit in the restaurant and the barber shop and talk about the money they made or lost on the cotton crop that fall.

AMADO JESÚS MURO

❦ ❦ ❦

*For a long time, Amado Jesús Muro submitted his stories
to the* Arizona Quarterly *or the* New Mexico Quarterly
*accompanied with a hand-written note saying apologeti-
cally that he was "not a professional writer" but only a
high-school-educated Mexican-American who was born in
1931 in Parral, Chihuahua, Mexico, and who, after his
father's death, came to the United States and went to work
on the railroad in El Paso. The stories had been written
in his spare time, he claimed. Certainly, he would add,
he "never made a living that way." Critics praised his
stories, such as "Cecilia Rosas," "María Tepache," and
"Sunday in Little Chihuahua," one going so far as to
observe that "Amado Muro . . . seems to have written
more good short fiction than any other young Mexican-
American." It was not until 1973 that the literary world
learned that, indeed, there was no such person as Amado
Muro. Hiding behind the mask of "Amado Muro" was
a most intriguing individual, a journalist named Chester
Seltzer. But the mask was not removed and the true identity revealed until Seltzer died of a heart attack on October
3, 1971.*

*Born in Ohio in 1915, Seltzer was the son of Louis
B. Seltzer, the politically powerful editor-in-chief of the*
Cleveland Press *and friend of Franklin Delano Roosevelt.
Chester Seltzer studied creative writing under the distin-
guished poet John Crowe Ranson at Kenyon College. His
was a life of diversity, filled with many twists and turns.
At the beginning of World War II, he declared himself a
conscientious objector and was sentenced to Lewisburg
Penitentiary. During his lifetime, he worked for numerous
newspapers, but also rode the rails and labored as a
migrant worker in the fields. Seltzer's sons, Charles and
Robert, confirm that their mother, Amada Muro Seltzer,*

160

did more than lend their father her name for his writing. Although Seltzer had, in fact, lived in Mexico for several years, his wife "helped him a great deal in understanding the Mexican culture," and acted as a kind of informal research assistant, helping him with Spanish phrases and Mexican customs. Seltzer's stories ring true; what gives them a sesne of truth and reality is his sympathy for the dispossessed, no matter which side of the border they happened to live on. He had a deep respect for the poor who struggled not only to feed themselves but also to maintain their dignity in the face of a situation that was constantly assulting it.

María Tepache

In San Antonio, I got off a Southern Pacific freight train near the tracks that spidered out from the roundhouse turntable. When I quit the train it was almost five o'clock, and the sky was dark with the smoky pall of thunderheads. I was tired and chilled and hungry. I hoped to find something to eat and then get on to Houston.

Nearby was a small white-frame Mexican grocery with a corrugated tin porch held up by a few warped scantlings. The window displayed lettuce heads and coffee in paper sacks, and near the door was a wire bin of oranges. A dog lay on the porch before the door. I went in and asked a buxon, gray-haired woman with a round face and untroubled eyes if she could spare some day-olds.

"Ay, Señora Madre de San Juan, I just fed four hoboes and I can't feed no more," she said.

I started out the door then, but she called me back. She stared at me, her dark eyes becoming very round. "*Hijole, paisanito*, what spider has stung you—you look sad and burdened like the woodcutter's burro," she said. "Well, I don't blame you. When bread becomes scarce so do smiles."

The gray-haired woman wore a blue dress that was cut straight and came to her knees, and she had on huaraches. She told me her name was María Rodríguez, but she said people all called her María Tepache because she liked Tepache with big pineapple chunks in it so well. We talked of different things—about where she came from was one. She came from a Durango village populated mostly, she said, by old men, old women, and goats.

"I was born in one of those homes where burros sleep with Christians," she said. "I can read and eat with a spoon, but I'm not one of those women meant to live in homes that would be like cathedrals if they had bells. In our adobe hut village, we lived a primitive life with no more light than the sky gives and no more water than that of the river. But my father never stopped feeding me because he couldn't give me bonbons or clothing me because he couldn't dress me in silks."

She asked me where I was from, her face intent with strong interest. When I told her, she appeared surprised. "*¡Válgame San Crispín!* I'd never have guessed it," she said.

When I asked why, she smiled and said: "Most Chihuahua people don't talk so fast as we of Durango. But you talk fast, and with the accent of *Santa María de todo el mundo.*"

After that she put on a cambaye apron with a big bow in back, and led me to the back of the store where all the living was done. "This is your humble kitchen—come in," she invited.

The place was like all the homes of poor Mexicans that I'd seen in Texas. There was a broken-legged woodstove, a shuck-tick bed, a straight-back chair, a mirror with the quicksilver gone, and a table covered with oilcloth frayed and dark at the edges. Beyond the stove and to one side was an old cupboard with the doors standing open. The kitchen's bare floor was clean, and the walls were painted wood with only a calendar picture of Nicolás Bravo that hung crookedly from its nail as decoration. On a tiny shelf in a corner was a gilt-framed picture of Maria Guadalupana and a crucified Christ.

The window had burlap curtains, and Doña María explained why she put them up long ago. "In a place where there aren't any curtains on the windows you can't expect children to turn out well," she said.

She lit a coal-oil lamp, and set it on the table. Outside it was beginning to rain. Wind blew the rain in through the window and made the lamp burn unevenly and smoke the chimney. The chimney blackened until only a ring around the base gave off light. Doña María closed the window and afterward stood near the lamp and told me she was a widow. Standing there very still with heavy lashes lowered, she spoke of her husband and her voice was husky. The dog that had lain on the porch was curled on the floor by the bed, his head resting on his outspread paws and his eyes watching her.

"In our village my husband was an *adobero*, and he came here to earn *dolarotes* in the pecan mills," she said. "I wasn't one of those model Mexican wives who leave their wills in the church, but we were happy together and I never worried that he'd fall in love with another *chancluda* prettier than me. He couldn't read or write, but I went through the fourth grade at the Justo Sierra School and I taught him about numbers so he could count the stars with our first son. When our centavos married and multiplied, he talked about going back to Mexico. '¡Ay Mariquita! If we can go back someday I swear I'll climb Popocatepetl on my hands,' he told me. 'We could go to Puebla on the other side of the volcanoes, and buy land near the *magueyes* and *milpas*. We'll buy three cows, and each will give her three *litros*. Our *chilpayates* will never dance the Jarabe Moreliano with hunger.' "

Her eyes softened in a reflection of faraway dreaminess. She said her husband made Puebla sound like Bagdad, and talked of singing to her with twenty mariachis.

"Now I live with no more company than my own sins," she said. "I pass my life tending the store, and mending the clothes of my many grandchildren." She broke off and lowered her lids over her eyes, veiling them. Her mouth grew set, a thin, straight line; she passed her hands over her forehead as though awakening from sleep. Her gray hair was in a tangled cloud about her face and she looked older than I'd thought at first seeing her. But when she looked up toward me, she was smiling again and her dark eyes were calm and reflective. "My grandchildren are less brutal than I," she said. "All of them know how to speak the gringo.

I hung my crumpled crush hat on a nail behind the

kitchen door and went out in the backyard to split
stovewood. The backyard was cluttered with piled-up
packing boxes and crates, and the grass was yellow with
sand. There was a stumpy cottonwood near the water
tap, and a row of sweetpeas clinging to a network of
strings tacked on the fence. The cottonwood leaves had
turned yellow, but they were still flat with green streaks
showing in them. Every once in a while the wind would
shake the branches and a flurry of dry leaves and dust
funneled up near me.

I split wood, carried out ash buckets, and brought
water in a zinc pail. While I worked, Doña María bent
over a larded frying pan and told me about her father.

"He was a shepherd and a good man—never ambitious
for the centavos," she said. "He was happy and con-
tented with no more ambition than not to lose a lamb
and go down to Santiago Papasquiaro two or three times
a year to hear the mariachis play in the plaza and listen
to the church bells."

When I finished the chores, night was coming and the
rain was heavier. There was lightning, vivid flashes that
scarred the sky, and I could see San Antonio's lights
golden on oil lamps beyond the new Braunfels Bridge.
The rain fell through the yellow lamplight streaming from
the kitchen window and cars, their lamps wet gems,
moved slowly across the high bridge. Their headlights
seemed to draw the raindrops, like moths. I looked at
them for a moment, rain spattering off my shoulders,
then went inside.

Doña Maía had finished setting the table. She wiped
sweat from her forehead with a fold of her apron, and
began to fan herself. Then she motioned me to a plate
filled with refried beans, rice, and blanquillos.

"*Esa es mecha,*" she said. "It will make you feel like
shouting, '*Yo soy Mexicano,*' in the middle of a crowded
street. Eat—one can think of nothing good when he's
hungry."

I ate so fast I grew short of breath. Doña María
watched me with her arms wrapped in her apron and
crossed over her chest. She looked solemn except for a
faint flicker of a smile at the corner of her mouth. The
dog sat on his haunches beside her bare legs.

When I finished, she gave me an ixtle shopping bag

filled with *tamales de dulce, nopalitos,* a milk bottle of *champurrado,* and a *tambache* of flour tortillas wrapped in a piece of newspaper. I tried half-heartedly to refuse it. But she insisted I take it.

"I have enough for today, perhaps tomorrow, and another day too," she said. "After that, God will say."

When I thanked her, she smiled her mild smile and told me to say the prayer of San Luisito every day.

"May the Indian Virgin who spoke with Juan Diego protect you and cover you with her mantle," she said when I went out the door, "and may you become rich enough to drink chocolate made with milk and eat *gorditas* fried in Guadalajara butter."

Cecilia Rosas

When I was in the ninth grade at Bowie High School in El Paso, I got a job hanging up women's coats at La Feria Department Store on Saturdays. It wasn't the kind of a job that had much appeal for a Mexican boy or for boys of any other nationality either. But the work wasn't hard, only boring. Wearing a smock, I stood around the Ladies' Wear Department all day long waiting for women customers to finish trying on coats so I could hang them up.

Having to wear a smock was worse than the work itself. It was an agonizing ordeal. To me it was a loathsome stigma of unmanly toil that made an already degrading job even more so. The work itself I looked on as onerous and effeminate for a boy from a family of miners, shepherds, and ditchdiggers. But working in Ladies' Wear had two compensations: earning three dollars every Saturday was one; being close to the Señorita Cecilia Rosas was the other.

This alluring young woman, the most beautiful I had ever seen, more than made up for my mollycoddle labor and the smock that symbolized it. My chances of looking at her were almost limitless. And like a good Mexican, I made the most of them. But I was only too painfully

aware that I wasn't the only one who thought this saleslady gorgeous.

La Feria had water fountains on every one of its eight
floors. But men liked best the one on the floor where
Miss Rosas worked. So they made special trips to Ladies'
Wear all day long to drink water and look at her.

Since I was only fourteen and in love for the first time,
I looked at her more chastely than most. The way her
romantic lashes fringed her obsidian eyes was especially
enthralling to me. Then, too, I never tired of admiring
her shining raven hair, her Cupid's-bow lips, the warmth
of her gleaming white smile. Her rich olive skin was
almost as dark as mine. Sometimes she wore a San Juan
rose in her hair. When she did, she looked so very lovely
I forgot all about what La Feria was paying me to do
and stood gaping at her instead. My admiration was decorous but complete. I admired her hourglass figure as
well as her wonderfully radiant face.

Other men admired her too. They inspected her from
the water fountain. Some stared at her boldly, watching
her trimly rhythmic hips sway. Others, less frank and
open, gazed furtively at her swelling bosom or her
shapely calves. Their effrontery made me indignant. I,
too, looked at these details of Miss Rosas. But I prided
myself on doing so more romantically, far more poeti-
cally than they did, with much more love than desire.

Then, too, Miss Rosas was the friendliest as well as
the most beautiful saleslady in Ladies' Wear. But the
other salesladies, Mexican girls all, didn't like her. She
was so nice to them all they were hard put to justify their
dislike. They couldn't very well admit they disliked her
because she was pretty. So they all said she was haughty
and imperious. Their claim was partly true. Her beauty
was Miss Rosas' only obvious vanity. But she had still
another. She prided herself on being more American
than Mexican because she was born in El Paso. And she
did her best to act, dress, and talk the way Americans
do. She hated to speak Spanish, disliked her Mexican
name. She called herself Cecile Roses instead of Cecilia
Rosas. This made the other salesladies smile derisively.
They called her La Americana or the Gringa from Xochi-
milco every time they mentioned her name.

Looking at this beautiful girl was more important than

money to me. It was my greatest compensation for doing work that I hated. She was so lovely that a glance at her sweetly expressive face was enough to make me forget my shame at wearing a smock and my dislike for my job with its eternal waiting around.

Miss Rosas was an exemplary saleslady. She could be frivolous, serious or demure, primly efficient too, molding herself to each customer's personality. Her voice matched her exotically mysterious eyes. It was the richest, the softest I had ever heard. Her husky whisper, gentle as a rain breeze, was like a tender caress. Hearing it made me want to dream and I did. Romantic thoughts burgeoned up in my mind like rosy billows of hope scented with Miss Rosas' perfume. These thoughts made me so languid in my work that the floor manager, Joe Apple, warned me to show some enthusiasm for it or else suffer the consequences.

But my dreams sapped my will to struggle, making me oblivious to admonitions. I had neither the desire nor the energy to respond to Joe Apple's warnings. Looking at Miss Rosas used up so much of my energy that I had little left for my work. Miss Rosas was twenty, much too old for me, everyone said. But what everyone said didn't matter. So I soldiered on the job and watched her, entranced by her beauty, her grace. While I watched I dreamed of being a hero. It hurt me to have her see me doing menial work. But there was no escape from it. I needed the job to stay in school. So more and more I took refuge in dreams.

When I had watched her as much, if not more, than I could safely do without attracting the attention of other alert Mexican salesladies, I slipped out of Ladies' Wear and walked up the stairs to the top floor. There I sat on a window ledge smoking Faro cigarettes, looking down at the city's canyons, and best of all, thinking about Miss Rosas and myself.

They say Chihuahua Mexicans are good at dreaming because the mountains are so gigantic and the horizons so vast in Mexico's biggest state that men don't think pygmy thoughts there. I was no exception. Lolling on the ledge, I became what I wanted to be. And what I wanted to be was a handsome American Miss Rosas could love and marry. The dreams I dreamed were imaginative mas-

terpieces, or so I thought. They transcended the insipid
realities of a casual relationship, making it vibrantly
thrilling and infinitely more romantic. They transformed
me from a colorless Mexican boy who put women's coats
away into the debonair American, handsome, dashing
and worldly, that I longed to be for her sake. For the
first time in my life I revelled in the magic of fantasy. It
brought happiness. Reality didn't.

But my window ledge reveries left me bewildered and
shaken. They had a narcotic quality. The more thrillingly
romantic fantasies I created, the more I needed to create.
It got so I couldn't get enough dreaming time in Ladies'
Wear. My kind of dreaming demanded disciplined con-
centration. And there was just too much hubbub, too
much gossiping, too many coats to be put away there.

So I spent less time in Ladies' Wear. My flights to the
window ledge became more recklessly frequent. Sometimes I got tired sitting there. When I did, I took the
freight elevator down to the street floor and brazenly
walked out of the store without so much as punching a
time clock. Walking the streets quickened my imagination, gave form and color to my thoughts. It made my
brain glow with impossible hopes that seemed incredibly
easy to realize. So absorbed was I in thoughts of Miss
Rosas and myself that I bumped into Americans, apolo-
gizing mechancially in Spanish instead of English, and
wandered down South El Paso Street like a somnambu-
list, without really seeing its street vendors, cafes and
arcades, tattoo shops, and shooting galleries at all.

But if there was confusion in these walks there was
some serenity too. Something good did come from the
dreams that prompted them. I found I could tramp the
streets with a newly won tranquillity, no longer troubled
by, or even aware of, girls in tight skirts, overflowing
blouses, and drop-stitch stockings. My love for Miss
Rosas was my shield against the furtive thoughts and
indiscriminate desires that had made me so uneasy for a
year or more before I met her.

Then, too, because of her, I no longer looked at the
pictures of voluptuous women in the *Vea* and *Vodevil*
magazines at Zamora's newsstand. The piquant thoughts
Mexicans call *malos deseos* were gone from my mind. I
no longer thought about women as I did before I fell in

love with Miss Rosas. Instead, I thought about a woman,
only one. This clear-cut objective and the serenity that
went with it made me understand something of one of
the nicest things about love.

I treasured the walks, the window-ledge sittings, and
the dreams that I had then. I clung to them just as long
as I could. Drab realities closed in on me chokingly just
as soon as I gave them up. My future was a time clock
with an American Mister telling me what to do and this
I knew only too well. A career as an ice-dock laborer
stretched ahead of me. Better said, it dangled over me
like a Veracruz machete. My uncle Rodolfo Avitia, a
straw boss on the ice docks, was already training me
for it. Every night he took me to the mile-long docks
overhanging the Southern Pacific freight yards. There he
handed me tongs and made me practice tripping three-
hundred-pound ice blocks so I could learn how to unload
an entire boxcar of ice blocks myself.

Thinking of this bleak future drove me back into my
fantasies, made me want to prolong them forever. My
imagination was taxed to the breaking point by the heavy
strain I put on it.

I thought about every word Miss Rosas had ever said
to me, making myself believe she looked at me with
unmistakable tenderness when she said them. When she
said: "Amado, please hang up this fur coat," I found
special meaning in her tone. It was as though she had
said: "Amadito, I love you."

When she gave these orders, I pushed into action like
a man blazing with a desire to perform epically heroic
feats. At such times I felt capable of putting away not
one but a thousand fur coats, and would have done so
joyously.

Sometimes on the street I caught myself murmuring:
"Cecilia, *linda amorcita*, I love you." When these surges
swept over me, I walked down empty streets so I could
whisper: "Cecilia, *te quiero con toda mi alma*" as much
as I wanted to and mumble everything else that I felt.
And so I emptied my heart on the streets and window
ledge while women's coats piled up in Ladies' Wear.

But my absences didn't go unnoticed. Once an execu-
tive-looking man, portly, gray, and efficiently brusque,
confronted me while I sat on the window ledge with a

Faro cigarette pasted to my lips, a cloud of tobacco smoke hanging over my head, and many perfumed dreams inside it. He had a no-nonsense approach that jibed with his austere mien. He asked me what my name was, jotted down my work number, and went off to make a report on what he called "sordid malingering."

Other reports followed this. Gruff warnings, stern admonitions, and blustery tirades developed from them. They came from both major and minor executives. These I was already inured to. They didn't matter anyway. My condition was far too advanced, already much too complex to be cleared up by mere lectures, fatherly or otherwise. All the threats and rebukes in the world couldn't have made me give up my window-ledge reveries or kept me from roaming city streets with Cecilia Rosas' name on my lips like a prayer.

The reports merely made me more cunning, more doggedly determined to city-slick La Feria out of work hours I owed it. The net result was that I timed my absences more precisely and contrived better lies to explain them. Sometimes I went to the men's room and looked at myself in the mirror for as long as ten minutes at a time. Such self-studies filled me with gloom. The mirror reflected an ordinary Mexican face, more homely than comely. Only my hair gave me hope. It was thick and wavy, deserving a better face to go with it. So I did the best I could with what I had, and combed it over my temples in ringlets just like the poets back in my hometown of Parral, Chihuahua, used to do.

My inefficiency, my dreams, my general lassitude could have gone on indefinitely, it seemed. My life at the store wavered between bright hope and leaden despair, unrelieved by Miss Rosas' acceptance or rejection of me. Then one day something happened that almost made my overstrained heart stop beating.

It happened on the day Miss Rosas stood behind me while I put a fur coat away. Her heady perfume, the fragrance of her warm healthy body, made me feel faint. She was so close to me I thought about putting my hands around her lissome waist and hugging her as hard as I could. But thoughts of subsequent disgrace deterred me, so instead of hugging her I smiled wanly and asked her in Spanish how she was feeling.

"Amado, speak English," she told me. "And pronounce the words slowly and carefully so you won't sound like a country Mexican."

Then she looked at me in a way that made me the happiest employee who ever punched La Feria's time clock.

"Amadito," she whispered the way I had always dreamed she would.

"Yes, Señorita Cecilia," I said expectantly.

Her smile was warmly intimate. "Amadito, when are you going to take me to the movies?" she asked.

Other salesladies watched us, all smiling. They made me so nervous I couldn't answer.

"Amadito, you haven't answered me," Miss Rosas said teasingly. "Either you're bashful as a village sweetheart or else you don't like me at all."

In voluble Spanish, I quickly assured her the latter wasn't the case. I was just getting ready to say "Señorita Cecilia, I more than like you, I love you" when she frowned and told me to speak English. So I slowed down and tried to smooth out my ruffled thoughts.

"Señorita Cecilia," I said. "I'd love to take you to the movies any time."

Miss Rosas smiled and patted my cheek. "Will you buy me candy and popcorn?" she said.

I nodded, putting my hand against the imprint her warm palm had left on my face.

"And hold my hand?"

I said "yes" so enthusiastically it made her laugh. Other salesladies laughed too. Dazed and numb with happiness, I watched Miss Rosas walk away. How proud and confident she was, how wholesomely clean and feminine. Other salesladies were looking at me and laughing.

Miss Sandoval came over to me. *"Ay papacito,"* she said. "With women you're the divine tortilla."

Miss de la Rosa came over too. "When you take the Americana to the movies, remember not to speak Christian," she said. "And be sure you wear the pants that don't have any patches on them."

What they said made me blush and wonder how they knew what we had been talking about. Miss Arroyo came over to join them. So did Miss Torres.

"Amado, remember women are weak and men aren't made of sweet bread," Miss Arroyo said.

This embarrassed me but it wasn't altogether unpleasant. Miss Sandoval winked at Miss de la Rosa, then looked back at me.

"Don't go too fast with the Americana, Amado," she said. "Remember the procession is long and the candles are small."

They laughed and slapped me on the back. They all wanted to know when I was going to take Miss Rosas to the movies. "She didn't say," I blurted out without thinking.

This brought another burst of laughter. It drove me back up to the window ledge where I got out my package of Faros and thought about the wonderful thing that had happened. But I was too nervous to stay there. So I went to the men's room and looked at myself in the mirror again, wondering why Miss Rosas liked me so well. The mirror made it brutally clear that my looks hadn't influenced her. So it must have been something else, perhaps character. But that didn't seem likely either. Joe Apple had told me I didn't have much of that. And other store officials had bulwarked his opinion. Still, I had seen homely men walking the streets of El Paso's Little Chihuahua quarter with beautiful Mexican women and no one could explain that either. Anyway it was time for another walk. So I took one.

This time I trudged through Little Chihuahua, where both Miss Rosas and I lived. Little Chihuahua looked different to me that day. It was a broken-down Mexican quarter honeycombed with tenements, Mom and Pop groceries, herb shops, cafes, and spindly salt-cedar trees; with howling children running in its streets and old Mexican revolutionaries sunning themselves on its curbs like iguanas. But on that clear frosty day it was the world's most romantic place because Cecilia Rosas lived there.

While walking, I reasoned that Miss Rosas might want to go dancing after the movies. So I want to Professor Toribio Ortega's dance studio and made arrangements to take my first lesson. Some neighborhood boys saw me when I came out. They bawled "*Mariquita*" and made flutteringly effeminate motions, all vulgar if not obscene. It didn't matter. On my lunch hour I went back and took

my first lesson anyway. Professor Ortega danced with
me. Softened by weeks of dreaming, I went limp in his
arms imagining he was Miss Rosas.

The rest of the day was the same as many others before
it. As usual I spent most of it stealing glances at Miss
Rosas and slipping up to the window ledge. She looked
busy, efficient, not like a woman in love. Her many other
admirers trooped to the water fountain to look at the
way her black silk dress fitted her curves. Their profane
admiration made me scowl even more than I usually did
at such times.

When the day's work was done, I plodded home from
the store just as dreamily as I had gone to it. Since I had
no one else to confide in, I invited my oldest sister, Dulce
Nombre de María, to go to the movies with me. They
were showing Jorge Negrete and Maria Felix in *El Rapto*
at the Colon Theater. It was a romantic movie, just the
kind I wanted to see.

After it was over, I bought Dulce Nombre *churros* and
hot *champurrado* at the Golden Taco Cafe. And I told
my sister all about what had happened to me. She looked
at me thoughtfully, then combed my hair back with her
fingertips as though trying to soothe me. "Manito," she
said, softly. "I wouldn't . . ." Then she looked away and
shrugged her shoulders.

On Monday I borrowed three dollars from my Uncle
Rodolfo without telling him what it was for. Miss Rosas
hadn't told me what night she wanted me to take her to
the movies. But the way she had looked at me made me
think that almost any night would do. So I decided on
Friday. Waiting for it to come was hard. But I had to
keep my mind occupied. So I went to Zamora's news
stand to get the Alma Nortena songbook. Pouring
through it for the most romantic song I could find, I
decided on *La Cecilia*.

All week long I practiced singing it on my way to
school and in the shower after basketball practice with
the Little Chihuahua Tigers at the Sagrado Corazón gym.
But, except for singing this song, I tried not to speak
Spanish at all. At home I made my mother mad by saying
in English, "Please pass the sugar."

My mother looked at me as though she couldn't
believe what she had heard. Since my Uncle Rodolfo

couldn't say anything more than "hello" and "goodbye" in English, he couldn't tell what I had said. So my sister Consuelo did.

"May the Dark Virgin with the benign look make this boy well enough to speak Christian again," my mother whispered.

This I refused to do. I went on speaking English even though my mother and uncle didn't understand it. This shocked my sisters as well. When they asked me to explain my behavior, I parroted Miss Rosas, saying, "We're living in the United States now."

My rebellion against being a Mexican created an uproar. Such conduct was unorthodox, if not scandalous, in a neighborhood where names like Burgiaga, Rodriguez, and Castillo predominated. But it wasn't only the Spanish language that I lashed out against.

"Mother, why do we always have to eat *sopa, frijoles, refritos, mondongo,* and *pozole?*" I complained. "Can't we ever eat roast beef or ham and eggs like Americans do?"

My mother didn't speak to me for two days after that. My Uncle Rodolfo grimaced and mumbled something about renegade Mexicans who want to eat ham and eggs even though the Montes Packing Company turned out the best *chorizo* this side of Toluca. My sister Consuelo giggled and called me a Rio Grande Irishman, an American Mister, a gringo, and a *bolillo* Dulce Nombre looked at me worriedly.

Life at home was almost intolerable. Cruel jokes and mocking laughter made it so. I moped around looking sad as a day without bread. My sister Consuelo suggested I go to the courthouse and change my name to Beloved Wall which is English for Amado Muro. My mother didn't agree. "If *Nuestro Señor* had meant for Amadito to be an American he would have given him a name like Smeeth or Jonesy," she said. My family was unsympathetic. With a family like mine, how could I ever hope to become an American and win Miss Rosas?

Friday came at last. I put on my only suit, slicked my hair down with liquid vaseline, and doused myself with Dulce Nombre's perfume.

"Amado's going to serenade that pretty girl everyone calls La Americana," my sister Consuelo told my mother and uncle when I sat down to eat. "Then he's going to take her to the movies."

This made my uncle laugh and my mother scowl.

"*Qué pantalones tiene* (what nerve that boy's got)," my uncle said, "to serenade a twenty-year-old woman."

"La Americana," my mother said derisively. "That one's Mexican as pulque cured with celery."

They made me so nervous I forgot to take off my cap when I sat down to eat.

"Amado, take off your cap," my mother said. "You're not in La Lagunilla Market."

My uncle frowned. "All this boy thinks about is kissing girls," he said gruffly.

"But my boy's never kissed one," my mother said proudly.

My sister Consuelo laughed. "That's because they won't let him," she said.

This wasn't true. But I couldn't say so in front of my mother. I had already kissed Emalina Uribe from Porfirio Díaz Street not once but twice. Both times I'd kissed her in a darkened doorway less than a block from her home. But the kisses were over so soon we hardly had time to enjoy them. This was because Ema was afraid of her big brother, the husky one nicknamed Toro, would see us. But if we'd had more time it would have been better, I knew.

Along about six o'clock the three musicians who called themselves the Mariachis of Tecalitlán came by and whistled for me, just as they had said they would. They never looked better than they did on that night. They had on black and silver charro uniforms and big, black, Zapata sombreros.

My mother shook her head when she saw them. "Son, who ever heard of serenading a girl at six o'clock in the evening," she said. "When your father had the mariachis sing for me it was always two o'clock in the morning—the only proper time for a six-song *gallo*."

But I got my Ramirez anyway. I put on my cap and rushed out to give the mariachis the money without even kissing my mother's hand or waiting for her to bless me. Then we headed for Miss Rosas' home. Some boys and girls I knew were out in the street. This made me uncomfortable. They looked at me wonderingly as I led the mariachi band to Miss Rosas' home.

A block away from Miss Rosas' home I could see her father, a grizzled veteran who fought for Pancho Villa, sitting on the curb reading the Juarez newspaper, *El Fronterizo.*

The sight of him made me slow down for a moment. But I got back in stride when I saw Miss Rosas herself.

She smiled and waved at me. "Hello, Amadito," she said.

"Hello, Señorita Cecilia," I said.

She looked at the mariachis, then back at me.

"Ay, Amado, you're going to serenade your girl," she said. I didn't reply right away. Then when I was getting ready to say "Señorita Cecilia, I came to serenade you," I saw the American man sitting in the sports roadster at the curb.

Miss Rosas turned to him. "I'll be right there, Johnny," she said.

She patted my cheek. "I've got to run now, Amado," she said. "Have a real nice time, darling."

I looked at her silken legs as she got into the car. Everything had happened so fast I was dazed. Broken dreams made my head spin. The contrast between myself and the poised American in the sports roadster was so cruel it made me wince.

She was happy with him. That was obvious. She was smiling and laughing, looking forward to a good time. Why had she asked me to take her to the movies if she already had a boyfriend? Then I remembered how the other salesladies had laughed, how I had wondered why they were laughing when they couldn't even hear what we were saying. And I realized it had all been a joke, everyone had known it but me. Neither Miss Rosas nor the other salesladies had ever dreamed I would think she was serious about wanting me to take her to the movies.

The American and Miss Rosas drove off. Gloomy thoughts oppressed me. They made me want to cry. To get rid of them I thought of going to one of the "bad death" cantinas in Juárez where tequila starts fights and knives finish them—to one of the cantinas where the panders, whom Mexicans call *burros*, stand outside shouting "It's just like Paris, only not so many people" was where

I wanted to go. There I could forget her in Jalisco-state style with mariachis, tequila, and night-life women. Then I remembered I was so young that night-life women would shun me and *cantineros* wouldn't serve me tequila.

So I thought some more. Emalina Uribe was the only other alternative. If we went over to Porfirio Díaz Street and serenaded her I could go back to being a Mexican again. She was just as Mexican as I was, Mexican as *chicharrones*. I thought about smiling, freckle-faced Ema.

Ema wasn't like the Americana at all. She wore wash dresses that fitted loosely and even ate the *melcocha* candies Mexicans liked so well on the street. On Sundays she wore a Zamora shawl to church and her mother wouldn't let her use lipstick or let her put on high heels.

But with a brother like Toro who didn't like me anyway, such a serenade might be more dangerous than romantic. Besides that, my faith in my looks, my character, or whatever it was that made women fall in love with men, was so undermined I could already picture her getting into a car with a handsome American just like Miss Rosas had done.

The Mariachis of Tecalitlán were getting impatient. They had been paid to sing six songs and they wanted to sing them. But they were all sympathetic. None of them laughed at me.

"Amado, don't look sad as I did the day I learned I'd never be a millionare," the mariachi captain said, putting his arm around me. "If not that girl, then another."

But without Miss Rosas there was no one we could sing *La Cecilia* to. The street seemed bleak and empty now that she was gone. And I didn't want to serenade Ema Uribe even though she hadn't been faithless as Miss Rosas had been. It was true she hadn't been faithless, but only lack of opportunity would keep her from getting into a car with an American, I reasoned cynically.

Just about then Miss Rosas' father looked up from his newspaper. He asked the mariachis if they knew how to sing *Cananea Jail*. They told him they did. Then they looked at me. I thought it over for a moment. Then I nodded and started strumming the bass strings of my guitar. What had happened made it only too plain I could never trust Miss Rosas again. So we serenaded her father instead.

NATALIE PETESCH

❦ ❦ ❦

Born in 1924 in Detroit, Natalie Petesch was the youngest child of Russian immigrants who lived and worked in the city's ghetto. As a child, she was deeply affected by the early death of her mother, who died at the age of thirty-five without having learned how to read or write. When she was sixteen, Petesch graduated from Northern High school and left home. She worked her way through college, first at Wayne State University and then at Boston University where in 1955 she received a bachelor of science degree, magna cum laude. Having been awarded a scholarship for her fiction, she earned a master's degree from Brandeis University in 1956, and in 1962 she received a PhD in English literature from the University of Texas at Austin. In addition to teaching at several universities, Petesch has published nine books of fiction and is the recipient of numerous awards, including the University of Iowa School of Letters Award for Short Fiction for After the First Death, There Is No Other *(1974), and the* New Letters *Book Prize for* Seasons Such As These *(1979), and the Swallow's Tale Press Short Fiction Award for* Wild with All Regret *(1985). "Moving to Antarctica" was published in* Best American Short Stories *in 1978. Petesch's most recent publication is* Justina of Audalusia and Other Stories *(1990), a collection of Hispanic stories set in Spain and Mexico. Also in 1990, her "The Laughter of Hastings Street: An Autobiographical Memoir" appeared in Volume 12 of* Contemporary Authors Series. *Currently, the author lives in Pittsburgh, Pennsylvania, with her husband, Donald, and their two children.*

Ramón El Conejo

Dawn, Ramón felt, was perhaps not the best time to get a hitch, since in the unfolding darkness, curled and echoing as a conch, a figure as small as he was, with what must appear to be a rucksack on his back could scarcely impress the speeding tourists from Laredo. Yet he was glad he had worked all night as usual, and had finished out the week at La Hoja Verde—collecting the three dollars pay which would, if necessary, buy him a bus ticket to San Antonio. By the time his mother and his stepfather had realized that he was missing, he would be nearly to Miami. He only hoped that his disappearance would cause his stepfather much trouble with the law on the American side of the bridge—though whatever they did to the *cabrón* would not be enough; it could never erase those weeks and months of humiliation, the foul names boiling like lava in Ramón's memory—nor the brutal mark of the boot heel in his back. When he had got rich as a waiter in Miami, Ramón resolved, he would return to Mexico, kill his stepfather, and rescue his little brother Mauricio.

Except for the thought of his mother's grief, he could relax and enjoy in detail his triumphant departure from Nuevo Laredo: how for the last time he had thrown the crudely starched waiter's uniform of La Hoja Verde into the laundry bin, then had taken a thick crayon and had scribbled into illegibility those words in the men's room which had mocked him for two years:

Puercos y perros
Mean por los suelos

Then he had carefully rolled his own father's cape, the *muleta* of the bullfight, with its leathery congealment of his father's blood still mingled with that of the bull which had killed him, so that the black shroud of satin with its sanctifying stain lay rolled inward, while the brave crimson which had challenged the bull now lay shining on

179

Ramón's back: a signal of courage in the mist of morning darkness fleeing before the first light of the sun.

As he bent toward the highway, he twisted his body into a scythe and raised his thumb into an imploring signal. A couple of returning tourists whipped by, their yellow SANBORN'S INSURANCE stickers flashing victoriously, like pennants. . . . Soon, he indulged himself in the reflection, his mother would be knocking at the door of every cousin in Laredo. "Have you see my Ramón, my little rabbit?" she would say. "He slept not to his home last night. Last pay night Aguijón took away from him again the three dollars. 'He eats here, let him pay: is he a pimp to live on his mother's work?' Aguijón said. So my *conejo* jumped and kicked him right here— *los hombres temen mucho sus cojones, tu sabes*—an' I thought sure Aguijón was goin' beat him to deat' for that, *el pobrecito*." . . . Ramón allowed the illusion of his mother's voice to lull him, echoing in his consciousness like a brook followed by a quick chirrup of a bird bathing. . . . But he knew his thoughts were not true ones: *la madre* never pitied him; rather, she had always seemed to fear pity as though it were a form of spiritual bankruptcy, like drunkenness or gambling: the more a man used it, the more he needed it. Nevertheless, he enjoyed the image he had created more than reality, as one enjoyed the marvels of mescal; and he would have gone on weaving *la madre's* odyssey into endless epics of love-rewarded, except that he was reminded by the slashing of gears as a van crested the hill that here was a chance for the long hitch.

The crunch of the truck spewing gravel as it came to a halt before him made him feel like a hero; he stood transfixed by a sense of his own power, marveling at what he had wrought: the truck's thickly groined tires, raised like relief maps, had stopped level with Ramón's eyes; its fog lights still burned watchfully in the waning light; on either side glared restive warning lights, red and lethal as the eye of a bull; and within the cowl of the truck sat the hunched figure of the driver, staring sightlessly down at him from behind a green spread of sunglasses, wide as a mask across his temples.

Ramón said a hurried, breathless prayer as he stood by the opened door.

"Climb up. I'm goin' straight to San Antone with this here load. Been ridin' all night. Think you might could keep us awake till we get there?"

That was all there was to it. Ramón was to fire the consciousness of the machine with a wakeful din while the driver sat immobile, a robot rotted to his leather seat cushion, his arms on the steering wheel like mountain cacti—club-shaped, thick, spiny and bursting with strong juice: the sun-bleached hairs stood up in porcine hackles. . . . The truck now roared through unresisting lateral space. . . . "No Riders Allowed," Ramón read on the door, and at once pitched his voice to a rising strophe of gratitude.

For more than two hours he blew his lungs out, his mouth dry and unbreakfasted; it was a strange kind of torture based on prestige and a sense of honor: without his voice flailing the wind, the over-sized toy at his side would tremble, and with a final click-click, counterclockwise, spin into a silent sleep. Suddenly the machine stopped.

"They got a river here. The Frió. Great for bustin' you in the eyes with a cold bath. I'm gonna have me a swim in 'er."

To Ramón's astonishment the mammoth-haired robot began to strew his clothes around like a madman, wrenching himself loose from the wet undershirt gummed to his skin like tar. For stunned seconds he watched as a bolt of flesh torpedoed the sunlit water, then surfaced, snorting and blowing a spume of water. Then again the barrelled curve of the back sluiced through the waters, turned suddenly with piscean ease and rested its arms oarlike on the surface; motionless the body floated in the sunlight, the eyes closed in still absorption: a buddha.

Gaining courage by the fact that the floating body really ignored him, Ramón hid behind a tapestried willow branch dipping in the riverbank, then plunged into the cool, gently-crescented waves. The water charged at his skin, flayed him with its ice, stripped him of identity: while at the same time his warm blood rushed to the surface to meet and merge with its primordial element. It filled him with a sense of having already accomplished great things to think that this water, perhaps, would go all the way to the sea—starting here with this river, dipping into an estuary at the Nueces River, and so on into a surging flood outside Corpus Christi and the Gulf. El Frió: the Cold One.

He dried himself with his T-shirt, which he noted had begun to thresh small holes under the arms. Then he lay on the river bank and waited for the driver to dress. . . . His brain rang with the cicadas teasing and burring in the sage around him; with his senses he absorbed the world: the pure white yucca blossoms and the womby splash of red gilias, the lissome swoop of the willow branch, all fretted and whirred by an ecstasy of birds. Across the river a lonely gnarled manzanita reared its scuffy black head to the sky.

The intensity of the morning blurred his vision—it was like an eclipse of pain; and he was sure that in all his life he had never been so happy.

Nevertheless, he tried to be greedy about it, to point out to himself that if this patch of earth brought such wonder, what must Miami be? . . .

He was somber and silent as the now wakeful driver revved the motor to a steady roar, as if on an endless elevator climb: they proceeded the short distance to San Antonio in silence.

When they hit the outskirts of San Antonio, the driver asked him where he wanted to get off. Ramón looked around desperately. He wanted to appear as if he knew the city at least well enough to know where to get off. But he could think of only one or two places. . . .

"Just by the Alamo, it'd be a'right. I gotta lot of places to go first."

"Don't want to drive this big load through the middle of town. Look, whyn't you just get out right along here— hop one of them buses into town, they go along Espada Road."

The driver stopped in front of a local cemetery, very neglected and rambling. Ramón would have protested; he had a superstitious fear of burial grounds, but with a conscious rise of valor, he leaped from the truck onto the cracked earth. Evidently it had not rained here in a long while. . . . A network of puffy-headed red ants, looking like a form of future life which was to survive man's extinction, rushed around sending furious messages of invasion. Ramón stamped his feet, shaking them from his sneakers; he could remember how in *la madre's* chicken house, they could pick a piece of chicken clean in a few hours, then perforate and atomize the bones.

With a startling belch, the truck jerked forward; the green-glassed driver nodded from the rear view mirror and was gone.

Ramón's situation depressed him; he saw no indication that this was a bus stop. The scraggly cemetery, scattered wtih sage and an occasional mesquite tree might have been in the middle of a Mexican prairie for all he knew; but a black American car glittering with chrome in the summer sunlight cheered him by its spectacle of efficiency and its apparent geographical sense. He began walking in the same direction. The cemetery seemed endless; however, it abutted suddenly on the stone stilts of a dun-colored house in front of which a clothesline flurried signs of inescapable life: a cotton shirt, diapers with round holes through which scraps of sunlight oddly capered, a pair of bright red woman's panties—strangely unrecked and shameless in the early light. There was no other sign of life in the morning silence: the clothesline with its crude effigies fluttered across the earth filled in turn with its dead; it waved, it fluttered; it struggled to move, and subsided.

Ramón knocked at the door, hoping to get directions and perhaps breakfast: his stomach felt like cracked glass. A Mexican woman, incredibly uncombed, came out, looking at him with eyes still puffy with white scars of sleep; but her voice was charged with a strangely garish and cheerful energy. She pointed in the direction the black car had taken.

"You goin' fishin'? Need worms?" She showed Ramón their sign, making a cannon of her fist from out of which she shot her index finger. WORMS: FOR BAIT. The sign was meaningless to him. "Here, I'll give you some *free*, give me good luck—start the day with a blessin'. 'Give somethin' away: have *good*-luck today!' " she chimed. She thrust a small can, Hunt's Tomatoes, into his hands, and quickly shut him out.

Ramón hurried away from the woman whom he thought of as a madwoman, a *loca*; he was consoling himself, however, with the thought that at least she had

offered him food, when he raised the jagged lid of the
can and saw the squirming, writhing clot of worms.

"Dios mío!" he breathed, his heart stopping with horror. There was something diabolical, sacrilegious about
it—was the woman a *bruja*, a witch, living on the nearby
human flesh? He could imagine her suddenly, with that
wild clutch of hair, late at night, digging, digging . . . for
the worms which toiled at the bottom of her necrophilis.

He threw the can with all his strength; he heard it hit
the side of a tombstone, then roll in the sandy earth. He
stood by the side of the road; the glass in his stomach
heaved and cracked, but fortunately he had had no
breakfast. . . . It would have been an unlucky way to
begin his first day of freedom, he thought. With the
patience of certainty, a cleansing ritual to rid himself of
the ill effects of this brief encounter with doom, he began
to tell his rosary beads, feeling a sweet swell of gratitude
toward his God for having furnished in His foresight,
such an infallible restorative. For good measure he lightly
tapped the St. Christopher medal inside his T-shirt, and
felt himself again in complete control of his fate.

The bus did come, finally, and he sat down in its fan-
tastical coolness; he found that his experience had
swathed him in perspiration; he shivered, but the air-
conditioning which wafted around his feet felt good, and
he removed his sneakers, allowing the jets of air to tingle
his toes. He was just becoming accustomed to this miraculous inversion of temperatures—winter in July—when
the bus had stopped, everyone got off, and Ramón stood
barefoot in the streets of downtown San Antonio.

Dazzled by the sunlight and the traffic he stood in the
street a moment, uncertain where to go, when to his
immense delight he saw a familiar sign: Mexican Tour-
ism; he crossed the street and looked into the window as
if it were an outpost from Home. Inside, he could see
an elderly lady with carefully screwed curls dilating her
forehead, sitting at a large desk; another American
woman sat in a chair beside the desk, a baby on one
arm, a small blue and white canvas bag in the other,
labeled PAN AM. The floor was what magnetized
Ramón: polished as the human eye it lay in tessellated
squares, a dark pool of reflected light, surely as cool to
the bare feet as the river Frío. In the very center of the

polished redwood wall had been laid a mosaic of the
Holy Family, a gleaming rondure of semi-precious stones:
the blue eyes of the baby Jesus were made of sharp slices
of sapphire; His eyes, one realized, were meant to pierce
the Darkness, nothing was to remain hidden to Him. . . .
The ascendancy of the Christ child, and the mystic glow
emanating from the floor made the place a paradise. For
was it not as Father Sebastian had told him was described
in the *Book of Revelations:* "In Heaven the floor is laid
with diamonds, real diamonds; their brightness is blind-
ing; it is all light, but still cool, very cool, and you walk
your way along this path of diamonds till you see
Jesus. . . ."

The sight of the Infant Jesus reminded him that he
wished to offer up a long prayer before he caught the
train to Miami. Opposite the tourist office was the place
the bus driver had called out, St. Anthony's: was not St.
Anthony one of the earliest of Catholic saints? Its proximity was surely a good omen. . . . He started for the
corner, so as to cross, this time, with the traffic light.

He paused at Travis and St. Mary's, feeling mildly edi-
fied by this posting of holy names by the wayside, like the
Stations of the Cross. A city saturated with holy relics: he
knew people who had brought home splinters from the
San José mission, and had performed miracles with
them. . . . His problem now was so simple that he
flushed with shame. He could not find the doors to what
he had thought was a church—and stood with amazement
as there passed in front of him on the *sidewalk*, a huge
black car, as long, it seemed, as a mule team and wagon,
driving straight into the hallowed vault of this building.
Ramón could see, just ahead of it, dozens of other cars,
honking, idling, pushing slowly but aggressively forward,
shouldering their way through the crowd. The rear of the
car was in the street; he wished he could touch its shiny
flank, graceful and silent as a cropping horse, but he
dared not. Instead, he walked around it, nearly four feet
into the street where the sloping rear panel had stretched
itself.

He stood for a moment staring into the faces of the
people driving into St. Anthony's; he gazed at them with
an almost religious awe, as though they were white Spanish Gods, bringing arms and horses and commerce and

misery to his people; but they did not notice him. They
were relaxed; blue-haired, black-hatted, as white and
clean as boiled rice. They spoke to each other gently;
there was no noise within the automobile, one could see
that, except for their voices; the blue windows held out
the sun, sealed in the cold air. Ramón saw a hand, the
color of burnt hay, like his own, adjust the air condi-
tioner to the new cool of the garage, and for a split-
second Ramón gazed into the eyes of the chauffeur,
brown eye to brown eye, eyes of my people—and there
was an exchange, an understanding between them, silent
and subterranean, like the soundless explosion of rifles
in a dream. . . . Ramón, stunned by the intensity of this
look, stood alone at St. Mary's.

He saw at once that St. Anthony's was not, after all,
a church, and he laughed at himself, though troubled by
his sacrilegious error as he hopped through the door, a
door sliced like a giant grapefruit into four equal parts,
spinning on its axis.

He stood uncertainly in the lobby of St. Anthony's,
his sneakers around his neck, his bare feet upon the red
carpet; his eyes clouded with shame when he saw he had
left two sooty footprints, so small they reminded him of
his little brother Mauricio's toes. He could scarcely
believe that it was he, Ramón, a grown boy, who had
thus dirtied the carpet: when the dapper brass-buttoned
desk clerk raised his plucked eybrows at him, it made
him feel like a dog. *Puercos y perros*. . . . With an illumination of memory, as of a sign of Braille raised by the
heat of shame to living words, he remembered something
Father Sebastian had read to him in English: " 'Juárez
could not forgive me,' " Santa Anna said, " "because he
had waited on me at table at Oaxaca in 1829 *with his feet
bare on the floor.*' " The great Juárez, too, had run away
when he was twelve—and like Juárez he, too, stood now
shivering with shame, his feet bare on the floor, and
expecting the brass-buttoned desk clerk to throw him
into the street. . . . As fast as he could Ramón slipped
into his sneakers, tied the rotting laces into a knot; then
he felt respectable: he cultivated a slow dignified stroll,
trying to look as if he were waiting for someone. He
even sat in one of the green leather chairs with its winged
bronzed back soaring above his head, its graceful concav-

ity to his back; he put his head back on the brass-nailed
trimming: not very comfortable, but *caramba*, it was cool
against the skin. As he slid off suddenly, violently, his
own wet skin made an inadvertent rasping sound against
the leather; so that again Ramón stood frozen with
shame, involuntarily shaking his head in denial and going
through the comedy of repeating the sound on purpose
so that the elevator boy would see how he had accidentally made the noise with his bare skin.

But he became at once indifferent to the judgments of
the elevator boy as his eyes fell on a beautiful bronze
statue of a woman (the sign said *Roman* and he was glad
it had been no Mexican *mala hembra* who had posed for
it) with one exquisite breast exposed while with the left
hand she held up a lamp as bright as the sun. Her breast
was round and high and looked soft to the touch as the
inside of a melon; but it would never have occurred to
Ramón to touch it: he knew that though she was nearly
naked it was nevertheless a thing of beauty—as when *la
madre* exposed the spurting curve of her breast to Mauricio—and not to be profaned by inquisitive hands.

Ah, how he wished, though, that he might take one
long, gliding run on the red carpet, but he dared not;
the faint nervous nausea of his stomach reminded him
that the excitement of the beautiful place had not fed
him. He had begun to drag his sneakers slowly along the
carpet toward the incredibly symmetrical radii of the
door when he noticed a pair of vases taller than himself—
surely the most beautiful urns in the world. Father Sebastian had once told him that in the days of Rome just
such urns were filled with rose petals, or even with one's
own tears and preserved: the memory of one's grief distilled to aromatic bliss.

He longed to look deep inside, and raised himself on
tiptoe, clinging to the lip of the vase for balance, and
peered into the darkness. He whispered into it, his susur-
rating breath returned to him like a dead voice from out
of the past; he tried to make a tear, so that like the
ancients, his sorrow would be sanctified forever. But he
felt no grief, only ecstasy; so instead, with his tongue he
scooped up a small bubble of saliva from the soft of his
cheeks and dropped it with a tiny *plick* into the bottom
of the vase.

It was for this that the hotel clerk threw him out. That was all right—he had to do that, Ramón realized, and felt neither fear nor humiliation for the rude ejection: he had reached the point where he could feel only hunger. So he quickly adjusted his manly pride by inhaling a robust whack of air and raced at top speed for several blocks, in a wild exuberance of freedom. He stopped short at the river, and leaned most of his small body over one of San Antonio's myriad bridges. There, on the opposite side of the river, was a Chinese restaurant. Calm and commercial, a Mexican boy travestied an Oriental waiter in white jacket and silk flowered Bermudas. On the near side, immediately under him lay stretched along the turbid river, *La Casa Mía* Fine Mexican Food.

La Casa Mía—the name attracted him, made a spasm of violent homesickness in his belly: he could hear his mother calling him and Maurico *Vengan hijos a la casa, a comer.* . . . Almost hopping with delight Ramón descended the granite stairs of the bridge and sat down at one of the tables inlaid with mosaic. Beside him were round tables rooted to the floor by a single stone base, and on the wide diameters of their surfaces, Aztec gods, birds, Zodiacs, Virgins, had been wrought in mosaic. From where he sat perched in his iron chair, he could see on the table next to him the hundred eyes of a peacock's tail, glinting in the sun; piece by piece it had been created, by tireless hands for whom each dainty piece meant a tenth of a peso.

A young couple sat down opposite Ramón: a blonde-haired girl with bangs like a scythe across her forehead smiled at him tenderly, glancing down at his tongueless shoes. The waiter came, hesitated, looked around helplessly, grinned at the blonde girl, who was nodding meaningfully. "So O.K. niño, you want tortillas, we got 'em, plenny of 'em. *Con mantequilla*," he added in the tone of a man describing a Christmas tree; and had vanished before Ramón could protest against the butter; it would cost too much, especially in this place.

The waiter brought tortillas, toasted crackers and several mounds of butter; from the table next to him where the beautiful blonde-haired angel was still smiling at Ramón, the waiter transferred more crackers and a soft drink which *el angel* pushed into his hand. Ramón devoured this rapidly, and left a five-cent tip.

He was about to leave when blind tears stung his eyes, and he realized with a shock that they had simply sprung like a tincture dilating the surface at the very moment the Mariachi music had struck his ears: they were serenading the couple at the next table. While his stomach ecstatically digested the tortillas, he took in at every pore the elixir of sound: oh sweet Mexico, to find you on this river. . . .

The *guitarrón* was strumming a hat dance, his fingers working with casual perfection. The singing tenor, flamboyantly decked out as a *vaquero* (*we* had cowboys before they did, Ramón silently boasted), stood beside a beautiful Mexican lady adorned with traditional tiara and mantilla. . . . In fact, they looked more Mexican than any Mexicans Ramón had ever seen—his people, masquerading as themselves. Ramón left the restaurant feeling crushed. There had been something about the Mariachis which had reminded him of his father—the pale, yellow resoluteness of their faces, and the sweating back of the *guitarrero*, whose silk shirt had clung to him in a wet, arrow-like wound, like Papa's shirt at the *corrida*. . . . He was trying, not rationally, but with a leap of personal apprehension to grasp the relationship between those two orbing wounds of sweat; thus he hardly noticed that he had taken over an hour, as he strolled up St. Mary's Street, to find a church, and even then he did not look at the name—it sufficed for him that he saw two nuns emerging in black robes, their heavy crucifixes hanging at their sides.

As he opened the door and stood in the transept of the church the cool beatified air, exempt from earthly heats, swept around him. He dipped his fingers into the holy water, glad his hands had been cleansed by El Frío; then he advanced to the Communion rail where he knelt and offered up a fervent prayer for courage in the new land.

At last he rose from his knees, satisfied that he had been heard. He sat down in one of the polished pews, lucent as amber, and feasted his eyes on God's earthly Temple: on the blue velvet altar cloth with the chastened glow of the chalice and the softly breathing flames flick-

ering like souls from out the red glasses, and beyond it
all, above him, a cross of gold on which Christ hung in
agony.

From the pocket of his jeans he pulled out the frayed
train schedule he had kept hidden for months, ever since
his stepfather had first slept at their house. He had studied the schedule many times, had supplemented his
uncertain comprehension with patient inquiry darkly
reticulated in the pockets of conversations till the information had returned to him repeated, axiomatic: take
the Southern Pacific to New Orleans; switch for the
Louisville-Nashville; watch out for railway guards and
queers. His head nodded over the long-familiar schedule,
and while the filtered light from the mullioned window
rained silence, he dozed. . . . When he awoke, he was
in terror a moment, not knowing how long he had slept;
so he jumped to his feet and began running, running as
fast as he could, spurred by the vision of vanishing freight
cars. He ran, sweating with fear and speed, the entire
two blocks to Commerce Street, where at the railway
yard, he stopped.

Fortunately he had not missed his train; that would
indeed have been a bad omen. What remained now was
merely to find a place to wait, so that when the train
approached and the railway guards flew their lanterns of
consent, he too would fly, silent as the hawk, and
descending upon the box car with a swift swoop of arm
and limb, would lift himself into the car and be—free.

When the train came at last, it proved to be intermina-
bly long—freight after freight of cotton, lumber, oil products, and Texas beef—freshly slaughtered, flash-frozen,
to be made into steaks worthy of a nation of conquerors.
The thought of steak made his stomach rage suddenly
with hunger; but he had not time to think of his stomach
now; for he must be watching, watching, for the moment
when the flares descended and the cars bumping together
in their blind haste would begin to move forward. Now
the train jerked, spattered, steamed like the ejaculation
of a bull, and began to move—one car following another
like some thundering herd hard behind its leader.

The noise was terrifying, but even more terrifying was
the possibility that this controlled acceleration of a miracle might vanish without him. . . . So he leaped . . . and

the roar and motion of the cars was like an earthquake,
in the midst of which he clung, clung to the opened door,
till a momentary stalled jerk of the car allowed him to
pull his legs up; and he let go. He was flung with a lurch
into deep sawdust, for which his brain flashed a marveling wink of admiration as the shavings cushioned his fall.
The train roared on, and he found himself alone, triumphant, looking outward from where he lay on the floor.

Keeping his head out of sight, he gazed on the city
from his vantage point. The usual railroad outskirts
pricked his vision, kaleidoscopic and searingly familiar as
they sped by, ugly shack upon ugly shack, like his very
own street, spotted here and there with geranium pots:
a huge scab covering the wound of the City, healed now
and then with a concentric beauty and health only to
break open from time to time in suppurating disease as
they sped away from the festering little homes and ruts
of streets out into the infinity of Texasland, a land as
wide as the Salt Sea. . . .

When they were out on the open road, Ramón felt at
last protected against vagrant eyes that might wish to
take over his squatters' rights. . . . Stacked on one side
of the car were a single bushel basket, and several empty
pinewood boxes with various labels: Texas Peaches,
Buford's Huisache Honey, 100% Pure, and Sam Slaugh-
ter's Packing House: Fresh Frozen Produce. He was
kneeling in the sawdust, looking for any stray bits of food
that might have been set adrift in the boxes when he
heard the cars come to a screeching stop. Without a second's hesitation, Ramón rolled himself like a pill bug
under the empty peach basket and lay there without
breathing while he listened to grunts, groans, heaves and
what seemed to be the rolling wheels of a dolly. After
about twenty minutes (which felt infinitely longer) the
marching and dragging subsided and darkness shrouded
the staves of his basket. He was safe; for the first time
in his life his small unfleshed body had been an asset; he
squatted for a moment on his haunches, then stood up,
chilled with relief, his hands cold from the prolonged
fear. . . .

On their way out they had slammed the doors to, all
the way, and locked them, and in the gloom he could
not at first make out what food his benefactors had left

him; but as he raised his head he collided with the flayed
and dangling limbs of a cow, evidently so recently killed
that it had not yet begun to smell dead; as he stood
beneath it a drop of blood, like a raindrop, fell to the
sawdust. Such was the inert company they had brought
to share his vault: he saw them clearly now, hanging
from hooks in the ceiling on which were skewered the
delicacies of edible flesh: hams and shoulders and legs of
mutton and carcasses of beef: there were even two or
three blue-eyed, rosy-cheeked heads of porkers spiked to
the side walls like condemned victims beside a medieval
drawbridge. A whole hennery of fowl lined the wall, and
a rabbit, which for some reason had not yet been
skinned. It hung head down, slender-footed paws nailed
to an iron tree, its delicate nostrils and fine whiskers still
alert with fear. The other animals, stripped of their deep
cow-eyes and bleating tones, were mere anonymous flesh
meant to renew and construct the body and mind of man;
but the rabbit's fur was still dappled grey, stippled with
the colors of the prairie, dogwood blossom and cenizo-
colored leaf. . . . Ramón felt suddenly a great desolation
and wished they had left the door open for him so that
he could stare out at the rolling escarpments of color—
at the orange clay and blue gentians and purple paint
brushes and yellow star grass and white shreds of thistle,
so that he might close his mind to what seemed to him
the still echoing shriek of the slain animals, their not
even memorable grief—the mere pitiless pain of the char-
nel house.

He had found a softly rotting peach, but in spite of his
hunger, he could not eat it. The grizzly spectacle had
chilled him to the bone; he realized suddenly, that his
teeth were clenched and chattering, though he could feel
drops of nervous perspiration congeal under his thinly
woven T-shirt. He shivered and tried the door, eager for
the now-fading sunlight, but as he had suspected, it was
immovable. If only there were a window through which
he could watch the moonlight and stars during his all-
night vigil across the Louisiana delta: twelve hours before
their arrival in New Orleans, and he would not once see
the glory of the heavens.

More practically, he murmured to himself, if there
were a window he could dry his perspiration, hold back

this progressive chill: was he getting a fever, hot and cold as his body seemed to be? He unrolled his father's cape and enveloped himself in it, with the black side, the side with Papa's blood close to his heart; but still his teeth did not cease to chatter; his hands remained stiff and cold. It was odd, too, that the *muleta* had no smell: almost always, and especially on hot, humid days, the smell of the dust and blood of doomed bull and father would pervade his nostrils; but now he could smell nothing. He breathed only the icy fumes of his own nostril; his breath made a cotton-like burr which eased away from him, refusing to cohere.

As he sat on the sawdust floor, shivering and peering longingly at the sharp blade of light slitting the throaty darkness of the door, he became aware of a humming in his ears, a bedtime murmuring as if *la madre* rocked him, cunningly, to sleep. Was it the sound of the wind—or the sound of a motor? He rose, gasping painfully at the cold which now burned at his chest like dry ice—he felt he would not be able to endure it, and he began whimpering softly to himself, clutching his rosary in rigid hands: *oh hace frío, o god, oh Jesús, hace frío.*

He remembered suddenly that moving about might keep him warm, and he began, not walking but hopping—his left leg had scraped against the side of the boxcar and now was numb with pain—hopping to and fro beneath the contorted limbs of the friable bodies. He was still stubbornly hobbling back and forth in the car when with a loud shriek the train began to cross a trestle and threw him against the wall. His hands clutched the wall in amazement: it was lined with coils and covered with a light, damp frost, like rail tracks in mid-winter; and his fingers pulled away with an icy burn.

In despair he threw himself down on the sawdust-covered floor, sobbing. *Oh Jesús help me*, he prayed with blue lips that made no sound as he moved them; but as the unarticulated prayer sounded in his heart, he clutched the sawdust which oozed through his fingers like sand: like sand that one could burrow in and be warm. With a sudden rush of energy, he moved all the hanging bodies to one side of the car, and with his arms and shoulders began shoving the sawdust into a corner of the car. The floor had been liberally covered with sawdust, and he

murmured little orisons of gratitude as he swept. And *oh
Jesús mío,* how good it felt to crawl into it, submerged
almost to the chest. Covered by the black and red cape
and buried in the sawdust, he felt as content, almost, as
when swimming in El Frío—when beneath him, sus-
taining his body, had reposed the infinite shales of
immovable time, and above him, skittering across his
naked chest like dragonflies, had darted the sunlight. . . .
And as he had trusted then to the maternal, caressing
rills of sunlight, he trusted now to the ooze and ebb
of the blood of his body, the very treachery of whose
congealment seemed to warm him as he slept, lifeless,
his rosary in his rigid hand.

MARY GRAY HUGHES

❦ ❦ ❦

Mary Gray Hughes was born in 1930 and grew up on the border between Texas and Mexico in Brownsville, where she attended public schools. In 1951, she earned her BA from Barnard College, graduating magna cum laude. The same year she was awarded a Fulbright Scholarship to study at Oxford University. A recipient of many honors for her writing, she was awarded a National Endowment for the Arts Fellowship in Creative Writing in 1978, served as writer-in-residence at the University of Illinois from 1977 to 1980, and was elected in 1983 to the Texas Institute of Letters. Hughes has published two collections of stories: The Thousand Springs *(1971) and* The Calling *(1980). Two of her stories have been anthologized in* Best American Short Stories: *"The Judge," which is included in this anthology and first appeared in* The Atlantic, *was the selection for 1972.*

When asked to comment on how she used her Mexican-American experiences in her fiction, Hughes wrote: "I don't feel I had Mexican-American experiences and I never, consciously, 'use' them. Mexican-Americans simply were part of my life, like the Anglos around me, like the landscape of South Texas, where I was born. Like the books I read, like the particular individuals I came to know well within my family or in the schools I went to, all filled with Anglos and Mexican-Americans. Like all the events of my life. Together, these form a background I draw upon unthinkingly as the writing demands." The story "The Judge" reflects these experiences and is one of her most successful.

195

The Judge

The Mexican's name was Baille. "Pronounced 'Buy-ye,'" the Judge liked to explain with amusement, and for the past three months now, at least once every week, the Judge had driven out through the flat country-side to where the Mexican lived to try and make him sign some papers. So far the Mexican would not do it.

"You'd think I was trying to sell him snake oil," the Judge said. "The old charlatan. I can't help liking him. Last time he came out with the statement that he didn't even have any rights in the claim at all. Just after I had shown him, with genealogical charts, how I had traced him. He says he's Basque, but that's nonsense. The name is pure Spanish. You find it all over this part of the state and in northern Mexico, going back, with a few ortho-graphic variations, for two hundred years. There were never any Basques around here."

The Judge would know. He knew about languages and races and the origins of people and their names. He had made a study of such things. He could speak five lan-guages and read two more. He knew Baille personally, too, though it was only in the last year that he had come to know the Mexican well. "It's not that he's an impor-tant claimant," the Judge said. "His portion is one of the smaller ones. But when it is a question of the heirs in a petition against the States, then it looks better to have all the heirs file. He's the only one who won't sign. One hundred and twenty-seven depositions I've got, two of them from as far away as the state of Oaxaca, and a brief that is easily the most complicated ever submitted in this jurisdiction, and I'm held up by a country school janitor. It's good I can appreciate the humor of it. Nonetheless, time is getting short. I must try to move him along this Sunday. I'll tell you one thing, if I have to drive out to that place of his many more times, I'm going to get the county to do something about that road."

Not the highway. The Judge did not mean that. The highway was fine; laid flat and dead straight on the ground, it fell before him across the countryside like a clap of thunder, splitting the gray brush in two. On Sunday afternoons it was usually empty, and the Judge's solitary car hummed along at the fifty miles an hour advised by the instruction book as best for breaking in a new car. They had offered to let him keep a state car when he resigned. "No, no," the Judge had said, "you know me better than that."

The first turn off the highway to Baille's came just beyond the railroad crossing. From there the Judge's car followed a gravel road past the country school where the Mexican was janitor. Beyond that there was a bend crowded by willow trees and then a sharp right turn onto a narrow dirt road. Dust spilled out under the wheels and rose up beside the car like a giant gray dog and ran around the curves with it, brushing against the bushes in the narrow places. When the Judge stopped at last before the Mexican's house, dust poured up and over and through the car and on ahead down the road before collapsing back down into the ground again.

The Judge spat out the window to clear his mouth and honked the horn once, then again. Nothing happened. He knew Baille would not come out. He honked again, longer.

"Baille," the Judge yelled out the car window. "Hey, Baille."

"You know, I took a Sears catalogue out there to him once. And a big black pencil in case he didn't have one. I told him to put a check by all the things in the catalogue he wanted, just go ahead and mark everything he would like to have, anything and everything, and to keep on marking, and I would tell him to stop when he had used up the money I could make for him in one single year. He wouldn't do it. He wouldn't even look at the catalogue. Wouldn't even open it."

The Judge sat in the car staring at the shack and rubbing his nose, which he did in a very distinctive way. He held his hand still and moved his head gently up and down, sliding his nose between his thumb and forefinger. It was occurring to the Judge that it would be all a great deal easier if the Mexican had more of the world's goods, for then there would be more places where pressure could be applied.

The Judge honked again, and called, "Baille," louder, but without really expecting any result. He got out of the car and started over to the gate. A short man, with most of his height from the waist up, the Judge walked with his back rigid and his big powerful stomach firmly leading so that he looked in profile like a chair being pushed steadily forward.

Around his feet two bulbs of dust spouted onto his shoelaces and his trouser legs and then settled back down on the tops and sides of his shoes when he stopped before the fence. It was a fence made of barbed wire and mesquite. The wire was a dull color, with rust exploding around the base of each barb, and the untrimmed mesquite posts were knobbed and twisted and so dried up that the old shallow, hand-dug post holes gaped open around them.

The Judge established himself by the main gate post to wait. He lifted a foot to rest it comfortably on one of the lower strands, but the wire twanged loose onto the ground, throwing the Judge forward.

"Damn," the Judge swore. And yelled, "Baille!"

"It's true that it is not precisely flattering to be kept cooling my heels outside his fence until it suits him to come out. I need my old baliff to hail him for me. Still, they have a sense of dignity and pride, these Mexicans. It denies our tempo of doing things. They insist on time, they respect it. And let me make one other point: he has some strange, absolutely perfect sense of just when it is the right time to come out."

The Judge pressed his stomach against the gate, moving it back on the tripled loops of wire that served as hinges. His hand eased along toward the latch. From around a corner of the shack the Mexican appeared, walking quickly with little low steps that moved him over the bare ground with no up-and-down movement at all but simply a fast unbroken propulsion forward as steadily efficient as the towing along of rakes or harrows after tractors, or the dragging of dead things behind the low rear bumpers of cars.

He was a man in his fifties, and so short he was forced to tip his head back to look up at the Judge. When he did, the Mexican showed his face with all the flattest angles exposed, showed his quick blinking eyes and soft squashed nose.

"How can you stand the heat out here?" the Judge said in a friendly tone.

The Mexican stared at him with the wild surprise the Judge's lisping Castilian always brought to him, for how was it this man could go on sounding like a drunken bird every time he spoke?

"Doesn't it bother you?" the Judge said again.

"You don't like the heat?" the Mexican said finally, hopefully.

"I can take the heat. It's the dust I really don't like. I swear, if you don't start acting sensibly, Baille, I'm going to get this road blacktopped."

The Mexican peered in amazement at the thin dirt road running along his fence and beneath the Judge's car, for the Judge had just announced that he intended to take an oath to do away with the road in darkness with a coating of perpetual obscurity.

"You don't like the dust then?" the Mexican said, trying again. "There is certainly much dust here. Much dust. You should stay in town. You stay in town, and I will come to visit you there."

"There is an innocence, or rather an obviousness that reminds one of innocence, in some of his ploys. At times it is terribly poignant. A touch . . . not of childishness, they are not childish, these people, he's a grown and very tough man, but a touch of the basic, unconcealed, open human being that can be very moving. Would any of you believe that I feel I have actually learned from him?"

"I think not," the Judge said to the Mexican. "I think not. You might forget to come. But I never forget, do I?" And the Judge began to fan himself slowly, swinging his hat in wide arcs. His clothing was sweated through. "Listen," the Judge said, "why won't you trust me? All I want is to make some money for you. Why won't you do what I tell you?"

"Don't think the irony of it has escaped me. Mrs. Easterbury reminded me only the other night that I was the one who got him his job. Otherwise he might not even be around here. Well, I don't regret it. He came to me for help about two years ago. I'd hardly spoken to him before, but he knew who I was, so of course I had to help

*him. His wife had just left him, and he had some scheme
in mind, some absurd plan for getting her back. I got him
the job as janitor. I told the school board he would never
steal. I took the responsibility for that and gave them my
assurance, and he never has stolen a thing."*

"No papers," the Mexican said, shaking his head. "No
papers for signing. Absolutely no."

"You can sign your name," the Judge said. "I've seen
it written down at the courthouse."

The Mexican neither moved nor spoke, but the Judge
became instantly alert, for he knew, just as he would
have in a courtroom, that the Mexican was running
inside, running and running while he was standing still.
The Judge was sure of it.

"What's the matter with your name on the records?"
the Judge said. "Hm? What's wrong with it?"

"Nothing, nothing," the Mexican said. "It's my mother's name for me, why not? So if you don't like it, what
will you do? Shoot me?" And he burst into a fit of giggles
snuffled out against the back of his hand. For the phrase
in Spanish was *Fuegame*, and it could mean either "fire
me," as from a job, or "shoot me," as with a gun.
Months ago when the Mexican had first said it, the Judge
had been so delighted he had laughed out loud, and after
a few seconds of uncertainty, Baille had joined in, laughing harder and harder.

*"Their humor. Even when used as the most pathetically
obvious smoke screen, still it is always appealing. Superb,
poised, and proud. It's dour and simple, yet with sophistication, too, and with that special cast of appreciating language. That's what I relish most of all, the gift of language
that they have. You see it right from the earliest days of
the nation's history and down through all the major shifts
in the language itself. They have a racial genius for language. Do you realize that even the poorest, most unedu-
cated Mexican uses the subjunctive tense?"*

"Fuegame," the Mexican said again, giggling behind
his hand.

"Maybe, maybe," the Judge said. "Or better than
that, if you don't act sensibly, I might have a look at
those records in the courthouse. The ones with your
name." He said it pleasantly, and aware that the expression on his face was one of brightness and humor, with

his eyes twinkling, yet he wanted a threat in his words, and there was. The Mexican was running again inside.

"How old are you?" the Judge asked suddenly, trusting it was the right question.

Intelligence flicked and vanished in the Mexican's face the way a lizard's tail slips away between sun-baked rocks, and the Judge was left gazing at the place where understanding had been. And slowly, with exquisite precision, the Judge's mind eased open and gave up to him his secrets in the order in which he needed them: the Mexican's age did not match his name. This Mexican's age was decades short of what was needed to match those yellowing, smudged courthouse records. He had "bought his name," as the Mexicans put it, and his papers were forged.

The Judge was home free.

I was reminded of the last will and testament of one of the first Spanish conquistadores. 'Before us,' he had written, 'there was no evil, now there is no good.' A moving sentiment, but is it history? The Aztecs could not have been conquered if the majority of the Indians in the Valley of Mexico had not joined Cortez' crew precisely because the Aztec rule had been so cruel; so evil, indeed, that they were willing to follow anyone else in order to overthrow that rule. Our Spanish testator erred in the way we all do—what we do not understand, we always simplify.

"Has the Sheriff ever looked at those records of yours in the courthouse?"

There was no more running now inside the Mexican, just the quick blinking of his eyes, the rabbit caught, and waiting.

"You look to me, Baille," the Judge said, "like a man who may have himself some trouble."

The Mexican waited.

"Listen," the Judge said, "I could go on away from here right now without any signature of yours on any papers. I don't need it. I can prove from the records in the courthouse that I don't need it. But I'm not going to do that. I've made up my mind to help you. I know all about you, and you'll have to do what I say. Do you understand?"

"It would be all right if you went away from here now," the Mexican said. "You can do that."

"Don't think it is just altruism on my part," the Judge said. "If I don't get your signature on the papers, it will not look right, because there are people who know your name should be in this case. So if you do not sign, I will have to explain why you did not, and I will have to tell about your records. Do you see? I will have to tell, and then the Sheriff will know about you, and then he would come for you. Understand?"

The Judge set himself to sound absolutely commanding, and it was easy because he had come to that key moment when he knew he was winning and was enjoying his skill at closing a case.

"Now, you go on in there and change your clothes," the Judge said firmly. He knew better than to give the Mexican any time. "I am going to take you with me into town to sign those papers." The Mexican's fast-blinking eyes kept wavering away, glancing off toward the road and the brush around. "Oh, yes," the Judge said, "yes, right now. You go put on something else, something cleaner that you can wear to the courthouse. Go on. Now. And while you're changing, I'll go take a look at your lake."

"Mud pond—that's what I usually call these unimproved water holes when I'm not trying to be nice to the people living near them. Little indentations in the ground they are, no deeper than the hollow in a beggar's palm and filled with thick brownish water evaporating away from the muddy banks. Often one end will go deeper, keeping a permanent water supply, and willows grow up all around it. Any of you noticed these little ponds? Ah, you should. These sites are going to be worth good money one of these days."

The Judge crossed the road and walked alongside it, and the soles of his shoes snapped down the brittle grass that grew and burned and grew again out in the sun beside the road. Once into the shade of the willow trees the grass thickened and made a soft cushion under the Judge's feet. He went straight to the deep part of the pond. As he went he kicked in the reeds and fallen tree limbs for frogs or turtles or any signs of the small animals that exist in the banks near water. Just at the end of the pond, there was a little rise of ground. It was not more than three feet high, but in the midst of the violent flat-

ness of the countryside around it seemed higher, and the
Judge, coming out from the fringe of willows and putting
aside their frail branch tips with the side of his hand,
pulled himself up onto it with his short legs and felt he
could see a long way, felt he could see for miles. He
looked across the pool to the low brush beyond and the
dense trees of pale green and gray on the other side. He
would have been embarrassed to say how stirred he was
by the countryside, or how much beauty he saw in the
tangle of mesquite trees growing in a solid cloud on their
thin, crooked trunks. He would not have wanted to tell
of a game he played, when he was out in the country,
of letting his eyes rise only slowly, slowly along the low
line of brush and small mesquite, and inch by half-inch
go along the solid mass, then slowly lift to the first few
broken spaces in between, and moving faster, a little
faster and rising again, up and farther along, and going
with joy now, joy, up and faster and off over the mesquite and willow to the horizon and the dumb unbeliev-
able idiot palm trees grinning like God, he told himself,
over the long flat landscape running beneath them all the
way to the sea.

*"It wasn't easy. I tried just about everything on him. I
made three trips out to the school to see the principal, and
I made sure each time that Baille saw us together. That
preyed on him. He would hang around in the hall pretending to sweep out but watching us. That fool principal
spent all the time carrying tales to me against Baille. He
told me the Mexican sneaks the lock shut on the boys'
washroom once a week or so, and then hangs around in
the hall to watch the fun. I was supposed to be shocked
at this. Especially shocked because Baille thinks it's funny.
The principal is naive. He doesn't understand their
humor. More than that, I think it bothers him that I like
Baille. He can't understand why I want to help him. At
heart, the principal has no feeling for them."*

The Judge's attention was caught, by a sound? a smell?
and he turned his head and the Mexican was there beside
him. The Judge opened his mouth to speak, thinking to
ask why the other was in the same clothes and had not
changed, when all at once the whole of the Mexican—
body, head, shoulders, arms, legs—came leaping into the

Judge and jolted him so hard that he hurt all through his body. The two of them fell, not backward and so down the slope of the little hill and into the shallow water as the Judge thought they would and the Mexican intended, but straight onto the muddy lips at the deep edge of the water, just below where the Judge had been standing. For the Judge had been felled absolutely, had had his short legs collapse right under him and had fallen with the Mexican on top of him. They rolled from side to side on the muddy ground, and the willows shaded them some of the time, and the position of sky and lake and trees kept shifting in their line of vision.

All the time the Judge kept grunting and trying to get his breath to say something like: but this is an accident and I accept your apology for stupidly and clumsily and accidentally knocking into me; I understand; while the Mexican pulled at the Judge's head and shoulders trying to haul and shove him further forward into the water, deep enough to cover his head and face entirely. Reeds at the water's edge snapped beneath the Judge's head, and a rock under his shoulder made him arch his back up in pain as he tried to roll free from the Mexican's hands which fled from his head and face back to his arms and tugged and pushed at him again, moving him forward once more, further into the water.

This time the Judge realized what was happening, and focused his eyes finally on the Mexican's face close above his own. The Judge's body jerked rigid and then turned frantic with terror. He grabbed at the Mexican's wrists, uselessly, then tried to get a hold anywhere on the skin that was thin and taut over muscle and bone, and not able to do that, clutched at the worn overalls, but he could not grasp hold of the Mexican in any way. "Knee him in the groin, knee him in the groin," yipped some part of the Judge's mind, delighting him with his own tough knowledge. But his legs thrashed foolishly and uselessly up and down, miles, it seemed, away from the Mexican straddling his chest. The Judge could not even kick the man in the back. The Judge pulled again, and again with no effect, at the Mexican's small hard wrists. With a hiss the Mexican shoved and slid him another few inches into the water and once more tried to submerge the heavy, golden head. There was not enough water, simply not enough water, and in a rage of despair the Mexican grabbed the Judge's head and pressed it deep into the mud. The shallow sludge filled the Judge's left ear and shut one eye, and the nostril on that side was plugged as solidly as by a finger. But the Judge's entire head would not go under. His free eye saw a reed inches in front of his face. It seemed gigantic, the strands that formed it long and beautifully green, and the edges of it the most incredible sharp yellow. The Judge strained toward it, moving with great effort, his head rising out of the mud and water. The Mexican hissed by his ear and got a different grip under the Judge's shoulders and hauled him forward again, deeper into the water. The Judge could feel mud under his shoulders now and dampness down to his waist, and water washed against his neck and up to his ears. With a deep grunt of satisfaction the Mexican pushed the Judge's head down again, hard, and this time the whole head and white face went beneath the water.

It was shocking. The Judge's eyes shut at first, but his ears heard all the sounds water takes in from the air but does not give back to it. He could hear hands thrashing in the water, and the sound of the Mexican's voice cursing. He opened his eyes, and he could see the Mexican, could see everything; it was there, but changed because of the layer of water over his face. The Judge went limp and the Mexican, too ignorant, too eager. (*"Poor son of a gun. They're so often like that, defeating themselves by lack of experience or lack of self-control"*), pushed forward too fast, thinking it was over, thinking to finish it, rushing, and so rising up on the Judge's neck too high and getting himself off balance for just that instant (*"Timing has always been one of my greatest courtroom assets, you know"*), so the Judge gave a heave of his powerful stomach and short legs and rolled up and over his own shoulder, tossing the two of them backward, half-somersaulting, and crashing through the reeds and over the muddied lip of the pool and down into the clearer, deeper water. Wet now to hip, to chest, and at any minute over the head possibly, but the Judge was not to know, for the Mexican had turned and flung himself at the shore, crying out for it, lunging back to the bank with the Judge hanging on around his hips while the Mexican grasped and tugged on the reeds, pulling great, sucking chunks of them out of the mud and lunging back again at them and seizing thick sheaves of them in his hands. And all the time the Mexican kept making hoarse, gasping noises, steadily louder, until with a burst of strength he tugged the two of them out of the lake and plunged onto the muddy bank where they fell crushing the reeds down into the mud.

The Judge propped himself on his knees but kept hard hold of the Mexican as they panted side by side. Streaks of mud curled down the sides of the Judge's face. "Listen," the Judge gasped. "Listen." But he could not get enough air for the words. He was bursting, bursting with joy. He had had a fight. He, the Judge, at his age, had had a fight, like any man, and with a Mexican.

"Listen," the Judge said, holding on to the Mexican's arm just under the shoulder, holding tight, lovingly. "Don't be frightened," the Judge said. "I understand. I am a man, too. I won't bring any charges against you for that. I know how you feel. I won't call the Sheriff. Understand? I know you had to fight."

"Have you ever seen a Mexican cry? A Mexican man, I mean? A grown man? Not the way we do, but with a little 'hee hee hee' noise. Sitting back on his heels with his head pressed against his knees and crying 'hee hee hee,' like that. Just like that."

"See here. Now, see here," the Judge said. "It's going to be all right. It's going to be fine. You can trust me."

The Mexican would not move or lift his head from his knees.

"I'll come out her tomorrow," the Judge said. "At ten. Ten in the morning. And I'll take you to town. And I'll call the principal personally and explain to him that you won't be at work so you won't have any trouble there. You be ready at ten sharp. Understand? Then you can sign those papers. Look, it will be fine. Fine. Don't be scared. Don't . . . Don't make noises. Please. Don't. Why listen, listen, you may have . . ." and he stopped. "Saved my life," the Judge wanted to say, but inexcusably he could not remember the verb "to save" in that sense is Spanish. "You may have kept me from drowning," he said. "Saved my life," he remembered, "that's it. You may have saved my life."

The Mexican at least stopped making the noise. The Judge shook his arm in comradely fashion.

"That's right. That's right," the Judge said. "See?"

"No, of course we didn't shake hands. They don't make agreements in that fashion. But by an old, mutually understood joke I became his attorney. Yes, that's it, that's the truth, I was made his counselor by humor, and to be honest, I don't have a better contract, I can swear to that. It was an extraordinary experience; he's an unusual man. All the same, I think I may take up judo on the side if my practice continues in this way."

"Of course you understand now," the Judge said. "Certainly. You probably saved my life, and so I want to help you, too. I'll come out here for you tomorrow at ten. Ten in the morning. You be ready. Hear? You be ready, or I'll have to go get the Sheriff to shoot you. Our joke. Right? Ha ha. Our joke."

In the morning the Judge changed his mind. It seemed to him the best and most courteous thing would be to save the Mexican the trip into town and to the courthouse. Instead, the Judge decided to take his secretary, who could act as notary, and the necessary papers, and go out into the country and let the Mexican sign the papers there. The Judge liked the idea of the gesture. He would meet the Mexican more than halfway. And in any case, the Judge did not know how he and the Mexican, with the closeness that they had between them now, would manage in town, for the town was not ready for that yet.

The Judge went first thing, as he always did, to get his morning newspaper. The newsstand attendant was waiting for him. An obese man, he was squeezed into the narrow doorway of the shop with the Judge's paper held folded and ready.

"You heard?" the attendant asked eagerly. The Judge, as was his custom, dropped a quarter into the brass bowl although the paper cost only ten cents. The attendant kept hold of the paper until he could finish his story. "Haven't you heard? Really? They's a Messgun drowned in the river. Sheriff says it's one you know. Says you know him for sure. I was the second one down to the bridge to see him. I could see him plain as I see you.

He was washed up nearest the American side, and he still had a bundle with his things in it tied around his wrist. He was curled up and lying real funny, sort of right on his head and knees, like a little brown snail, and down back of him there was a trail going all the way he'd come out of the river. Everyone wondered where his hat was, but I told him any idiot would know a hat would be the first thing to float on off. Isn't that the truth, Judge? Any idiot ought to know that. But you know something I don't get, how come Messguns don' learn to swim since they keep crossing back and forth in that river all the time? You'd think they'd learn to swim, I say. Now, you take my sister's boy, he's learned to swim good and he's only fourteen. If they'd have learned to swim, them Messguns, none of them would have never drowned."

The Judge stood on the sidewalk with his feet planted square and carefully apart. He had a wide staring look on his face as if an arrow had shot straight through him from back to front going at a great speed and he was looking way off in the distance after it for some vital part of him that was being taken away faster and faster and faster away over the long, flat Texas landscape. Then the Judge gave a sudden, violent jerk, as happens sometimes when falling asleep, or waking.

"So what I say," the attendant said, "is someone ought to teach them to swim. That's what I say."

The Judge turned and began walking away, stamping off with hard steps pounding on the sidewalk.

"Want your paper?" the attendant called after him. "Judge?"

The Judge did not answer. He was getting into his car. He turned it around in the middle of the street and started straight out into the country to the Mexican's home.

He drove the distance in the same way that he always did, at the same carefully restrained rate of speed. There were not even many other cars on the highway, and he got there in the same time that it took him on the quiet Sundays.

There was no sign of life from the shack or from the treeless area of dirt around it. The gate hung open, slanting crookedly onto the ground. The Judge turned off the engine of his car.

"Baille!" he yelled at the shack. "Baille!"

The Judge got out and slammed the door hard and began to walk through the sparse grass and the dust which heat and wind had worn to a powder. He walked cautiously, as if at any minute he expected to be struck lame by a stiffening in both knees, an affliction he had felt creeping up on him from a long time past and which he dreaded because he knew that like old rusted locks, it was something no oil or ointment or paid-for expert he might hire was ever going to loosen for him again.

"Baille!" the Judge yelled.

There was no point in standing still before the open gate. The Judge went through it into the yard where he had never been before. He walked toward the corner of the shack around which he was used to seeing the Mexican come. He supposed there must be some sort of door on the other side. When he turned the corner he saw a square black opening in the wall before him. "Baille?" he called again, when he had reached the door, "Baille?" and there being no reply, he lowered his head and plunged into the darkness inside.

There was no one there. The Mexican was gone. And the second shock was the size of the room. For somehow the Judge had always imagined rooms and rooms expanding within the small frame of the shack. In his mind the Judge had thought of the Mexican waiting for him while sitting in a living room or small reading room, with a kitchen off to his left somewhere and at his back a bedroom. The Judge had placed the Mexican there, sitting comfortably, reading perhaps, or walking around at his ease while he waited for the Judge to come so he could match wits with him again. But there was instead a square of space marked off by gray wooden boards and covered with a tin roof and with the bare ground underfoot. There were not even windows cut in the walls. Threads of light spun themselves down through gaps in the roof, and a block of light fell through the doorway like a hunk of wall collapsed onto the floor.

The Judge's eyes adjusted to the dimness, and he could see every part of the room. Quite obviously the Mexican was gone, gone and had meant to go. He had left a coat the Judge had given him, and a pair of pants the Judge had given him, and two black shoes the Judge had given him. But all the rest was gone except the heavy things he could not carry, a table made of railroad ties and next to it a three-legged stool; an old kerosene stove that was thick with rust; a brass bedstead with no mattress.

A cup, still half filled with coffee, was on the table, and the Judge put his palm against its side. It was cold.

"Damn him," the Judge said. He struck the cup a flat blow, lifting it up through the air to smash into the wall. "Damn, damn, damn him," and the Judge kicked the small three-legged stool. It rolled under the table. The Judge kicked one of the table legs, but the table stood firm on thick square legs. The Judge bent over and caught the edge of the table to upend it, but it would not move. He could not budge it. He tugged again, heaving on it, and when it still stood motionless he bent lower, his head just above its surface, and pulled harder, his mouth strained open with the effort and his face glazing with sweat as he pulled and pulled—and he was seeing through the bright sunlight his car just beyond the gate, and realized he had been seeing it for several seconds before he understood that it was possible, that he had been seeing it with that special clarity of vision given by a peephole, a tiny tear-shaped opening between two warped boards.

And he understood that the Mexican had seen him this way. The Mexican had sat there in the dark at this table and had seen him, the Judge; had watched and waited, all the time looking out through the little hole, and seen the car arrive and the Judge get out of it, and watched it all in a flood of garlic-smelling sweat and terror while his heart leaped and raced all over the place inside his frozen, terrified fraud's pose of stillness.

"Your simple Mexican has a grace of bearing and manner that is hard to believe if you have not seen it. Or experienced it, perhaps, is a better way of putting it. Let me give you an example. I drive up to his house, you see, and of course he hears the car, but first I have to sit and wait. There is to be no rushing. Finally, I get out and walk to the gate, and sometimes I call out to him. Nothing happens. Some ethnic formality of time has to be satisfied first, some proper amount of respect allowed for. Then he

*emerges and comes forward to meet me at the gate. But
it is always just as I become restless and impatient, yet
more receptive, that he appears. He comes when I am
most alert, most open to meeting with him. He knows this
somehow. Then he comes forward, and every time it is
done with pride."*

"Damn him." The Judge slammed his palms down on
the table so hard his cheeks quivered with the blow.
"Damn him for a rotten fraud. Damn him." He leaned
forward over the table with his arms braced stiffly
straight on it. "Damn him to hell, I swear if I could I'd
kill him . . ."

He stared straight ahead at the empty air, and slowly
his body sagged down onto the thick black table. His
hands slid across the rough surface to the opposite side
so that he was half lying on it, almost embracing the
wood, with his heavy stomach pressed against the edge.

"I wonder when he started packing?" the Judge said.
"I wonder what he used to make the bundle—a second-
hand gunny sack and some old begged-for, handed-down
rotten piece of twine?"

The Judge's cheek rested flush against the table. Suddenly he stretched out his tongue and licked across a
section of the surface, violently hoping it was thick with
germs.

He raised his head, and drawn irresistibly, put his eye
to the peephole and looked out again through the bright
sunlight that was another dimension of his country, and
saw his new blue empty chrome-iced car winking and
flashing back at him.

"St. John of the Cross," the Judge said, "as we know
perfectly well from the writings of Alonso de la Madre
de Dios and the dissertation of the brilliant medievalist
Jean Baruzi, made a point of choosing for himself the
smallest, meanest, darkest cell in the monastery because
he knew that from there, when he looked through the
tiny window out over the fields of Spain, he would see
visions. Visions."

DANNY SANTIAGO

❁ ❁ ❁

*Danny Santiago's "The Somebody" first appeared in the
February 1970 issue of* Redbook. *When it was reprinted
in* The Best American Short Stories of 1971, *the biographical notes said: "Danny Santiago supplies no vital
statistics. He has said of himself, 'When it comes to biography, I am "muy burro" as we say in Spanish which
means worse than mulish.' 'The Somebody' is his only
published work, but several other stories of his have been
mimeographed and are currently floating around in East
Los Angeles." Then, Danny Santiago disappeared. The
young Chicano writer did not surface again until 1983
when Simon and Schuster published Danny Santiago's
first novel,* Famous All Over Town, *in which the final
chapter is a reworking of "The Somebody." The critics
praised* Famous All Over Town *as a classic novel of initia-
tion. One critic noted: "Danny Santiago has written a love
letter, in Chicano." The following year, the judges for the
Richard and Hinda Rosenthal Foundation Award given
by the American Academy and Institute of Arts and Letters agreed.* Famous All Over Town *was cited for having
added "luster to the enlarging literary genre of immigrant
experience, of social cultural and psychological
threshold. . . . The durable young narrator spins across a
multi-colored scene of crime, racial violence and extremes
of dislocation, seeking and perhaps finding his own space.
The exuberant mixes with the nerve-wracking; and throughout sly slippages of language enact a comedy on the theme
of communication." John Gregory Dunne later commented in the* New York Review of Books *that "Danny
Santiago did not show up at the ceremony to pick up the
$5,000 check that came with his Rosenthal Award. His
absence was in keeping with a long established pattern of*

reclusiveness. There is no photograph of Danny Santiago on the dust jacket of Famous All Over Town. *His agent and publisher have never laid eyes on him. Neither have they ever spoken to him on the telephone. Danny Santiago claims to have no telephone. His address is a post office box in Pacific Grove, California, a modest settlement on the Monterey penninsula. . . . Danny Santiago refuses to be interviewed and therefore did no publicity on behalf of* Famous All Over Town. *It is as if Danny Santiago did not exist, and in a sense he does not."* In his essay, entitled *"The Secret of Danny Santiago,"* Dunne takes off the mask of Santiago, the brash, young Chicano from East Los Angeles. Therein, he reveals, *"I have known the author of* Famous All Over Town *for the past eighteen years. . . . Danny Santiago, strickly speaking, is not his name. He is not a Chicano. Nor is he young. He is seventy-three years old. He is an Anglo. He is a graduate of Andover and Yale. He was the only member of the Yale class of 1933 to major in classical Greek. He is a prizewinning playwright. He is the co-author of the book of a hit musical comedy [*"Bloomer Girl"*] that played 654 performances on Broadway."*

The author's real name is Daniel James, which, of course, is *"Danny Santiago"* in Spanish. James had been a Hollywood screen writer. In the thirties he joined the Communist party, although he later resigned, in 1951 he was blacklisted by the House Committee on Un-American Affairs, meaning that he could no longer work at his trade. For years after that, he and his wife lived quietly in Mexican-American barrios in East Los Angeles where James got to know—inside and out—his Mexican-American neighbors. He became, in a sense, one of them. And he wrote of those barrio experiences in the stories which he published under his pseudonym.

Was using a pseudonym deceptive? Dunne asked Daniel James if he *"had considered the possibility of being accused of manufacturing a hoax. [James] shrugged and said the book itself was the only answer. If the book were good, it was good under whatever identity the author chose to use, the way the books of B. Traven were good. Nor would he consider that* Famous All

Over Town *was a tour de force. 'I spent thirty-five years working on this book,' [Daniel James] said, 'twenty years learning what it was all about, the last fifteen writing it. You don't spend thirty-five years on a tour de force.' "*

The Somebody

This is Chato talking, Chato de Shamrock, from the Eastside in old L.A., and I want you to know this is a big day in my life because today I quit school and went to work as a writer. I write on fences or buildings or anything that comes along. I write my name, not the one I got from my father. I want no part of him. I write Chato, which means Catface, because I have a flat nose like a cat. It's a Mexican word because that's what I am, a Mexican, and I'm not ashamed of it. I like that language, too, man. It's way better than English to say what you feel. But German is the best. It's got a real rugged sound, and I'm going to learn to talk it someday.

After Chato I write "de Shamrock." That's the street where I live, and it's the name of the gang I belong to, but the others are all gone now. Their families had to move away, except Gorilla is in jail and Blackie joined the navy because he liked swimming. But I still have our old arsenal. It's buried under the chickens, and I dig it up when I get bored. There's tire irons and chains and pick handles with spikes and two zip guns we made and they shoot real bullets but not very straight. In the good old days nobody cared to tangle with us. But now I'm the only one left.

Well, today started off like any other day. The toilet roars like a hot rod taking off. My father coughs and spits about nineteen times and hollers it's six-thirty. So I holler back I'm quitting shcool. Things hit me like that—sudden.

"Don't you want to be a lawyer no more," he says in Spanish, "and defend the Mexican people?"

My father thinks he is very funny, and next time I make any plans, he's sure not going to hear about it.

"Don't you want to be a doctor," he says, "and cut off my leg for nothing someday?"

"Due beast ine dumb cop," I tell him in German, but not very loud.

"How will you support me," he says, "when I retire? Or will you marry a rich old woman that owns a pool hall?"

"I'm checking out of this dump! You'll never see me again!"

I hollered in at him, but already he was in the kitchen making a big noise in his coffee. I could be dead and he wouldn't take me serious. So I laid there and waited for him to go off to work. When I woke up again, it was way past eleven. I can sleep forever these days. So I got out of bed and put on clean jeans and my windbreaker and combed myself very neat because already I had a feeling this was going to be a big day for me.

I had to wait for breakfast because the baby was sick and throwing up milk on everything. There is always a baby vomiting in my house. When they're born, everybody comes over and says: *"Qué* cute!" but nobody passes any comments on the dirty way babies act or the dirty way they were made either. Sometimes my mother asks me to hold one for her but it always cries, maybe because I squeeze it a little hard when nobody's looking.

When my mother finally served me, I had to hold my breath, she smelled so bad of babies. I don't care to look at her anymore. Her legs got those dark-blue rivers running all over them. I kept waiting for her to bawl me out about school, but I guess she forgot, or something. So I cut out.

Every time I go out my front door I have to cry for what they've done to old Shamrock Street. It used to be so fine, with solid homes on both sides. Maybe they needed a little paint here and there but they were cozy. Then the S.P. railroad bought up all the land except my father's place because he was stubborn. They came in with their wrecking bars and their bulldozers. You could hear those houses scream when they ripped them down. So now Shamrock Street is just front walks that lead to a hole in the ground, and piles of busted cement. And

Pelón's house and Blackie's are just stacks of old boards waiting to get hauled away. I hope that never happens to your street, man.

My first stop was the front gate and there was that sign again, the big S wrapped around a cross like a snake with rays coming out, which is the mark of the Sierra Street gang, as everybody knows. I rubbed it off, but tonight they'll put it back again. In the old days they wouldn't dare to come on our street, but without your gang you're nobody. And one of these fine days they're going to catch up with me in person and that will be the end of Chato de Shamrock.

So I cruised on down to Main Street like a ghost in a graveyard. Just to prove I'm alive, I wrote my name on the fence at the corner. A lot of names you see in public places are written very sloppy. Not me. I take my time. Like my fifth-grade teacher used to say, if other people are going to see your work, you owe it to yourself to do it right. Mrs. Cully was her name and she was real nice, for an Anglo. My other teachers were all cops but Mrs. Cully drove me home one time when some guys were after me. I think she wanted to adopt me but she never said anything about it. I owe a lot to that lady, and especially my writing. You should see it, man—it's real smooth and mellow, and curvy like a blond in a bikini. Everybody says so. Except one time they had me in Juvenile by mistake and some doctor looked at it. He said it proved I had something wrong with me, some long word. That doctor was crazy, because I made him show me his writing and it was real ugly like a barb-wire fence with little chickens stuck on the points. You couldn't even read it.

Anyway, I signed myself very clean and neat on that corner. And then I thought, Why not look for a job someplace? But I was more in the mood to write my name, so I went into the dime store and helped myself to two boxes of crayons and some chalk and cruised on down Main, writing all the way. I wondered should I write more than my name. Should I write, "Chato is a fine guy," or, "Chato, is wanted by the police"? Things like that. News. But I decided against it. Better to keep them guessing. Then I crossed over to Forney Playground. It used to be our territory, but now the Sierra have taken over there like everyplace else. Just to show them, I wrote on the tennis court and the swimming pool and the gym. I left a fine little trail of Chato de Shamrock in eight colors. Some places I used chalk, which works better on brick or plaster. But crayons are the thing for cement or anything smooth, like in the girls' rest room. On that wall I also drew a little picture the girls would be interested in and put down a phone number beside it. I bet a lot of them are going to call that number, but it isn't mine because we don't have a phone in the first place, and in the second place I'm probably never going home again.

I'm telling you, I was pretty famous at the Forney by the time I cut out, and from there I continued my travels till something hit me. You know how you put your name on something and that proves it belongs to you? Things like school books or gym shoes? So I thought, How about that, now? And I put my name on the Triple A Market and on Morrie's Liquor Store and on the Zócalo, which is a beer joint. And then I cruised on up Broadway, getting rich. I took over a barber shop and a furniture store and the Plymouth agency. And the firehouse for laughs, and the phone company so I could call all my girl friends and keep my dimes. And then there I was at Webster and Garcia's Funeral Home with the big white columns. At first I thought that might be bad luck, but then I said, Oh, well, we all got to die sometime. So I signed myself, and now I can eat good and live in style and have a big time all my life, and then kiss you all good-bye and give myself the best damn funeral in L.A. for free.

And speaking of funerals, along came the Sierra right then, eight or ten of them down the street with that stupid walk which is their trademark. I ducked into the garage and hid behind the hearse. Not that I'm a coward. Getting stomped doesn't bother me, or even shot. What I hate is those blades, man. They're like a piece of ice cutting into your belly. But the Sierra didn't see me and went on by. I couldn't hear what they were saying but I knew they had me on their mind. So I cut on over to the Boys' Club, where they don't let anybody get you, no matter who you are. To pass the time I shot some baskets and played a little pool and watched the television, but the story was boring, so it came to me, Why not write my name on the screen? Which I did with a squeaky pen. Those cowboys sure looked fine with Chato de Shamrock written all over them. Everybody got a kick out of it. But of course up comes Mr. Calderon and makes me wipe it off. They're always spying on you up there. And he takes me into his office and closes the door.

"Well," he says, "and how is the last of the dinosaurs?"

Meaning that the Shamrocks are as dead as giant lizards.

Then he goes into that voice with the church music in it and I look out of the window.

"I know it's hard to lose your gang, Chato," he says, "but this is your chance to make new friends and straighten yourself out. Why don't you start coming to Boys' Club more?"

"It's boring here," I tell him.

"What about school?"

"I can't go," I said. "They'll get me."

"The Sierra's forgotten you're alive," he tells me.

"Then how come they put their mark on my house every night?"

"Do they?"

He stares at me very hard. I hate those eyes of his. He thinks he knows everything. And what is he? Just a Mexican like everybody else.

"Maybe you put that mark there yourself," he says. "To make yourself big. Just like you wrote on the television."

"That was my name! I like to write my name!"

"So do dogs," he says. "On every lamppost they come to."

"You're a dog yourself," I told him, but I don't think he heard me. He just went on talking. Brother, how they love to talk up there! But I didn't bother to listen, and when he ran out of gas I left. From now on I'm scratching that Boys' Club off my list.

Out on the street it was getting dark, but I could still

follow my trail back toward Broadway. It felt good seeing Chato written everyplace, but at the Zócalo I stopped dead. Around my name there was a big red heart done in lipstick with some initials I didn't recognize. To tell the truth, I didn't know how to feel. In one way I was mad that anyone would fool with my name, especially if it was some guy doing it for laughs. But what guy carries lipstick? And if it was a girl, that could be kind of interesting.

A girl is what it turned out to be. I caught up with her at the telephone company. There she is, standing in the shadows, drawing her heart around my name. And she has a very pretty shape on her, too. I sneak up behind her very quiet, thinking all kinds of crazy things and my blood shooting around so fast it shakes me all over. And then she turns around and it's only Crusader Rabbit. That's what we called her from the television show they had then, on account of her teeth in front.

When she sees me, she takes off down the alley, but in twenty feet I catch her. I grab for the lipstick, but she whips it behind her. I reach around and try to pull her fingers open, but her hand is sweaty and so is mine. And there we are, stuck together all the way down. I can feel everything she's got and her breath is on my cheek. She twists up against me, kind of giggling. To tell the truth, I don't like to wrestle with girls. They don't fight fair. And then we lost balance and fell against some garbage cans, so I woke up. After that I got the lipstick away from her very easy.

"What right you got to my name?" I tell her. "I never gave you permission."

"You sign yourself real fine," she says.

I knew that already.

"Let's go writing together," she says.

"The Sierra's after me."

"I don't care," she says. "Come on, Chato—you and me can have a lot of fun."

She came up close and giggled that way. She put her hand on my hand that had the lipstick in it. And you know what? I'm ashamed to say I almost told her yes. It would be a change to go writing with a girl. We could talk there in the dark. We could decide on the best places. And her handwriting wasn't too bad either. But

then I remembered I had my reputation to think of.
Somebody would be sure to see us, and they'd be laughing at me all over the Eastside. So I pulled my hand
away and told her off.

"Run along, Crusader," I told her. "I don't want no
partners, and especially not you."

"Who are you calling Crusader?" she screamed. "You
ugly, squash-nose punk."

She called me everything. And spit at my face but
missed. I didn't argue. I just cut out. And when I got to
the first sewer I threw away her lipstick. Then I drifted
over to the banks at Broadway and Bailey, which is a
good spot for writing because a lot of people pass by
there.

Well, I hate to brag, but that was the best work I've
ever done in all my life. Under the street lamp my name
shone like solid gold. I stood to one side and checked
the people as they walked past and inspected it. With
some you can't tell just how they feel, but with others it
rings out like a cash register. There was one man. He
got out of his Cadillac to buy a paper and when he saw
my name he smiled. He was the age to be my father. I
bet he'd give me a job if I asked him. I bet he'd take
me to his home and to his office in the morning. Pretty
soon I'd be sitting at my own desk and signing my name
on letters and checks and things. But I would never buy
a Cadillac, man. They burn too much gas.

Later a girl came by. She was around eighteen, I think,
with green eyes. Her face was so pretty I didn't dare to
look at her shape. Do you want me to go crazy? That
girl stopped and really studied my name like she fell in
love with it. She wanted to know me, I could tell. She
wanted to take my hand and we'd go off together just
holding hands and nothing dirty. We'd go to Beverly
Hills and nobody would look at us the wrong way. I
almost said "Hi" to that girl, and, "How do you like my
writing?" But not quite.

So here I am, standing on this corner with my chalk
all gone and only one crayon left and it's ugly brown.
My fingers are too cold besides. But I don't care because
I just had a vision, man. Did they ever turn on the lights
for you so you could see the whole world and everything

in it? That's how it came to me right now. I don't need to be a movie star or boxing champ to make my name in the world. All I need is plenty of chalk and crayons. And that's easy. L.A. is a big city, man, but give me a couple of months and I'll be famous all over town. Of course they'll try to stop me—the Sierra, the police and everybody. But I'll be like a ghost, man. I'll be real mysterious, and all they'll know is just my name, signed like I always sign it, CHATO DE SHAMROCK with rays shooting out like from the Holy Cross.

FRANCISCO JIMÉNEZ

❦ ❦ ❦

Francisco Jiménez was born in 1943 in the village of San Pedro Tlaquepaque in the state of Jalicso, Mexico. At the age of three, he moved with his parents to Santa Maria, California, to begin their lives as migrant workers. At the age of six, Jiménez joined his parents, brothers, and sisters following the seasonal migrant circuit, picking strawberries during the summer in Santa Maria, grapes in the early autumn around Fresco, and cotton in Corcoran during the winter until they all returned home to Santa Maria in time to harvest carrots and lettuce. The long hours of work in the fields and the constant movement from town to town as well as his inability to speak English took their toll on the child: He failed the first grade. Although the authorities declared him mentally retarded, he persevered and quickly mastered his second language only to suffer another devastating setback. When he was in junior high school, he was removed from the classroom by an immigration officer—Jiménez, after all, was an illegal alien—and deported to Mexico. Determined, he returned and became an American citizen. His excellent academic performance in high school gained the attention of a high school counselor. Through his efforts, Jiménez earned three scholarships which sent him to the University of Santa Clara. With the assistance of several fellowships and awards, Jiménez earned his MA and PhD in Spanish and Latin American Literature and went on to become a distinguished scholar and teacher, the author of several textbooks, co-founder and editor of Bilinqual Review, and advisor to Bilinqual Press. "The Circuit" is an "autobiographical story based on my childhood experiences. The action takes place during a time when my family and I were migrant workers. 'Roberto' is the name of my older brother; 'Panchito' is my nickname. The idea for the story

222

*originated many years ago when I was studying English in
Junior High School in Santa Maria. Miss Bell, my English
teacher, encouraged me to write about my personal experiences. Although English was difficult for me, I liked writing and forced myself to write about what I knew most
intimately, what I knew best. And that was the life of the
migrant worker. Miss Bell's positive attitude stimulated me
to continue writing even after I finished junior high."* Perhaps, Jiménez will one day continue.

The Circuit

It was that time of year again. Ito, the strawberry share-
cropper, did not smile. It was natural. The peak of the
strawberry season was over and the last few days the
workers, most of them *braceros,* were not picking as
many boxes as they had during the months of June and
July.

As the last days of August disappeared, so did the
number of *braceros.* Sunday, only one—the best picker—
came to work. I liked him. Sometimes we talked during
our half-hour lunch break. That is how I found out he
was from Jalisco, the same state in Mexico my family
was from. That Sunday was the last time I saw him.

When the sun had tired and sunk behind the mountains, Ito signaled us that it was time to go home. "*Ya
esora,*" he yelled in his broken Spanish. Those were the
words I waited for twelve hours a day, every day, seven
days a week, week after week. And the thought of not
hearing them again saddened me.

As we drove home Papá did not say a word. With both
hands on the wheel, he stared at the dirt road. My older
brother, Roberto, was also silent. He leaned his head
back and closed his eyes. Once in a while he cleared
from his throat the dust that blew in from outside.

Yes, it was that time of year. When I opened the front
door to the shack, I stopped. Everything we owned was
neatly packed in cardboard boxes. Suddenly I felt even
more the weight of hours, days, weeks, and months of

work. I sat down on a box. The thought of having to move to Fresno and knowing what was in store for me there brought tears to my eyes.

That night I could not sleep. I lay in bed thinking about how much I hated this move.

A little before five o'clock in the morning, Papá woke everyone up. A few minutes later, the yelling and screaming of my little brothers and sisters, for whom the move was a great adventure, broke the silence of dawn. Shortly, the barking of the dogs accompanied them.

While we packed the breakfast dishes, Papá went outside to start the "Carcanchita." That was the name Papá gave his old '38 black Plymouth. He bought it in a used-car lot in Santa Rosa in the winter of 1949. Papá was very proud of his little jalopy. He had a right to be proud of it. He spent a lot of time looking at other cars before buying this one. When he finally chose the "Carcanchita," he checked it thoroughly before driving it out of the car lot. He examined every inch of the car. He listened to the motor, tilting his head from side to side like a parrot, trying to detect any noises that spelled car trouble. After being satisfied with the looks and sounds of the car, Papá then insisted on knowing who the original owner was. He never did find out from the car salesman, but he bought the car anyway. Papá figured the original owner must have been an important man because behind the rear seat of the car he found a blue necktie.

Papá parked the car out in front and left the motor running. *"Listo,"* he yelled. Without saying a word, Roberto and I began to carry the boxes out to the car. Roberto carried the two big boxes and I carried the two smaller ones. Papá then threw the mattress on top of the car roof and tied it with ropes to the front and rear bumpers.

Everything was packed except Mamá's pot. It was an old large galvanized pot she had picked up at an army surplus store in Santa María the year I was born. The pot had many dents and nicks, and the more dents and nicks it acquired the more Mamá liked it. *"Mi olla,"* she used to say proudly.

I held the front door open as Mamá carefully carried out her pot by both handles, making sure not to spill the cooked beans. When she got to the car, Papá reached out to help her with it. Roberto opened the rear car door and Papá gently placed it on the floor behind the front seat. All of us then climbed in. Papá sighed, wiped the sweat off his forehead with his sleeve, and said wearily: *"Es todo."*

As we drove away, I felt a lump in my throat. I turned around and looked at our little shack for the last time.

At sunset we drove into a labor camp near Fresno. Since Papá did not speak English, Mamá asked the camp foreman if he needed any more workers. "We don't need no more," said the foreman, scratching his head. "Check with Sullivan down the road. Can't miss him. He lives in a big white house with a fence around it."

When we got there, Mamá walked up to the house. She went through a white gate, past a row of rose bushes, up the stairs to the front door. She rang the doorbell. The porch light went on and a tall husky man came out. They exchanged a few words. After the man went in, Mamá clasped her hands and hurried back to the car. "We have work! Mr. Sullivan said we can stay there the whole season," she said, gasping and pointing to an old garage near the stables.

The garage was worn out by the years. It had no windows. The walls, eaten by termites, strained to support the roof full of holes. The dirt floor, populated by earth worms, looked like a gray road map.

That night, by the light of a kerosene lamp, we unpacked and cleaned our new home. Roberto swept away the loose dirt, leaving the hard ground. Papá plugged the holes in the walls with old newspapers and tin can tops. Mamá fed my little brothers and sisters. Papá and Roberto then brought in the mattress and placed it on the far corner of the garage. "Mamá, you and the little ones sleep on the mattress. Roberto, Panchito, and I will sleep outside under the trees," Papá said.

Early next morning Mr. Sullivan showed us where his crop was, and after breakfast, Papá, Roberto, and I headed for the vineyard to pick.

Around nine o'clock the temperature had risen to almost one hundred degrees. I was completely soaked in sweat and my mouth felt as if I had been chewing on a handkerchief. I walked over to the end of the row, picked up the jug of water we had brought, and began drinking. "Don't drink too much; you'll get sick," Roberto shouted. No sooner had he said that than I felt sick to my stomach. I dropped to my knees and let the jug roll off my hands. I remained motionless with my eyes glued on the hot sandy ground. All I could hear was the drone of insects. Slowly I began to recover. I poured water over my face and neck and watched the dirty water run down my arms to the ground.

I still felt a little dizzy when we took a break to eat lunch. It was past two o'clock and we sat underneath a large walnut tree that was on the side of the road. While we ate, Papá jotted down the number of boxes we had picked. Roberto drew designs on the ground with a stick. Suddenly I noticed Papá's face turn pale as he looked down the road. "Here comes the school bus," he whispered loudly in alarm. Instinctively, Roberto and I ran and hid in the vineyards. We did not want to get in trouble for not going to school. The neatly dressed boys about my age got off. They carried books under their arms. After they crossed the street, the bus drove away. Roberto and I came out from hiding and joined Papá. *"Tienen que tener cuidado,"* he warned us.

After lunch we went back to work. The sun kept beating down. The buzzing insects, the wet sweat, and the hot dry dust made the afternoon seem to last forever. Finally the mountains around the valley reached out and swallowed the sun. Within an hour it was too dark to continue picking. The vines blanketed the grapes, making it difficult to see the bunches. *"Vámonos,"* said Papá, signaling to us that it was time to quit work. Papá then took out a pencil and began to figure out how much we had earned our first day. He wrote down numbers, crossed some out, wrote down some more. *"Quince,"* he murmured.

When we arrived home, we took a cold shower underneath a waterhose. We then sat down to eat dinner around some wooden crates that served as a table. Mamá had cooked a special meal for us. We had rice and tortillas with *"carne con chile,"* my favorite dish.

The next morning I could hardly move. My body ached all over. I felt little control over my arms and legs. This feeling went on every morning for days until my muscles finally got used to the work.

It was Monday, the first week of November. The grape season was over and I could now go to school. I woke up early that morning and lay in bed, looking at the stars and savoring the thought of not going to work and of starting sixth grade for the first time that year. Since I could not sleep, I decided to get up and join Papá and Roberto at breakfast. I sat at the table across from Roberto, but I kept my head down. I did not want to look up and face him. I knew he was sad. He was not going to school today. He was not going tomorrow, or next week, or next month. He would not go until the cotton season was over, and that was sometime in February. I rubbed my hands together and watched the dry, acid stained skin fall to the floor in little rolls.

When Papá and Roberto left for work, I felt relief. I walked to the top of a small grade next to the shack and watched the "Carcanchita" disappear in the distance in a cloud of dust.

Two hours later, around eight o'clock, I stood by the side of the road waiting for school bus number twenty. When it arrived I climbed in. Everyone was busy either talking or yelling. I sat in an empty seat in the back.

When the bus stopped in front of the school, I felt very nervous. I looked out the bus window and saw boys and girls carrying books under their arms. I put my hands in my pant pockets and walked to the principal's office. When I entered I heard a woman's voice say: "May I help you?" I was startled. I had not heard English for months. For a few seconds I remained speechless. I looked at the lady who waited for an answer. My first instinct was to answer her in Spanish, but I held back. Finally, after struggling for English words, I managed to tell her that I wanted to enroll in the sixth grade. After answering many questions, I was led to the classroom.

Mr. Lema, the sixth grade teacher, greeted me and assigned me a desk. He then introduced me to the class. I was so nervous and scared at that moment when everyone's eyes were on me that I wished I were with Papá and Roberto picking cotton. After taking roll, Mr. Lema gave the class the assignment for the first hour. "The first thing we have to do this morning is finish reading the story we began yesterday," he said enthusiastically. He walked up to me, handed me an English book, and asked me to read. "We are on page 125," he said politely. When I heard this, I felt my blood rush to my head; I felt dizzy. "Would you like to read?" he asked hesitantly. I opened the book to page 125. My mouth was dry. My eyes began to water. I could not begin. "You can read later," Mr. Lema said understandingly.

For the rest of the reading period I kept getting angrier and angrier with myself. I should have read, I thought to myself.

During recess I went into the restroom and opened my English book to page 125. I began to read in a low voice, pretending I was in class. There were many words I did not know. I closed the book and headed back to the classroom.

Mr. Lema was sitting at his desk correcting papers. When I entered he looked up at me and smiled. I felt better. I walked up to him and asked if he could help me with the new words. "Gladly," he said.

The rest of the month I spent my lunch hours working on English with Mr. Lema, my best friend at school.

One Friday during lunch hour Mr. Lema asked me to take a walk with him to the music room. "Do you like music?" he asked me as we entered the building.

"Yes, I like *corridos*," I answered. He then picked up a trumpet, blew on it and handed it to me. The sound gave me goose bumps. I knew that sound. I had heard it in many corridos. "How would you like to learn how to play it?" he asked. He must have read my face because before I could answer, he added: "I'll teach you how to play it during our lunch hours."

That day I could hardly wait to get home to tell Papá and Mamá the great news. As I got off the bus, my little brothers and sisters ran up to meet me. They were yelling and screaming. I thought they were happy to see me, but when I opened the door to our shack, I saw that everything we owned was neatly packed in cardboard boxes.

ROLANDO HINOJOSA-SMITH

❦ ❦ ❦

Rolando Hinojosa-Smith is considered by many to be the dean of Mexican-American literature. No other American of Mexican descent has written and published so diversely or extensively, or received such critical attention, recognition, and awards, not only in the United States but in Europe and throughout Latin America as well. Born in Mercedes, on the border between Texas and Mexico, in 1929, Hinojosa is the son of Manuel Guzman Hinojosa, a Mexican-American, and Carrie Effie Smith, an Anglo. He grew up in a totally bilingual, bicultural atmosphere and had a distinguished academic career, earning his PhD in Spanish from the University of Illinois. Hinojosa-Smith has taught and held administrative positions at a number of universities, including Trinity in San Antonio, Texas A and I in Kingsville, and the University of Minnesota. He has been at the University of Texas at Austin since 1981, where he currently serves as the Director of the Texas Center for Writers and is the Ellen Clayton Garwood Professor of Creative Writing. Estampas del Valle y otras obras: Sketches of the Valley and Other Works, *his first novel, won the 1973 Quinto Sol Prize for Best Novel.* Klail City y sus alrededores, *published first in Havana, won the Casa de las Americas award for Best Novel in 1976, and in 1982,* Mi querido Rafa *won prize for the Best Writing in the Humanities awarded annually by the Southwest Latin American Studies Conference. In 1983, he was elected to membership in the Texas Institute of Letters. His latest novel,* Becky and Her Friends, *was published in July 1990.*

In the Pit with Bruno Cano

"What do you mean, you won't bury him?"

"You heard me."

"Sure, we heard you, but you have to bury him. There's nothing else you can do."

"Let him figure it out. I'm not burying him. Have someone else do it . . . You, for example. The Church will not bury him."

"The Church or you, don Pedro?"

"Me, the Church; it's all the same."

"It's not the same thing at all. It's you, isn't it?"

"Yes, it's me; but don't come around here telling me that I'm not right. To think that he cursed my mother to my face."

"Yeah, don Pedro, but if anyone can forgive, it should be you. The priest."

"Yes, sure. The priest. But I'm also a man."

"And who doubts that? C'mon, bury him and we can have a drink."

"I don't know."

"C'mon. Cheer up, don Pedro. You and don Bruno were good friends. Besides, the whole mess happened because he was drunk."

"I don't know."

"What can it cost you? Here, Lisandro and I'll take you to the cemetery, okay? How about it? Say yes, don Pedro."

"Look, don Pedro, we won't even bring him to church. From Salinas' place, we'll take him straight to the cemetery and there you can bury him for us with your prayers and all."

"Now, you're sure you won't bring him to church?"

"Promise."

"Word of honor."

"Okay, take him from Salinas' and I'll go to the cemetery within a quarter of an hour. Have you seen Jehú? I'll need him for the responses."

"He should be around here somewhere throwing rocks

at birds or running an errand. Let him be, don Pedro. I'll do it."

"Remember now, not a word. Within a quarter of an hour and into the ground . . . That's really something, swearing at a fully vested priest of our Holy Mother Church."

"Much obliged, don Pedro. Don't worry about a thing and thanks, okay?"

The two returned downtown without saying a word to each other or to anyone who greeted them. They arrived at Germán Salinas' tavern and announced: "It's done. There'll be a funeral. Call the Vegas'; have them bring their biggest hearse. Step on it, spread the word to everyone."

Don Bruno Cano, a native of Cerralvo, Nuevo León and neighbor of Flora, Texas, whose marital status was that of a widower and who was without progeny or heirs, died, according to the doctor, of a heart attack. Of an infarct that rendered him as lifeless as a puppet. Those who really knew him would say that he died from envy and from going around making fun of people.

The night that Cano died, he and another friend, Melitón Burnias, had agreed to dig up a small lot that belonged to doña Panchita Zuárez, bone setter, midwife on the side, and a talented mender of slightly used but still serviceable girls. Aunt Panchita, according to the people from Flora, had a treasure hidden in her patio. This "swag," the name given to treasures around Flora, was hidden since the time of Escandón, according to some; since the time the General Santa Ana, according to others; and according to still others, more recently, since the time of the Revolution . . . a treasure that was hidden by some anxious merchants recently emigrated, etc. It seems that Bruno Cano and Burnias, between drinks, decided to dig up the land, as had so many others, in search of the aforementioned treasure. Melitón Burnias swore that he knew some infallible chants for those endeavors.

It's difficult to imagine two more disparate men: Cano was fat, pink, a certified miser, a merchant and the owner of the slaughterhouse, "The Golden Ship"; in short, one of the first self-made men in town. Burnias was altogether different; he was somewhat deaf, skinny, very short, of unknown occupation and more wizened than goat turds in August. He was also poor and unlucky. When Tila, his eldest girl, took off with Práxedis Cervera, Cervera returned with Tila and together they kicked Burnias out into the street. The man, they say, shrugged his shoulders, went out and slept in the watermelon patch. That same night, of course, there was a hailstorm, Melitón Burnias, nonetheless, was not greedy and it must have been for that reason that Bruno Cano selected him as his partner in the search for the swag.

They were both drinking at Salinas' when they suddenly realized how late it was. When the cuckoo clock struck eleven, the two went to get their picks, shovels and other tools needed to dig up doña Panchita's land.

It was around three o'clock and Bruno Cano was down in the pit shoveling the dirt out. Deaf Burnias was up above, spreading it as best he could, when Bruno heard a *thunk*. He dug further and again, *thunk*, then another and still another.

"Melitón! Melitón, did you hear that? I think we're gettin' close."

"Did I hear anything? Did I hear what?"

"I said we're gettin' close."

"Okay, what should I chant?"

"What?"

"What do I chant?"

"What do you mean, what do I chant?"

"You heard something pant?"

"Pant, you say?"

"What panted? Omigod!"

Saying this, Burnias fled, abandoning his shovel and his companion. He began to shout, convinced perhaps that a ghost was panting down his neck. He ran through patios taking fences with him, slipping in puddles, bounding across alleys, waking up dogs and leaping like a pregnant rabbit until he got to the watermelon patch where he began to pray loudly.

Meanwhile, Bruno Cano was standing there with his mouth hanging open. (What panted?) (A ghost?) As soon as caught his breath, he began to shout and cry, "Get me out! Get me out of here! Help! Goddammit, get me out!"

While this was going on (it was almost five o'clock in

the morning), don Pedro Zamudio, the parish priest of
Flora, was crossing doña Panchita's lot on his way to the
church when he heard Bruno's cries. Picking up his cassock so it wouldn't get in his way, he went over to the
hole and asked the person in the pit:

"What's going on? What are you doing there?"

"Is that you, don Pedro; It's me, Cano. Get me out."

"Well what are you doing in this neighborhood?"

"Help me out first, then I'll tell you."

"Did you hurt yourself when you fell in?"

"I didn't fall in . . . help me."

"All right, son, but then how did you get down there?
Are you sure you're not injured?"

"As sure as I can be, father, get me outta this son of
a . . . excuse me."

"What were you going to say, my son?"

"Nothin', father, nothin'. Now, get me out."

"I don't think I can do it by myself; you're kind of
fat."

"Me, fat? Your mother's the fat one!"

"My whaaaaaat?"

"Get me out, goddammit! C'mon."

"Let's see your mother get you out!"

"You shithead, go fuck your own mother!"

Don Pedro made the sign of the cross, knelt down
close to the hole and began to recite ". . . take this sinner
into your heart . . ." when Bruno Cano cursed his
mother again. So clearly was the curse uttered that even
the birds stopped warbling. Don Pedro, in turn, took out
his rosary and began reciting the Creed. At this Cano
got beet-red and burst out with another thunderous "go
fuck your mother" as round and resonant as the first.
He was about to let loose with another when don Pedro
arose extending his arms in the form of a cross while
reciting "take this sinner into your heart." At that point
Bruno Cano stopped talking and all that could be heard
were deep gasps like bellows whooshing. Don Pedro
ended the prayer, leaned over the hole and said: "Don't
you see? Prayer brings peace. It's almost daybreak. In a
little while they'll come for you."

Bruno did not pay any attention to him. He did not
even hear him. Bruno Cano had kicked the bucket
between one of the mysteries of the rosary and one of

his curses, surrendering his soul to God, the Devil or his
mother; whoever wanted him.

As might have been supposed, no less than thirty people had witnessed the scene. They had remained at a
respectable distance while the one prayed and the other
cursed.

But, nevertheless, they buried him and in hallowed
ground at that. Much to don Pedro's dismay, the funeral
was well attended. The affair lasted almost seven hours.
There were twelve orators and four choruses all decked
in white (one of boys and one of girls, another comprised
of the Ladies of the Perpetual Candle and the fourth
made up of members of the Sacred Heart of Jesus). The
Vegas' brought Bruno's body in their purple hearse
fringed with a grey curtain. Besides don Pedro, twelve
of us altarboys went, each dressed in a starched black
and white chasuble. Everyone from the other towns in
the Valley soon realized that something was going on in
Flora and they came in droves—hitchhiking, by truck,
and by bicycle. Some people from Klail even rented a
Greyhound that was already filled with people from
Bascom.

Three vendors appeared and began selling sno-cones
to combat the sun which was so hot that it melted the
tarred streets. Estimating conservatively, the crowd was
at least four thousand strong. Some, to be sure, didn't
know whom they were burying; the rest didn't even know
Cano; the fact of the matter is that people like a little
excitement and they don't waste any opportunity to get
out of the house.

Don Pedro couldn't put up with all this and so recited
at least 300 Our Fathers in between his Hail Marys and
Glorias. When he began to cry (whether from anger,
hysteria or hunger, God only knows) the people, taking
pity, prayed for him. The orators repeated their eulogies
several times and each of the sno-cone vendors had to
buy three more hundred pound blocks of ice in order to
have enough for everyone. Sometimes they wouldn't
even add syrup. The people would eat the ice just the
same, with or without the syrup. For their part, the
choruses soon exhausted their repertories; and, so as not
to waste the opportunity, they sang the *Tantum Ergo*
which did not fit the occasion and the even less fitting,

"Come, Good Shepherd, Celestial Redeemer," heard only on Easter. Finally, the choruses joined forces and then they sounded much better.

In spite of the intense heat, the dust, the shoving and the milling crowd, things went rather smoothly: a fight here and there, of course, but without knives. The most serious problem was people falling: there were at least 34 who fainted. It was, all in all, a decent burial.

The only one that did not attend was Melitón Burnias. As he often said later, "I had other things to do that day."

Hardly anyone paid him any attention.

RON ARIAS

❦ ❦ ❦

Ron Arias was born on November 30, 1941, in Los Angeles, California, but his roots are planted on the border between Mexico and the United States. His father was from Ciudad Juárez, across the Rio Grande from El Paso, where his mother was born. His step-father was from Nogales, on the border between Arizona and the Mexican state of Sonora. As a young child, he lived with his grandmother in El Paso, where he spoke Spanish almost exclusively. Of that period of his life he has noted, "I was even put with the 'Mexican only' first grade class at Ascarate grammar school and later when I returned to L.A., I remember getting off the train at Union Station and not being able to speak English." However, once back with his family in California, everything changed. At home, the Arias family spoke English because "everyone from my parents' generation on spoke primarily English. Those early years living in Texas in a predominately Mexican-American culture provided Arias with a firm foundation even though his life after that was a rather restless one, as his step-father was a career soldier and the family moved from post to post, all over the United States and in Europe. Arias earned a BA in Spanish from the University of California at Berkeley and an MA in journalism from UCLA. However, as he has said, "My true education—at least as a writer is concerned—took place in travel, work, and in all kinds of books I picked up here and there." He began his writing career as a journalist writing for high school and university newspapers. Later, he worked as a reporter on newspapers in Los Angeles, Buenos Aires, and Caracas as well as for the Associated Press. Those experiences as well as his undergraduate studies in Spanish and Hispanic literature led him to the works of contemporary writers like Arreola, Borges, Cor-

tazar, Fuentes, Rulfo, and García Márquez, whose works—Garcia Márquez's One Hundred Years of Solitude *and Rulfo's short stories—have been, he readily admits, a tremendous influence on his own fiction. "The Wetback" is an excellent example. In 1971, it was awarded first prize in the First Chicano Literary Contest sponsored by the Spanish and Portuguese Department at University of California at Irvine. Later, it was included as a chapter in his distinguished novel* The Road Tamazunchale, *published in 1975 and nominated for the National Book Award.*

Many critics feel that The Road to Tamazunchale *is the outstanding novel written by a Mexican-American. In assessing Arias's work, Cordelia Candelaria has noted that Arias "is concerned with chronicling the urban Chicano experience in all its bittersweet contradictions, and his major themes are the struggle between imagination and rationalism and the transcendent possibilities of ethnic pluralism. His themes reveal Arias to be a well-read student of both Anglo and Latino histories and mythologies of the Americans. His fusion of North and South American identities has produced a remarkable* mestizaje *(a term for the admixture of Spanish and Indian blood once used pejoratively) that philosopher José Vasconcelos has recognized as the dynamic synthesis of racial, historical and cultural products of the hemisphere's indigenous (Indian) and immigrant (European and African) roots."*

The Wetback

That afternoon Mrs. Rentería's neighbor's grandchildren discovered David in the dry riverbed. The young man was absolutely dead, the children could see that. For a long time they had watched him from behind the clump of cat-'o-nine-tails. His body lay so still even a mouse, picking into one dead nostril, suspected nothing. The girl approached first, leaving behind her two brothers. David's brow was smooth; his gray-blue eyes were half closed; his hair was uncombed and mixed with sand;

his dark skin glistened, clean and wet; and the rest of him, torn shirt and patched trousers, was also wet.

"He drowned," the girl said.

The boys ran over for their first good look at a dead man. David was more or less what they expected, except for the gold tooth in front and a mole beneath one sideburn. His name wasn't David yet; that would come later when the others found out. David was the name of a boy who drowned years ago when Cuca predicted it wouldn't rain and it did and the river overflowed, taking little David to the bottom or to the sea, no one knew, because all they found was a washtub he used as a boat.

"How could he drown?" one of the boys asked. "There's no water."

"He did," the girl said. "Look at him."

"I'm telling," the other boy said, backing away.

The boys ran across the dry sand pebbles, up the concrete bank and disappeared behind the levee. Before the crowd of neighbors arrived, the girl wiped the dead face with her skirt hem, straightened his clothes as best she could and tried to remove the sand in his hair. She raised David's head, made a claw with her free hand and raked over the black hair. His skull was smooth on top, with a few bumps above the nape. Finally she made a part on the right side, then lay his head on her lap.

Tiburcio and the boys were the first to reach her, followed by the fishman Smaldino and the other men. Most of the women waited on the levee until Tiburcio signaled it was okay, the man was dead. Carmela helped Mrs. Rentería first, since it was her neighbor's grandchildren who had discovered David, then she gave a hand to the other older women. Mrs. Rentería, who appeared more excited than the others, later suggested the name David.

For some time they debated the cause of death. No bruises, no bleeding, only a slight puffiness to the skin, especially the hands. Someone said they should remove the shoes and socks. "No," Tiburcio said. "Leave him alone, he's been through enough. Next you'll want to take off his clothes." Tiburcio was overruled; off came the shoes, a little water and sand spilling out. Both socks had holes at the heels and big toes.

"What about the pants?" someone said.

In this way they discovered the man not only lacked a

small toe on one foot but also had a large tick burrowed in his right thigh and a long scar running from one hip almost to the naval. "Are you satisfied?" Tiburcio asked.

Everyone was silent. David was certainly the best looking young man they had ever seen, at least naked as he now lay. No one seemed to have the slightest shame before this perfect shape of a man. It was as if a statue had been placed among them, and they stared freely at whatever they admired most. Some of the men envied the wide chest, the angular jaw, and the hair, thick and wavy; the women for the most part gazed at the full, parted lips, the sunbaked arms, the long, strong legs and of course the dark, soft mound with its finger of life flopped over, its head to the sky.

"Too bad about the missing toe," Tiburcio said. "And the tick, what about that?" Mrs. Rentería struck a match and held it close to the whitish sac until the insect withdrew. There were oos and ahhs, and the girl who had combed the dead man's hair began to cry. Carmela glanced at the levee and wondered what was keeping her uncle Fausto.

They all agreed it was death by drowning. That the river was dry occurred only to the children, but they remained quiet, listening to their parents continue about what should be done with the dead man. Smaldino volunteered his ice locker. No, the women complained, David would lose his suppleness, the smooth, lifelike skin would turn blue and harden. Then someone suggested they call Cuca, perhaps she knew how to preserve the dead. Cuca had cures for everything, why not David?

"No!" Mrs. Rentería shouted, unable to control herself any longer. "He'll stay with me." Although she had never married, never been loved by a man, everyone called her Mrs. out of respect, at times even knowing the bite of irony could be felt in this small, squarish woman who surrounded her house with flowers and worked six days a week changing bedpans and sheets at County General. "David is mine!" she shouted for all to hear.

"David?" Tiburcio asked. "Since when is his name David? He looks to me more like a . . ." Tiburcio glanced at the man's face. ". . . a Luis."

"No senor!" another voice cried. "Roberto."

"Antonio!"

"Henry."

"Qué Henry, Enrique!"

"Alejandro!"

Trini, Ronnie, Miguel, Roy, Rafael . . . the call of
names grew, everyone argued their choice.

Meanwhile Mrs. Rentería left her neighbors, who one
by one turned away to debate the issue. After kneeling
a moment beside David, she stood and wrung out the
sopping, gray shorts, then began slipping his feet through
the leg holes, eventually tugging the elastic band past the
knees to the thighs. Here she asked for help, but the
group didn't seem to hear. So with a determination
grown strong by years of spinsterhood, she rolled David
onto one side, then the other, at last working the shorts
up to his waist. The rest was the same, and she finished
dressing him by herself.

When the others returned no one noticed the change,
for David appeared as breathtaking dressed as he did
naked. "You're right," Tiburcio announced, "his name
is David . . . but you still can't have him."

About this time Fausto arrived, helped by Mario, a
goateed boy whose weaknesses were stealing cars and
befriending old men. The two figures stepped slowly
across the broken glass and rocks. Fausto, winking at his
niece, immediately grasped the situation. David was a
wetback. Yes, there was no mistake. Hadn't he, years
ago, bought at least a dozen young men from Tijuana—
one, sometimes two at a time, cramped into the trunk of
the car? Of course Fausto knew, for even after they
found work, months later, they would return to the house
dressed in new clothes, but always the same type of
clothes. Fausto wasn't too quick to recognize women illegals, but the men, like young David there, were an easy
mark.

"How can you tell?" Smaldino asked.

The old man raised his staff and pointed to the gold
tooth, the cut of hair, the collar tag, the narrow trouser
cuffs, the thickheeled, pointy shoes. "It's all there. You
think I don't know a *mojado* when I see one?" As a last
gesture, he stooped down and closed the dead man's
eyes. "Now . . . what will you do with him?"

"No, *hijita*, he's too old for you."

Mrs. Rentería repeated her claim, placing her body

between David and the others. Before they could object, Fausto asked in a loud voice what woman among them needed a man so greatly that she would accept a dead man. "Speak up! Which of you can give this man your entire love, the soul of everything you are? Which of you, if not the senora here who has no one?"

The wives looked at their husbands, and the girls and unmarried women waited in awkward silence.

"Then it's settled," Fausto said with unusual authority. "You, Tiburcio . . . Smaldino, and you, Mario, take this man to her house."

"Hey, I ain't touchin' no dead man," Mario said.

Carmela stepped forward. "Yeah, you'll steal cars, but you won't help your own kind."

"Alright, Alright," Mario muttered, "one time and no more."

That evening so many visitors crowded into the small, frame house next to the river that latecomers were forced to wait their turn in the front yard. Even Cuca, her stockings rolled down to her ankles, had to wait in line.

Mrs. Rentería had bathed and shaved David, clipped his hair and lightly powdered his cheeks. He wore new clothes and sat quietly in a waxed and polished leather-recliner. The neighbors filed by, each shaking the manicured hand, each with a word of greeting, some of the men with a joking remark about the first night with a woman. And most everyone returned for a second, third and fourth look at this treasure of manhood might not survive another of summer heat.

Like all discoveries, it was only a matter of time till David's usefulness for giving pleasure would end, till the colognes and sprays would not mask what was real, till the curious would remain outside, preferring to watch through the window with their noses covered, till the women retreated into the yard, till the men stopped driving by for a glance from the street, till at last only Mrs. Rentería was left to witness the end.

Happily this was a solitary business. For several days she had not gone to the hospital, her work was forgotten, and she passed the daylight hours at David's feet, listening, speaking, giving up her secrets. And not once did he notice her wrinkled, splotchy hands, the graying hair nor the plain, uninspired face. During the warm after-

noons David would take her out, arm in arm, strolling
idly through the lush gardens of his home, somewhere
far away to the south. He gave her candies and flowers,
kissed her hands and spoke of eternity, the endless pulse
of time, two leaves in the wind. At night she would come
to him dressed as some exotic vision, a sprig of jasmine
in her hair, and lay by his side till dawn, awake to his
every whisper and touch.

On the third day Fausto knew the honeymoon was
over. "Señora," he called at the door, "it's time David
left."

Mrs. Rentería hurried out from the kitchen. Her hair
was down in a carefree tangle and she wore only a bath-
robe. "You're too late," she said with a smile. "He died
this morning . . . about an hour ago."

Fausto examined her eyes, quite dry and obviously
sparkling with something more than grief.

"He died?"

"Yes," she stated proudly. "I think it was too much
love."

The odor of death was so strong Fausto had to back
down the steps. "Señora, I'd be more than happy to take
him away for you. Leave it to me, I'll be right back."
He turned quickly and shuffled toward the sidewalk.

"Wait!" she shouted. "David's already gone."

"I know, but I'll take him away."

"That's what I mean. The boy, that *greñudo* friend of
yours, carried him off just before you came."

"Mario?"

"I think so . . . he's got *pelitos* on his chin?"

"*Está bien, señora*, your David will get the best burial
possible."

Mrs. Rentería said she insisted on going with him, but
Mario refused.

"Don't worry," Fausto said, "we'll take care of him.
The body does, but the soul. . . ."

"I know, his soul is right here . . . in my heart."

"Señora, keep him there, because if you ever lose him,
watch out for the other women."

"He'll never leave. You see, I have his word." She
pulled a folded scrap of paper from between her breasts
and studied the scribbled words.

Fausto asked if he should say something special at the burial. "Some prayer . . . a poem?"

Mrs. Rentería answered with a toss of her head, and for a moment the glassy eyes were lost in the distance. Then she closed the heavy, wooden door, clicked both locks, dropped the blinds behind the big bay-window and drew them shut.

But David was not buried. He left the valley as fresh and appealing as he had arrived. A man so perfect should not be buried, Fausto told Mario, and with the boy's help and using a skill more ancient than the first Tarahumara Indian, the old man painstakingly restored David to his former self. Even the missing toe was replaced.

By late evening the restoration was complete. Only one chore remained. Carmela brought the pitcher of water into the yard and wet the dead man's clothes, the same shabby clothes he wore when he arrived.

"More water," Fausto said. Mario took the pitcher and skipped into the house. David was about his own age, and ever since Mrs. Rentería had taken him home, Mario's admiration for the dead man's quiet sense of confidence had grown. The *vato* is cool, Mario thought.

After the second pitcher of water was poured, Fausto asked for the egg—a dried quetzal egg Mario had plucked from the Exposition Park ornithology hall.

"What's that for?" Carmela asked.

"Oh, Cuca once told me that you do this"—and here Fausto lightly brushed the egg on the dead man's lips"—and it brings him good luck. I don't believe it . . . but just in case. . . ."

Mario struggled with the body, lifting it over one shoulder. "Is that it?"

"Follow me," Fausto said.

Carmela opened the picket-fence gate and silently watched the two silhouettes walk into the darkness. "Tío!" she called. "Where you taking him?"

"Further down the river," came the faint reply, ". . . where others can find him."

Mario, Fausto and David—once again the best-looking dead man this side of Mexico—crossed the street and disappeared under the broken street lamp.

SANDRA CISNEROS

❀ ❀ ❀

Sandra Cisneros was born in 1954 and has lived most of her life in Chicago. The daughter of a Mexican father, a Mexican-American mother, and sister to six brothers, she—as she says of herself—is "nobody's mother and nobody's wife." The recipient of two fellowships for poetry and fiction from the National Endowment for the Arts, she is also a fellow of the Karolyi Foundation of France and of the Texas Institute of Letters. She has worked as a teacher to high school dropouts, a college recruiter, an arts administrator, and, most recently, as a "migrant professor," teaching as writer-in-residence at California State University at Chico, the University of California at Berkeley and Irvine, the University of Michigan. When she is not teaching she lives in San Antonio, Texas. Among her books are My Wicked Ways *and* The House on Mango Street, *winner of the 1985 Before Columbus Foundation American Book Award. Critic Phillip Lopate has commented that* The House on Mango Street—*which includes "Geraldo No Last Name," a selection in this anthology—"is a beautiful book. Rarely have I read anything that came so closely to reviving the ache of childhood. The metaphoric imagination is ripe, the details are accurate, and it manages to operate on the twin planes of dreams and reality with great sophistication. It also speaks to all those exiles . . . who feel both ashamed of the poor neighborhood they grew up in, and inadequate to its beauty."*

Regarding her own work, Cisneros says, "I write the kind of stories I didn't get growing up. Stories about . . . people I knew and loved, but never saw in the pages of the books I borrowed from the Chicago Public Library. Now that I live in the southwest, I'm even more appalled

244

*by the absence of brown people in mainstream literature
and more committed than ever to populating the Texas
literary landscape, the American literary landscape with
stories about* mexicanos, Chicanos, and Latinos.*"*

Geraldo No Last Name

She met him at a dance. Pretty too, and young. Said
she worked in a restaurant, but she can't remember
which one. Geraldo. That's all. Green pants and Saturday shirt. Geraldo. That's what he told her.

And how was she to know she'd be the last one to see
him alive. An accident, don't you know, Hit and run.
Marin, she goes to all those dances. Uptown. Logan.
Embassy. Palmer. Aragon. Fontana. The Manor. She
likes to dance. She knows how to do cumbias and salsas
and rancheras even. And he was just someone she
danced with. Somebody she met that night. That's right.

That's the story. That's what she said again and again.
Once to the hospital people and twice to the police. No
address. No name. Nothing in his pockets. Ain't it a
shame.

Only Marin can't explain why it mattered, the hours
and hours, for somebody she didn't even know. The hospital emergency room. Nobody but an intern working all
alone. And maybe if the surgeon would've come, maybe
if he hadn't lost so much blood, if the surgeon had only
come, they would know who to notify and where. But
what difference does it make? He wasn't anything to her.
He wasn't her boyfriend or anything like that. Just
another *brazer* who didn't speak English. Just another
wetback. You know the kind. The ones who always look
ashamed. And what was she doing out at three a.m. anyway? Marin who was sent home with her coat and some
aspirin. How does she explain it?

She met him at a dance. Geraldo in his shiny shirt and
green pants. Geraldo going to a dance.

What does it matter?

They never saw the kitchenettes. They never knew

about the two-room flats and sleeping rooms he rented, the weekly money orders sent home, the currency exchange. How could they?

His name was Geraldo. And his home is in another country. The ones he left behind are far away. They will wonder. Shrug. Remember. Geraldo. He went north . . . we never heard from him again.

Hugo Martínez-Serros

❦　❦　❦

Hugo Martínez-Serros was born in 1930 and grew up during the Depression in a poverty-stricken working class community on the far south side of Chicago, in the shadow of the steel mills and railroad yards. After graduating from public high school, he entered the University of Chicago on a scholarship and received his BA in 1951. He has a PhD in literature from Northwestern University, and has taken courses in phoenetics, advanced Spanish grammar, and literature at what is now the Universidad de las Americas in Mexico. Martínez-Serros has taught at several universities and is currently a professor of literature at Lawrence University in Appleton, Wisconsin.

Regarding his short stories, he has noted, "I learned to write fiction very late in life." His first stories were published in 1980, when he was fifty years old. "Richardo's War" is included in his first collection, published in 1988, The Last Laugh and Other Stories. *The stories are set in a Mexican-American barrio in South Chicago during the 1940s and, as one critic has noted, reflect a "concern for the injustice, poverty and discrimination that have characterized the Hispanic experience in the United States." Another critic adds, "Martínez-Serros' stories hold promise of a fervent Hispanic voice to be heard and acknowledged. As he continues to write and publish his rich, blistering indictments of racism, Martínez-Serros will only increase his stature as a pioneer of Mexican-American literature."*

Ricardo's War

Ricardo pulled on his coat in the lobby. Something was going on outside and he hurried through the big door of the movie theatre to see what it was. Then he heard the news boys: "Extra! Extra! Japs bomb Pearl Harbor! War! War!" Newspapers under their arms, they barked their message over and over. Everywhere people swarmed around them and traffic slowed in the streets. The air was charged with commotion.

Alarm gripped Ricardo and he felt a deep instantaneous chill. He buttoned his coat, turned up his collar and looked fearfully into the night sky. He fought back his tears as a single thought slashed at him: *War! War! That's what they're sayin'; it's war! I'll never get home! I'm too far away, never!* He was eleven and had never left the city, had ridden in an automobile twice, and had never seen a plane up close. But he knew about war—it changed everything right away, destroyed everything in a flash. At the corner, close to panic, he boarded a streetcar.

That afternoon in the bright sun the streetcars had carried him along, swaying from side to side when they sped, making him smile because he swayed with them. He had always felt safe in streetcars, liked the feeling of independence they gave him. Now it was dark and he pressed his face to the window, searched the sky for bombers. *I'd rather see them in the daytime*, he thought, *know where they are so I can get ready.* He felt trapped in that red and yellow cage—so much glass and steel that ran along on tracks—and felt his fear grow. They flew at him from his memory, planes he had seen dropping bombs—newsreel planes that for years had been bringing the wars in Europe and Asia to everyone who went to the movies, and picture-card war planes.

When he was younger he had collected bubblegum picture cards of those far-off wars. He was thinking now of the two most terrifying cards: one, its background a burning mountain of human bodies, showed a horde of naked

248

yellow men firing rifles at onrushing tanks and infantrymen; in the other, planes were bombing a city, buildings everywhere exploding, crumbling, frightened people fleeing in confusion. His eyes continued to search the sky. Each time they found what they were looking for, he stiffened, drew in his breath, listened and waited. But the blinking lights moved across the black sky and nothing happened. He exhaled slowly and looked around at the other riders. Their composure mocked him, appalled him, and he dried his hands on his coat.

From the streetcar everything looked unchanged. Familiar buildings stood where they always had and there were no signs of rubble. But time had slowed. This ride home had always been fast and now it was taking forever. In his mind he sped on in search of his house, and, where it should have been, he found a hole. Two transfers and a long time afterward he finally spied his house. Before the streetcar came to a full stop, its doors swung open and he jumped from it, ran across the street, pushed through the front door and hurried up the stairs, not knowing what he would find. He entered the flat. Nothing had changed. He undressed silently and went to bed.

Bombers and tanks hunted him. He was naked but did not feel cold. In the dark he ran looking for a street that would lead him out of the city. A street unknown to him. If he did not find it before dawn they would see him. They were in hot pursuit when he opened his eyes.

Monday morning. *I must be crazy*, he thought, his heart racing. It seemed no different from other mornings. He got out of bed, heard the others' voices, then he heard it on the radio. It was true! Buttoning his shirt, he tried not to listen to the radio. It terrified him with details. He plugged his ears with his hands, pressing hard, and went to the kitchen. From the table the newspaper fired its headline at him: JAPS BOMB PEARL HARBOR! His hands fell from his head, his arms dropped to his sides. The radio blared.

At school he found things exactly as he had left them on Friday. There were no barricades. No gun emplacements. No troops stationed close by to protect the children, to guard the steel mills, two short blocks away, from surprise attacks. What would they do, Ricardo wondered, against guns and bombs and tanks? What if he

never saw his family again? It had happened to his
mother and father—in Mexico, the Revolution. They had
told him. Without warning, the machine-guns started.
Children running in the streets, dropping books, caught
in crossfire. Shells. Falling buildings, people inside. They
came with guns, looking for food and money. Killed. At
night too, when nobody expected them. And the stink
of dead bodies.

Before the week was out Germany had declared war
on the United States. Ricardo was struck dumb with fear.

It baffled Ricardo that they were not afraid, wounded
him that they were so unfeeling, so different from him.
More than anything, it shamed him, shamed him to
speechlessness, separated him from them, casting him
deeper into fear and shame. How could he tell them?
How could he explain to them what they could see?—
that everything was unprotected! They would laugh at
him, single him out, call him names. *Coward*! He buried
his head in his hands. ¡*Cobarde*! It was the worst thing
his father could say of anyone. ¡*Cobarde*! What his
mother called him when he struck his younger sister.
¡*Corbarde*!

There it was, his terror. He wanted to push the war
away. If he didn't think of it, didn't hear or read about
it, it would go away. News of defeat terrified him, and
reports of victory only meant that the war went on. He
would avoid it, it was the only way.

In the early months of the war, a current events class
was held once a week, more often than that if the fighting
was fierce. Using large maps, the teachers tracked the
war for the children. They answered questions and
explained why America would win: "We've never lost a
war because we're the most powerful nation in the world.
We've never had to fight a foreign war on our own soil.
And we're the world's first democracy, the land of the
free and the home of the brave." They explained how
America was winning the war even when it seemed that
she was not: "We've just begun to fight. Wait until we
reach full production. They sneaked up on us, but things
will be different now that we know what's what."
Ricardo tried not to hear, thought of the park, movies
he had seen, the swimming pool at the YMCA.

As if to mock Ricardo, the whole school was suddenly caught up in "the war effort." "Patriotism" became a common word and the principal, Mr. Fitts, spoke of it repeatedly in assemblies that were held often now. In the auditorium, principal, teachers and students gathered to sing songs ("God bless America," "Anchors aweigh," "Over hill, over dale, as we hit the dusty trail," "From the halls of Montezuma," "O, semper paratus," "Off we go into the wild blue yonder"), to hear stories of American bravery and heroism, to cheer the teams of students that, armed with rifles and sabres and American flags, performed crisp drills. There was no let up.

All those assemblies made Frederick Douglass Sneed important. He was as big and strong as a man and never misbehaved in class, and Mrs. Gleason, the English teacher, put him in charge of a crew of boys to set up the stage on assembly days and to put things away afterward. She said it was a job for the boys who had learned all they ever would in class, those who didn't mind straining their backs or getting dirty and would do more good in the auditorium. Freddie, who had complete control of the boys, made Ricardo his "lieutenant," and Lalo, Mario and Manny rounded out the "squad."

Calls for national cooperation, vigilance and sacrifice reached Ricardo's classrooms from the White House. His teachers, their voices like bugles, sounded the alarms that came from Washington: "Now, children, we must be careful, we must all work together. Chicago is the most important city in the entire war effort because of our steel mills and railroads. It's something the enemy knows. We must be on our guard against spies and sabotage. Look out for strangers who ask about the steel mills. Tell the police. Tell your fathers not to talk about their work to strangers. Don't repeat anything your brothers in the service say about troop movements. Remember, 'A slip of the lip might sink a ship.' "

These warnings fueled Ricardo's fears, which flamed like the fires in the steel mills, burning day and night now and filling the sky with smoke. They were things he had to know for his protection, but he didn't want to know them.

One day the windows, eyes that looked out from the numbing drudgery of the classroom, began to be blinded one by one. Ricardo watched every detail of the operation. Measurements were taken, the blades of the big shears cut cleanly, cement was applied carefully. It took time, but in the end every window was blinded with a heavy gauze-like cloth. Now everybody was protected. In an air raid nobody would be slashed by flying knives of glass. The wounded-looking windows, bandaged like casualties of the war, oppressed Ricardo. He could no longer look out; he would not see *them* when they came. He would have felt much safer with a battery of anti-aircraft guns on the playground.

The air raid drills were orderly, full of urgency and fearful excitement. At the sound of the alarm the teachers, like platoon sergeants, quickly moved the children to prearranged areas. Taking shelter in the building, they shunned its most vulnerable spots—open spaces, windows—and found cover under tables and desks, along inner walls, in the basement. For several minutes—while imaginary planes flew overhead and until the all-clear signal sounded—they all curled up on the floor. Ricardo could hear some of the others whispering:

"If they come for the mills, we'll never escape, we're too close. My father says so. They'd hit us too."

"If they come! But they won't. They can't fly that far. Across the ocean."

"They take off from carriers. It'd be easy to get here"

"We'd shoot 'em down before they got this far!"

"Yeah! Like we did at Pearl Harbor!"

Easily stirred, Ricardo's imagination filled the skies with planes that dropped bombs on the steel mills. He curled up more tightly, pressing his hands to his ears, and waited for his bomb, knowing it would blow him to pieces when it found him. He remembered Fourth-of-July firecrackers he had set off under glass jars.

The war filled Ricardo's world. Day after day it made its way into everything, touched everybody's life. Young men over eighteen disappeared into the services, their lives represented by blue stars displayed in windows, their deaths by gold stars, and there was a lot of talk about blue-star and gold-star mothers. The dark green pack of Lucky Strike cigarettes abruptly turned white because "Lucky Strike green has gone to war." Suddenly there were more jobs than workers, and *braceros*, laborers from Mexico, appeared everywhere. In mills and factories women took over the work of men, carried lunch pails, began to drive taxicabs and trucks. Ricardo's father sometimes worked seven days a week and his older brothers found jobs. Debts of many years standing were finally paid off and, for the first time, worrylines disappeared from his mother's face. His father now kept a couple of bottles of beer in the icebox. Certain things that his mother needed became scarce or were rationed—sugar, coffee, meat, soap, paper goods. Some people bought them at high prices on the Black Market. For Ricardo's teachers it became harder to buy nylons, cigarettes, and gasoline; they did not hesitate to ask their students for ration coupons that their parents did not use. More than anywhere else, Ricardo heard the war in popular songs that filled the air: "Dear Mom, the weather today . . . all the boys in the camp"; "They're either too young or too old"; "There's a star-spangled banner waving somewhere"; "Praise the Lord and pass the ammunition"; "Comin' in on a wing an' a prayer"; "Rosie, the riveter"; "There'll be bluebirds over the White Cliffs over Dover." Ricardo, who loved the movies, seldom went now because movies about the war filled screens everywhere. Unendingly, the war dragged on.

Ricardo knew that the Japanese and the Germans were "the enemies of freedom." Everybody knew it. The Japanese even more than the Germans, because they were so sneaky. He did not know a Japanese; there were none in his school. But he knew what they looked like from newsreels and pictures in the paper. Mrs. Gleason explained that they were "just like Chinks, only smaller." Now, whenever he could, he would look through the window of the Chinese laundry a half block from the YMCA and feel that he was looking at "the enemies of freedom." Along with everybody else, Ricardo learned that the Japs were doubly yellow—they had yellow skins and they were cowards. *¡Cobardes!* Sneaks especially, that's what they were. Mrs. Gleason never tired of telling her students that "The lesson of Pearl Harbor is that those little animals can't be trusted. That's what we mean when we say, 'Remember Pearl Harbor!' We can't trust little animals anywhere in the world! It's like 'Remember the Alamo!' " And this made Ricardo very uneasy.

Japp's Potato Chips had been a part of Ricardo's life as long as he could remember. Their blue and gray waxed-paper bags hung temptingly on little stands in every store. Now suddenly they became Jay's Potato Chips. And now his older brother Ramiro called him Tojo when he got angry at him. It wasn't just that he, Ricardo, wore glasses. There was something more. "You look Japanese," Ramiro would say. "Look at your eyes, it's there. Hasn't anyone ever told you?" When he was alone, Ricardo searched his face in the mirror. And he studied Japanese faces whenever he saw them. In the end he saw that Ramiro was right; it was in his eyes— they were tipped and slightly puffy. And he was dark like some of them, had their dark eyes and black hair.

"What we gonna play?" somebody asked. It was recess and they were on the playground.

"Remember Pearl Harbor! Let's play war!"

"We need some Japs. Who's gonna be the Japs?"

Ricardo moved away slowly, hoping they wouldn't call him back. He took off his glasses and cleaned them.

"Hey Freddie, you be a Jap!"

"You crazy? I can't be no Jap, I'm colored an' big!"

"Well I can't be no damn Jap neither! My eyes ain't slanted or swolled up."

"Who's ever the Japs can win the battle!" somebody offered.

"Then you be a Jap, you're so interested!"

The bell rang, ending their quarrel.

The Germans were different. Not like the Japanese. Nobody said the Germans were sneaky. They were big, blond, blue-eyed, like many Americans; but they looked tougher. Everybody said they were smart, said their scientists were the best in the world. Only the Americans were smart enough and tough enough to beat Germany. Ricardo knew some Germans, German-Americans, had always known some because they went to his school. Ernie Krause and Olga Schmidt were in his class. Nobody said anything to Olga, she was quiet; but everybody jeered Ernie, called him Kraut, Heinie, Nazi, traitor, whenever he said, "The Germans got the best fighting force in the world. You'll see, they'll win the war." Nobody hit Ernie when he talked that way; his classmates argued with him, got angry with him the way they would have if he had cheered not his own but another school's team.

Ricardo wondered why nobody changed the names of German rye and sauerkraut. Wouldn't sabotage be easy for the Germans if they looked like Americans? And weren't they more dangerous than the Japanese if they were smarter? Someone was always willing to be a German in war games. And why didn't anyone say anything when children goose-stepped back and forth in front of Jake Bernstein's dry goods store, arms raised obliquely in front of them, palms open and down, shouting, "Heil Hitler, Heil Hitler!" until the old man, quivering with rage, came out with a broom and chased them away?

Germany made Ricardo think. He didn't want to, but he couldn't help it. The only way to understand the Germans was by accepting what others said—that even though they were wrong in what they were doing, you had to admire the Germans for opposing all Europe and beating the hell out of it. Ricardo understood the importance of force. It was what he and his schoolmates understood best. The trouble with this explanation was that it led you to conclude that Japan, which was smaller than Germany, deserved greater admiration because it had not only taken on some big countries, but had attacked the United States directly. It made no sense, what people said of the Germans and Japanese. Just as it made no sense, no sense at all, for people not to be afraid of war.

Everybody participated or wanted to participate in the war effort. People talked of how hard it was to do with less, and yet many seemed to have more. When he was finally forced to accept the reality of the war, Ricardo timidly began to think of how he might help. Some children felt themselves directly involved in the fighting every time they bought defense stamps and bonds. The teachers said everyone had to buy them. Anyone who didn't wasn't patriotic and wouldn't pass at the end of the semester. But few had money to help in this way and, in any case, they were not Ricardo and his friends. Mostly they were the *güeros*, those who looked like their teachers and had always boasted that they were the *real* Americans. Now they flaunted their patriotism in the faces of those who did not buy. Ricardo and his friends kept silent.

One day Ernie Krause made those who did not buy defense stamps and bonds feel good. In class one morning Ernie suddenly raised his hand. "What'll happen to the defense stamp an' bond money if we lose the war?" he asked. His tone was genuinely curious, his eyes inquisitively unblinking.

"That's a stupid thing to ask! How can we lose the war? They would take everything from us if we lost the war. Everyone would lose everything! Our defense stamps and bonds would be worth nothing!" Mrs. Gleason answered in a voice that had tightened, her eyes flashing with indignation.

"Suppose, just suppose. I mean, will the people who buy defense stamps an' bonds be treated worse'n the people who don't, I mean if the Germans find out who did an' who didn't?" Ernie insisted, unruffled by Mrs. Gleason's anger.

"How would I know that?" she snapped. "It's a horrible thing to ask! Shut up, shut up! Not one more word out of you! Why, that's impossible and you know it, you know it!"

Ricardo wondered if the war would ever end. Although his fear had receded, he had not learned to relax, and an adverse turn in the war would bring on old feelings. Air raid drills no longer aroused fear and uncertainty in the others. The teachers, annoyed by it all, no longer curled up on the floor with the students. One day Ricardo noticed that the cloth that covered the panes of glass in windows and doors had been pulled up in some corners. Occasionally, a clouded eye spied into an unsuspecting classroom from the corner of one of the door panes.

Toward the end of the second year of the war a scarcity of paper brought the war effort to the very door of Ricardo's school. A national call for an all-out effort to salvage cardboard and paper was aimed at school children. Ricardo's principal, Mr. Fitts, visited every classroom to explain what had to be done: "We need paper to win the war, mountains of paper! Paper for messages, paper to keep records, paper for maps, for war books and military manuals, paper to pack and ship things— food, equipment, clothing. Can we win it? Can we?"

"Yes! Yes! We can!" the children assured him, their voices ringing.

"Good! I knew I could count on you," he confided. "It'll be hard work," he added, "but we must do it, we must, for as long as it's necessary," and he clenched his fist and waved it at their enemies.

Mr. Fitts gave the children one afternoon off every two weeks to collect cardboard, newspapers, magazines, and to bring them to school, where they would be stored until a truck arrived to haul them away. For months Mr. Fitts and his teachers had worked to cultivate love of country in the children. The success of the paper drives rested on the strength of that love and the principal wondered how deep it went.

In Ricardo's class the first drive was a very great success. Spurred by patriotic zeal and a keen sense of purpose, the children hunted their prey like new warriors eager to prove their valor. They searched basements, attics, coalsheds, garages, and by three o'clock they returned to school with great piles of paper. They came with their arms full, stopping along the way to rest; they came pulling wagons, pushing wheelbarrows and buggies, all shouting, "We'll win the war with paper! We'll win the war with paper!" They collected so much that most of them had to make several trips to get it to school. Freddie, Ricardo, Mario, Lalo and Manny worked as a team and brought more paper than anybody else. But in all the commotion, in all the coming and going, the stacking, the shouting and laughing, the working and horsing around, nobody noticed it. And nobody noticed that Ernie Krause refused to have anything to do with "all that silly shit."

It was Ricardo who realized that the area where they lived, and beyond, had become their battleground. It was he who told his four friends that what they did in the drives would be their part in the war: "It'll be like fightin', really fightin', an' not any of that stamp an' bond stuff." They had been a working crew; now they would be a fighting squad. It was the turning point in the war for Ricardo.

Freddie, narrowing his eyes and talking through his teeth, said what they all felt: "Them bastards, Walker an' Ryan an' Pelky an' their friends! Think they're so goddamn American. Think, they're the only Americans aroun' here."

"We look for paper whenever we can, seven days a week. Then we store it until we pick it up drive-day," Ricardo explained to his friends after the first drive. They were in a corner of the school playground.

"Yeah, 'cause all that easy paper's gone now. Everybody got it. Everybody's gonna wanna get it an' there ain't gonna be that much," Manny added, gently moving his head in agreement. His eyes were shining with seriousness.

"We don't want nobody else comin' with us, right?" Freddie asked, the tone of exclusiveness hard in his throat.

"Right! We're a team! Only good team I ever been on. We don't need no damn güeros on it," spat Mario.

"While they're playin' an' screwin' aroun', we'll be fightin'. We'll be whippin' Jap ass an' Kraut ass with all that paper." Lalo's voice was steady, the words clear. He was jabbing the ground with a stick. Suddenly he laughed and said, "An' we'll be whippin' güero ass too!"

His voice bright with a motion, Ricardo told them, "I know where we can get a big goddamn wagon with iron wheels!"

Ricardo became their leader. He thought about where they might find paper and how they would collect and store it. "We go first to the houses with blue an' gold stars. They wanna help more'n anybody else, 'specially them blue-star an' gold-star mothers." He thought more about the whole thing than they did and he gave orders and they obeyed. Time began to slip away from him, to move forward too quickly.

It was harder to find paper for the second drive, and this discouraged many students. By the third, the fun was gone from their enterprise and grumbling became commonplace.

"Who ever heard of paper bombs?"

"Maybe they're shootin' spitballs at the Japs an' Krauts."

"We shouldda won the war long ago! Who are the Japs an' Krauts? Nobody!"

"Must be a lotta shittin' goin' on, all that paper our side's been usin'!"

"I'd show them Japs an' Krauts! Jus' gimme a machine-gun!"

Ricardo memorized a speech like the one Mr. Fitts had given, and he and his team went everywhere—to stores, taverns, restaurants, factories, packing houses, barbershops, beauty parlors, filling stations. Like guerrillas, they learned more with each drive, broadened the range of their operations and became more single-minded in carrying out their mission.

In Mrs. Gleason's class only Ricardo and his men brought back larger and larger piles of paper with each drive. This puzzled her. She had expected the *most American* of her pupils to collect the largest quantities of paper, the pupils who got the best grades and bought most of the defense stamps and bonds. Something was wrong in all this, she knew it.

After the third drive she had devised a system for grading the paper-collecting effort of each student. Using colored stars, she inverted the color-order assigned to grades in class work. Those who brought no paper were dishonored with a gold star ("It means you're dead"); a silver star designated those who brought a modest amount ("At least you're moving"); a blue star went to those who really did their share("You're fighting like our boys"); a red star honored Ricardo, Freddie, Lalo, Mario and Manny ("You're our commandos, school commandos").

When Ricardo and his squad returned to school with mountains of newspapers, cardboard and magazines in their wagons, they did it proudly, confidently, stirred by the approval and disbelief of fellow students:

"Wow! Lookit that paper!"

"Damn! Where'd you guys get all that paper?"

"You been savin' it for months!"

"Boy! You guys could start your own junkyard!"

Freddie's unassuming "Shhiiit! Ain't nothin' like the

paper we bringin' nex' time!" expressed exactly the feelings of his fellow commandos.

Now the days rushed by for Ricardo. He had put his fear behind him and followed news of the war with the keenest interest. When America or the Allies suffered a setback, he would rouse his commandos to an intense search for paper and cardboard, hoping to offset the defeat.

One afternoon Mrs. Gleason announced to her class that they no longer would take part in the drive since they were bringing in so little paper and staying out of class all afternoon. She made one exception—Ricardo and his squad. "After all," she told the others, "they're bigger and stronger than most of you and they know where to find it."

Mr. Fitts learned about the mountains of paper the five boys unfailingly delivered and he called them to his office to commend them. It forced Mrs. Gleason to get them larger red stars, and a bit later she named them the "Commando Reserves Enlisted To Increase National Strength." She entered their names on a special list with this title and displayed it prominently on the bulletin board. All this gave the boys a real sense of their worth, finally bringing them the official recognition they craved.

Then it occurred to Mrs. Gleason that the undue attention heaped on the five boys was working to the detriment of her best students. After all, they had feelings too; in fact, they were probably more sensitive. To put an end to bruised sensitivities, she bluntly addressed the class: "Now, all of you know that there's backwork and there's headwork. Let's put things in their proper perspective. Those of you who do backwork well should go on doing it, and those of us who do headwork well should get on with *it*. War turns everything upside-down. Do I make myself clear?"

Soon after this she began matter-of-factly to call Ricardo and his crew "the CRETINS," an acronym that filled them with pride. Without a single exception, their schoolmates called them "the COMMANDOS."

ESTELA PORTILLO

❦ ❦ ❦

Estela Portillo was born in 1936 in El Paso, Texas, where she has lived all of her life. She earned a master's degree in English and American literature at the University of Texas in El Paso and taught high school for many years. For a while, Portillo had her own "very political" talk show on an El Paso radio station and was resident dramatist at the community college, where she staged a number of her own plays. Portillo began publishing in the early 1970s, her works—poems, short stories, and excerpts from plays—appearing in El Grito, *the pioneering literary review from the University of California at Berkeley devoted to publishing literary efforts by Mexican-Americans. In 1972, she received the Quinto Sol Award for literature. The following year, she edited and wrote the introduction to a special issue of* El Grito: *"Chicanas en la Literatura y el Arte," the first collection of literature by Mexican-American women. Her controversial drama,* The Day of the Swallows, *was first published in 1976 in* Contemporary Chicano Theatre, *edited by Roberto Garza.* Rain of Scorpions and Other Writings, *her first collection of short stories—and the first published collection of stories by a Mexican-American woman—appeared in 1975. Feeling that the stories needed polishing, Portillo revised and even rewrote them, and in May 1991, the collection was republished under the same title, including a new story, "Village." "The Pilgrim," which appears in this anthology, is excerpted from her novel,* Trini (1986), *and relates the struggles of a Tarahumara woman who, late in her pregnancy, crosses over illegally into Texas in order that her child, Rico, may be born in the United States. Rico appears again as the central character in "Village." Estela Portillo's most recent work,* Masihani, *the result of three*

261

years of research in Mexico, traces the origins of and offers new insights into the popular Hispanic folktale of La Llorona, adding a new dimension to Portillo's already extensive and diverse oeuvre.

The Pilgrim

Trini walked with stumbling feet behind La Chaparra. They had followed a network of alleys through El Barrio de la Bola overlooking the western bank of the Rio Grande. The adobe *choza* on top of the sandhill gaped empty, roofless, without windows or door. A gaunt cat sitting on a pile of adobe stared at them with the frugal blank eyes of starvation. It was unusual to see a cat in this barrio. They were usually eaten by the starving people who lived in the makeshift cardboard and tin huts scattered along the hill. La Chaparra, her back against the wall, slid down to the ground, out of breath. The barrio ended on top of a hill that overlooked the smelter across the river on the United States side. Trini, tired, brooding, followed the path that led to the river with her eyes, shading them against the harsh sun. La Chaparra had brought her to the easiest crossing. The boundary between Juárez and Smeltertown in El Paso was no more than a series of charcos extending about fifty feet.

"You sure you want to do it?" La Chaparra's voice was skeptical. She muttered under her breath, "You're crazy, no money, having a baby in a strange land—you're crazy."

Trini turned to reassure the seasoned wetback, though her body was feeling the strain of the climb. "Everything will be fine, now that I know the way, thanks to you." She would wait for the pains of birth, then her pilgrimage would begin to the Virgin across the river. Somewhere in El Paso was a church, el Sagrado Corazón. She would be led. For her, destiny was an intuitive pull, a plan with a dream, sometimes without practical considerations. But practical considerations were luxuries in life. She could not afford to think of the dangers ahead, the suffering. She must just go.

On the way back home, La Chaparra cautioned her of the dangers—watch out for *la migra*, stay away from the highway. If they catch you, you might have the baby in jail if they don't process you back soon enough. Day crossings were easier through El Barrio de la Bola. La Chaparra wished her well and left her at the entrance to El Arroyo Colorado.

The birth pains came before dawn a few days later, a soft, late autumn dawn that wove its mysteries for her between pains. She took a streetcar at six that left her on the edge of El Barrio de la Bola. From there she walked all the way down the sandhill through the arrabales leading to the river. The river was not a threat. Most of the water had been banked upstream into irrigation ditches that followed newfound fields converted into farmland from the desert.

This was the point of safe crossing, safe from deep water, if not completely safe from the border patrols who made their morning rounds on the highway that followed the river. Still, her chances were good. Her pains were coming with regularity, but at distant intervals. From the Juárez side of the river she could see the small, humble homes scattered in the hills of Smeltertown. She rested under a tree on the edge of the river, her pores feeling the chill of the coming winter. She leaned her head against the tree, a lilac tree, of all things, in the middle of nowhere! For an instant, she seemed to feel a force from the earth, from her hold on the tree. She laughed, then pain cut sharply through her body. It sharpened and focused her instinct. Failure was impossible.

She took off her shoes and waded across a shallow area until she came to a place where the water was flowing uniformly downstream. She made her way carefully, looking for sure footing, her toes clutching at cold sand. Brown mimosa seeds floated on the surface of the water. Then, without warning, she felt herself slipping into the river. As she fell, a pain broke crimson, a red pain that mixed and swirled with the mud water that was up to her breasts now. She had lost the shoes she was carrying. Her feet sank into the deep soft sand, and she kicked forward to free herself. The steady flow of water helped pull her toward a dry section of riverbed. She was but a few feet away from the American side. Then, she was across.

Shoeless, drenched through and through, holding a wet rebozo around her, she made her way, breathless and cold, to a dirt road leading to the main highway. She looked both ways for any sign of a patrol car, but saw none. She sighed with relief, searching around for a place to rest. Ahead, she saw an abandoned gas station with a rusty broken-down car by its side. She could hide there until a bus arrived. She sat behind the car with the high-way before her; looming across the highway was a mountain carved by the machinery of the smelter, contoured by time, veined with the colors of a past life. Its granite silence gave her comfort. She understood mountains. Like trees and the earth, they bound her, gave her their strength. Pain again. It consumed her as she clutched the edge of a fender, the metal cutting into her palm.

While the pain still wavered, she saw a bus approaching far away along the stretch of highway. She wiped the perspiration from her face with the wet rebozo, her body shivering, her vision hazed as she fixed her eyes on the moving, yellow hope that came toward her. Her blood was singing birth, a fading and then a sharpening of her senses. She felt weak as she raised her heavy, tortured body and made her way to the edge of the highway. She stood, feet firm, arms waving. Oh, Sweet Virgin, make it stop! She waited, eyes closed, until she heard the grind-ing stop. Thank you, Sweet Mother. She opened her eyes to see the door of the bus swing open. When she got on, she saw the driver's eyes questioning. Words came out of her mouth; the clearness of her voice surprised her. "I have no money, but I must get to a church."

For a second, the bus driver stared at the pregnant woman, muddied and unkempt, standing her ground. He simply nodded, and the bus went on its way. She saw that the people on the bus were mostly Mexican like herself. Their eyes were frankly and curiously staring. A woman came up and helped her to a seat. She asked with concern, "Is there anything I can do?"

Trini looked at her with pleading eyes. "Where is the church?" She was breathing hard against the coming of another pain.

"A Catholic church?"

Trini nodded. The pain came in purple streaks. She bent her head, her face perspiring freely.

"It's your time," the woman whispered. "There's a hospital near."

"No, no, no, the church." Trini's plea swirled with the pain. She whispered, "The Virgin told me."

"*¡Jesucristo!*"

It seemed that the bus driver was going faster without making his usual stops. No one protested. The church was the destination now. Trini leaned her head against the window, hardly conscious of buildings interlacing light and sounds. At a distance, a church steeple rose south of the maze of city buildings. Someone said, "Over there, El Sagrado Corazón."

Joy danced on the brink of Trini's pain. El Sagrado Corazón! She had been led. She had been helped. She was certain now that her child was meant to be born in the church. The pain pierced, bounced, and dispersed. Then she breathed freely. The bus had stopped. The driver was pointing out directions. "Just go all the way down the street, then turn left."

The woman helped Trini off the bus as voices called out words of sympathy and good luck. As the bus took off again, Trini's legs gave way. She fell on bended knee on the sidewalk. The pains were almost constant now. She looked up at the woman with pleading eyes as the woman cleansed her brow, encouraging, "Just a little way now, *pobrecita.*"

"I have to find the Virgin . . ." The words were dry in her throat.

"The rectory . . ."

"No, the church." Trini shook her head in desperation, breathing hard. "The Virgin."

The woman said no more, bracing herself to hold Trini's weight. Through a wave of nausea, Trini saw the church before her. *Ave María, Madre de Dios, bendita seas entre todas las mujeres*. The prayer came like a flowing relief. They were climbing the steps slowly. Happy moans broke from Trini's throat as her legs wavered and her body shook in pain. She could feel herself leaning heavily on the woman. The woman opened the door of the church, and they walked into its silence. Before them were the long aisles leading up to the altar, a long, quiet, shadowy path. The woman whispered, "Can you make it?"

Trini looked up and saw what seemed like miles before her, but in front of the altar to the right was the Virgin Mary holding out her arms to her. The same smile on Her face as when She had looked down at Trini in the Juárez church. The pain was now one thin tightrope made of colored ribbons that went round and round, swirls of red and black. Reflections from the stained glass windows pulsed their colors, hues of mystery, creation. Colors wavered and swam before her eyes, the Virgin's heartbeat. Yes, she would make it. She stretched out her hand, feeling for the side of a pew to support herself. There was peace now in spite of the pain. The candles flickered, dancing a happiness before the Virgin. But now her body made its own demand, one drumming blow of pain. She fell back in a faint, and the woman broke her fall to the floor as two priests ran down the aisle to see what the matter was. Yes, the Virgin had been right all along . . .

Trini held the piece of paper in her shaking hand. It was in English so the words meant little to her, but the name Ricardo Esconde written in black ink stood out bold and strong. Her eyes, radiant in her triumph, looked for a second into the unconcerned eyes of the clerk, then flickered away. "Gracias."

Thank you, God—thank you, clerk—it was all over. Her son's birth had been registered. She walked away unsteadily, the weight of the baby in her arms, the paper held tightly in her hand. She made her way to a chair in the corner of the office, a queasiness commanding, stomach churning, the taste of vomit in her mouth. She let herself fall into the chair as she tightened her hold on the baby. Her breath came in spurts. She raised her head, throwing it back, mouth half-open to draw in air, her body withstanding many things—fear, hunger, fatigue. She had run away from the priests. Her mind retraced the time of her escape as her shaking hands carefully folded the birth certificate.

It was now in the pocket of her skirt. She had run away, not because the priests had been unkind. They had helped with the birth on the floor of the church, angry questions lost among sympathetic murmurings. After that, sleep overtook the pain. When she awoke, the priests placed a son in her arms, clean, wrapped in a kitchen towel. She had smiled her gratitude and had gone back to sleep. Later, she eagerly drank the hot soup and ate the bread they offered her, the baby close and warm by her side. But then the priest who spoke Spanish told her that the immigration people had to be notified. It was the law. The woman had told them that she had crossed the river.

When they had left her alone, she had simply taken the baby and walked away, out of a side door into an empty street in the early afternoon. She had walked south. When she could walk no more, she sat on a corner bench to rest. A Mexican woman sat next to her, waiting for a bus. She looked at Trini and the baby with interested eyes but said nothing until Trini asked, "Where do I register my baby as a citizen?"

Instantly, the woman understood. She shook her head as if to push away the futility of things, but answered, "City-county building." The woman was pointing north. "It's closed now."

"How far?"

"About twelve, thirteen blocks north, on San Antonio Street." The woman's eyes were troubled. "Just walk up, then turn left, but watch out for *la migra*. You look like you just came out of the river."

The bus stopped before them, and the woman disappeared behind its doors. Trini looked around and saw warehouses with closed doors, parking lots yawning their emptiness. She had the urge to cry, to give up, but the sun was falling in the west, and the baby in her arms told her differently. She sat numb, without plan, without thought as buses came and went, loading and unloading passengers. She sat on the bench until dark, putting the baby to her breast before she set out again. How insatiable was her drowsy, grey fatigue. She set one foot before the other without direction as gauze clouds were swallowed by the night. The night had swallowed her and the baby too. She made her way to an alley, away from the wind, and there in a corner slept, the baby clasped tightly in her arms.

*   *   *

That had been yesterday. Now it was all over. She had
found the building—the baby was registered. A thought
came to her like the climbing of a mountain, steep and
harsh. What now? What now? She caught the stare of a
woman waiting for the clerk. Then Trini noticed the
clerk's eyes on the baby. The man was clasping his hands,
then unclasping them, then tapping his fingers on the
counter as if he were deciding to call the authorities.

Wan and pale, Trini drew the baby closely to her and
made her way to the door marked "Vital Statistics." Her
hands were trembling out of weakness and fear. The
baby began to cry as Trini made her way out of the
building, shouldering her way through people, avoiding
eyes. She was a curious sight, a muddied, barefoot
woman with wild hair and feverish eyes, holding a baby,
running for dear life. She ran along the streets that took
her away from tall buildings, from uniforms, from American people. She was going south again. Her mouth felt
dry and raw, and the towel the baby was wrapped in was
soaking wet. Oh, my baby, I have to change you, feed
you, her heart cried. But still, she ran until she could
run no more, standing against the wall of a building to
catch her breath, avoiding the curious stares of people.
Before her was a street sign. The words were distended
images, visions of hope: "Santa Fe."

Holy Faith! The name of the street was Holy Faith!
An omen—a guiding force—a new decision. The hope
was as feverish as her body. She would follow the street
to its very end. She started on her way again, feet heavy,
body numb, the baby now crying lustily in her arms.
People had been left behind. Only one man passed her,
unconcerned. Before her was a railroad yard, across the
street a bar, beyond that an old familiar bridge, El
Puente Negro! Strange, the circle of her life. The end of
Santa Fe had brought her to a dead end. She did not
want to cross the bridge. She did not want to go back.
She had to find a place nearby to rest, to look after the
baby's needs.

Behind a warehouse was a lumberyard fenced off with
sagging, rusty wire. She made her way through one section where the fence had sagged to the ground, her feet
stepping over a desiccated piece of lumber, half-buried

in dry mud. She sat down against the wall of the building and hushed her baby with soft tones of love. The baby had to be changed. She raised her skirt and jerked at the cotton slip underneath. It did not give. The baby lay on the ground crying harder. She pulled at a shoulder strap, tearing it, repeating the process until both straps gave. She pulled the garment from the knees, stepped out of it, then tore it in pieces to make a diaper. With quick fingers she unpinned the wet towel, flinging it over a pile of lumber. Afterwards she placed the dry pieces of cloth on the ground and lifted the baby onto them. He was whimpering in tired, spasmodic little sobs. Her breasts were hard and sore in their fullness. Now she rested against the building, picked up the baby and turning him tenderly toward her. The nipple touched his lips. He took it eagerly, drops of milk forming on the sides of his little mouth. Then she dozed with the baby at her breast.

After a while she awoke with a start, aware of the greyness of the day. She sat quite still, the baby fast asleep. Her arms felt cramped and stiff, so she laid the child low on her lap and stretched out her legs.

Through half-closed lids she saw El Puente Negro at a great distance, like a blot against the greyness of the day. Her mind was a greyness too, things not yet clear or distinct. Thoughts ran: a world in circles, a black bridge standing, pulling through a dark hole, Santa Fe—faith, faith and the burning of a fire, a plan. Perhaps it was all useless, this trying. She felt as if she were a blot lost in space. All she wanted was a chance, a way to stay in the United States, to find a piece of land, to have a family.

It had taken her friend Celestina fifteen years to buy a thirsty, ungiving piece of land in Mexico—fifteen years! No, there was a better way in the United States where the poor and hungry did not have to stay poor and hungry. Something had pulled her to this country of miracles. It was all still shapeless, meaningless, beyond her. But things would take shape. She would give them shape. A blot in space was the beginning of many things in all directions. She looked down at the sleeping child, her son, Rico.

Village

Rico stood on top of a bluff overlooking Mai Cao. The whole of the wide horizon was immersed in a rosy haze. His platoon was returning from an all-night patrol. They had scoured the area in a radius of thirty-two miles, following the length of the canal system along the Delta, furtively on the lookout for an enemy attack. On their way back, they had stopped to rest, smoke, drink warm beer after parking the carry-alls along the edge of the climb leading to the top of the bluff. The hill was good cover, seemingly safe.

Harry was behind him on the rocky slope. Then, the sound of thunder overhead. It wasn't thunder, but a squadron of their own helicopters on the usual run. Rico and Harry sat down to watch the planes go by. After that, a stillness, a special kind of silence. Rico knew it well, the same kind of stillness that was a part of him back home, the kind of stillness that makes a man part of his world—river, clearing, sun, wind. The stillness of a village early in the morning—barrio stillness, the first stirrings of life that come with dawn. Harry was looking down at the village of Mai Cao.

"Makes me homesick . . ." Harry lighted a cigarette.

Rico was surprised. He thought Harry was a city dude. Chicago, no less. "I don't see no freeway or neon lights."

"I'm just sick of doing nothing in this goddamned war."

No action yet. But who wanted action? Rico had been transformed into a soldier, but he knew he was no soldier. He had been trained to kill the enemy in Vietnam. He watched the first curl of smoke coming out of one of the chimneys. They were the enemy down there. Rico didn't believe it. He would never believe it. Perhaps because there had been no confrontation with Viet Cong soldiers or village people. Harry flicked away his cigarette and started down the slope. He turned, waiting for Rico to follow him. "Coming?"

"I'll be down after a while."

"Suit yourself." Harry walked swiftly down the bluff, his feet carrying with them the dirt yieldings in a flurry of small pebbles and loose earth. Rico was relieved. He needed some time by himself, to think things out. But Harry was right. To come across an ocean just to do routine checks, to patrol ground where there was no real danger . . . it could get pretty shitty. The enemy was hundreds of miles away.

The enemy! He remembered the combat bible—kill or be killed. Down a man—the lethal lick: a garotte strangling is neater and more quiet than the slitting of a throat; grind your heel against a face to mash the brains. Stomp the ribcage to carve the heart with bone splinters. Kill . . .

Hey, who was kidding who? They almost made him believe it back at boot camp in the States. In fact, only a short while ago, only that morning he had crouched down along the growth following a mangrove swamp, fearing an unseen enemy, ready to kill. Only that morning. But now, looking down at the peaceful village with its small rice field, its scattered huts, something had struck deep, something beyond the logic of war and enemy, something deep in his guts.

He had been cautioned. The rows of thatched huts were not really peoples' homes, but "hootches," makeshift temporary stays built by the makeshift enemy. But then they were real enemies. There were too many dead Americans to prove it. The "hootches" didn't matter. The people didn't matter. These people knew how to pick up their sticks and go. Go where? Then how many of these villages had been bulldozed? Flattened by gunfire? Good pyre for napalm, these Vietnamese villages. A new kind of battleground.

Rico looked down and saw huts that were homes, clustered in an intimacy that he knew well. The village of Mai Cao was no different than Valverde, the barrio where he had grown up. A woman came out of a hut, walking straight and with a certain grace, a child on her shoulder. She was walking toward a stream east of the slope. She stopped along the path and looked up to say something to the child. It struck him again, the feeling— a bond—people all the same everywhere.

The same scent from the earth, the same warmth from

the sun, a woman walking with a child—his mother, Trini. His little mother who had left Tarahumara country and crossed the Barranca del Cobre, taking with her seeds from the hills of Batopilas, withstanding suffering, danger—for what? A dream—a piece of ground in the land of plenty, the United States of America. She had waded across the Rio Grande from Juárez, Mexico, to El Paso, Texas, when she felt the birth pangs of his coming. He had been born a citizen because his mother had had a dream. She had made the dream come true—an acre of riverland in Valverde on the edge of the border. His mother, like the earth and sun, mattered. The woman with the child on her shoulder mattered. Every human life in the village mattered. He knew this not only with the mind but with the heart.

Rico remembered a warning from combat training, from the weary, wounded soldiers who had fought and killed and survived, soldiers sent to Saigon, waiting to go home. His company had been flown to Saigon before being sent to the front. And this was the front, villages like Mai Cao. He felt relieved knowing that the fighting was hundreds of miles away from the people in Mai Cao—but the warning was still there:

Watch out for pregnant women with machine guns. Toothless old women are experts with the knife between the shoulders. Begging children with hidden grenades, the unseen VC hiding in the hootches—village people were not people; they were the enemy. The woman who knew the child on her shoulder, who knew the path to her door, who knew the coming of the sun—she was the enemy.

It was a discord not to be believed by instinct or intuition. And Rico was an Indian, the son of a Tarahumara chieftain. Theirs was a world of instinct and intuitive decisions. Suddenly he heard the sounds of motors. He looked to the other side of the slope, down to the road where the carry-alls had started queuing their way back to the post. Rico ran down the hill to join his company.

In his dream, Sergeant Keever was shouting, "Heller, heller . . ." Rico woke with a start. It wasn't a dream. The men around him were scrambling out of the pup tent. Outside most of the men were lining up in uneven formation. Rico saw a communiqué in the sergeant's hand. Next to Keever was a lieutenant from communications headquarters. Keever was reading the communiqué:

"Special mission 72 . . . for Company C, platoon 2, assigned at 22 hours. Move into the village of Mai Cao, field manual description—hill 72. Destroy the village."

No! It was crazy. Why? Just words on a piece of paper. Keever had to tell him why. There had to be a reason. Had the enemy come this far? It was impossible. Only that morning he had stood on the slope. He caught up with Keever, blurting out, "Why? I mean—why must we destroy it?"

Sergeant Keever stopped in his tracks and turned steel-blue eyes at Rico. "What you say?"

"Why?"

"You just follow orders, savvy?"

"Are the Viet Cong . . ."

"Did you hear me? You want trouble, private?"

"There's people . . ."

"I don't believe you, soldier. But OK. Tell you as much as I know. We gotta erase the village in case the Viet Cong come this way. That way they won't use it as a stronghold. Now move your ass . . ."

Keever walked away from him, his lips tight in some kind of disgust. Rico did not follow this time. He went to get his gear and join the men in one of the carry-alls. Three carry-alls for the assault—three carry-alls moving up the same road. Rico felt the weight and hardness of his carbine. Now it had a strange, hideous meaning. The machine guns were some kind of nightmare. The mission was to kill and burn and erase all memories. Rico swallowed a guilt that rose from the marrow—with it, all kinds of fear. He had to do something, something to stop it, but he didn't know what. And with all these feelings, a certain reluctance to do anything but follow orders. In the darkness, his lips formed words from the anthem, "My country, 'tis of thee . . ."

They came to the point where the treelines straggled between two hills that rose darkly against the moon. Rico wondered if all the men were of one mind—one mind to kill . . . Was he a coward? No! It was not killing the enemy that his whole being was rejecting, but firing machine guns into a village of sleeping people . . . people. Rico remembered only the week before, returning from their usual patrol, the men from the company had stopped at the stream, mingling with the children, old men, and women of the village. There had been an innocence about the whole thing. His voice broke the silence in the carry-all, a voice harsh and feverish. "We can get the people out of there. Help them evacuate . . ."

"Shut up." Harry voice was tight, impatient.

The carry-alls traveled through tall, undulant grass following the dirt road that led to the edge of the bluff. It was not all tall grass. Once in a while trees appeared again, clumped around scrub bushes. Ten miles out the carry-alls stopped. It was still a mile's walk to the bluff in the darkness, but they had to avoid detection. Sergeant Keever was leading the party. Rico, almost at the rear, knew he had to catch up to him. He had to stop him. Harry was ahead of him, a silent black bundle walking stealthily through rutted ground to discharge his duty. For a second, Rico hesitated. That was the easy thing to do—to carry out his duty—to die a hero, to do his duty blindly and survive. Hell, why not? He knew what happened to men who backed down in battle. But he wasn't backing down. Hell, what else was it? How often had he heard it among the gringos in his company.

"You Mexican? Hey, you Mexicans are real fighters. I mean, everybody knows Mexicans have guts . . ."

A myth perhaps. But no. He thought of the old guys who had fought in World War II. Many of them were on welfare back in the barrio. But, man! did they have metals! He had never seen so many purple hearts. He remembered old Toque, the wino, who had tried to pawn his metals to buy a bottle. No way, man. They weren't worth a nickle.

He quickly edged past Harry, pushing the men ahead of him to reach the sergeant. He was running, tall grass brushing his shoulder, tall grass that had swayed peacefully like wheat. The figure of Sergeant Keever was in front of him now. There was a sudden impulse to reach out and hold him back. But the sergeant had stopped. Rico did not touch him, but whispered hoarsely, desperately in the dark. "Let's get the people out—evacuate . . ."

"What the hell . . ." Keever's voice was ice. He recognized Rico, and hissed, "Get back to your position soldier or I'll shoot you myself."

Rico did as he was told, almost unaware of the men around him. But at a distance he heard something splashing in the water of the canal, in his nostrils the smell of sweet burnt wood. He looked toward the clearing and saw the cluster of huts bathed in moonlight. In the same moonlight, he saw Keever giving signals. In the gloom he saw the figures of the men carrying machine guns. They looked like dancing grasshoppers as they ran ahead to position themselves on the bluff. He felt like yelling, "For Christ's sake! Where is the enemy?"

The taste of blood in his mouth—he suddenly realized he had bitten his quivering lower lip. As soon as Sergeant Keever gave the signal, all sixteen men would open fire on the huts—machine guns, carbines—everything would be erased. No more Mai Cao—the execution of duty without question, without alternative. They were positioned on the south slope, Sergeant Keever up ahead, squatting on his heels, looking at his watch. He raised himself, after a quick glance at the men. As Sergeant Keever raised his hand to give the signal for attack, Rico felt the cold metallic deadness of his rifle. His hands began to tremble as he released the safety catch. Sergeant Keever was on the rise just above him. Rico stared at the sergeant's arm, raised, ready to fall—the signal to fire. The crossfire was inside Rico, a heavy-dosed tumult—destroy the village, erase all memory. There was ash in his mouth. Once the arm came down, there was no turning back.

In a split second, Rico turned his rifle at a forty-degree angle and fired at the sergeant's arm. Keever half-turned with the impact of the bullet, then fell to his knees. In a whooping whisper the old-time soldier blew out the words, "That fucking bastard—get him." he got up and signaled the platoon back to the carry-alls, as two men grabbed Rico, one hitting him on the side of the head with the butt of his rifle. Rico felt the sting of the blow, as they pinned his arm back and forced him to walk the path back to the carry-all. He did not resist. There was a lump in his throat, and he blinked back tears, tears of relief. The memory of the village would not be erased.

Someone shouted in the dark, "They're on to us. There's an old man with a lantern and others coming out of the hootches . . ."

"People—just people . . ." Rico whispered, wanting to shout it, wanting to tell them that he had done the right thing. But the heaviness that filled his senses was the weight of the truth. He was a traitor—a maniac. He had shot his superior in a battle crisis. He was being carried almost bodily back to the truck. He glanced at the thick brush along the road, thinking that somewhere beyond it was a rice field, and beyond that a mangrove swamp. There was a madman inside his soul that made him think of rice fields and mangrove swamps instead of what he had done. Not once did he look up. Everyone around him was strangely quiet and remote. Only the sound of trudging feet.

In the carry-all, the faces of the men sitting around Rico were indiscernible in the dark, but he imagined their eyes, wide, confused, peering through the dark at him with a wakefulness that questioned what he had done. Did they know his reason? Did they care? The truck suddenly lurched. Deep in the gut, Rico felt a growing fear. He choked back a hysteria rising from the diaphragm. The incessant bumping of the carry-alls as they moved unevenly on the dirt road accused him too. He looked up into a night sky and watched the moon eerily weave in and out of tree branches. The darkness was like his fear. It had no solutions.

Back on the post, Sergeant Keever and a medic passed by Rico, already handcuffed, without any sign of recognition. Sergeant Keever had already erased him from existence. The wheels of justice would take their course. Rico had been placed under arrest, temporarily shackled to a cot in one of the tents. Three days later he was moved to a makeshift bamboo hut, with a guard in front of the hut at all times. His buddies brought in food like strangers, awkward in their silence, anxious to leave him alone. He felt like some kind of poisonous bug. Only Harry came by to see him after a week.

"You dumb ass, were you on loco weed?" Harry asked in disgust.

"I didn't want people killed, that's all."

"Hell, that's no reason, those chinks aren't even— even . . ."

"Even what?" Rico demanded. He almost screamed it a second time. "Even what?"

"Take it easy, will you? You better go for a Section eight." Harry was putting him aside like every one else. "They're sending you back to the States next week. You'll have to face Keever sometime this afternoon. I thought I'd better let you know."

"Thanks." Rico knew the hopelessness of it all. There was still that nagging question he had to ask. "Listen, nobody tells me anything. Did you all go back to Mai Cao? I mean, is it still there?"

"Still there. Orders from headquarters to forget it. The enemy were spotted taking an opposite direction. But nobody's going to call you a hero, you understand? What you did was crud. You're no soldier. You'll never be a soldier."

Rico said nothing to defend himself. He began to scratch the area around the steel rings on his ankles. Harry was scowling at him. He said it again, almost shouting, "I said, you'll never be a soldier."

"So?" There was soft disdain in Rico's voice.

"You blew it, man. You'll be locked up for a long, long time."

"Maybe . . ." Rico's voice was without concern.

"Don't you care?"

"I'm free inside, Harry." Rico laughed in relief. "Free . . ."

Harry shrugged, peering at Rico unbelievingly, then turned and walked out of the hut.

LIONEL G. GARCÍA

❦ ❦ ❦

Lionel G. García was born in 1935 in San Diego, a ranching and farming community in South Texas. He grew up in an extended family which included parents, brothers, sister, grandparents, aunts, uncles, and great numbers of cousins. His grandmother's house, he recalls, was "a constant refuge for many a character. Parientes arrimados, *they are called in Spanish. All manner of people from all walks of life, but mostly the down and out. And many of them have wandered back again into my fiction." His first stories were published in his high school paper, and he continued to publish stories in the literary magazines at Texas A and M University, where he earned his BA. García received a doctorate in veterinary medicine from A and M in 1965 and stayed on to teach veterinary anatomy, all the while continuing to write, and publishing two stories in* Latitudes. *In 1968, he left teaching to enter private veterinary practice. He currently lives in Seabrook, Texas, on Galveston Bay where he is a dedicated veterinarian by day, and a dedicated writer at night. In 1983, García was awarded the P.E.N. Southwest Prize for his novel-in-progress,* Leaving Home, *which was published by Arte Publico Press in 1985. García's other published works include* A Shroud in the Family *(1987) and* Hardscrub *(1990) which in 1991, was named the novel of the year by The Texas Institute of Letters. His stories have appeared in numerous journals, including* Americas Review, *and in the anthologies* Cuentos Chicanos *and* New Growth.

The Apparition

Father Procopio jiggled his eyebrows once more, a sure sign that he had changed images in his mind, gone from the infamous brown and white apparition that he had been seeing every morning for the last week against the church wall, gone to the many-colored picture of his mother coming at him with his father's belt, her hand raised in passion, ready to strike him anywhere on the head. Father Procopio, aware that his mother was about to hit him, jumped from his bed in the morning heat, feeling his stupor melting, and fell on his knees on the floor next to his wrinkled shoes. He reached over and gathered his pants from the chair next to his bed and brought along with his pants the frayed white shirt that rested on top. In the solitude of the darkness of his room he instinctively took out from his pants' pocket his miniature rosary and begin to pray as he stayed on his knees and attempted with difficulty to put his clothes on before the nosey Pimena entered the room with his coffee. He looked at the clock on the dresser and saw five o'clock in the morning. The old rooster had not yet crowed. The mosquito that had bothered him all night long rested, his rear-end upright, next to his pillow. He took the rosary and swatted at it in anger and it flew away unharmed, disappearing from his focus right in front of his very eyes. He followed the sound as the mosquito droned his way up toward the rafters of his room to hide for the day. Father Procopio felt of his body where the insect had taken enough of his blood during the night to last for a week. Outside the door he could hear the housekeeper, Pimena, picking up the tufts of hair that the cats had deposited in the hallway during the day. He could smell the cup of coffee in her hand.

"Cats, cats, cats," he could hear her complain as she swept cat hair from the floor of the hallway with her hand. "First it was collecting bottles and then cats and then collecting fleas from the cats and putting them in bottles and now we are into bedbugs and putting the bedbugs in little tin boxes. When he doesn't collect one thing he collects another. He reminds me of the raccoon. The next thing we know he'll be washing his food at the table before he eats it. It's a good thing the Bishop is coming to see about the apparition. When the Bishop sees the rectory he's going to make the good Father consent to clean it up. And I need extra help. The Bishop will see that. I've been working on cleaning the attic for the last two weeks. A lot of good it does to clean only the attic. There were more bottles and bottles with fleas and little tin boxes with bedbugs and cat hairs than any human would believe."

Having heard her, Father Procopio crossed himself twice with the small bronze crucifix and said a minuscule prayer for Pimena, a prayer to make her mind her own business. Before Pimena could knock, Father Procopio gauged the motion of her actions, imagining through the wooden door as the elderly lady raised her hand to knock. "Enter, by all means," he said as Pimena held her hand in check.

"This man knows everything," she said, filled with mystery, as she opened the door, walking stooped from having had to clean the house of the cat hairs for three years.

"How are you this morning, Pimena?" the good Priest asked her.

"Fine, Father," Pimena responded. "How long have you been praying?"

"Just now," Father Procopio said, adjusting the sleeves of his long shirt. "I have just now started."

"By the time you finish, the coffee will be just right," Pimena said, wiping the table top of cat hairs and placing the coffee next to the clock. "And don't forget to say a little prayer for me. And for my back and for all the work I had to do in the attic."

"I already did," Father Procopio told her. He moved his weight from one knee to the other, rocking from one side to the other. "I think that I'm getting too old to do this anymore," he informed Pimena. "Maybe God will forgive me, if I pray sitting down."

"You know very well the Bishop has written that it takes ten prayers sitting down to equal one kneeling down," Pimena reminded him.

Of course he knew, goddammit, irritated that the ignorant Pimena presumed to remember better than he. Had it not been he that had read the Bishop's letter to the congregation, the ten-page letter that explained in detail how one should pray not only the prayer itself but how one must chose the proper stance, the proper lighting to aid in the comfort of the task? "The light must fall over the left shoulder," the Bishop had written. His mind was suddenly distracted at how irritatingly ignorant the Bishop was. These people were doing good to come to church and sit down, much less be preoccupied with the light coming over the left shoulder. "If one knows how to read, the holy book should be at least eighteen inches from the front of the eyes. Any shorter distance will tire out the vision. One must remember that the idea behind prayer is that one must be comfortable not only with the written word but in God's presence. However, too much comfort can impede prayer. Here I am referring to the practice that some people have of praying sitting down. This is well and good and our Father recognizes such prayers. However, it is my contention that prayers recited while kneeling are found more receptive by our Father. If someone would ask me for exact figures I would be hard pressed to answer, but taking a wild guess I would venture to say that our Father considers a prayer offered kneeling down to be ten times more effective than one sitting down."

"How is it outside?" he asked, nervously skipping over from the first to the last mystery of his tedious rosary.

"There are only a few out there," Pimena answered as she went to look out the window at the churchyard below. "The true believers. But it's very early. Wait and see at eight o'clock when the sun has been out a few hours."

"Of all churches . . . that it would have to happen to this one. The one with the most lunatics," he said as he sat on the bed to put on his shoes.

"The Ladies of the Altar Society will begin selling snow cones today. I saw Olivia and Sixta trying to buy ice yesterday," Pimena told him.

Father Procopio jiggled his eyebrows and changed mental gears. He was now seeing the Altar Society reserving ice for today, the large Olivia, her gold medal-

lion swinging from breast to breast as she led the group
of four women through the dusty streets of San Diego.
Not only were they looking for ice, they were in search
of volunteers, someone to patrol the churchyard now that
the Mother Superior and her three nuns had gone on
vacation for the summer.

"If only the Mother Superior was here," Pimena
lamented, knowing well that she was irritating the Priest
and that all his morning prayers would be canceled on
their way to Heaven by Father Procopio's anger.

"Don't even say that," Father Procopio replied as he
stood up, gritting his teeth. He jammed his rosary into
his pants' pocket. It would be blasphemous to continue
praying.

"And your rosary?" Pimena asked as she picked cat
hairs from her arms.

"I'll just have to pray it later on," the harried Priest
informed her.

"You'd better do it before sunup because you know
how many people will be in the courtyard today. Word
of the apparition has reached all of South Texas. Every
day more and more come."

Father Procopio adjusted his suspenders over his
shoulders and took a sip of coffee. "I know," he murmured to himself.

"Father?"

"Yes, Pimena."

"Well, I don't know whether to ask you or not. Maybe
you've already thought about it and have rejected the
idea."

"What are you talking about?"

"Some of the people in my poor neighborhood have
been asking me to ask you. But it's up to you and the
Mutualists. Whatever you say goes. You know that,
don't you, good Father."

Father Procopio looked at her with much hate. She
had ruined his rosary. He was tired of hearing her complain about his cats. She was not keeping the rectory
clean. It was not he, it was she, Pimena, that was dirty.
Twenty cats was not too much for one household, not
one where there was almost nothing to do except to move
dust around.

Father Procopio whistled softly and this time the noise

of nineteen cats was heard as they ran down the stairs in anticipation of the morning's blessing and the milk that he would give them. Only the faithful Princess, his most favorite cat, the one that had come to him one night as he walked and prayed for his soul, stayed behind. Father Procopio realized what a prize she was. Any cat that would prefer him to milk and blessings in the morning had to be special.

Princess walked into Father Procopio's room very deliberately, seductively, her back arched, and went over to the legs of the dresser and rubbed her body around the them. She meowed twice and went over to Father Procopio to be stroked and kissed on the top of the head.

"Now what were you saying, Pimena?" Father Procopio asked her as he continued to stroke and love Princess.

"I was just talking, good Father," Pimena replied, embarrassed as usual at seeing Father Procopio show so much love to an animal.

"What were you going to ask?" Father Procopio wanted to know as he stroked his beloved cat.

"I was saying about you and the Mutualists. And how whatever you say goes."

"I know that what I say goes, Pimena. I wish to God that you would understand that I know that. I know everything, Pimena. As far as you are concerned, I know everything."

"That is exactly what I tell everyone in town, good Father. That you know everything. You even know when I'm about to knock on the door, as though you could see through wood."

Father Procopio put the cat down and finished his coffee in one large swallow. He smacked his lips, felt Princess's cat hair sliding down his throat, and said, "I can see through wood. And I know how to anticipate. I know everything that is going on about me."

"And the apparition? How do you explain that, Father Procopio?" Pimena teased the good Father.

Father Procopio buttoned the top of his shirt and made a grunting sound as though he was thinking about picking up something with which to hit the woman. Princess ran out of the room when she heard the unfamiliar grunt. Pimena stepped back indecisively, but with much respect.

She knew how frustrated he was in trying to explain the apparition. Instead of venting his anger on her he lit a cigarette and pointed the match at her. "I tell you, Pimena, that that is the only thing that has ever baffled me in my life."

"It is religion," Pimena said innocently, surprised that the Father had not at the very least burned her with his cigarette as he did the Altar Boys. "Only God knows those things. I myself thank God for making me ignorant, if you must know. I wouldn't know what to do if I was in the Altar Society. So much knowledge. It would break my head."

"Not necessarily," Father Procopio corrected her. "There really isn't that much knowledge to go around," he said.

"But religion," Pimena worried, "look at all that there is to it. Look at this apparition of our Blessed Mother that has taken over the wall of the church. How do we account for that?"

"I'll find out," Father Procopio informed her. "Religion is more of a science than you ignorant people think," he said.

"I've always said to the neighborhood and everyone that will listen that you know everything, Father Procopio."

"Oh, that it were true," the good Priest had to admit now that he was in control of his frustrations and at the present forgiving Pimena for destroying his morning prayer.

Pimena scraped cat hair from her tongue and cleaned her wet finger on her apron. "And the people that ask me about the Wheel of Fortune . . . well, I say to them, 'Let the good Father worry about that. Maybe he's thought of that already and has dismissed the idea.' 'It would make money,' some say. 'Now's the time to drag it out. There are many people making a pilgrimage to San Diego. What harm would it do?' 'No,' I say to them. 'Father Procopio in his own time will decide if the wheel should come out. Andres García is dead,' they say. They say, there is no opposition to the Wheel of Fortune."

Father Procopio had not listened to Pimena. He had been lost in his thoughts about the apparition. Pimena took the empty cup and saw the cat hairs that stuck to the bottom and shook her head. "The cats will be the ruination of this house one day," she said.

Father Procopio took a huge drag from his cigarette and blew smoke at Pimena. "Just leave the cats alone," he said. "They are my life. I could not live without them and you know that."

"Well, Father, that was what you said about the bottles and now look at where they're at . . . hidden in the attic behind the boxes. Abandoned and dusty with no one to look over them. You haven't been to see them in over a year."

The Priest took in what he felt was the disgusting sight and smell of the old lady. "I tuck my cats to sleep every night. I go into the attic," he scolded her.

"But good Father, you never go to where the bottles are anymore," Pimena responded as she took the cup and tried to sweep cat hair from the tabletop. "You don't move them around or look at them like you did when you first started."

"I don't have to if I don't want to. The bottles are mine. Leave them alone. I don't want anyone touching them."

"Have no fear, Father. I didn't touch any of your precious bottles."

"Good," Father Procopio said, "I don't want anyone touching them except me."

"And the fleas and the bedbugs, good Father?" Pimena asked him.

"The fleas and the bedbugs are mine also. I have a reason for saving them."

"Whatever you say, good Father," Pimena agreed with him. "Like I always say. 'Father Procopio is a lot smarter than he looks.' "

Father Procopio looked through the rafters, past the mosquito, to the heavens and whispered, "Dear God what have I done to deserve this—the Bishop, Pimena, San Diego, and now the apparition. I wonder if the Baptists need a Catholic priest?"

"What did you say?" Pimena asked.

"Nothing," Father Procopio answered her brusquely.

"I thought I heard you speak."

"You need to clean your ears, Pimena."

"Yes, good Father. Like I cleaned the attic for the cats and the Bishop's beast."

"Yes," Father Procopio said bitterly, "the Bishop's beast. Did you make a bed for him?"

"Yes, good Father," Pimena said hurriedly, "I cleaned up real good right where he's going to sleep. I arranged a feather pillow for him just as you asked."

"Not as I asked," Father Procopio reminded her, "as the Bishop demanded."

"And the cats, good Father?" Pimena worried. "Will they do fine sleeping with the beast?"

The Priest looked out the window at the faint outline that was beginning to take shape on the church wall. He said, "The cats will do fine. They've done it before ... slept with the beast, I mean. And besides, the attic is their home. I'm not going to move them just because of the Bishop's beast. And that is that. Bishop or no Bishop."

"I understand, good Father. But don't be so angry just because the Bishop is coming."

"It's not the Bishop. You make me angry. You think you'd know by now that the cats are not to be moved for any reason at all. And especially not for the Bishop's beast."

Pimena looked at the Priest with some distress. She said, "You never know, good Father. I just wondered if the cats and the horrible beast would get along, it's been so long."

"I'll worry about that, Pimena," said the Priest. "You're beginning to make me angry so you'd better leave."

Pimena started to bow and walk backward toward the door when she said, "Don't get so upset about the Bishop. You shouldn't hate him so much. Please don't argue with the Bishop. We would like to keep you as our Priest. You know how violent the Bishop can become."

"Just leave me alone, Pimena. Please," he pleaded. "Just leave me alone with my cats."

"Here," Pimena said, "I almost forgot." She had reached into her apron and pulled out a small glass jar. Father Procopio knew instantly what it was. "This came for you this morning from the crazy Bernabe."

Father Procopio's eyes danced as he counted the tiny bedbugs inside the jar. "Fifteen," he whispered.

"That's all he could find last night, he said," Pimena explained.

Father Procopio sighed and said, "Well, along with the other ones that I have in the attic that ought to be enough."

"It's a mystery to me, but whatever you say, good Father," Pimena told him. She picked cat hairs from the sleeves of her blouse and held them at the tip of her fingers before shaking them to the floor. "But Father, look at this. The whole house is covered with cat hairs. It will ruin our health someday. It can't be normal to live with twenty cats."

Father Procopio puffed on his cigarette and flipped the ashes on the table. He grunted again in anticipation of his thoughts, scaring Pimena. "Just leave my cats alone," he said with so much conviction that Pimena backed out of the room using the empty cup of coffee as a shield. And as she did so, she stepped on Princess, who had been waiting for Father Procopio in the hallway by the door.

"Watch what you're doing!" the good Father shouted at the old woman as she ran down the hallway, flew down the stairway to the first floor, and cried her way into the kitchen.

She screamed from the kitchen as she ran, scattering the other cats waiting for their milk: "Forgive me, Father. I didn't mean to step on your precious cat."

"It is Princess that has to forgive you," Father Procopio yelled down at her from the top of the stairs. "Look at the poor cat. Afraid of being hurt again. Ready to go hide in the attic. Come Princess, my beauty, we must have our morning's blessing and our milk. Pimena is mean, don't you think? I won't let her touch you again. I promise."

Pimena was right. By eight in the morning, when the sun had cleared the tops of the salt cedars that surrounded the rectory, the apparition was perfectly formed on the church wall and with the apparition came the people, some with large medallions in the shape of body parts, others with the less expensive body parts made of small tin pieces, others with photographs of loved ones in need of medical help or long-ago dead. Some came from the front gate of the rectory on their knees to touch the wall.

Father Procopio looked out through the window of his small downstairs office at the crowd, at the abhorrent spectacle, and crossed himself. He thought for a moment and then looked at his watch. He got out of his office and went into the kitchen and looked for Pimena and then through the window he saw her standing outside talking to Carmen, the youngest of the Ladies of the Altar Society. Pimena was crunching on a yellow snow cone, which meant to Father Procopio that she had been recruited by the Ladies of the Altar Society as a volunteer to keep order on the church grounds.

He hurried up the stairs and the cats ran with him. He flung open the attic door and there on the floor by the window was the feather pillow that Pimena had fluffed for the Bishop's beast. Trembling, he opened four jars of fleas and poured the little insects into the pillow as the cats, licking themselves, watched in fascination. He took four tin boxes full of bedbugs plus the glass jar that Pimena had given him and ran out of the attic to the room across the hall where the Bishop was to stay. Quickly, he threw off the sheets and scattered the starved bedbugs on the mattress.

He went back to his office, looked out to see Pimena still munching on her yellow snow cone leaning against the ice box and probably telling everyone how smart Father Procopio really was. He put on his coat and walked out the rear door in order not to be seen. Still a few old ladies saw him and stopped him to bless their rosaries and the images of body parts. He waved his hand over the icons that they dangled in front of him, whispering the sign of the cross in Latin as the ladies offered him money, money that he turned down.

From the rear gate he could see Pimena now helping the four women of the Altar Society as they erected their tent under which they would sell their snow cones. He tried not to look at them to see if by God's good grace they would not see him. He opened the gate hurriedly, walked out into the street, and closed the gate behind him. As he did so, he turned up the street to walk to the depot and saw the Fat Amandito, Don Andres García's dog walking next to him. Amandito, upon seeing the Priest, ran over to the fence that Father Procopio was crowding. As Amandito approached him Father Procopio said, "I don't have time to talk this morning. I'm on my way to meet the train and the Bishop."

"Heaven help us then," Amandito prayed as he made the sign of the cross and then kissed his thumb. "I just now got through telling my dog that this would not be a good day for you Father Procopio."

"That's presumptuous of you, Amandito, don't you think?" the Priest scolded him as he hurried on his way.

"Whatever that means, good Father," Amandito replied.

"Presumptuous, Amandito. To think that you know what will happen to me. I didn't know you could tell fortunes. The next thing we know you'll be joining the Ladies of the Altar Society and start explaining Catholicism to the old ladies."

Amandito kept up with the Priest stride for stride. "All I know is what I feel," he informed the Priest.

"Just be quiet," Father Procopio suggested. "Don't say a word. You're starting to irritate me."

Amandito, ignoring the Priest, let out a sigh as his inherited dog cut out in front of him. "This dog will be the death of me," he said, changing the conversation. "You just watch, good Father, one day they will find me dead in the street. I will have tripped over the dog and hit my head on a rock and killed myself."

"I don't have time to talk about your dog. I've already told you that I'm on my way to meet the Bishop."

"That must be hard on you, Father Procopio, as much as you hate the man."

"I don't hate the man, Amandito. Where did you get that idea?" he asked, thinking of the bedbugs.

"Oh, there is the talk about town. You know how everyone knows everything. And I myself can tell you hold no love for the man."

"We don't agree on some aspects of religion, if that's what you mean," Father Procopio informed Amandito. Feeling guilty, he quickened his pace to see if Amandito would stay behind.

"If you don't mind, good Father, I'll accompany you as far as the barber shop."

"Suit yourself, Amandito," Father Procopio said as he wiped the hair of twenty cats from his coat. "After all, this is a public street."

"It must be hard on you not to agree with the Bishop on religion," Amandito kept on.

"It's none of your business, Amandito," Father Procopio let him know. "Whenever you start going to church, then you can make it your business."

"Anyway, it's not good for the Bishop and the Priest not to agree on religion," Amandito told the Priest as the dog bounced in front of him and almost tripped him again. "Goddamn dog," he muttered so that the Priest was sure to hear.

"Don't curse in front of me, Amandito," Father Procopio warned him.

"I'm sorry Father," Amandito said remorsefully, "but this dog will be the death of me."

Father Procopio studied the dog's rear and said, "You haven't castrated him like Don Andres asked you on his deathbed."

"How could I?" Amandito pleaded. "You know that the doctor won't allow the dog in his office."

The dog weaved his way between Father Procopio's legs and made the Priest stumble. "See what I mean, good Father?" Amandito said. "The dog is constantly between ones's legs or in front of one or behind one. He's always in the way. Always in some mischief. Just like the poor late Don Andres."

"You could take him to the veterinarian in Alice," Father Procopio said, jumping over the dog.

"But that would cost more than the doctor," Amandito informed him.

"Well, suit yourself," Father Procopio said. "I just don't like him hanging around my doorsteps."

"I knew it!" Amandito cried. "I knew he was over at your house when he disappears."

"Just don't let him bother my cats," the Priest threatened him.

"I won't, Father," Amandito promised, feeling guilty for owning the dog.

The dog weaved his way around Amandito's legs and then came from behind and smelled Amandito's rear end and then started to sneeze and couldn't stop, embarrassing Amandito. The Priest had seen what the dog had done but was content to ignore the indelicacy, hoping that ignoring the dog would spare him the act that the dog had performed on Amandito. But the dog was smarter than to be ignored and he knew instinctively that the ultimate embarrassment was to embarrass a Priest. So he quit sneezing and went over to the Priest and, almost tripping him, smelled his crotch and acted as though he were gagging.

Amandito adjusted his pants and retucked his shirt all around his waist as the dog went over to the fence and spit up a white froth. "What about the apparition, good Father? What is the meaning of such an important event? And in San Diego no less."

"I don't know," the good Father replied, trying to ignore what the dog was doing.

"Is it a good sign or a bad sign to have an apparition?"

"It depends on how it came about."

"Like what do you mean?"

"Well, is it a true apparition or is it false?"

"What if it's false?"

"Then we must expose it for what it is," Father Procopio said. "Contrary to what you ignorant people believe, religion is based on the truth. And the truth never hurt anyone."

"What will happen then, if the people find out the truth?"

"Nothing. They'll accept it for what it is."

"Is this where you and the Bishop do not agree, Father?" Amandito asked as his dog came running to get in front of him.

"I suppose so, Amandito," Father Procopio said, jiggling his eyebrows and ducking out of the way as once more his mother swung the leather belt at his head.

Amandito stepped on the dog's foot and the dog gave out a shrill but short yelp. Despite the pain that made him limp, the dog refused to give ground, continuing to swing back and forth on three legs in front of the two men.

"Your dog, Amandito," Father Procopio concluded, admonishing the owner rather than the beast, "is very obtrusive."

"I'm sure you're right, good Father," Amandito agreed,

looking down at the many-colored dog. "Whatever the word means."

Amandito and his limping dog stayed at the barber shop where the pair was greeted by the ne'er-do-wells that inhabited the town in great numbers. Father Procopio heard the screams run out of the small building as the men greeted Amandito and his dog. One of the men, who had never worked a day in his life, came out and shouted at Father Procopio that the train had not come in. Father Procopio, not knowing whether the drunk was lying or not, ignored the drunkard and kept on, not wanting to be made a fool.

As the Priest continued to the depot in the early heat of the day, he felt the morning sun against his black frock. He felt of the hot frock and without realizing it he brushed away at the cat hairs on his sleeves as he wondered if he had used enough bedbugs on the Bishop's bed.

On his way he could not remember whether he had heard the train whistle or not. When he arrived at the depot he found Don Tomas sitting quietly by himself on the bench, his wife having brought him over early in the morning so that he could talk to any passenger that might have the misfortune to have to wait for the train.

The drunkard at the barber shop had been right. The train had not arrived. If it had, the Bishop would have been there hugging his yapping beast and Don Tomas would surely have gotten hold of him by now. He cursed to himself so that God would not hear him, cursed that he had to find out for himself because the drunkards in this town were not to be trusted. In any other town, he assured himself, he woule have turned back at the barber shop and saved himself the trip.

Just for that he would not take out the Wheel of Fortune.

He knew better than to let Don Tomas get started in conversation. He turned and ran out of the depot as soon as he saw the man, not giving Don Tomas a chance to get started on the diatribes on snakes breeding like dogs and possums fornicating through the nose and coyotes defecating on their offspring and the pee of the spider. He had heard all of this dirty talk before when he had had to kick Don Tomas out of the Mutualists. He couldn't take Don Tomas any more than he could take the apparition, Amandito's dog, the Bishop, the Bishop's beast, Pimena, Amandito, Bernabe, Fecundo, Faustino, and the Ladies of the Altar Society and their large gold medallions.

Father Procopio heard a slight sound, like a "Hey, Father," from Don Tomas as he ran away from the depot.

He returned to the rectory taking a different route, not by way of the barber shop where the drunkards would laugh at him, but by way of the park and the kiosk where Andres García had been flogged.

From the park across the street he could see the mass of people already invading the churchyard. He could hear the Ladies of the Altar Society lining up the people that wanted to buy snow cones. Pimena was at the front gate letting people in one by one, crunching the ice of a red snow cone. He crossed the street and went around the church, through the rear, around the parochial hall where he kept the Wheel of Fortune, and from there he ran to the rear door of the rectory. Fortunately for him no one saw him except for Amandito's dog, who had mysteriously beat him back to the rectory and was lying at the doorsteps.

From the upstairs window he could see the image he had been observing for the past mornings: A very slight resemblance of the Virgin Mary projected on the wall during the early morning hours when the sun cleared the tops of the salt cedars that surrounded the rectory. One had to catch it before eleven o'clock at the latest. By that hour it would have moved and faded and disappeared.

Faustino, the drunkard, and Bernabe, the crazy one, had discovered it as they weaved their way home one morning. They had shown it to Pimena as she watered the salt cedars. To show it to Pimena had been the equivalent of showing it to the world. By the end of that day everyone in town knew about it. By the second day the surrounding communities knew about it. By the third day the newspapers from Alice and Corpus Christi knew about it and had sent reporters. By the fourth day the Bishop, sitting in the Bishopric in Corpus Christi having breakfast, had read the Corpus Christi newspaper. An hour later he had sent a telegram to Father Procopio inviting himself over to see for himself what the apparition looked like, since the paper's photograph did not show anything and had to be doctored in order for the reader to see what the photographer had seen. And naturally, the Bishop and his beloved beast expected to stay with Father Procopio for a few days.

Father Procopio heard the train whistle as he jiggled his eyebrows and studied the figure intently. It fascinated him to see the downward movement that accompanied the apparition. Gradually he could see it work its way down so that by his watch, at eleven o'clock when the sun was almost overhead, the figure would disappear into the church ground and the faithful people would leave. The jiggling of his eyebrows turned his thoughts to his abandoned bottles and without bothering the lounging Princess and the other nineteen cats he went into the attic and worked his way through the twenty cat boxes, the cat hair, and the feather pillow full of fleas that he had prepared for the Bishop's beast. He stepped over cartons of files—death certificates, birth certificates, church documents, marriage licenses—all from years and years ago. Not being able to climb over the wall of boxes he began to move some of them out of his way in order to clear a path to the bottles.

Opening the path was a revelation. Pimena had lied. She had cleaned the bottles and had rearranged them differently, stacking most of them on the floor in rows of fours and fives, lining some of them on the windowsill. Father Procopio cursed under his breath, raked cat hair from his tongue with his fingers, and wiped the fingers on his thigh. He noticed the beam of light cutting across the room and looked to his left at the source. The sunlight, broad beamed, was coming into the room through the window on his left, crossing through the row of bottles, emerging as a converted thin beam across the room into the row of bottles on the opposite window, the one on the Priest's right. Cautiously, Father Procopio approached the beam of light. Without touching it or disturbing it in any way he studied the intensely bright beam as it crossed in front of him from the left window to the right. He ducked under the beam and studied it from the opposite side and then he jiggled his eyebrows twice. Very carefully he went over to the right window and studied where the focused beam was entering one of the old hair-oil bottles that he had collected from the trash at the barber shop. After coursing through the glass, the beam was then directed downward and out over the churchyard and like a lover sitting in the balcony of a cheap theater he could see the white-hot fan of light piercing the air to create the projected image on the movie screen—the church wall.

In order to satisfy himself, Father Procopio very gently placed the fingers of his right hand over the top of the hair-oil bottle and without disturbing the path of the beam he rotated the bottle ever so slightly as he watched the image below. Immediately he heard the roar from the crowd.

The effect had been unpredictable. The rotation of the apparition was something that no one had seen before. People began to faint and mass hysteria took over. The crowd, urged on by the Ladies of the Altar Society and the few old Mutualists that could leave home on their own, began to back away from the moving apparition. Father Procopio, looking down and smiling, slowly turned the bottle in the opposite direction and everyone began to scream and run.

The Ladies of the Altar Society were shoving the crowd away, yelling for everyone to leave the churchyard before the church exploded. Their tent and the icebox with the shaved ice and the snow-cone syrup were knocked down by the running crowd. The wrought iron fence that Father Procopio loved, the one that had been brought over from the cemetery, was torn down by the weight of the people that were trying to scale it. Pimena, who had been standing by the gate eating another snow cone, had been the first to run and could be seen ahead of the pack running toward the center of town.

In a matter of seconds Father Procopio had cleared the churchyard except for the old intact dog that Don Andres García, on his death bed, had given Amandito.

Just for spite, Father Procopio turned the bottle slowly and then rapidly back and forth and made the image disappear and reappear on the church wall as the growling dog watched the visual spectacle with unusual interest.

Across from where he stood, through the front window of the attic, Father Procopio could see a man dressed in white walking in a crouched, intimidated way, carrying a suitcase, hugging tightly against his chest his beloved beast, the ugly Pug named La Poochie. It was the Bishop walking toward the church, wondering what all the commotion was about and what this congregation of humanity was doing running toward him. Father Procopio could see the Bishop tighten his hold on his dog as if to protect her, as if anyone would bother to steal a dog so ugly that she looked as though she had been sired by the Bishop himself. Nonetheless, La Poochie, not knowing that she was ugly, braced herself for the crowd that ran toward her and her master. As her heart quickened, she closed her eyes and prayed, expecting the worst. She felt the Bishop tighten his grip on her and she could hardly breathe through her short fat black nose. Then she felt the heaviness of his stride, her large head bobbing and weaving painfully, as the Bishop began to run. The crowd was screaming words that made no sense to her. When she finally opened her eyes the Bishop had stopped running and she recognized the front of the rectory, except that now the gate and the wrought iron fence had been torn down by some mysterious force. Out of the corner of her large globular right eye she saw Amandito's dog as it growled and moved its head first to one side and then to the other as Father Procopio played with the apparition on the wall. Instantly she recognized that this dog would cause her trouble during her stay, a stay that she had not wanted considering the condition of the Rectory every time she visited, knowing that she had to endure not only the twenty cats and their hair but the pillow full of fleas. (Oh yes, she knew that Father Procopio hated her as he did the Bishop and added fleas to her pillow and bedbugs to the Bishop's bed, but she had no way of relaying the information to the Bishop.)

By the time the Bishop reached the door, Father Procopio was there to open it.

"Where is Pimena?" the Bishop asked as he took La Poochie from inside his coat and placed her on the floor.

"You didn't see her?" Father Procopio asked the Bishop. "She was at the head of the crowd that greeted you."

"What was that all about?" the Bishop wanted to know. "Did it have to do with the apparition?"

"Yes," smiled the satisfied Father Procopio. "It had all to do with the apparition."

"Then you must tell me, Father. I am very excited about this apparition if you must know. It is the talk of all South Texas. On the train all I could hear was the people talking about it. The train was full, by the way."

"It's been full for the last days. People are coming from all over, Your Excellency," Father Procopio said. Then looking at the Bishop's dog he said, "But not for long. This thing is about to end."

"Hogwash," the Bishop informed him. "You're always having a defeatist attitude, Father Procopio. Look at this as a gold mine . . . and heaven-sent too. Remember that everything that happens is the Lord's will. Take it. Take the opportunity that the good Lord gives you, Father. I would think that the episode of the Wheel of Fortune would have cured you by now."

"Don't you think you ought to take La Poochie out to do her business?" Father Procopio asked the Bishop as the poor dog panted her desire to go relieve herself.

"You're so right, Procopio," the Bishop said, picking up La Poochie and taking her outside.

"Remember, Procopio," the Bishop spoke as he and Father Procopio watched as La Poochie tried to relieve herself in the churchyard, "that this is a golden opportunity for your church and our diocese."

"I'm afraid I don't agree," Father Procopio replied.

"What do you mean, you don't agree?" the Bishop demanded to know.

"I don't agree at all. Wait until you see what I've discovered, Your Excellency."

"What do you mean?"

"Your trip may have been for nothing. I have solved the mystery of the apparition."

"The mystery, Father?"

"Yes, Your Excellency."

"I don't want to know about it. I don't want to know. Father Procopio, keep the information to yourself."

"Your Excellency, I can't. I have to show you."

"Father, I'm ordering you not to force me to look."

"I'll force you if I have to," Father Procopio informed the Bishop as the Bishop watched his beloved beast relieve itself of all that she had accumulated during the train ride.

"May I remind you, Father, that you are talking to your Bishop?"

"I don't mean to be disrespectful, Your Excellency."

"I wonder, Procopio," the Bishop said, stroking his chin. "I wonder. There are rumors, you know."

"I know, Your Excellency," Father Procopio admitted.

"You know what I'm referring to, good Father?"

"Yes," Procopio replied.

"The other Priests have told me and it hurts me, Procopio."

"I know the other Priests have told you, Your Excellency."

The Bishop strolled around the churchyard taking in the disarray left behind by the large crowd. He shook his head. "We could make a fortune in snow cones, icons, little tin legs and arms, miniature automobiles, farm animals, tacos, lemonade, photographs. If only there were instant photographs," he murmured the recitation to himself and then jabbed his right fist into his left palm. And to Procopio he turned and asked, "Just where is this apparition?"

"At the wall, Your Excellency," Father Procopio said, "right by where the ugly dog is sitting."

The Bishop tried to shoo Amandito's dog away from the wall by stomping his feet but the dog recognized the Bishop and growled and refused to move. The Bishop picked up a rock and threw it at the dog as La Poochie barked from behind the Bishop's legs. "That's right, Poochie," the Bishop praised her. "Get that ugly mean dog. Let me throw another rock at him and see if he doesn't move."

La Poochie stayed behind the Bishop, clawing at the dirt to show everyone that she had finished her business and was now in the process of running off Amandito's dog. The expereienced dog saw the odds against him and he went quietly to the back of the church.

Now that the dangerous dog was gone La Poochie contentedly followed the Bishop's every step, proud to belong to the Bishop, disgusted that she had to come to such an insignificant town and put up not only with the cats and the fleas but now with a mongrel dog in her own yard. It was at moments like this that she wished she could talk to her master.

Amandito's dog had not left entirely. Instead he had gone to hide under the pomegranates to observe this strange little creature with the bashed-in face and bulging eyes that always came with the Bishop. He looked at the Bishop and then at La Poochie and wondered how they ever became related.

"And this is where the apparition appears?" the Bishop asked as he ran his hand on the wall.

"Yes, Your Excellency," Father Procopio informed him.

"And where is it now? Where is the apparition?"

"I've made it disappear," Father Procopio admitted.

The Bishop touched the wall and shook his head in disgust. "This, good Father Procopio, could mean a fortune for the church . . . for the railroad . . . for the town. Just think of it."

Father Procopio had remained by the shade of the Rectory and from there he said, "It would be a lie, Your Excellency."

The Bishop felt of the wall and then checked the palm of his hand. "So?" he murmured, dusting one hand with the other.

"I couldn't put up with that," Father Procopio said.

"It's God-sent," the Bishop replied as he thought and walked over to where Father Procopio stood.

"I don't believe that," Father Procopio replied. "I must insist on showing you what the problem has been."

"What if I refuse to go with you?" the Bishop asked him as he picked up his dog.

"You'll go," Father Procopio told him. "You know that you can't live in a lie."

The Bishop looked at the good Father and, raising one of his large thick eye-brows, corrected him. He said, "It's been done before, Procopio. It's been done before."

Procopio, jiggling his eyebrows, braced himself as he saw Amandito's dog stand up from under the pomegranates and begin to walk away, growling. "I won't allow the apparition anymore," he informed the Bishop.

"In that case," the Bishop said, "I may have some bad news for you . . . But let me see what you've discovered.

It's the least I can do, Procopio . . . the least I can do before I relieve you of this church."

Father Procopio swallowed the thick spittle that had accumulated at the back of his throat. He had not anticipated that the Bishop would be so quick to condemn him. He said, "I didn't know that the apparition meant this much to you, Your Excellency."

"That's your trouble, good Father," the Bishop smiled, stroking his beloved Pug, "you don't know where to make your stand. Now let's see the strength of your convictions. Do we go along with the lie or do we tell the truth?"

In the attic Father Procopio showed the Bishop his dog's bed. The Bishop placed his dog on the floor and asked her to go smell the bed and La Poochie, knowing more than the Bishop, refused to go near the pillow. "It's all right, Poochie," the Bishop said to her, "it's a feather pillow like the one you use in Corpus. Don't be afraid." But La Poochie knew what was in store for her. She could see the fleas that the Bishop didn't. The Bishop, trying to help ease her fears, shoved the little dog's face into the pillow and she felt the barrage of starving fleas attack her pugged nose.

Father Procopio was nervously moving more boxes out of the way to allow the Bishop, in his white frock, to get into the back of the attic without dirtying his habit. The Bishop had let go of his dog and was waiting for Father Procopio to clear the way.

"This is where the mystery is," Father Procopio said as he cleared the last box and invited the Bishop to come in. "Right here," he said as he walked and stood between the two windows.

The Bishop looked at the good Father and said, "What are you talking about?"

Father Procopio, heavily worried about losing his church, looked around and said, "Well, Your Excellency, you can't see it now. The sun is overhead. But in the mornings, when the sun clears the salt cedars, sunlight strikes this window and the bottles on the ledge. Somehow the light is filtered and condensed and a very intense beam is created. This thin beam goes across the room here and goes to the opposite window and goes through this old bottle of hair oil. From here the image is projected, just like a projector at the movies, down to the wall below. Naturally, as the sun travels overhead the image moves farther and farther down on the wall. By eleven in the morning the image disappears."

The Bishop stood silently for a while and looked back to find his dog. He picked up La Poochie and stroked the top of its head. "And . . . and how did this all come about, good Father?" he asked.

"Pimena," Father Procopio shrugged. "She cleaned the bottles and set them up just as you see them."

"Divine Providence," the Bishop said, smiling.

Father Procopio jiggled his eyebrows three times and the thought of losing his church became secondary to his principles. "If this is Divine Providence, then it's not worth it for me to stay in this parish anymore," he said.

"As you wish," the Bishop said, shaking his head at the disloyal Priest. "And by the way, good Father," he continued, "now that the Rectory is mine once more, I will sleep in your room. It's much more comfortable than the one you always give me. I just hope that your room is not as heavily infested with bedbugs as the bed you always give me."

Father Procopio swallowed the new white froth that had formed in back of his throat during his ordeal and replied, "Whatever you say, Your Excellency."

"And," the Bishop added, "I'll just have Poochie sleep with me instead of having the poor dog sleep with all of your cats."

"I'll be sure and tell Pimena about the arrangements when she returns," Father Procopio replied.

"I was just thinking," the Bishop said as he stroked his chin, "that as adamant as you are about destroying the apparition, I am going to forbid you to come into this attic anymore."

Father Procopio sighed and asked in desperation, "And my cats?"

The Bishop checked La Poochie's eyes and wiped the mucus from them and rubbed it off against one of the boxes. "They," he said, "can sleep wherever they please."

"They love to sleep in the attic, Your Excellency," Father Procopio replied.

"Very well," the Bishop concluded, "they can sleep

here. But I forbid you from coming into this attic. I don't
want you forcing your idealistic, your iconoclastic ways
by destroying the apparition. Early in the morning I will
come in this place and I will be sure that the apparition
appears on the wall. Do you understand, Father
Procopio?"

"Yes, Your Excellency. Whatever you say," Father
Procopio answered.

"Where's your fight now, Procopio?" the Bishop
sneered. "Where is your strength?"

"My strength is within me, with my Savior," the good
Father responded. "I don't need to show it off."

"What will you do without a church? Where will you
go?" the Bishop whispered as he stroked his beloved
dog.

Father Procopio jiggled his eyebrows and said, "I'll go
wherever I'm sent."

"I'm going to send you," the Bishop said with a hatred
born of the glee of seeing Father Procopio defeated,
"where I've never sent anyone before. It'll take me a
while to figure out where, but I'll figure it out. You'll
see, Procopio."

Pimena returned exhausted as the Bishop and Father
Procopio were sitting in the darkened kitchen without
saying a word. She greeted the Bishop with much fan-
fare, kneeling and kissing his ring.

"Oh, Your Excellency, I'm sorry that I was not here
to greet you when you arrived. But we had such a scare."

The Bishop smiled and said, lying, "I saw you,
Pimena. I saw you running at the head of the pack."

"You did?" Pimena wondered. "Where were you,
Your Excellency?"

"Why on my way to the Rectory, Pimena," the Bishop
laughed.

"Heaven and earth," she said. "I never saw you. Here,
let me make you some coffee.

"I would love that," the Bishop replied, "since Father
Procopio has not even offered me a glass of water."

"Shame on you, Father Procopio," Pimena scolded
him as she began to take out the parts of the old coffee
pot. "The least we can do is make the Bishop comfort-

able . . . How long are you staying, Your Excellency?"
she asked.

"It depends," the Bishop said, eyeing Father Procopio.

Pimena rinsed the coffee pot and removed the cat hairs
that were stuck to the inside. "You must tell our good
Father here about keeping so many cats, Your Excellency," she complained. "Look at all the cat hairs everywhere. The cats will be the ruination of all of us. Mark
my words, Your Excellency."

The Bishop laughed as he put his dog down on the
floor. La Poochie went over to the back door and
through the screen smelled the foul odor of stale urine
on Amandito's dog as he rested contentedly against the
door. "I'm afraid that Father Procopio is as concerned
with his twenty cats as I am with my Poochie," the
Bishop said, watching proudly as La Poochie continued
to smell and growl across the screen at Amandito's dog.
Then to Father Procopio he asked in a whisper so that
Pimena could not hear, "What are you going to do with
your cats? Wherever I'm sending you, you won't be able
to take them with you."

Father Procopio cupped his nervous hand over his
mouth and whispered to the Bishop so that Pimena could
not hear: "As long as I have my Princess I'll be all right
wherever I go."

"You must confess me, Your Excellency," Pimena told
the Bishop as she faced toward the sink and filled the
coffee pot with water. "You know, Your Excellency, that
you are the only one that can hear my confession. As
much as I love Father Procopio, I would never allow him
to know my most intimate of thoughts."

The Bishop threw his large head backward and laughed.
He said, "My dear Pimena, I'm sure that Procopio has
heard it all by now."

Pimena nervously put the coffee pot on the fire and
finally turned on the lights. "Not from me he hasn't,"
she said.

The Bishop leaned toward Procopio and whispered, "I
think I will send you to the farthest ranch in the deepest
brush in all of south Texas."

Father Procopio jiggled his eyebrows and swallowed
the spittle that had once again gathered in the back of
his throat. "Whatever you say, Your Excellency," he

replied, wondering what it would take to become a Protestant in order to keep his Princess and his nineteen other cats.

Over coffee the Bishop said, "Pimena, I think I will turn in early. Would you please make my bed ready?"

"We're not going to eat, Father Procopio? Surely you want me to fix supper?" Pimena asked.

"Whatever the Bishop wants, Pimena," Father Procopio said. "For my part, I'm not the least hungry."

"I'm not hungry either, Pimena," the Bishop informed her. "Poochie's not hungry either. If she gets hungry during the night I'll get up and get her a bowl of milk."

"The bed is ready, Your Excellency," Pimena said. "I made up your bed in the small bedroom yesterday."

The Bishop cleared his throat and looking at Father Procopio said, "Father Procopio has been nice enough to offer me his room for my stay."

"Heaven and earth be elevated," she prayed. "It makes my heart sing to hear that both of you are on such good terms."

"Don't jump to any conclusions, Pimena," the Bishop warned her before she could further express her joy. "Right, Father Procopio?"

Father Procopio took some coffee and thought of his mother and her eternal belt. He felt his beloved Princess rub against his leg and he picked here up and began to stroke her. Amandito's dog, peering inside through the screen door, saw Princess being picked up and he barked twice and let out a sorrowful moan that scared La Poochie back into the Bishop's lap.

"You make a sight," Pimena said, surveying the two men at the table. "Such important men with a dog and cat on their laps."

"We're putty in the hands of these wonderful little animals," the Bishop said as he kissed La Poochie on the top of her large head.

"Pimena," Father Procopio said, admiring how much the Bishop loved his little ugly dog, "you'd better make up the bed in the small bedroom for me."

"But I already did, good Father," Pimena replied. "I made it up for His Excellency."

"No you haven't," Father Procopio said. "Go look for yourself."

"Good Father," Pimena said mildly, "if you are right then I'm ready for the house for the insane. This apparition is getting the best of me."

"Get ready to pack then," Father Procopio advised her, secure in the knowledge that it had been he that had undone the bed to spread the bedbugs on the mattress.

At night the Bishop tossed in his bed, trying to extract the hair from twenty cats from all the areas of his body, cat hair that to Father Procopio had become an essential part of his sleep. The Bishop tried combing the cat hair from his own hair, tried to scrape cat hair from his own tongue, tried to rub it off his torso, his legs, his feet, his arms, from around his neck, from his back. Sleep was impossible. He was wishing now that he had taken the small bedroom along with the starving bedbugs that Father Procopio saved for him. He looked across the bed and could see that La Poochie was not asleep. She was having difficulty breathing with all the cat hair around her.

In the small bedroom Father Procopio said his rosary as the bedbugs feasted on his body. He could hear the Bishop across the hall cursing him and he smiled as another bedbug got him between the toes.

At precisely three in the morning, when the Rectory clock struck the hour, Father Procopio, still awake and slapping at the infinitely small bedbugs, saw the Bishop through the wooden door, as he saw Pimena every morning, as the Bishop walked into the hallway, dressed in a white gown and carrying La Poochie. He heard the Bishop knock very gently. "Procopio," the Bishop whispered through the door. "Procopio . . . are you awake? I can't sleep with the infernal cat hair. You should have warned me. That was the least you could have done . . . Are you awake? Procopio?"

"Yes, Your Excellency," Procopio replied, as he sat up and moved to the edge of his small bed.

"Procopio . . . We can still be friends. Be reasonable. Think of the people."

"I'm going to try to go to sleep," Father Procopio answered.

"Very well," the Bishop said. There was a long pause as the Bishop waited in vain for Father Procopio to give

in. Then the Bishop sighed through the door at the good
Father and walked away disappointed.

At four in the morning Father Procopio was awakened
by the Bishop's noise in the hallway. He heard the mild
footsteps as he saw through the wall as the Bishop
walked downstairs carrying the hungry Poochie. Father
Procopio lay silent, a bedbug in his ear. He cursed himself for having put all these little creatures in the Bishop's
bed. God had punished him. He could hear the Bishop
tripping around downstairs and cursing the darkness. He
lay very still, ignoring the bedbugs that were happily
chewing at his body, trying to understand what the
Bishop was doing at this hour. He could hear Poochie
barking. He heard a loud noise, like a scream, but then
his mind told him that it could not be a scream, that it
was a cough, the Bishop clearing his throat of all the cat
hair that he had swallowed during the night. He heard
the noise again. And then again. And again. It was more
than a cough. He distinctly heard the deep shouting voice
of a man, the Bishop, as if he were talking very loudly to
someone. He heard the noise made from frantic footsteps
running on hard floors. He heard the running footsteps
under his room, then toward his office, then back on the
downstairs hallway. He heard the Bishop screaming at
the top of his voice for someone to stop. He heard the
panting as someone ran up the stairs. The Bishop was
right behind whoever it was. At the top of the stairs he
heard the Bishop scream for Father Procopio's help.
Father Procopio jumped from the bed and ran to the
door. He threw the door open just in time to see Amandito's dog running by the door heading for the attic. He
had La Poochie clamped between his jaws. The dog hit
the door with such an impact that it flew open. The
Bishop, running after Amandito's dog, trying to save La
Poochie's life, was so winded that he was clutching his
heart and could not speak. The Bishop raised his right
hand and Father Procopio saw the blood where the dog
had bitten the Bishop. Father Procopio was frozen
momentarily at seeing the attack on La Poochie and at
seeing the blood on the Bishop's hand.

At first the good Father heard La Poochie's weak cries
coming from the attic, fearful little whimpers, no longer
the fierce barks that she had shown the whole town ear-

lier in the day. She sounded near death inside the mouth of the much larger dog. Then he heard the commotion as twenty cats ran wildly around the crowded room. Father Procopio heard boxes fall, cats scream, Amandito's dog growling ferociously.

The Bishop and Father Procopio ran into the attic and began chasing Amandito's dog while La Poochie screamed in pain. Amandito's dog escaped through the alley that Father Procopio had made of the boxes in order to get to the bottles. The Bishop dove at the dog as La Poochie screamed for him to save her. Father Procopio was able to grab the dog by one of the hind legs and all of them— the Bishop, Father Procopio, Amandito's dog, La Poochie—crashed against the left window knocking down all the bottles off the ledge. Then to the right they went, the dog dragging both Father Procopio and the Bishop with an unnatural power. The snarling, howling group crashed against the right window this time and knocked the bottles off the ledge. Father Procopio, as if by Divine Intervention, finally remembered the dog's weak point. He grabbed Amandito's dog by the testicles and twisted them around and around and then yanked them up toward the tail. The dog let go of La Poochie immediately and started on Father Procopio. Father Procopio ran out, the dog in pursuit, and he flew down the stairs without touching them and ran down the hallway to the back door. He opened the door and took one step to the outside. As the dog followed right behind him, Father Procopio stopped, stepped to one side and the dog ran out past him and tumbled over the back doorsteps. He yelped in pain as he rolled for several yards on the hard ground. Father Procopio jumped back inside and closed the door.

"Damn dog," he said. "Wait until I tell Amandito about you. He's going to take you and see that your testicles are removed."

He made sure that both the screen door and the wooden door were locked. At that moment, as he made sure Amandito's dog had run away, he heard the Bishop scream in agony and he ran upstairs to see what had happened. As he ran he prayed for La Poochie's life. What would the Bishop do without her?

In the middle of the attic the Bishop, his own hand

bleeding, held the bleeding Poochie to his chest and cried. Father Procopio walked slowly toward the Bishop and could see that La Poochie's whole limp body was covered with blood and saliva. As Father Procopio tried to take the dog away from the Bishop the Bishop objected. He would not let the dog go. Father Procopio took the stunned Bishop by the arm and led him into the bathroom. There the two of them cleaned La Poochie under the warm stream of the sink. Her right front leg was broken. She had been bitten mostly on her head. The whites of both her little eyes were bleeding from the trauma. The Bishop collapsed by the sink, fell to his knees and began to pray as he cried. His hand had been washed when they had cleaned La Poochie and Father Procopio could see the teeth marks on the Bishop's palm.

Father Procopio worked on La Poochie all the rest of the night, stroking her, keeping her warm, exhorting her not to die, and by daybreak, when Pimena came to work, the little dog was resting comfortably under the covers made from the Bishop's nightgown. The Bishop sat on the floor by her and stroked her little head.

"What in heaven's name happened here last night?" they could hear Pimena ask. "It looks as if a hurricane slept in here. What could have happened?"

"Your Excellency," Father Procopio said to the Bishop, "we must take Poochie to the veterinarian in Alice."

"No," he said, tired and forlorn, "I need to take her as soon as possible to Corpus. To her own veterinarian where she belongs. Do you think she can travel?"

"I'm sure of it," Father Procopio replied, looking at La Poochie as she licked her wounds, as she shuddered at how close to death she had come.

"Heaven and earth," Pimena said as she walked upstairs, "look at all this mess and blood. Something sure stirred up the cat hair last night."

In one hour the Bishop had packed and was ready to leave for Corpus Christi. He and Father Procopio had made a crude splint and had wrapped La Poochie's leg.

"Pimena," the Bishop cried as he looked for the housekeeper. "Pimena, I'm leaving. Father Procopio is walking with me to the depot."

Pimena walked slowly from upstairs, crying.

"What is it, Pimena?" Father Procopia asked her. "What has happened? Why are you crying.?"

Pimena wiped the tears with her apron as she walked. "Oh, good Father," she cried. "If you only knew."

"What happened, Pimena? In God's name," the Bishop demanded.

"Father Procopio," Pimena cried, "it's Princess." She began to gag but managed to get the words out. "I found her dead. A box fell on her and crushed her."

Father Procopio ran upstairs to the attic as the Bishop began to nervously run around the room. "Oh my God!" he cried. "Poor man. And it's all my fault. How he must feel!" he said as he stopped and thought about Father Procopio. He ran around the room some more as Pimena tried to quiet him down.

Upstairs, they heard the cries of Father Procopio as he gazed at the crushed Princess for the first time. "She's dead!" they could hear him cry. "She's dead . . . all that I had is dead. Why is God so cruel?"

The Bishop, on hearing the screams of the Priest upstairs, ran for his dog and cradled it in his arm. With the other hand he picked up his luggage and hurriedly ran for the door. There was no use staying there for the aftermath.

As he held the door open with his foot he said: "Pimena, tell the good Father that I couldn't wait. Tell him how I feel for him. Offer condolences . . . anything. How the poor man must feel . . . Tell him to forget about the apparition. Tell him that whatever he wants to do is fine with me. Tell him he's right . . . as always."

Pimena had never seen the old Bishop move as fast as he did that morning. Both fascinated and repulsed by his speed, she had not had time to reply. By the time she had collected her thoughts the Bishop was a blur running up the street toward town and the train depot. In his right arm he carried the injured dog and dangling from his left hand, like a tow sack, was his patent leather bag.

Two weeks later Father Procopio received the letter from the Bishop. La Poochie's bite wounds had healed. Her little crooked leg had been set and placed in a cast. She was able to take short walks. He could tell that she hurt because she would bark at him after a few blocks and he would have to pick here up and carry her the rest

of the way. His hand was healing nicely but he had had
to be vaccinated against tetanus just as La Poochie had.
He had just one complaint about San Diego: Father Procopio should not allow the old man, the one known as
Don Tomas, to loiter at the depot. It was bad enough
that Don Tomas had bothered him when he first arrived
from Corpus Christi but waiting for the train as he had
had to do was too much. The old man had pestered the
Bishop unmercifully. The Bishop wrote: "In the condition that La Poochie and I were in, I did not appreciate
anyone asking me if I knew that snakes have sexual inter-
course like dogs and whether I knew that the possum
breeds through the nose, the coyotes defecate on their
young and in particular I don't care, nor does the
Almighty God care, whether the spider pees or not. But
nothing I could say or do could convince the man to
leave me alone. P.S.: How is the congregation taking to
the loss of the apparition?"

Father Procopio jiggled his eyebrows for the hundredth time since he had found Princess's crushed body
in the attic. He took a pen and paper and wrote: "Your
Excellency: I am happy for you and La Poochie and
expect that she will be back to normal in a short time.
Take care of your hand. You know what happened to
Father Diaz at Alton when he did not take care of his
bite wound and he had to be hospitalized and almost
lost his arm. For Your Excellency's information, I had
Bernabe, the crazy one, bury Princess by the side of the
church where I used to see her sleeping during the day.
You will be happy to know that Amandito and I took
the dog to Alice and had him castrated as per Don
Andres García's deathbed instructions. I have not seen
him around the Rectory since. P.S.: The loss of the apparition has not deterred the ladies of the congregation.
They are even more devout now than before, coming to
pray at the wall instead of inside the church. You can
imagine what that does to the collection plate! What's
more, they are eagerly expecting another apparition very
soon. You can tell, Your Excellency, that I did not have
the heart to tell them the truth."

DAGOBERTO GILB

❦ ❦ ❦

Dagoberto Gilb was born in 1950 in Los Angeles where he attended high school and junior college before entering university to study philosophy and religion. In 1976, Gilb received a master's degree, after which, he has written, "I was lucky enough (it seemed to me then) to find a laborer's job that paid $50 a day. Ditches. But I worked hard and learned and for twelve years made my living in construction as a highrise carpenter." For the last ten years, he has lived with his wife and their children in El Paso, Texas, where he writes and occasionally teaches remedial writing courses at the University of Texas at El Paso. Of his work, Gilb has written, "I often use the culture I live in [in this case, Mexican-American] for settings because it is the one most familiar to me. My writing is self-exploratory and questioning, and I suppose, given that, it makes what I write about somewhat inevitable. Maybe also it has to do with my father (whom I didn't live with), an Anglo, who told me to lie and say my mother was Spanish because being Mexican (especially in the Los Angeles of their day) would keep me down, while my mother, who raised me, raised me to be proud and unashamed." Most of Gilb's fiction has appeared in literary journals such as The Threepenny Review *and* Fiction Network, *which are published in the San Francisco/Berkeley area, where, Gilb says, "there is still an independent literary scene." While he is "still New York (i.e. 'nationally') unknown," he has received his share of success. In 1984, he received California's prestigious James D. Phelan Award in Literature, awarded annually to the outstanding native California writer under age thirty-five. Of his fiction, one commentator noted that Gilb explores "a world of frustrated but loving fathers, friends who also are enemies, lovers,*

311

drugs, laborers, Mexican-Americans, Anglos, feuding
neighbors, and lonely children, all of them too aware of
life's downside, yet somehow blessed with hope—
survivors."

Vic Damone's Music

Our house just fits between two buildings that keep us
in shade almost all day long. There used to be
another house with a big yard and a new fence on the
side of us, but it was torn down and replaced by a popcorn factory, which means we smell popcorn all the time.
When they first started things up over there, the owner
would give my mother and me huge bags of it, and I
liked that then. These days I don't feel one way or the
other about the smell, but please don't offer me any. On
the other side of us an older fence with the same mesh
separates our chunky grass from the laundry that's been
there since I was born and before that, and its red brick
walls seem to me to take up most of Cordoba Street.
This is the place I know the best. Even as a little kid, if
I didn't go in to visit my mother during working hours,
I'd climb over the fence when the plant was closed and
find a way inside. There was never anything I wanted,
even when I had the nerve to think about it, so all I did
was wander around the cement floors, touching those
secret machines that either washed, dried, squeezed,
ironed, folded, or bundled the sheets and towels, pants,
shirts, tablecloths or napkins. You can't imagine how big
the place is. Each workroom must be at least two of my
house, and there are seven different areas that size, and
still there are all these other places where a few more
people could work. It was a whole world to disappear
into. I did have to be careful though, because it seemed
like there was always someone there. Sometimes that's
what I did: I'd see who was around while I was hiding
from them, I'd find spots I wouldn't be discovered.

My mother has worked at the folding table in the cor-

ner for as long as I can remember. It was only recently
that I realized this was a place of recognition, that it was
reserved for the best-looking women in the plant. While
most of the others work near hot steam, these women
hand-fold dry, clean towels and linen the company owns,
or the finer things a restaurant or club has done there,
or maybe some personal belongings those at the top have
done for themselves. They get to do this near an open
window, without any machine too close to them, and
they can move around and talk and laugh, all those privi-
leges the other women don't have. The way I understand
it now, my mother's appearance had a lot more to do
with my getting to work here three years ago, at thirteen,
than I'd like to admit.

During school, I work three or four hours a day and
eight on Saturday. They never let me work more than
eight hours because of the law, but during vacation I
work all six days full-time. We need the money, even
though it's only my mother and me. My aunt used to live
with us and help when she could, though she practically
stopped knowing us once she got married. That was
about the same time I started in the sorting room, which
is where all the dirty laundry is unloaded off the trucks
in heavy sacks, which are untied and dumped onto the
cement floor. Men gather around the pile and sort,
throwing one kind of thing into a wooden cart and
another kind in another cart, the colored things into
another, like that. My first hour was almost my last. I
was standing near this heap of greasy restaurant rags that
were still hot, and all around them was wiggling rice,
something which I'd never seen before. *Gusanos,* a short
man next to me smiled. Maggots, a tall black man nearby
said. He offered to work where I was and he went
through them with gloves on, and I let him.

The short guy that spoke Spanish was Victorio, who
was from Panama. We've worked together since that first
day. He liked it when I was there because he didn't speak
English well and they put him with the black crew in the
sort room. That was because he worked hard and never
said anything that would have given anybody the idea,
at least in English, that he didn't want to be there, even
though at lunch and breaks he'd go over with the Spanish-speaking guys, which was most of the other employ-

ees. Another reason he stayed with them as long as he
did was that the black guys liked him. Victoria was very
short around them, but he was always telling them how
big his dick was, which made everybody break up. Also
Victorio could sing with the confidence of someone
naked in the shower, and everyone who could hear him
enjoyed that, whether it was in Spanish or English. He
knew a lot of old songs in Spanish, but the black guys
preferred his Righteous Brothers imitations, and he tried
to please them. He himself said his favorite singer was
Vic Damone, not only because of the name, but because
he was a lady's man.

Victoria and I work together with Raúl in the shake
room now. He's happier because there are women all
around us, and everyone speaks Spanish except the foreman. Victoria does miss the weekly sort through the
Playboy Club, which all the guys liked because of the
souvenirs, those plastic cocktail stirrers with the Playboy
symbol at the top of them, and because once somebody
found a bunny outfit, though it had to be returned, and
one other time a twenty-dollar bill, which got kept. I
suppose the work over here is harder, worth the nickel
more an hour, because it takes more muscles and endur-
ance than going through the hospitals' bloody greens or
their sheets or pillowcases, which is what our old crew
still does. Here the sheets are damp and knotted up in
the wooded carts. We have to pull them out and stack
them in a way so that the women who work the mangle
in front of us can each take a corner of one and feed it
through to be pressed and dried and folded on the other
side. And no matter what we do or don't, no matter
what the weather is outside, in this room we're sweating.
The women don't seem to care for that much, but none
of us minds it. In fact Raúl thinks it's good for him
because he plays soccer and works out with weights, and
Victorio because he thinks the women get sexually
excited on account of it, and I don't care because I don't
have plans to stay here.

Maybe you already know how it is when you hear
someone like Victorio constantly singing the same songs.
In the shake room he couldn't sing as loud because of the
windows above us where the owner and his secretar-
ies worked and watched us, but he could sing loud

enough for me and Raúl to hear. He'd bought this
album, *Vic Damone Live at Basin Street East*, wherever
that is. It has his favorite song on it, "Adiós," but it also
had a few new ones that Victorio liked, for instance,
"When Your Lover Has Gone," which he memorized
right away, and one called "You and the Night and the
Music." This was one he struggled with, that he listened
to every day to figure out a new word or two. He'd
learned the opening very quickly.

> *You and the night and the music*
> *thrill me with flaming desire*
> *setting my being completely*
> *on fire*

After that Victorio was having his troubles, though we
all knew it started out with those lines again and that
sooner or later hearts would be guitars, because that was
another line he'd learned.

Pulling wet sheets out of a cart may not sound hard,
but really it is. After a few hours of doing it, especially
in that heat, all the usual tough-guy or great-lover talk
doesn't leave the mouth. Victorio, though, would sing or
hum during these times, and it was that tune he was
stuck on. I never felt one way or the other about Vic
Damone's music before Victorio, but my opinion was
forming by the day. I'd tell him that if he had to, to sing
a few Spanish ones, but he told me he was trying to learn
the others because sometimes he got to sing at some
nightclub, and at the nightclub the American songs were
what were making him famous. I couldn't blame him for
that, and I didn't want to be the one to discourage him.
Anybody with any sense should try to get out of this
work. There were way too many people stuck here for
no other reason than that they wouldn't quit. Inez, as an
example, has worked the left side of the mangle I work
in front of for as long as I can remember. She stands
there and takes her corner of a sheet and feeds it to the
hot rollers. She and her partner Rosita, who has worked
her side more than a few years, talk a little in the morning and a little in the afternoon and that's how they pay
their bills. The same attitude is true of my mother. Her

main excuse is that we live next door and it's easy for her.

It isn't that easy for her because my mother was once the owner's lover. I think I probably knew this for a long time, but it's only recently that I gave the words to it. Not out in the open. I wouldn't talk about it to anyone, and if I did, who knows what I'd have to do or say. And naturally nobody brought it up with me. Not that they weren't aware of it. They told me, with their eyes and indirect questions. Last year, when I first put it together in my mind, I made a point of flirting with this woman at the job the guys said was a prostitute. I'd wink and look her up and down and ask about prices and times. I wanted everyone to see, including my mother. Mostly the woman waved me off and told me to shut up and go back to work, but she did smile. Nothing happened between us, and my mother never said a word to me about it either. She only acted a little sadder than she usually was.

The owner is married to a woman his age. Yet he always seems to have a young one to hang around with. In the few years that I've worked here, it's been one of the other women that works at the folding table where my mother works. Her name is Juliana, and she's from Costa Rica. I don't know how many different ones there have been over the years, or how he manages to interest them and then give them up, but he does. Most of the men who work here admire him for it openly, even say they'd do the same if they could, and that the women do better for it, get new clothes, jewelry, a better job on the floor. I can't say about that, but to me he's an ugly old man who'd be spit on if he didn't drive a Lincoln Continental.

The way I was reading it, Juliana was being replaced by Mercedes, who fed napkins into the mangle in the corner, closest to the wall of dryers, which is about the hottest spot a woman can work. Mercedes is eighteen and just from Vera Cruz. She doesn't have papers, which is common for many of the people who work in the plant. I doubt if I'd have noticed her if I hadn't seen the owner talking to her one morning before the whistle. The only ones I even thought of paying attention to were the obvious ones, and they weren't even near my age, though

Mercedes wasn't either. She was more like a woman. Also her eyes were crossed. I don't go around thinking I'm the greatest-looking guy in the world, but I suppose my tastes are normal enough to not want a girlfriend that's going to be stared at for bad reasons.

Once I overlooked Mercedes' defect, I saw the rest of her, and I saw what the owner probably did, that she was pretty and she had a good body. So each day I spent more time looking at her. I've been on dates with girls from school, and I probably could have a steady girlfriend from there if I wanted to, but I've already mentioned that I have plans, and they don't include getting all mixed up with a female. I know too much about what can happen at the worst, and at the best it's like Raúl, who's only twenty-one and is married and has a kid and still works in this place.

This is what I did: Victorio was singing that song to himself and I was pulling sheets so fast and hard that sweat soaked through my pants. It seemed everyone around was hypnotized by their routine. The women behind the mangles were folding, near them a guy was tying counted piles, blue paper top and bottom. Another man opened the round windowed doors of the dryers and tipped the spinning drums so that the whirling sheets dropped into the wooden carts. Women stood in a line in front of their mangles, leaning, tired, lazy, or bored, this way or that, those huge rollers in front of them turning and steaming. Mercedes was with them, her black hair more shiny than the older women's near her. I walked over there to steer a cart to our work area and, without really asking myself about the right or wrong of it, I went up behind her and ran two of my fingers across the hard seam of her pants between her legs. She hopped and took an angry swing at me, and the other women at the trough of the machine jumped on each side of me, chattering like I'd touched them. I ran with that cart back to Victorio and Raúl and didn't say anything. My heart pumped and I felt as stupid as that Vic Damone song.

Clumsy and crude, it worked, even though I didn't plan that it would—I just did it. The next day the women were smiling and Mercedes was watching me whenever I glanced over. After I explained to him, Victorio got excited, singing for Raúl and me as though he'd fallen in love. To be honest, I was confused. I wasn't sure what to do next, what I wanted from Mercedes. But like some obligation, at break I went over and ate with her in the lunchroom where all those women held back their stares and voices, as best as they could. Though I really did like her, I didn't want to like Mercedes so publicly, didn't want all these people judging my taste or intentions. At the same time, I wanted all to see. Both these feelings intensified when I let myself think about my mother's opinion.

That afternoon I finally couldn't stand Victorio's broken verses and I offered to listen to the song and get the words for him. He brought me the album the next day. When I told him that I was going to invite Mercedes over to my house for lunch so we both could listen to it, he acted like I announced a wedding.

Mercedes agreed to come over to the house with me as though we'd been doing that regularly, which wasn't the only thing that was different about being with her. Another was how I felt right away. Not young or old, but from up here, from this side, and therefore more natural and more like a man. I don't mean like *bad*, like *chingón*, just like a man with a woman. My usual worries, in other words, weren't playing with me since she didn't live with parents, didn't think about my style or crowd or cash. In fact she made me feel proud of our house next door, proud just as I knew my mother was that at the very least it was ours, wherever it was. She brought whole new fears and confidence out of me. Passing the time clock, I couldn't miss the owner tilting and swiveling toward us seriously in that chair, and through the door, moving on the sidewalk beneath the open lunchroom windows, I was more conscious of those women squealing and gaping than of my feet walking. Mercedes, on the other hand, seemed to be in complete control.

I hadn't played our record player in the living room in so long that dust covered it and the book that'd been sitting on it, a hardbound picture book of President Kennedy's one thousand days. The dust didn't affect Mercedes in the slightest, and I wished my mother could see that. Because she trusted me, I knew she wouldn't say anything about bringing Mercedes over, but that she'd be very upset about her being in the house without it being cleaned up first. I imagined she'd be very upset about that, that she'd use extra words to tell me how wrong it was to bring someone over to a dirty house, and she'd go on about it. And I already imagined my standing near her, listening, telling her that the house isn't so dirty, that she shouldn't worry so much. And finally she'd say that the owner wasn't going to like it that we came over here during lunch because we're supposed to go right back to work, that it was a break from work. And I'd have to say that the owner doesn't pay us during the lunch break, and that some of the guys go over to the stand down the street to buy food, not everyone stays in the building, so what's the difference? That besides, he never cared when I came over here by myself, or when you did, he knows we can hear the five-more-minutes whistles fine from any room in our house. And then she'd stop arguing with me about it.

Mercedes and I listened to the first song, Victorio's, on the album twice, then let the rest of it play through. I made sandwiches in the kitchen and she shared her lunch with me. We small-talked, drank soda, thumbed through the sad pictures of the book about the president. I started the album over again to hear Victorio's song one more time. I sat on the couch next to her, and I kissed her before we heard the two whistles telling us to go back.

That afternoon, Victorio, his dark face lit up, asked me as though it were one question whether I'd understood the words to the song and whether anything happened between Mercedes and me. I didn't say yes or no that day or any of the following ones that she and I took our lunch at my house. I worked on it for him though, until finally I had the words and almost Mercedes.

> *You and the night and the music*
> *fill me with flaming desire*
> *setting my being completely*
> *on fire*
>
> *You and the night and the music*
> *thrill me but will we be one*
> *after the night and the music*
> *are done*

*Until the pale light of dawning and day lights
our hearts will be throbbing guitars
morning may come without warning
and take away the stars*

*If we must live for the moment
love till the moment is through
after the night and the music die
will I have you*

I had a problem with that last line. I didn't know if it
was supposed to have a question mark. At first it seemed
obvious that it did, but after I'd heard it so many times
I couldn't be sure. Even though she didn't know English,
I asked Mercedes if she could tell, but she couldn't
either. I kept listening, and the more I did the less certain
I was. And then I had another problem. I couldn't get the
song out of my head. It played over and over and over
without the record player. And as it did I kept seeing Mercedes. Now she and the song were connected just as Victorio had joined them, and my thoughts twisted between.
Dislike or like of one became dislike or like of the other.
Doubt about one was doubt about the other.

Victoria was happy when I gave him the words, but I
told him to please not sing it, that if he had to, to sing
anything else. He couldn't understand how I wouldn't
want to hear Vic Damone, even after I told him it had
nothing to do with that. One day he came to me
exclaiming that my sweetheart Mercedes loved his version of the song he'd just sung for her and he offered it
as proof of how wonderful Vic Damone's music was and
that I should be grateful. I begged him to not sing any
of it around me. He acted hurt, like I was rejecting Mercedes' love. She was so beautiful, the song was so beautiful, he told me so sincerely. I tried to say he didn't
understand, and yet he was right, somehow.

Everybody waited for me to make a move, I knew it.
The owner, my mother, Victorio, Raúl, Inez, Rosita, all
the women at the mangles and at the tables. Mercedes
waited. I just wasn't sure. How could I know what to do?
I wanted and I didn't want. It was that simple and that
hard. It was not exactly like working in the shake room,
where that hot steam pours out of everything and we sweat,

wondering why we should let it run off our legs and arms for hardly enough money, and then again why not, why once we've already got a job and know how to do it, aware or not of what other possibilities are out there.

This is what I did: I invited Mercedes to my house for dinner. I asked my mother to make something special and I went out and bought all the ingredients. I helped her clean the house, I helped her set the table, I told her to relax because it was only a dinner. It was my favorite meal, and the whole house smelled of sauces for hours. I brought Mercedes over and I swore my mother was happy for the first time in years, in so long a time. We ate flan with the TV on.

It was still light when I offered to take Mercedes home. She didn't live very far so I told my mother we were going to walk. When we got out the front door I told Mercedes to follow me. I helped her climb the fence so she wouldn't tear the dress pants I'd never seen her wear before. I led her through the side entrance of the laundry—I'd used this same way so many times—and we walked the concrete floors we both knew well during the day, but which at night seemed cool with the machinery down, and wider with no one working around them. It was in a useless corner of the building, a spot good enough to store towels but not much else, close enough to mangle that towels passing through it could get bundled and stacked there. The pile was seven feet high toward the front, and we climbed a stairway of them, then rolled down to where the pile sloped beneath a window and leveled out like a mattress. Under us were towels that I imagined to have been there for ten years or more, ones I'd climbed on when I knew nothing of sex. I took a bundle from the high, recently stacked part and broke the string that kept them together and spread the clean towels around. I showed Mercedes how we could see around an edge of the pile and almost be certain no one could see us unless they knew to look here, which nobody ever had, and how through the window we could see my house and the street. A perfect place, I told her.

We lay on the towels and we kissed and touched. Finally we had our clothes off. We made love. With her eyes closed, Mercedes was the most beautiful woman I could ever imagine wanting to be with. I looked around the tall edge of the bundled towels and could tell the light was on in the owner's office by the way it reflected on the work floor below. In the other direction I could see the lights on at home, where my mother was alone either in the living room, still watching TV, or in the kitchen, washing dishes. I could smell the chemical and soap in the towels under us, and the popcorn outside, and the perfume Mercedes wore. Then I thought of how pleased Victorio would be, and then I thought of that song. That stupid song that had nothing to do with what I thought about or what I liked or even, if anything made sense, this event in my life. Unwillingly I went through the verses with Vic Damone's voice and intonations, and I could hear the hollow rhythm of the bass and the forced harmony of the brass instruments, and I followed a snare drum, a piano, and Vic Damone's voice rising, rising, lengthening a note, another, and then it was over, and it really was for a moment, longer than that, and I felt as good as I thought was ever possible, until the music began again.

Hollywood!

Santa Monica beach was clean and quiet. The sand was moist, the air cool, the ocean as gentle as a bay, and Luis was happy that he didn't have to pay for the parking.

"The sun's out," he said. "Just look what a pretty day it is."

"It's still *cold*," Marta told him, making sure he didn't get away with it. She was trying to wrap her sweater around their son Ramón, who wasn't about to cooperate and was about to cry because his mommy wouldn't leave him alone.

"He'll be all right," Luis said to ease her worry. "It's good for him just to get out."

"It's not good for him to catch a cold!" Marta was mad at Luis for insisting that Ramón wouldn't need any more than shorts and a T-shirt at the beach.

"He won't. Look at how happy he is." That was the kind of reasoning Luis liked to use.

Ramón was, in fact, happy. His plastic grader tore through the sand, slicing out a smooth road for his Matchbox cars. He didn't seem the least bit cold.

Marta had learned long ago that she couldn't fight with Luis's logic. She lay down on the old blanket she'd never convince him to replace, draped the sweater over herself, and looped her arm over her eyes. The sun *was* out. She felt pained.

Fishing boats bobbed on the near horizon. Helicopters battered the air. Joggers came and went along the wet part of the shore.

"If they worked like us they wouldn't have to run," Luis said of the joggers.

"At least they move to keep warm," Marta shot back.

"We've got the whole beach to ourselves. Think of what memories he'll have."

She scoffed. Ramón's cars vroomed and squealed and crashed into themselves and mounds of sand.

"The beach is just great," Marta shivered. "I can't wait to tell everybody at home what a great experience our first vacation ever was." It was Luis's idea to visit California in the winter because the motels were said to be cheaper and everyone said it was warm anyway.

"He's gonna remember this forever," Luis said. Just to make sure, he went over to his son. "You wanna go see the ocean up close?"

Ramón looked over to his mommy. He seemed to know, even at his very young age, that his daddy didn't always have the best ideas.

Luis picked Ramón up and carried him to the breakwater. "Now those boats out there—they look like the ones you have for your bath, don't they?" Luis felt pretty clever thinking of that. It was always better to describe things to a child in a way he could understand. "Those boats go around and catch fish so that people can eat. It's just like at home at the groves. Except instead of nuts it's fish, like sardines. You know, those fish from those cans your mommy puts in my lunch sometimes."

Ramón seemed to listen and Luis was sure he was

getting through to him. He was determined to not lose
the momentum.

"And the seagulls, those birds that are flying around
out there, see? See how big they are? Those are called
seagulls and they go around and catch fish too, just like
those boats, and that's how they live."

Ramón was listening. He was watching the birds.

"The ocean's just like the land. Animals live in it. Men
make a living on it the same way I do working in the
groves for Mr. Oakes." Luis thought this over and realized he didn't know how to explain himself any better.
"The only important thing in life is hard work." That
was somehow what he was getting at, and in any case he
loved these kinds of statements, and he always sincerely
believed them.

Ramón started fidgeting.

"You wanna get down? Okay. You should get your
feet wet. These are nice waves . . ."

Now Ramón was crying. The water was very cold and
the little waves scared him. He ran up the sand to his
mommy.

"Why can't we go to Disneyland?" Marta implored
Luis back at the blanket. "It can't cost that much. He
would have such a good time, even if it is expensive. I
could pay with that money I saved . . ."

"It's not the money."

"Or we could leave a day or two earlier and with the
money we save by leaving . . ."

"No."

Marta rolled her eyes and shook her head. It was no
use. Even though every little boy and girl dreams of going
to Disneyland at least once, Luis had his ideas and this
was one of them: it was better for his son to learn the
important things first. What would a place like Disneyland
teach him besides cartoons? Of course Marta didn't believe
him for a second. She knew he was just being cheap.

A couple came wearing bathing suits and left with
warmer clothes on. They didn't stay long. A teenage couple came carting a portable stereo with a cassette player.
They listened to a tape of Tierra and felt each other up.
Luis finally couldn't stand it and told them to turn it
down and to make their sex private. They left, but once
he got a safe distance away the boy yelled something

obscene at Luis about his mother. Marta laughed. Ramón wanted a hot dog because the day before Luis had promised him one.

"They do too sell hot dogs up on that pier," Marta told him. "I saw that man coming down the stairs eating one."

"No they don't," Luis insisted. "Besides, we brought these sandwiches."

"You already told him you would!"

"Hey, look at all the birds landing around us," Luis said to his son, changing the subject.

Ramón stopped whining and looked. They were sea-gulls and pigeons. They waited in segregated clumps.

"Let's feed them! We can feed them some of the bread!" Luis pinched off chunks of the white bread from his sandwich and threw them at the birds. They squawked and flapped their wings and moved in closer. Ramón watched ecstatically. Seagulls hovered in the air and Luis tossed the balled-up crumbs so they'd catch them there. More gulls flew in from the ocean and more pigeons from the pier and then Ramón threw the pieces of his sandwich too.

Luis tried to show Ramón how to tear little pieces off the bread so he wouldn't go through the sandwiches too quickly, but the boy had already lost control. Pigeons were almost crawling on the blanket, and it seemed all the ocean's gulls waited by him while he talked and laughed, letting the pigeons eat from his hand and making sure each and every seagull got something.

Pleased as he was, Luis was also relieved when the last sandwiches were spared by three high-pitched beeps, and then music and song, which distracted Ramón from the feeding.

"Look!" Marta pointed. "They're making a movie over there on the pier. See the camera?"

Ramón went back to the birds. Luis looked at the film-ing area skeptically. Marta demanded that they go see it up close. Luis, watching his son take out another sand-wich from a plastic bag, gave in to Marta's wish and waved the birds away.

It was a commercial for A&W root beer but Marta didn't care. This was Hollywood! There were film people everywhere, standing by electronic machines and under wire cables. There was a fat director, dressed in a casual

velour suit, arranging scenes with waving hands and
arms. There was a cameraman, who wore a cowboy hat,
sitting on a rolling lift. And there were handsome young
actors and beautiful young actresses and a punk-style
woman dabbing them with makeup.

"They're all blonds," remarked Luis cynically.

"Those two men on the roller skates have dark hair,"
Marta corrected him. "And there's a black man."

"Boys. Those are all boys."

First came the beeps, then the music, and then the
action: cute, barelegged actresses drank from a can of
the soda and expressed amazement and pretended to sing
the jingle that screamed out of a speaker in front of
them. Other actresses jogged to a stop and one of the
actors twirled on his roller skates. They all moved toward
a park bench while the camera aimed down and away
from the crowded park bench.

They watched the actors do this several times before
Luis made them move to another area behind the rope.
He didn't like standing near the shirtless blond longhairs
with tattoos who, according to Luis, didn't do anything
more than smoke marijuana and drink beer.

After a while Luis stopped paying attention. He
watched a man below him driving a tractor across the
sand. He watched a truck collect the trash from the barrels on the beach. Then a uniformed guard was standing
next to him telling him something in English. Luis
noticed that the fat director was glaring at him, and when
he looked to his side for a translation he realized that
Marta and Ramón had left him alone. He stiffened until
the guard put his hand on his shoulder and slowly drew
out the word "move" and pushed Luis farther down the
rope.

"It's because you were in the picture," Marta
explained to him.

Luis still felt like everyone was looking at him. "The
boy should be playing on the beach. Maybe he'll want
to get wet in the ocean."

Marta frowned. "I want to see this a few more times.
He's hungry. Buy him a hot dog."

"There's still two sandwiches," he reminded her.

"He wants a *hot dog*."

Luis wanted to argue, but once Ramón had heard his

mommy mention hot dogs, he started whining again. Luis knew it was hopeless. He took his son to the nearby stand.

"One hot dog," Luis told the fry cook.

"The long or the short?" the man said in a hoarse foreign accent. "The sauerkraut, the chili, the cheese?"

Luis stared at him mystified. "I want one hot dog," he said in English.

The man stared back at Luis. "You wannit the long dog or the regular? You wannit the chili or the sauerkraut or the cheese? You wannit the plain or the mustard and relish?"

Luis looked down at Ramón in defeat. The fry cook, irritated, started to go over the options again, but before he finished, Ramón, in clear English, told him he would have a regular hot dog with ketchup only.

Luis returned to Marta with the news.

"He watches television, and a lot of friends talk to him in English," she said, unimpressed. "And when I baby-sit for Mr. and Mrs. Oakes, the children speak English to him. The Oakes speak Spanish to you, but not to their children."

Luis wished he could talk to either Ramón or Marta on the way back home, but a sore throat and fever kept his son whimpering the whole way and made Marta mad at him. So he drove fourteen straight hours, secretly not unhappy that they were getting back from expensive California two days earlier than they'd planned.

Late the next night, Ramón was tossing and turning on the bed between his mommy and daddy, who had been trying everything to get him to stop his crying.

"He used to go to sleep when you sang to him," Luis reminded Marta.

"Well, you see it hasn't been working this time," she said, tired. "Maybe you should tell him one of your stories. Tell him how much money we saved not going to Disneyland."

Luis, as always, ignored her sarcasm. But he liked the idea. He liked to tell what Marta called his stories, and he believed Ramón liked them too, because many times he did go to sleep hearing about the men Luis worked with or the animals they raised or the plants they grew. And,

according to Luis, this was good for him since they would
help him in the future, especially since Ramón went to
sleep with them. He considered talking about the wild burros he saw in the Mojave Desert, or those saguaros near
Picacho Peak, or the *piscadores* in the chile fields near the
Rio Grande. Any of these could have worked too.

"Remember when we were at the ocean, where the
waves ran up your legs? And the helicopters, and those
fishing boats?"

Ramón stopped whimpering.

"Remember those birds that flew around those boats,
and how they all flew onto the beach when you and I
started feeding them bread?"

Ramón seemed to listen, was quiet. Already Luis felt
a little like gloating to Marta, who'd rolled her head over
to watch. "Those birds make their life there, *mijo*, and
with their wings . . ."

But suddenly Ramón lost interest. He turned to his
mommy and cried about the sore throat and how hot he
was. Luis was sincerely disappointed.

Luis and Marta stared up at the darkness toward their
small bedroom ceiling. There were crickets outside, and
they could hear a hard breeze rustle the trees and bushes
around their house, a tumbleweed scraping against the
backdoor screen. A cat yowled louder than the boy and
that was comforting to them both.

Marta hummed a few unmelodic notes. "How did that
go?" she asked Luis softly. "A and double U . . ."

Luis didn't know the words, but he tried to remember
the music to the jingle. They'd heard it a dozen times or
more, but things like that didn't stay with him.

"A and double U root beer . . ." she whispered, hoping that maybe Ramón had finally fallen asleep because
he wasn't crying.

Marta kept trying. Luis would tell her when she didn't
have it, which was every time.

Then Ramón, with his eyes barely open, sang the first
words just loud enough for them all to hear.

Luis couldn't believe it. Marta laughed. She sang: "A
and double U tastes so fine, sends a thrill up my spine!
Taste that frosty mug sensation—uuu!" And she laughed
again, hummed the rest of it, laughing still more, and
Ramón fell asleep as she sang it over and over to taunt
Luis, who this night was happy to lose his battle.

ARTURO ISLAS

❦ ❦ ❦

Arturo Islas was born in 1933 in El Paso, Texas, where he was educated in public schools. A second-generation American of Mexican descent, he received a scholarship in 1956 to attend Stanford University where he was elected to Phi Beta Kappa and, in 1960, was graduated with distinction. With time out for work and travel, Islas continued on at Stanford to earn his PhD and became a tenured professor at the university, teaching American literature, creative writing for bilingual students, and the writing of autobiography for students from minority cultures. An outspoken supporter of affirmative action policies, Islas also was responsible for adding the literature of ethnic minorities to Stanford's curriculum. As Islas noted, "At last, universities like Stanford were recognizing the existence of 'minority' cultures in the U.S., thanks to affirmative action policies. Until then, Anglo males had been thriving in the privileged academies for decades with the aid of such programs. They just didn't call them affirmative action."

Islas's publications include essays on Chicano literature, poems, and book reviews on writers such as Carlos Fuentes and Mario Vargas Llosa. His first novel, The Rain God, *was selected one of the three best novels of 1984 by the Bay Area Book Reviewers Association. A chapter from that novel—"Rain Dancer"—appears in this anthology.* Migrant Souls, *(sequel to* The Rain God *and the second novel in a projected trilogy about the Angel family and the Texas-Mexican border, was published in 1990. His promising career as a writer ended with his death in 1991.*

Rain Dancer

Felix Angel, Mama Chona's oldest son, was murdered by an eighteen-year-old soldier from the South on a cold, dry day in February. They were in Felix's car in a desert canyon on the eastern side of the mountain, and they talked only briefly before the boy kicked him to death. Because of the mountain and the shadows it casts, it was already twilight in the canyon, but on the western side where Felix lived the sun was still setting in those bleak, final moments when he thought of his family and, in particular, of his youngest and favorite son, JoEl.

The border town where Felix spent most of his life is in a valley between two mountain ranges in the middle of the southwestern wastes. A wide river, mostly dry except when thunderstorms create flashfloods, separates it from Mexico. Heavy traffic flows from one side of the river to the other, and from the air, national boundaries and differences are indistinguishable.

Imagining his uncle's last moments while sitting in his study gazing out at the California dusk settling on the leaves of the birch tree and turning them blue, Miguel Chico felt the sadness of that time of day. There are no sounds in the desert twilight. On very cold or very hot days, the land and its creatures breathe in that dry acid air of the space between day and night and, as the first stars appear, resume their activities in one long exhalation. Felix loved those quiet moments at dusk as much as the smell of the desert just before and after a thunderstorm when the sky, charged with lightning, became fresh with the fragrance of the mesquite, greasewood, and vitex trees. He had never been able to describe the smell until one day JoEl, not yet five years old, had said, "They're coming. I smell them."

"Who? What are you talking about?"

"The angels."

"You mean the family?" Felix asked.

"No. The ones in the sky."

330

From then on, JoEl could tell them when it was going to rain.

When Felix was a child he would run outside and dance when the storm clouds passed over, while his brothers and sisters hid under the bed. Neither Mama Chona, nor later his own family, could stop him.

"You'll be struck by lightning," they said.

"Good. I'll die dancing."

Felix and the young soldier had met in a bar around the corner from the courthouse. The bar serves minors and caters to servicemen and has enough of an ambiguous reputation to be considered an interesting or suspicious place by the townspeople on the "American" side of the river. Usually, afraid to be seen in such places, the citizens north of the river went to the dives and nightclubs across the border in search of release or fantasy and returned to their homes refreshed, respectability intact, like small-town tourists a little hung over after a week in New York or San Francisco.

But Mama Chona's son Felix was not a respectable man. Constantly on the lookout for the shy and fair god who would land safely on the shore at last, Felix searched for his youth in obscure places on both sides of the river. He went to the servicemen's bar regularly after work at the factory. On payday he treated everyone to a round of drinks, talked and laughed in jolly ways, and offered young soldiers a ride to the base across town, especially when he paid visits to his mother's sister, Tía Cuca, out in the desert.

Felix had been irritable that day because of his argument with JoEl at the breakfast table. Ordinarily he approached his work and even the difficult disputes between laborers and bosses with a casual good humor his comrades at the plant appreciated. He had been a graveyard shift laborer when his daughters, Yerma and Magdalena, were very young, but after Roberto and JoEl were born he was promoted to regular shift foreman. In the last five years he had been put in charge of hiring cheap Mexican workers. He had accepted the promotion on the condition that these men immediately be considered candidates for American citizenship and had been surprised when the bosses agreed. After thirty-five years, he was content with his work at the factory.

The Mexicans he hired reminded Felix of himself at that age, men willing to work for any wage as long as it fed their families while strange officials supervised the preparation of their papers. As middleman between them and the promises of North America, he knew he was in the loathsome position of being what the Mexicans called a *coyote*; for that reason he worked hard to gain their affection.

A person of simple and generous attachments, Felix loved these men, especially when they were physically strong and naive. Even after losing most of his own hair and the muscles he had developed during his early years on the job, he had not lost his admiration for masculine beauty. As he grew older that admiration, instead of diminishing as he had expected, had become an obsession for which he sought remedy in simple and careless ways.

Before they were permitted to become full-time employees, the men were required to have physical examinations. These examinations, Felix told them, were absolutely necessary and, if done by him, were free of charge. He scheduled appointments for them at his sister Mema's place across the river. The physical consisted of tests for hernias and prostate trouble and did not go beyond that unless the young worker, awareness glinting at him with his trousers down, expressed an interest in more. The opportunists figured that additional examinations might be to their advantage, though Felix did not take such allowances into account later. In those brief morning and afternoon encounters, gazing upon such beauty with the wonder and terror of a bride, his only desire was to touch it and hold it in his hands tenderly. The offended, who left hurriedly, were careful to disguise their disgust and anger for fear of losing their jobs. He could not find words to assure them. In most cases, however, the men submitted to Felix's expert and surprisingly gentle touch, thanked him, and left without seeing the awe and tension in his face. It did not occur to them that another man might take pleasure in touching them so intimately.

Later, after the men were secure in their work, the more aware among them joked about the *examinaciones* and winked at each other when Felix passed by on his way in and out of the office. None but the most insecure harbored ill will toward him, because his kindness, of which they took advantage on days when they were inexcusably late or absent, was known to all. A few, feigning abdominal pains, returned for more medical care and found themselves turned away. Most forgot the experience, occasionally referred to him behind his back but affectionately as *Jefe Joto*, and were grateful for the extra money he gave them for the sick child at home.

On the day of his morning argument with JoEl, Felix had not responded to any of his men in the usual friendly manner. In an attempt to tease him out of his mood, one of them talked loudly about the phases of the moon. Felix stared at the man.

"Hey, *Jefe*, it was only a joke."

The young Mexican pronounced the English "j" like a "y" and Felix said to him angrily, "Hey, *pendejo*, why don't you stop being a stupid wetback and learn English?" Then, murmuring an apology, he walked toward the man as if to embrace him, gave him a strange look, and walked away.

Any disagreement with JoEl caused Felix to be irritated with everyone, even his wife Angie toward whom he felt the kind of tenderness one has for a creature one loves and injures accidentally. He was unbearably ashamed of his remarks to the young laborer. Alone in his office at the noon hour, eating the burritos Angie had prepared for him, he choked on his shame.

The beer at the bar was good enough to restore his spirits and it began to give him the calm he needed to mull over his quarrel with JoEl. Felix loved young people and did not understand why his son did not see that. Now that JoEl was fourteen and more rebellious than ever, their arguments became nightmares during which Felix said words he did not mean. JoEl replied in curt, distant phrases that cut him off and caused anger to rise from his belly into his throat with a vehemence that caught him off guard. Their arguments never directly confronted the deeper antagonism that had begun to grow between them. Sometimes, even without speaking to each other, the tension was so palpable that one of them was forced to leave the room.

"But I want to go on that trip," JoEl had said harshly.

"I don't have the money to give you for it," Felix answered in the same tone.

"You have the money for beer and for Lena whenever she wants it."

"Your sister is older than you and needs it for important things, not for football trips with gringos." Felix liked gringos and football. Why had he said that?

"Oh, yeah," JoEl replied, "important things, huh? Like a phony pearl necklace for her date with that *pauchuco* she's been seeing."

"He's not a *pauchuco*. He plays in the band she sings with, and it's important for her to look nice. She's got talent."

"She's got talent, all right." JoEl's face had been ugly when he repeated the word.

—My beautiful son, don't look like that. It will wrinkle your face like a prune and your eyes will harden and break my heart.

Felix saw JoEl's eyes floating in the warm darkness of the bar. He would borrow money from his younger brother Miguel Grande, who would lend it without any questions or conditions. Felix felt the cold air of the desert winter as someone came into the bar, but the glare from the light outside blinded him so that he saw only the silhouette of a young man in uniform cross the threshold. JoEl's eyes disappeared into the far corner of the room.

Felix and his first son Roberto did not quarrel. Berto, who was Angie's favorite, was happy and easygoing—not a thinker like JoEl—and they all enjoyed his company. He helped his father fix the car whenever anything went wrong with it and would talk to him quietly about his problems with girls. He was dark-skinned like his mother, very "Indian," polite and shy. Felix returned his love in a steady, uncomplicated way. Only JoEl, antagonism causing his cinnamon eyes to seem darker, persistently disagreed with Felix about almost everything.

"You are just like your father," Angie told him. "Stubborn and too proud for your own good." She spoke English with a heavy Mexican accent and used it only when she wanted to make "important" statements, not realizing that her accent created the opposite effect. After his first year in school JoEl learned to be ashamed of the way his mother abused the language. The others, including Felix, loved to tease and imitate her. Their English was perfect and Spanish surfaced only when they addressed their older relatives or when they were with their Mexican school friends at social events.

"Come on, Mother, say it again," Magdalena pleaded.

"No seas malcriada," Angie said and waved her hand close to Lena's cheek.

"No, Ma, not in Spanish. Say it in English." Lena and her summer boyfriend were on the front porch, seated side by side hardly touching, swinging slowly back and forth. Every night at exactly nine-thirty, Angie went to the screen door behind them and said, "Magdah-leen, kahm een." Lena shrieked with delight; the sad boyfriend smiled apprehensively.

"Oh, Mamá, just a few more minutes." She said "mamá" in the Spanish way.

"No, *señorita*. Joo mas kahm een rye now." More howls, as the boy said an embarrassed good night and slipped from the swing and the porch into the dark. Lena barely noticed. She was too taken up by her mother, whom she adored.

Of his two girls, Lena was more like his wife, small and dark, with eyes like JoEl's. From his room in the back on those hot desert nights, Felix loved hearing the women talk and laugh after the boyfriends left, and he followed them in his reveries before sleep as they walked arm in arm from the living room to the kitchen spraying mosquitoes and turning off lights.

Angie had painted the rooms brilliant colors to annoy Felix's sisters, knowing that Jesus Maria and Eduviges disapproved of her and thought her a "lower class Mexican." She had also chosen the colors for their names: *Perico Tropical* and *Sangrita del Rey*. Felix agreed to buy the paint because he could refuse her nothing and because he knew that she would keep her word and paint the rooms without anyone's help. Her daughters had long since despaired of teaching Angie the good taste they learned in their home economics classes at school.

"But Mother, the colors are too bright." Yerma, her older and more prudish daughter, was shocked as she walked in the door after school.

"I dun't care," Angie said in her best English. "I dun't like white rooms. They give me the suzie creeps."

"The what?"

"Joo know, the suzie creeps." When Yerma figured out that her mother had combined current slang with a French dessert, she was too amused to insist on a subdued version of the colors already drying on the walls. From then on, anything white they disliked gave them all the "suzie creeps." And Yerma, who secretly loved white, painted her own room a lighter version of the tropical parrot in the living room.

Angie and Lena walked through that room, then the purple dining room, and into the bright yellow kitchen to set the table for the next morning. Felix heard them getting ready for bed and fell asleep. Lena and Angie now slept in the same room, he and JoEl in the back porch they had walled in with cinder blocks, and Yerma in the front bedroom on the double bed where all but she had been conceived. Berto slept on the living room sofa. When JoEl was ten Felix bought him a bed of his own, but until then they had slept together.

From the time he was very young, JoEl had dreamed vividly. He had often come to his parents' bed and stayed there until at dawn he fell asleep out of fatigue, his terror diminished by the light and the warmth of his mother and father on either side of him. When his son's dreams were very bad, Felix learned not to ask him about them. Instead, he allowed JoEl to weep away his terror while he and Angie took turns rocking him. At first they had attempted to exorcise JoEl's demons by asking him to describe them, but they saw that this made him even more frightened and inconsolable. Gradually they arrived at the better solution, but it was difficult because his fear was monstrous in relation to his size and frightened them. The first time he awakened the household with his screams, Angie wept out of frustration because he could not tell her what he saw.

"JoEl, what's the matter? What it is? Tell me." It was clear that JoEl, eyes open, did not see her, and the more she begged him to name his monsters the louder he screamed.

He did name them once when he was just learning to speak. The week before, Yerma and Lena had been teaching him the words for bugs in Spanish and English. JoEl was fascinated by the sugar ants that created roadways in the kitchen every summer, and which Angie could never bring herself to poison. They had begun crawling over his legs as he sat on the floor observing them, and only Yerma saw that he was hypnotized by fear and not curiosity. She could tell by the color of his face, pale yellow with a blue cast under the eyes, which was also its color during his nightmares. She brushed the ants from his legs, saying their diminutive Spanish name, "*Hormiguitas, hormiguitas*, JoEl," and tickling him at the base of his spine in an attempt to make him laugh. He neither laughed nor cried, but the natural color returned to his face.

"*Moleecas,*" he had said, "*moleecas.*"

Yerma smiled. "Not *moleecas. Hor-mi-gui-tas.*" She kissed him.

"*Moleecas,*" he had repeated seriously.

Sitting up in bed in the desert night, frantically brushing over his legs and arms in rigid, measured gestures that awed the family as they stood around him, JoEl screamed, "*Moleecas.*"

Watching him, Felix's heart broke with the knowledge that his son was a poet. He motioned Angie not to touch him until the gestures stopped and the eyes lost their unearthly sheen. He then lifted JoEl from the cot with great tenderness and took him to their bed.

As the three of them slept more frequently together, Felix lost his passion for Angie, and he would wake during the night cradling JoEl on his side of the bed. His protective feelings for the child perplexed and disoriented him because they seemed stronger than his desire for his wife. In the beginning, Angie paid no attention and was touched deeply by Felix's love for their son. Slowly, without intending it, she stifled her own desires and lay awake watching her husband and son in their timeless embrace. In the summer the crickets kept her company and in the winter she listened to the wind.

Finally, she set up the cot for herself in Lena's room, helped Yerma move their double bed into the front room when she started high school, and never disturbed Felix again. "He's a good man," she confessed to her priest in

Spanish. "I have my children, my house, enough to eat.
What more do I need?" The priest said nothing.

She remained thin and small with the beautiful arms
of a medieval madonna, but she forgot to dye her hair
at times and laughed with the irony of the sexually
deprived. Her own desire for Felix cooled and, loving
both her husband and son, she knew her son's strength
and sided with her husband whenever they quarreled.

Felix ordered another beer as a North American ballad
the children liked to sing began playing on the jukebox.
Yerma, Lena, and JoEl had good voices and serenaded
him and Angie often, though lately JoEl had stopped
joining in.

He and his son began to quarrel after JoEl had been
in school for two years. "Leave me alone," JoEl had said
to him one evening when Felix tried to see what he was
reading. "Can't I have any privacy in his house?" The
whole idea was preposterous to Felix, as he was not prepared to believe that his youngest child could understand
the full meaning of those words in English or Spanish.
The more Felix hounded him, the more JoEl retreated
into his private world of books. Felix knew he was wrong
to be envious of that world, but he could not help
himself.

"JoEl, you read too much. You're going to ruin your
eyes. Let's go for a ride." He had just bought a new
Chevrolet. JoEl did not look up from his book.

Their fights wounded Angie most of all, and Felix saw
how careful she was not to intrude. She watched them,
however, ready to spring between him and JoEl when
Felix's frustration led him to begin undoing his belt.
After those occasions, when he and Angie sat alone in
the kitchen, she attempted to soothe him by talking to
him quietly. She told him that she hid from JoEl's laughter when the belt buckle struck him. Only later, when
she heard the boy crying to himself, was she reassured
that they had not lost him. She understood that a father's
pride did not allow him to apologize to his son, but
couldn't he allow JoEl some freedom to do what he
wanted?

"What freedom?" Felix asked her in Spanish. "Freedom to turn into a delinquent or to become a selfish little

brat? He belongs to a family and he must learn to share. I know what they're teaching kids in those schools. How to disobey parents and how to act like grownups when they're only children. And they also teach them to be ashamed of where they come from."

Angie defended JoEl by reminding Felix that he was only eleven years old, very intelligent, and most of the time a good son. But even while defending him, Angie agreed with Felix about the schools. Unlike Berto and the girls, JoEl did not come to her for comfort. He disdained it from all of them, and she attributed his distance to the ideas he was learning from the younger Anglo teachers. When JoEl taunted her sarcastically for putting up with Felix's injustices, she did not understand what he was doing. They did not seem injustices to her but simply the rights of a husband and father. Her duty was to suffer from his arbitrary nature so that she might enjoy greater glory in heaven. JoEl scorned her for doing her duty. Felix noticed how icily JoEl looked at Angie after he had berated her for spending her household money in foolish ways.

"Don't look at your mother like that."

"I can look at her any way I want."

"Don't talk back to me."

"Why?"

JoEl's most effective tactic was silence. Wordlessly, he let Angie know that she deserved the pain she endured and that she was no better than a worm for letting Felix take advantage of her goodness.

"You have no respect for us," she said to him in self-defense. *"Malcriado, muchacho malcriado."*

"Well, you brought me up," JoEl answered.

At this point if he was present, Felix undid his belt. "Don't talk to your mother like that."

But when the family was happy, the house sang and the sofa played music. Lena, who had perfect pitch, discovered that if you sat on it in a certain way, it played two notes. These they incorporated into the background music for their songs. Felix and JoEl laughed together in the old ways and the others became infected with the joy. After the evening meal, they sang for their parents the songs they learned in school. Angie understood that they were patriotic North American songs and praised and kissed her children even if she did not like the music.

Berto was a perfect audience because he liked everything they did. JoEl told them stories and riddles he had read or made up, or sometimes he recited poems which they pretended to understand. He made them feel sad and Angie would look at him and wonder what was to become of her youngest child. As he grew older and turned more to himself, her fears grew with him. Sadness stuck to JoEl like the smell of garlic, she said to Felix. There was no remedy. Neither lemon nor baking soda could reach his pain and she contemplated it while preparing the evening meal. This time of day—twilight—was the most melancholy time of the day to her. The aroma of the rice made her think of JoEl's poems. Felix watched her stir it as he hugged her from behind.

An old romantic Mexican ballad was playing on the jukebox now and reminded Felix of the days when he was courting Angie. As usual, the singer was suffering from love and Felix smiled at the sentimentality of the lyrics. "Ay, Papa, how can you listen to such corny music?" the children asked him at home. He was not ashamed to admit that he loved all music. He and Angie had danced to this song shortly before and after they were married. After three beers, he sang along.

"Hey, Felix," asked the bartender, "what does it mean?"

"You wouldn't understand, you stupid gringo," he said. To himself he thought how only a Mexican song could mix sadness and laughter like that so that one could cry and sing at the same time. Another beer came sliding down the counter toward him.

Felix and Angie had met at school. They were among the first large group of Mexicans (or, as their teachers referred to them, "first generation Americans") to graduate from the town's high school. He was an average student with an undisciplined talent for music and literature that was discovered too late by a teacher who liked his sense of humor. She recommended that he be allowed to take college preparation courses but was told by the head counselor that it was too late for him to enroll. She knew that it was not but did not argue, seeing that Felix's family circumstances would keep him from continuing his education. His family, though proud of him, expected him to find a job right away. His sisters were anxious to see him begin fulfilling his duty as family breadwinner, for their father had died when they first crossed the border and Mama Chona had suffered much to keep them all together. Jesus Maria and Eduviges were tired of the menial work they took on which interfered with their studies.

The week after he received his diploma, he announced to the family his intention to marry Angie. Only his youngest sister Mema shared his happiness and embraced him. His brothers were still too young to care very much one way or another. They had no desire to attend schools of any kind after their grammar school experiences and were looking forward to the day they could find jobs that would allow them to earn the money to buy a car.

Before she left the kitchen where they were all seated for lunch, Jesus Maria said to him, "How could you do this to us? After all the sacrifices we've made for you? Now you're going to marry that *India* and leave the burden of this household to us." Jesus Maria had light skin and anyone darker she considered an "Indian." She said she did not understand how Angie had even gotten through school. Obviously she belonged to that loathsome group of Indians who were herded through the system, taught to add at least since they refused to learn any language properly, and then let loose among decent people who must put up with their ignorance. Jesus Maria knew that her family was better than such illiterates and she would prove it by going on to college.

"Don't worry, Jessie, I'll still help. You'll see, we'll work things out." He tried to put his arms around her, but she pushed him away and left the room. Felix faced his mother now. Mama Chona had remained silent throughout her children's quarrel.

"Come here, son," she said to him in her refined Spanish. "Let me kiss you." He had not expected her to assent so readily. She stood up and continued to tell him that she wished his father were alive so that he could give Felix the family blessing. She, God forgive her, could not.

Felix watched his mother walk away from him, a small despair beginning to impinge on his love for Angie. "I don't need your blessing, Mamá," he said in English, knowing she understood. "With or without it, I'm going to marry her."

And he did, five years later, after he had gotten the job at the factory and all but Mema and Miguel Grande were graduated from high school. Yerma and Lena were born in the first two years of their marriage, Berto a year later and JoEl two years after him.

Mama Chona forgave Felix for marrying beneath him when she saw her granddaughter, for whom she would have felt unrestrained affection had Yerma's skin been lighter. Angie learned quickly not to be hurt by her mother-in-law's snobbery, but she did not like it when Mama Chona held Yerma in her arms and called her a little Indian. "Don't worry about it." Felix said to her. "It's just the pot calling the kettle black."

When Yerma was eight years old she began taking piano lessons from Mrs. Ramos, the wife of a wealthy boot manufacturer. She was a good pupil and her talent was recognized by all who heard her play on the old piano Tia Cuca had given them when she moved out to the desert on the other side of the mountain. When Mrs. Ramos raised her fee from fifty cents to two dollars an hour, Angie, who saved money for the lessons out of the household budget, was unable to afford the increase. She did not want to ask Felix for it because she knew he did not have it, so Yerma no longer made the weekly climb up the hill to the rich peoples' part of town. She began practicing on her own with a devotion that ignored how badly out of tune their piano was, and she relied on Lena's ear to tell her how it should sound. They commented on its steady decline. "Pretty soon, Yerma, we can transpose everything down a whole tone. I can't wait, my ears are killing me."

One afternoon, Angie took Yerma up to the Ramos mansion. They were met at the back door by one of the kitchen servants who led them to the music room on the ground floor. Angie, who had never been to the house because she was too ashamed of her clothes to attend the biannual recitals in the living room upstairs, almost lost her nerve in the face of so many beautiful things.

She had not dreamed of such furniture, and she calculated that her entire house could fit easily into this lower level. "What beauty," she said out loud to Yerma.

They waited outside the music room in an alcove with windows looking out onto a garden filled with flowers. Angie could not believe they were real. "Imagine," she said, "in this desert." Yerma was afraid her mother would ask permission to touch them and was about to insist that they go home and not bother Mrs. Ramos, when her mother's attention focused upon the sofa. It was the most comfortable Angie had ever known, of a pale orchid color, and she dared not lean back for fear of sinking too far and disappearing altogether. Later, she said to Felix that in the Ramos mansion, everyone sat on clouds. Yerma was embarrassed by her mother's reactions and remained silent. She did not want Angie to plead with Mrs. Ramos for anything because she was afraid her teacher would then dislike her. At the same time, she did not want to hurt her mother's feelings by denying her the chance to bargain for the lessons. But she wished that her mother would behave differently, as one did in church, with respect and a certain lack of enthusiasm.

After all the students finished their lessons, Yerma and Angie were admitted to the music room. There were three pianos in it, two uprights and a baby grand. The students were allowed to play the magnificent full grand piano upstairs during dress rehearsals and recitals, and so four times a year Yerma lovingly touched the most beautiful object she had ever seen.

"Señora Ramos, I am Yerma's mother," Angie began confidently in Spanish. She counted on the inspiration she had prayed for to give her the necessary words, but instead there followed a long silence that made Yerma want to cry.

Mrs. Ramos responded kindly, "How happy I am to meet you, Señora Angel." To Yerma she expressed her happiness at seeing her again. "I've missed you," she said warmly.

Angie, encouraged, continued in Spanish. "Señora, my daughter has practiced every day and plays well. Please listen to her."

"Of course."

Yerma sat down quickly and played a simplified version of Chopin's "Minute Waltz" which she had mastered on her own. When she finished, Angie asked Mrs. Ramos what she thought.

"Thank you very much, Yerma, you played that very well. I'm glad you have been practicing. Please wait outside for a few minutes, I want to talk to your mother." Mrs. Ramos spoke in Spanish out of courtesy to Angie.

Afterward, Yerma told Felix that these were the most difficult moments for her. She felt ashamed yet happy that Mrs. Ramos had praised her technique, since she knew her to be a good teacher who meant what she said. A few minutes later Angie emerged from the music room, took her arm, and led her out of the house. As they walked down the hill her mother told her that she would begin her lessons again the following week, and they hurried home to give the good news to the rest of the family.

Now, after every visit to the mansion, Yerma came home to find JoEl sitting on the piano bench, waiting impatiently to learn what his sister had been taught by the mysterious lady who lived on the hill.

In the bar, Felix saw them sitting together on the bench, his oldest and youngest children, arguing and disagreeing about a phrase, humming the melodies out loud in key, and then playing them to each other on that sad old piano. He would borrow the money somehow to get it tuned for them. Food was not enough for his children. They needed music.

The beer, the ballads, and JoEl's eyes floating through the air began to act as a balm for the irritations of the day. He wished JoEl were outside waiting for him so that they might drive out to Tía Cuca's together. Felix could not believe that JoEl was irrevocably lost to him. Yet he knew it was so by the way Angie had looked at him several weeks before and said, "That's enough. Let him go." How could he? To what? Who would protect him from his nightmares and his melancholy? Felix peered into the darkness of the bar for the first time in an effort to locate the young man who had entered earlier. He saw only a string of small Christmas lights, sad remnants which acted as permanent illumination for the far side of the room. He returned to his beer.

*　　*　　*

The lights on the tree, which was scraggly and already dried out after only three days, pleased JoEl. Yerma and Lena had stopped bickering long enough to complete the decorating with angel's hair. It gave the lights a strange brightness that made JoEl think of heaven. He knew little about religion yet, but they had told him of heaven where he would go if he were good, and of a devil who would throw him in the fire if he were bad. He sat on the sofa in a trance while the girls finished their fussing over the tree and stood back to admire their work. Too big for them to pick up and hug and too small to help, he was content to sit and enjoy the colored lights made fuzzy by the synthetic cobwebs.

From the kitchen, the aroma of their mother's cooking reached them. She had worked a long time on the batter for the tamales, whipping it smooth and creamy so that its redolent corn smell made them want to eat it before it was cooked. "You're going to get sick," Angie always warned them, but sneaking tastes from the batter was worth the stomachache, even if it would cause your *ombligo* to burst. Your *ombligo* was where you were born, and to JoEl it was the most sacred part of the body. Often, when he was frightened or very happy, he would twist his finger in its hollow until he made small suction noises. He loved his *ombligo*.

They ate the tamales before midnight mass, which he was not yet allowed to attend. Yerma opened his and cut it for him so that he tasted the meat and red chile inside even before he put them in his mouth. He was the official family taster.

"Is it good, JoEl?" Angie stood over him and watched as he ate the first bites. His silence and the look on his face reassured her of her accomplishment. Everyone else commented on the lightness of the dough and the especially good flavor of the chile that year, or the tenderness of the meat Angie had saved every cent to purchase from the best butcher in town. Felix put his arms around her waist as she stood by him with more tamales and told her what a splendid cook she was. The children loved it when their parents touched each other in front of them. Angie, of course, was able to find fault with her cooking. "Next year, they'll be better. You'll see," she said, trust-

ing that the yellow-white corn husks which were more
and more difficult to find would be available the following year. She could not imagine tamales without them.

In the morning, after the gifts were opened, Felix prepared *capirotada*. It was his annual rite in the kitchen
where for the rest of the year Angie reigned. JoEl was
the only member of the family permitted to watch his
father prepare the rich bread pudding, and sensing the
privilege from the beginning, he kept still as Felix chose
the best slices of dried bread and cut them into perfect
cubes.

They closely monitored the milk scalding on the stove,
for if it overheated it would have to be thrown out and
fresh milk brought in from the market. The brown sugar,
the freshly grated nutmeg, the cinnamon lay waiting in
small, carefully measured piles. They and sherry beside
them sent out fragrances that made JoEl drunk with pleasure. Sometimes their strength, particularly that of the
nutmeg, made his head ache, a fact he did not mention
to his father who would have ignored him. Felix went
into a trance when he cooked. He shelled and chopped
each pecan with precision, selected every raisin for its
apparent succulence, and mercilessly discarded all of the
imperfect. Looking upon their flaws with disgust, he
wondered aloud what the world was coming to. "I don't
know what those *cabrones* think. I'm no fool."

Who the *cabrones* were did not seem to matter and
JoEl did not ask why they ruined the raisins. Evidently
they were with the devil. *"Pobres cabrones,"* he said with
sympathy, and his father laughed long and loudly every
time he remembered the story or told it to Christmas day
visitors. Profanity from the mouth of a child never failed
to assure him that innocence, if not perfect raisins, still
existed in the world.

"Pobres cabrones," Felix said into his empty beer
glass.

"What did you say?" The young soldier, fair with light-
colored eyes, stood next to him while ordering another
beer.

"Cabrones"? It's just an expression we Mexicans have.
In English, you'd say something like 'poor bastards.' "

The boy did not respond. Instead, he ordered his beer
with the cockiness of someone underage, almost daring

the bartender not to serve him. Felix took to him immediately and offered to pay for it. The boy looked at him without smiling and thanked him in a sweet southern drawl.

"You're welcome," Felix said. "Where you from?"

"Tennessee."

The boy's voice and his guarded, tentative answers excited Felix. He enjoyed making these shy types respond to his warmth. Even when they reacted in a surly or defensive manner, he did not give up the chase. They were his greatest challenge. Usually these encounters ended when he made them smile, talk, and even laugh openly at his bad jokes, their fear gone, their suspicions laid to rest. Once he had assured them that he was not interested in them for any perverse reason, they fell into his charming trap. Later, when he did make sexual allusions or even put his hand on their thighs while driving them to the base, they either responded according to their needs and desires or in embarrassed abrupt ways. Felix did not force them to do anything they did not want to do.

Most of all, he loved their youth and lack of guile. Even the most experienced among them had a certain purity that gravity, not worldliness, pulled down with the passing of time. They were in their prime, and when he was in their company and they permitted him to touch them, he tasted his own youth once again.

"How old are you?"

"Twenty-one." The boy was lying. Felix knew he could be no more than eighteen.

"What's your name?"

The boy told him and Felix observed that he had the mouth of a young girl. He had long since stopped wondering why his pursuit of the past led him to young men instead of women. He was secure in the love of his children, even when they quarreled with him, and he knew that Angie loved him. He was not looking for any of them in this boy's mouth. He was looking for something else.

"Can I give you a ride to the base?"

"Sure. Thank you very much," the boy replied with southern courtesy.

"It's just about the sunset. Maybe we'll stop at the

canyon on the way. It's nice there this time of day." The
boy did not reply, and as Felix opened the door for them
to walk out into the crisp winter light, he could smell the
bright polish of the young soldier's boots.

It was one of his favorite times of year, the air clean
and stinging his nose as they walked to the car. He had
forgotten to phone his brother Miguel and ask for the
money, but he would drop by tomorrow and talk to
Juanita before Miguel got home. He usually visited his
sister-in-law every Friday after work. They were fond of
each other and he loved to make her laugh until tears
came out of her small brown eyes.

Felix drove along the mountain so that he would not
waste any time if the boy agreed too accompany him into
the canyon. The eastern sunset was fine now, but the
color would be gone by the time they got to his special
place. Soon the March sandstorms would begin and the
road would be closed. He detested those storms because
they made him feel buried alive, and JoEl had learned
not to tease him about his fear of them or the handkerchief he tied around his nose and mouth so that he would
not smell the dust. He hated its bitter taste.

In the twilight there was no wind at all, and he wàs
glad the young soldier did not smoke. They usually did.
The sky was a bleached-out blue and the granite on that
side of the mountain was a beige that made it difficult
to distinguish planes and depths. A brilliant red-orange
light outlined the edge of the mountain from the sun still
setting on the other side. Off in the distance, toward the
east, he saw the darkness coming at them.

"Ah don't think ah want to go into the canyon," the
boy said.

"Oh, come on, only for a few minutes. It's real nice
in there."

Felix took the boy's silence as an indication of consent
and he began the slow drive up the canyon road. He
maneuvered the car expertly, familiar with every turn
and obstacle. They reached his secret place just as a soft
quarter moon rose in the eastern horizon.

"Nice moon, isn't it?" Felix said and put his hand on
the boy's knee. The boy sat rigidly on his side staring at
the windshield and not the landscape. Felix sensed his
preoccupation with the hand as it stroked his thigh.

"Don't do that," the boy said in a quiet, even tone.

"Don't be scared. I'm not going to hurt you. Let's have some . . ." The blows began before he finished. They were a complete surprise to him, and the anger behind them stunned and paralyzed him. He began to laugh as he warded off the attack, then stopped when the moon took on a strange shape and color.

"Hey, come on. I was just kidding." He was vaguely aware that he spoke through a mouthful of stones. It did not occur to him to struggle or to fight back. He forced his door open and fell to the ground, kicked sharply in the kidneys from behind. The stones in his mouth looked like teeth as he spat them out, and he turned to avoid the blows to his back. The boy stood over him. The kicking continued and he felt great pain in his groin and near his heart. Then his mouth was full of the desert and then it was not. He could no longer see the boy. The pain in his loins and along his side seemed distant, blotted out by a queer painful sensation in his left ear. He tasted the dust.

—Angie, where is my handkerchief? I hate this smell.

The biting ache in his ear began to recede and it seemed odd to be falling from a great height while lying on the desert floor. The sound of walking on stones puzzled him because he was surrounded by water. Its reflection and the luster of the boots flashed before him in an irregular, rhythmic motion. The beautiful youth was gone. Felix had time to be afraid before he heard his heart stop.

The desert exhaled as he sank into the water.

ROGELIO GOMEZ

❦ ❦ ❦

Rogelio Gomez was born in 1950 in Castano, Coahuilla, Mexico, the son of Elivra Mondragon and Ireneo Gomez Saldana. Gomez moved with his mother and sisters to Chicago in 1956, to join his father who had gone there several years earlier—illegally—to find work and a "more rewarding life" for his family, including educational opportunities that he had never had. Unable to speak much English, Gomez had trouble in school and received little sympathy or understanding; a counselor told his parents that Rogelio was retarded. In 1965, Gomez became a naturalized American, answering correctly the only question that was asked of him: "Who was the first president of the United States?" He attended the University of Texas at San Antonio; where he helped found the university's first student literary publication, Cactus Alley, *and later received an MA in English from Southwest Texas State University in San Marcos.*

The Aztecs Are Coming

There was never a customs agent like Fidencio de Luna. His dedication was notorious. Mexicans knew better than to attempt sneaking into the United States through Laredo's International Bridge. This was Fidencio's outpost. Sworn to repel the invading hordes, he had earned the appellation Bloodhound of the Border.

No one could sniff contraband like Fidencio either. Even as a rookie fresh out of college, Fidencio had a nose for smelling illegal traffic. His first bust was an old man smuggling huaraches. He was a real con, that man. Not to draw attention, the old man would cross the border once a month wearing a new pair of squeaky sandals. Despite arguing these were his only shoes, that he was poor and used them only when visiting his brother in Laredo, Fidencio was not fooled. He knew the old man was smuggling huaraches one pair at a time. For his efforts, Fidencio's supervisors laminated his chrome badge. It shone in all kinds of weather.

"You have to watch 'em all the time," he told his supervisor.

"I'll tell you somethin' else, de Luna," his supervisor replied. "If we had more good men like you, we wouldn't be in danger of them taking over. Do you know last census reported a whopping sixteen million? That's right! Right here in the good ol' USA. And where they hidin', boy?"

Fidencio didn't need encouragement, however. He reveled in his work. He was prouder still to be an American, not naturalized, but a *real* "native" American. And with this ardent patriotism burning in his soul, Fidencio had set himself as sentry to the States. *Someone* had to take a stand. So he could not be blamed if he was a bit rough on Mexicans. Fidencio was just taking care of number one.

"Let them stay where they belong," he confided to friends at The International Beer and Eat—Truck Stop Café. "They've no right here. This is *our* land."

Each day Fidencio arose with a growing sense of self-worth. Each day he found new ways to make it harder for Mexicans to cross his bridge: a shiftless stance; a humble demeanor; smudged passports. Reasons abounded.

Thus, with his chromed badge glaring into Mexico, Fidencio would stand at his bridge screening undesirables. One day he spotted an old woman approaching whose appearance, for some unknown reason, raised the hair on the back of his neck. Even from a distance Fidencio perceived something peculiar. His instincts warned him. It wasn't her colorful red and green Indian skirt and white cotton blouse that particularly called his attention. Nor was it the brilliant amulets of copper and silver flashing in the sun. The woman's long graying hair, flowing loosely down her back, seemed no cause for alarm either. There was just something about her Fidencio disliked.

"Where you going?" Fidencio asked.

"Qué?" The old woman retorted. *"No hablo Ingles, mijo."*

Four semesters of college Spanish enabled him to reply, "I'm not your *mijo*. Where you going?"

Employing hand motions, the old woman tried to explain that she had an ill sister in Austin who needed rare medicine. She produced a small bottle from a leather pouch, and, holding it tightly with both hands, the old woman said, *"Mi hermana la necesita. Vengo desde Cholula. Por favor, déjeme cruzar."*

"Oh, so you don't think American doctors good enough for her, eh?"

"Qué? No entiendo. Qué dices?"

Fidencio knew she was lying. Why, *everyone* knows English. Mexicans just like to play dumb. They know damned well how to get on welfare. No, we don't want her type, he concluded. Besides, Fidencio remembered, he'd seen her cross the border not more than two weeks ago. He was sure of it. Then, when looking more closely at her bracelets, rings, and brooches, Fidencio was certain she was smuggling untaxed jewelry. He confiscated her passport.

Leading the old woman to the detention center, Fidencio left her waiting as he filled out the appropriate paperwork. The detention center was also the customs' lunchroom. When she overheard someone inform Fidencio that his lunch was left at a nearby table, the old woman prepared her revenge. Removing from her leather pouch a few minuscule dog hairs, she sprinkled them over Fidencio's plate.

Hatefully, the old woman's words fell like venom on Fidencio's food. *"Perro desgraciad,"* she cursed, "you will realize your worst fears. One day you will find yourself kicking at the end of a long ugly rope. And should there be anything in you worth redeeming, you'll not return to the human race before recognizing your horrible nature."

Upon finishing lunch and returning to his post, Fidencio began feeling a queer sensation. He felt hot and feverish. He saw a stout Aztec Indian approaching from afar. Wearing only a long skirt, sandals, and a leather headband, the Indian walked stoically toward him. A prominent nose dressed his stonelike face. Perched on his leather-encased left arm was an eagle with fierce black eyes.

"Well, I'll be damned!" Fidencio hollered. "Look here, captain, if it isn't the last of the Aztecs."

Intending to please his supervisor by ridiculing the Indian, Fidencio armed himself with taunting quips. He stood with his chest puffed awaiting his prey.

As they met, Fidencio found himself disgustingly pleasant. Embracing the Indian and patting him on the back, Fidencio turned the Aztec to face his captain. He could not believe what he was doing. Fidencio attempted to restrain himself as flattering words spilled from his mouth.

"Captain," he heard himself say, "this is my distinguished uncle Xicoco, Cultural Overseer of the great capitol of Tenochtitlan." Fidencio covered his mouth, his face flushing with embarrassment. He cringed as his captain shook the Indian's hand and escorted him away.

"Why, hell," the captain said, "any relative of Fidencio here is sure 'nough friend of mine."

Fidencio was petrified. With mouth gaping, he was aghast, horrified. Can't he sée? Fidencio wondered. This'll be the end of me. He touched his face and decided the sun had truly beat down on him. "I'm . . . hallucinating," he mumbled.

His condition worsened as the day progressed. The sun's given me a rash, too, Fidencio figured as he scratched more and more about the scalp, and particularly behind the ears.

Near dusk, Fidencio thought himself well enough to return to his post. But no sooner did he arrive than his eyes sparkled with delusion. An army of Aztec warriors marched toward the border. With drummers heralding the proud, leathery-looking horde, the Aztecs arrived in mass. A fierce column extended well into Mexico. Leading the band were the elite Jaguar legions. Draped in their animal skins, fanged cat-headdresses, and carrying deadly-looking obsidian weapons, the Meso-American soldiers struck fear in Fidencio's heart. Unwilling to question them for their passports, Fidencio stood immobile. A weak grin dressed his face.

For more than an hour Fidencio smiled as the military procession entered the States. He thought himself ill but greeted the warriors jovially nonetheless. It must have been those horrible enchiladas, Fidencio determined. I should know better than to eat Mexican food. Concluding to be sick, Fidencio shut his eyes to the spectacle and went home. He was glad to be off the following day. It had been a hard week.

When he arose the next day Fidencio saw that things had not only changed—but, to his dismay, society was completely transformed. Olmecan craftsmen lined the streets. Toltecs wearing feathery headdresses drove Yellow Cabs. Aztec businessmen read the *Aztlán Street Journal*. The Pumas had defeated the world-champion *Chichimecas* in double overtime.

Fidencio knew there was something wrong with him, but had no idea how to alleviate the problem. Wandering Laredo's streets, Fidencio roamed dispiritedly until finding himself irresistibly drawn to the psychiatric office of Y. Crasyquatl, High Priest. A force compelled him within. Entering, Fidencio found an Aztec priest sitting behind a walnut desk. Wearing a necklace of dried hearts and bloodied, matted hair extending to his ankles, Crasyquatl motioned Fidencio to lie down.

Fidencio stretched himself onto a miniature pyramid. After hearing Fidencio's detailed hallucinations, Crasyquatl concluded there was nothing wrong with him that a good sacrifice could not cure.

Puffing on a corncob pipe, Fidencio's analyst said in Nahuatl: "These are common delusions resulting from a bad heart." Drawing a sharp obsidian dagger, Crasyquatl added, "All we have to do is cut it out."

But Fidencio was fast running out the door. Hiding in his apartment, he searched his soul for an answer; and concluded that if the Aztecs had taken over, then he simply had to adjust himself to the new power. "Why sure, that's all," he said. "Tomorrow I'll look for a job with them. I'm sure they can use someone who speaks English." Fidencio felt better almost immediately. He laughed. "Why, we'll teach those gringos once and for all what's what. That's the spirit, Fidencio," he praised

himself. "Why, you're already even beginning to sound
like one of them."

Dancing about his apartment, Fidencio knew that
everything would soon improve. He took a brisk shower
and planned on a good night's sleep. The only thing that
kept him from truly resting was his inability to shave.
Having struggled in front of the mirror for over an hour,
Fidencio determined his razor was simply too dull. For
no matter how he attempted removing facial hair, there
just seemed to be more and more. Of course he still felt
himself a bit ill. Why else would his ears seem a bit
longer, more pointy? It was just a minor relapse, that's
all. By morning he expected recovery.

Still, Fidencio passed a restless night. He tossed and
turned and scratched all over. There must be fleas in this
bed, he thought, scratching drowsily. It was well before
dawn, however, when Fidencio found himself stirring,
unable to sleep. Jumping out of bed, Fidencio landed on
all fours and scurried into the bathroom. He feared worse
things had occured overnight, but he could not see himself in the mirror to determine. He only recognized an
irrespressible urge to mangle a cat.

He tried finding a job with the Aztecs but they simply
pelted him with rocks. His own boss didn't recognize
him. Kicking Fidencio in the side, the man let him know
he was unwanted. Total strangers spit on him. Even the
little Aztec children practiced their hunting skills as they
chased Fidencio with bows and arrows. When he returned
to his apartment, the Indian landlord attacked him with
a lance.

No one wanted Fidencio, and he roamed the streets
scavenging for food. Gradually, he began to think he was
losing his mind. Fidencio could tell. Little things showed,
like baying at the moon. And surely trying to bite the
tires of moving cars was not like him at all. Still, peeing
on fences and posts was not altogether unlike him, and
so it helped him endure. Fidencio lived on the fringes of
society. Except that a good hot meal and cold beer still
lured him into cafés and cantinas; where, however, being
beaten unmercifully, he finally decided to leave the
human race.

"I don't need anyone," Fidencio said. "Besides, it's
safer."

It was true. A little old man, for example, had persisted in trying to catch Fidencio. At first, Fidencio didn't know why. Then he recognized him as the huarache smuggler. So it's revenge, eh? Now that I've lost my job the old man wants his way with me, is that it? The old man truly offended Fidencio. Baiting him with scraps of food outside his door, the old man taunted Fidencio as if he were no better than a stray mutt. Fidencio did not mind lapping the old man's bowls of water once in a while, for Laredo was very hot; but he had to admit the food was awful. *Arrggh!* Fidencio wanted a good steak.

The old man continued until finally, one unsuspecting day, Fidencio was caught unaware. As hungry Fidencio wolfed scraps, the old man roped him about the neck. Fidencio put up a mighty struggle. Kicking his legs and jerking this way and that, Fidencio proved spunky indeed for a Chihuahua. But it was in vain.

He spent the following weeks in agonizingly brutal self-discovery. He was a dog after all, he concluded, and learned that he deserved no better. Yet the old man, Fidencio nonetheless admitted, was really not so bad after all. He treated him well enough, fed him whenever he was hungry; and when the old man came home drunk after visiting his brother, he even spoke to him like a human being.

"Fido," he would say as they watched *fútbol* on television, "we're a poor lot, you and me. We can't afford to fight each other." Fidencio would look at him from his corner of the room, wondering, with large watery brown eyes, what was left to fight.

In time Fidencio began to trust and even like his gentle master. And one winter night, as Fidencio heard his hungry pals howling throughout the barrio, he saw the little old man shivering, asleep beneath his sole raggedy blanket. Fidencio approached him cautiously, allowing his instincts to lead. And as he sniffed around the old man, suddenly feeling the need to show his appreciation, Fidencio jumped atop the bed and curled his hairy little body on his friend's cold feet.

CAROLYN OSBORN

❦ ❦ ❦

*Born in Nashville, Tennessee, in 1934, Carolyn Osborn
has lived in Texas since 1946. She has a BA in journalism
and an MA in creative writing, both from the University
of Texas at Austin, and has been a newspaper reporter, a
radio writer, and an English instructor at Texas. Her short
stories have been published in many literary magazines,
including the* Antioch Review, Georgia Review, Paris
Review, New Letters, *and* Shenadoah. *She has been a
frequent contributor to anthologies published in the United
States such as* Southwest Fiction *and* Gringos in Mexico,
*and her work has also appeared in anthologies published
in England, Belgium, and Peru. Three collections of her
short stories have been published:* A Horse of Another
Color *(1977) and* The Fields of Memory *(1984) and* Warriors and Maidens, *(1991). For a number of years, she
has offered readings from her works and directed master's
classes and writer's workshops, such as one during the
summer of 1978, at the Universidad de las Americas in
Mexico, participating with, among others, Vance Bour-
jaily, Tomas Rivera, Thomas Thompson, and Rolando
Hinojosa-Smith. Osborn's stories have won numerous
awards, including a 1985 P.E.N. Syndicated Fiction
Award. One of her stories was selected for* Prize Stories
1990, *the O. Henry Awards. She now lives in Austin.*

Overlappings

L et's go down to the corral. It's been a long time since I watched Leo shear." Bern walked across the room to the door.

Annie looked up at him. "You know we can't." They'll talk. The others will, even if Leo doesn't."

"So they will talk. I'm tired of being in the house."

"With me?"

"No. I'm only tired of being inside."

She watched him go. He refused to listen to her. He would do as he pleased unless she could prevent him, and she couldn't. Because he'd changed the rules. She realized that when he called from Mexico City. This time she, not Leo, had to meet his plane. The demand was flattering. It was also a way of forcing her to decide.

When Annie didn't return from the ranch at the expected time, Cliff waited awhile, then called the foreman. She was a woman who generally moved according to schedule, a more flexible one now that the children had gone to college. Still she usually came home when she said she would. He did likewise although he was known to miss a plane when a meeting ran late. His call to Poke was unsatisfactory.

"Last time I seen her, Cliff, was when I took her back to the house around dinnertime yesterday. I was down at the corral till about three. Had the doctoring to do and the marketing. We're short thirty-eight goats, and I've been riding all the pastures looking—"

For more years than Cliff could remember Poke had worked for Annie's parents. Now, he often said, what was left of him worked for Annie. Accustomed to his meanderings as he was to his taciturnity, Cliff let Poke talk about goats for sometime before he broke in. "I spoke to her about eight-thirty last night, maybe a little before. She said she was driving back this morning. I've already checked with the highway patrol. They haven't seen anything of her, not that they would, ordinarily. It's

six now. Take a look at the house for me. No one
answers out there, but that phone doesn't always work."

When he hung up he wondered why he'd been so slow
to begin searching. Annie wasn't an adventurous woman.
She was fond of the ranch, though, and liked to spend
the night out there alone occasionally. Every fall and
spring, she drove up to oversee the goat shearing, not
that much overseeing was required.

"I thought you were going down to the corral. Why
did you come back so soon, Bern?"

"Poke's there. His truck is parked on the other side
of the barn."

"We're out behind the barn." Her laughter rose and
just as quickly, subsided. "Thanks for—"

"That's all right. I'll see Leo at the noon break."

"Now I have to go to the corral."

"I know. *La patrona.*"

It was true. She was *la patrona* though all she did was
sit on the fence and watch. The shearers were more careful when she was around. Fewer goats were nicked.
Fewer wisps of mohair drifted out to the pasture. She
liked seeing the men work, liked seeing them peel away
the heavy, dirty coats. "Bern, I always—"

"I thought you were tired of always."

"I am, and I'm not. If staying here hurts your Latino
pride so much, come with me. Let Poke see you, let him
talk."

"Oh, Annie. Shut up. Shut up. You'll make us both
angry if you keep talking." He caught her by her arms,
held on a moment, then let go.

Alvarez was the head of the shearing crew. Leo Alvarez, Bern's younger brother. Honest, Cliff was certain.
He made his men keep correct count of the number they
sheared and worked alongside them. Some locals, some
wetbacks. Nothing to worry about there. All the ranchers
around Mullin used him. Annie loved to see Leo's truck
running up the low hill to the corral. "It looks like an
ancient rickety shearing machine, something Don Quix-
ote might have imagined rising out of those dusty Spanish
plains, Cliff. The panels tilt madly, and that old faded
pink canvas he still uses flaps in the wind. Everything

jolts, and rattles and squeaks. Then three or four men crawl out of the truck, all of them grinning." Anything strange tickled her, the sight of domestic ducks mingling with wild ones on the lake, a red oak tree that kept its leaves all through November, a peculiar question from one of the children, any foreign place. She'd loved Mexico ever since she'd gone to school down there, so they went back in the summers and took the children with them to Guanajuato, Oaxaca, Jalapa, anywhere it was cool and they could rent a house. Yet she also liked the things she knew. She kept the customs, particularly at the ranch. The Sawyers ran cattle mostly. They had run goats, too, for nearly ten years, so Annie wanted to keep on even though she'd left the ranch at eighteen, the same age he'd left Mullin. The Sawyers . . . both of them were gone. Except for a few aunts and uncles, he was Annie's family now. The ranch was her one real tie to the past, and he had encouraged her going out there when maybe he shouldn't have. But how could he keep her in Austin when she obviously wanted to go?

Annie stopped in the hall where pictures of her parents hung. She hadn't really looked at them for months. There was the only picture her Mother had made of herself wearing a hat, a green tilted straw with a huge brim and a bunch of cherries dangling. Glossy, dark-red cherries, she could see the color, though the picture was black and white. She'd thought they were real at first. What was it Mother said? Yes. "Your father goes around in a hat all the time. I thought I'd have the photograph made to remind him I have a hat to wear." She didn't have many occasions to wear an outrageous hat in Mullin County. All one spring, she wore it when she went shopping in Austin or San Antonio until Daddy begged her to buy another one. How she used to worry about Mother not coming home from San Antonio . . . so far from Mullin she had to spend the night. The picture had been taken at a studio there. Afterward she put the hat away. She hadn't known a defiant gesture when she saw one. Oh well, she was just ten and it was only a gesture, a shadow of her mother's longing for city life, for something richer. The rest she stifled the way some ranch women planted rose bushes, those one-summer blooms,

which they knew the next drought would wither. What
contrary moves we insist on making sometimes. One step
forward, one step back.

"What are you doing, Annie?"

"Looking at Mother's picture, thinking about her life
out here. She loves this place and hates it, too, sometimes. She didn't grow up on a ranch. She was from San
Antonio."

"Let me see." Bern stood beside her in the dark hall
in front of the walnut chest with its cracked marble top.
"She was beautiful." He sighed. "My mother never had
a hat like that."

"Not many women did. I guess that's why she bought
it."

Cliff caught himself reciting worries the way other people recited prayers. The Sawyer place was remote, a mile
and a half to the nearest neighbor, and there were plenty
of natural dangers—rattlesnakes, coral snakes, copper-
heads, scorpions, wasps, spiders—he'd killed a black
widow in the tack room the last they were there—three
horses that ran wild in the pasture where the house was,
a lame bull in the same pasture. Ah, he was letting his
imagination run wild. Anything could happen anytime.
Annie was careful. She was safer on home territory than
she was on the highway. But she would call, wouldn't
she? Or have somebody call. If it was car trouble, he'd
know by now. What kind of trouble could she be in?
Everything had seemed all right last night. But wasn't
that the way he wanted to think? To throw a reassuring
net over all. Annie accused him of that when he tried to
comfort her at times.

"Why are you calling Cliff?"

"It's hard to give up the things I've been doing for
twenty years."

"What I believe you mean is it's hard to give up Cliff.
You still love him."

"Of course I do. Don't expect me to give up loving
Cliff. There are many kinds of love, Bern. You know
that." She sighed. There were so few words for emotions,
for love, for grief. Only anger produced a lot of words,
and all of them the wrong ones. Much of her time with

Bern was misspent arguing. They had so little time, a few days each year, and every day he always said she must do what he asked . . . when she was not ready to. When Anita was alive, they were peaceful . . . in the summers. In the mountain towns where she'd rented houses all over Mexico, and they had come to visit. Then at the beaches Bern loved, where he and Anita insisted she and Cliff must visit them, must bring the children, must give way and let the servants wait on them. Because it was Mexico. That was what Anita used to say, "You must not take their work from them, Annie." She had to remind her everytime.

"I have to make this call, Bern. I'll say what I usually say. I'll tell Cliff how many pounds were sheared."

"All right. I'll wait for you on the porch. I can see from here the moon is coming out of the clouds."

The connection was bad. Cliff had to ask Evelyn to repeat herself.

"I said she's not out there. Poke just phoned from the ranch to ask me to tell you."

"Why didn't he call me from the ranch?"

"You know how he is about long distance. He hates to dial it. Says there's too many numbers. He always leaves one out."

"Well is there anything, any sign of where she might be?"

"I don't know how to explain this. The car is in front of the house, but all her stuff is gone. Poke says the house looks real neat. Locked up, too."

"I don't guess there was any—"

"There's a mirror propped up against one end of the couch over by the door like she meant to take it with her and forgot."

"Don't touch anything out there, Evelyn. Tell Poke not to, either."

"All right. Cliff, I'm sorry."

"For what?"

"Whatever. I hope she hasn't come to any harm."

"Did Poke see any signs of any other cars?"

"I don't know. I should have asked him."

"Evelyn, when Poke gets there, see that he calls me."

"All right."

She sounded shaken. He was shaken, himself. He would have to call the police now to report Annie was missing. They wouldn't even begin to look for her for twenty-four hours after he called. He'd have to convince them she'd been gone that long already. Should call the sheriff in Lampasas, too. The ranch house was in that county. First—before calling anybody—he'd have to hear more from Poke. Damn his foolishness about the phone. Probably had to get Evelyn to dial for him. At least he was sharp-eyed. He would notice every little detail. Used to tell him he'd make a good witness. Could she have been kidnapped? Why? A forty-year-old woman. Forty-two. Pretty still. Not especially rich. The land was worth a lot, but she'd never sell it. Crazies didn't care. Don't look at today's paper. Don't check on who's been raped, robbed, beaten, stabbed, murdered in one day. It all happens everyday. Don't think about the damned cases . . . the client whose son disappeared, the woman with all the knife wounds, the— Don't! Wait. Have a drink, have two. Wait for Poke to call.

"Why the mirror?" Bern ran a finger around the frame as if checking the finish for flaws.

"It was my mother's."

"Yes, all right. Why do you want to take it with you?"

"See the little holes in the frame? They were made by my father's shotgun. When I was a child, he brought it into the house loaded. He never did that again. The glass was shattered. Mother replaced it, but she kept the damaged frame."

"Was he shooting at her?"

"No, what a crazy idea. It was momentary carelessness. That's all. He was putting the gun on its rack. He'd forgotten there was a shell in the chamber. When he lifted it up, it slipped. His hand caught the trigger. Shot sprayed through the mirror and all around it on the bedroom wall. Haven't you ever noticed?"

"No. And you haven't told me why you want to take it."

"I'm leaving everything else." She was leaving her familiar place and going to his, and she wanted to take a piece of her own with her. Was that it? Or was she merely a woman running out of a burning house choosing something indiscriminately? No. That couldn't be true. She'd always chosen with great care—Bern, Cliff, Bern.

Poke Rabbin stood on the steps of the house Annie had been raised in. The sun had already set. All that was left was the show. Enough dust for a good one, too. Red and pink clouds smeared the southwestern rim of the sky. When she was little, Annie had ridden off that way to school every morning. He'd gone with her, watched her catch the bus, then taken the pony home. In the afternoon they repeated the trip, and when the weather got bad, either he or Bob made it down and back in the pickup with her. Neither one of them minded. It was part of the routine on the place, like calving, or feeding, or fencing. Only, he liked going after Annie better than doing any of the rest. He and Evelyn should have had a bunch of kids but they couldn't, so he got to share Annie, the only one Bob and Catherine had. She showed an early preference for men. Never wanted to stay in the kitchen and let Catherine teach her how to bake cookies. If he and Bob went hunting, she went with them. He'd taught her how to shoot a .22 first, then a .410, and even if she didn't like deer hunting, she knew how to handle a .30-30. Bob said a girl ought to know which end of a gun to point. When Annie was twelve—too young, Evelyn said—Bob taught her how to drive, gave her an old cranky Ford to get herself to the gate in. How long was it after that that the Alvarez boy showed up? A year or so. He started giving her rides home from school. Just to the gate. He was two or three years older than she was, and he knew he wasn't supposed to go further. What was that boy's name? Bernie? No. Bernado, and everybody called him Bern. Leo Alvarez' older brother. Sometimes Leo was with them when they drove to the gate in that beat-up truck.

Pulling out his tin of tobacco before he sat down, Poke lifted out just enough with one finger. Like an old goat chewing, Evelyn used to say. Then she got used to it and gave up on reforming him. He sat on the second step and put his elbows against the top step. He didn't like none of what was probably going to happen next, and he had to think on it. Replacing the tobacco, he patted his back pocket to make sure the letter Annie had left

was still there. He'd hand it over to Cliff himself.
Damned if he'd read a private letter to anybody over the
long distance telephone.

"Annie, why are you writing?"

"I have to let him know something, or he'll think—"

"What?"

"He'll think something disastrous has happened, Bern."

"I didn't know Cliff had such an imagination."

"Why not? Most people imagine something when a
person disappears. Remember, even if he's not a criminal
lawyer, a lot of people with criminal problems come to
him first."

"And—?"

"He listens. Later he refers them to someone else."

"You don't like for me to talk about Cliff, do you?"

"Sometimes you underestimate him."

"It's the weakness of a jealous man."

"Do you want to read what I've written?"

"To Cliff? No . . . Yes. No."

Poke moved up to the top step, wrapped his fingers
around his bony knees, and watched the afterglow. It
couldn't last. Annie and the Alvarez boy. At least he
hadn't told on them. Talk made its way and gossip traveled fastest. Bob told her no more riding around with
the Merican boy. We like them fine, but Anglos and
Mexicans don't mix here.

"She said I was prejudiced, Poke. I told her, damn
right I was. The Alvarezes are shearers, always will be.
They're Mexicans, always will be. What else was I to tell
her?"

He groaned inwardly. His daddy was a cowboy. He
was a foreman. Everybody didn't stay the same. Bern
was smart, smarter than a lot of the ranchers' sons. Most
of them hated him for it, too.

"What did Annie say then?"

"She said, things didn't have to stay the same. I told
her to wait awhile to see."

They quit riding around together. Saw each other at
school, at other places, he reckoned. She wasn't his
daughter; still having no children, Annie was, in some
way his. He was as relieved as Bob when Bern went off.

Some of his mother's people lived in Mexico still. He graduated top of his class from Mullin High School, went to college in Mexico City. Half the people in Mullin never dreamed there was a college down there. Leo stayed home, took over the shearing when his daddy died. Of course, Annie went away to college, too. Hated to see her leave. Seemed like there were big holes in the days when she was gone.

After that there was a lot of her life he knew nothing about. Had to be. She came home Thanksgiving, Christmas, Easter. In the summers, she was gone way off— Europe. Mexico. Somewhere down there, a place where there was a summer school, San Miguel . . . that was it. To learn Spanish better, she said. Was that when it happened? Did she pick up with Bern Alvarez that summer? If she did, then why did she come back and marry Cliff the next October? Of course she'd always known him. Everybody knew Cliff Mullin. Town was named after his granddaddy.

"Do you mind leaving all this?" Bern waves his arm to indicate the living room, the hearth, the old branding irons on the wall, the pictures of her grandparents in florid gilt frames, the furniture so carved in claws and curls that sometimes she was reminded of hulking animals sleeping . . . griffins, bears, lions. The zoo, her children called it; the museum, her mother said, because Daddy liked the room as grandmother had left it.

"Do you mind leaving your house, your ranch?"

"No. It will still be here, and it will still be mine, and one day it will belong to my children."

"Then leave the mirror."

But it was where she saw herself. Wasn't that why she chose it . . . to remember her father's accident, the shattering, the replacement. Wasn't that what she was doing? How carefully we choose things even when choosing unknowingly. By marrying Cliff, I stayed close to Bern. So? So, I have known that for a long time.

"Can't you give it up, Annie? It will be awkward to carry."

"All right." Do we ever truly leave? Has he ever really left? Will I? Am I the part of his past he chooses to take with him? Or do I choose him because he's part of mine? Memory is oppressive here. Maybe that's why I can go.

Poke stood up, stretched, and looked over at the windmill. Running too fast before the light, south wind. Blades whirling free in the air. Not a damn drop was being pumped. Sucker rod broke probably. He'd have to get hold of Patterson to work on it tomorrow.

He swung the door to his pickup shut, spat out the window, and drove into Mullin where Evelyn met him at the kitchen door.

"Cliff wants you to call him."

"She left a letter."

"I thought she might."

"What do you know about all this?"

"Not much more than you've put together probably." Evelyn sighed. "Only I can't . . . I can't quite figure it out. Maybe if you read Cliff the letter—"

"No. It's got his name on it. He has to read it himself. Call him for me, Evelyn. Tell him I'll meet him at Seward Junction."

"That's way over halfway for you."

"I didn't arrange the towns around here. Anyway he'll have to wade through all that Sunday-night traffic coming and going out of Austin. Tell him to meet me at that filling station there."

"Did you see any signs of—?"

"Like I told you. The place was real neat. Only the mirror on the floor. Couldn't tell anything by the road. Too dry and too windy to hold tracks. Besides the shearers was in and out yesterday. Annie drove that same road. So did I. Everything's all mixed up."

"Sure is." Evelyn smiled. "Don't be too upset, Poke. It was bound to happen sometime. Go on and get your supper while I phone Clifford."

All the way to Seward Junction, he wondered what she meant. Evelyn had a whole mysterious-woman side to her he'd never been able to figure out. What was bound to happen? He'd intended to ask her but was so hungry he'd let the remark pass.

Annie stood at the window watching the windmill blades blur together. It was moving too fast. Sucker rod was probably broken. She could call Patterson, the wind-mill man, to come out. Poke would notice and call him tomorrow when he came by to check on the goats. It was a sound she'd miss. Had Bern ever missed the sound of a windmill turning? She doubted he had. Bern disdained nearly everything in Mullin, Texas, not everyone though, not his family. He saw them each time. Leo met his plane and took him home for a day or so. They believed he returned to Mexico. Instead, he came to her at the ranch. Someone always had to be fooled. Her parents first, now his, and for the last five years, Cliff. She'd never liked the deceit. It was the price she paid for wavering, a com-mon guilt, and she was weary of it.

They could be direct, but it was something difficult. They responded to each other so quickly, too quickly often. Everything was easier when they were in bed. They were still good for each other even after how many years? Almost twenty she'd been married to Cliff. What a fury Bern had been in when he discovered they were getting married. It was as if he'd been betrayed. In a way, he was.

The phone call from Mexico was brief.

"Why are you marrying him?"

"Cliff's a kind man, and he loves me."

"You don't love him. You love me."

"Living in Mexico has changed you. You're harder to like."

"What has liking to do with this?"

"Everything."

The wires hummed through the thick silence between their words. He hadn't called since she'd left. What was she to think? She had believed . . . Oh, she'd believed he'd become impossible. Once he'd gone to Mexico City, he was quickly involved in machismo, that ridiculous strut, that cock-a-whammy version of male dominance. She hadn't realized how much solace he needed. Neither all his intelligence, nor all her attention, nor Cliff's steady friendship could save him from Mullin's careless tongues mumbling "Meskin." So he became Mexican truly and turned his back on the gringos.

What did he look like then? All she could see was the tall, thin young man, always wearing sunglasses, always dressed in white, always demanding. He had consumed her summer. When she refused to go with him into Mexico City anymore, he came to San Miguel. Flowers everyday, music two or three times a week—mariachis, violinists, and once two Indians playing reed flutes so plaintively she wanted to laugh and cry. The songs were alike though. Sometimes harsh, sometimes tender, all were outpourings of grief over the pain of love.

A part of courtship in Mexico, everyone told her. Yet she mistrusted such effusion. He would ask her to meet his family next if he was serious, they said without knowing who he was, without knowing she had already met his family in Mullin, Texas where his father and brother sheared her father's goats. In San Miguel her friends knew only his aunt and uncle, Lena Alvarez's brother, a successful coffee merchant from Jalapa who kept an apartment in Mexico City.

"Marry me!" cried the trumpets, the guitars, the violins, the flutes, the pink gladiolus, the yellow daisies, the roses of every color. She had refused. He was volatile, demanding, and after she'd slept with him, arrogant. He seemed to think he could plan their whole lives alone. "We will live in the city, have a house on the coast. In the summers we will—"

"Sometime we have to go back to Texas."

"No. Let them come down here."

"My parents will never—"

"Yes they will."

"You don't know my father."

"He is a proud man, and he has only one child. He will come to Mexico."

"I'm not so sure of that."

"If he won't, your mother will."

"My mother does as my father wishes."

"I wish you would be more like her."

"I have no intention of being like my mother. You are not like your father. Why would I copy my mother?"

Their quarrel grew and spread like the bougainvillea whose tenuous leaves turned to red flames flickering over the patio wall. So she left, went back to Austin to finish her last year at the university, to see Cliff Mullin graduate from law school, to marry him. Because she would not allow herself to marry Bern? Wasn't it a question of

her own pride? Taught to think and act for herself, she
could not imagine being half of a cock and hen pair.

Now, twenty years later, they had become a pair.
Impossible to explain. Cliff would never believe her.
He believed in explanations, in reasons. There was one
she could think of, but it was too unsatisfactory, too
indefinite to give him. She had grown up alone and so,
essentially, had Bern. There was no one remotely like
him in his family. When she joined him, they returned
together to their solitudes, which like feathers, like fans,
overlapped.

Evelyn straightened up her kitchen quickly after Poke
left. She was tired of kitchen work, worn out with pots,
and pans, and decisions about meals. At sixty-nine, she
guessed she had a right to be, though it seemed to her
she remembered being tired of all that when she was
thirty-five or forty. Most women she knew got that way
unless they were crazy about cooking. Like her, they
kept on throwing it all together. Poke was good to help
out even if he wasn't much on planning ahead. He was
a fried-egg-and-ham cook. The one who really planned
ahead was Annie. She came to the ranch with menus
made and all the food cooked. Because, she said, I don't
want to have to think about it for two or three days.
Evelyn remembered Annie's determined voice. But she
couldn't plan ahead for everything. Too much happened,
too many other people make plans of their own. Like
Clifford. He was patient. He knew how to wait.

Most of Mullin came to that wedding. People drove
up from Austin and from ranches all over Texas. It was
a natural match. Sawyers and Mullins, ranchers and
bankers, only Cliff was breaking away to be a lawyer.
Well, there was only room for so many on the land and
in the banks, and he had three brothers. The minute
Annie married Cliff, Bern Alvarez married a girl he
knew in Mexico. Leo told her, shook his head when he
did.

Of all the Alvarezes, Evelyn knew Leo best. He
sheared her six goats twice a year. They'd talk while he
worked out in the corral. Leo, kneeling on the board,
worked slowly because he was talking.

"My brother is a fool about Annie. It was right for her to marry Cliff."

"I don't know."

"Her parents wanted it."

"Sometimes Bob and Catherine, like a lot of other people, want what they think is best, and it isn't. But who am I to say?"

Leo shrugged. "Who is anyone? I know well as you about Bern and Annie."

"Something must have happened while she was in San Miguel."

Leo smiled, his clippers held in mid-air for a moment. *"Sí."*

It was the one Spanish word he permitted himself around Anglos.

"They quarreled, I guess."

Leo nodded, untied his goat, and reached for another one. "Here she is, the daughter of a rich man."

"She put on airs?"

"Not so much, but you know Annie. She gets her way. Maybe—"

"Maybe Bern wanted his way in his country."

Leo laughed.

Evelyn could still imagine him. Young, not so fat then, dark-headed, careful. Almost twenty years ago, on his knees in the corral laughing. Leo fit into his family, wanted to carry on when his father died. He'd always planned to. Nobody knew Bern's plans. He didn't look like the rest of them. Had Lena Alvarez . . . ? No use making up tales about some other woman. Lena said Bern favored her side of the family, and who could deny it since all of them lived in Mexico, still. Bern went back to his mother's people where he stayed, and according to Leo, he prospered.

"He's an engineer, Mrs. Rabbin. He takes care of the oil while I," he held both arms wide apart, "I take care of the goats."

Did he mind the difference in them? He didn't seem to. She ran into him at the feed store right after the big well erupted into the Bay of Campeche.

"Bern's down there. He's got plenty of trouble now. We won't get a visit from him for awhile." He smiled.

"Which is worse, do you think, the smell of goats or oil?"

She said she hardly knew and smiled back at him. Though neither of them admitted it, they both knew Bern flew in every fall and spring when Annie's goats were sheared. She hadn't gone out to the ranch snooping. She seldom went to the place at all when Annie was there. Maybe she was jealous. Poke had always protected Annie so . . . ever since she was a little kid. He was doing that now, keeping still, waiting. Because he hadn't told anybody about Bern's trips up, hadn't even told her. She'd found out by accident. Driving back from Lampasas in March, five years ago. The highway went right down by the airport, such a small landing strip, only big enough for private planes, and who was that? Leo Alvarez hugging a man taller than he was. Then she recalled the date. Shearing time at the Sawyers' wasn't it? Bern wasn't flying up just to visit his family. If he was, she'd see him in town and she didn't. Leo never mentioned his visits. Neither did any of the others. So Bern and Annie had been carrying on five years at least. How many more? What happened to his wife . . . anything? Leo hadn't said, and she wasn't of a mind to ask. Did Clifford know, or did he keep himself from knowing? Did he know and not know at the same time? Hard to tell about Cliff. He was a button lip like Poke, like most of the men she knew. Whatever bothered them the most, they hid the most.

Wonder if Clifford had called the police? Of course she was too curious. Hard not to be even though it was a small secret so far. She and Poke knew. The Alvarezes? Bern must see all of them when he flew up. Probably he didn't tell them anything. It took four or five hours to shear Annie's goats. She didn't have many over three hundred. They ran mainly cows and claves. Bern could stay out of sight at the house. After the shearing, he'd be free to roam anywhere on ten thousand acres.

Did he like it? Did Bern Alvarez like the country he'd been raised in? Annie did and didn't. Too dry, she said. Too hot in the summer, too rocky, and there were way too many snakes, she complained after she'd moved to Austin. But she knew how to look at a thing another way. There was a fairness about Annie. When they were talking that time she'd said, "Evelyn, you've done what my mother did. You've endured the droughts, the heat, ridden over the rocks and killed the snakes."

"I don't believe we'll ever get them all killed."

They both laughed.

"Maybe I like it here, Annie, because I haven't lived anywheres else. Maybe it's because I only know this part of Texas, so it's all right with me. People get used to their places."

True enough for her, not for Annie. She was restless. Bob and Catherine sent her to Europe for a whole year before she made that trip to Mexico. Sounded like from what she'd said she didn't much want to come home.

"You ought to see the cowboys in France way down in the south and the ranches in Spain. Splendid! Especially the ones where they raise the fighting bulls."

She went on and on about France and Spain, but she didn't have much to say about Mexico when she got back. San Miguel was cool, pretty, yes, there were lots of churches, and she'd learned real Spanish. That was about all. Then, just as the heat was breaking in late October, she married Cliff. Must have been something . . . something unfinished between Annie and Bern, or maybe it couldn't be finished.

Cliff waited on the asphalt drive running around the station at Steward Junction, a noplace almost. There was a shack advertising barbeque. He and Annie had tried it once.

"The old Texas con game," Annie said. "Bake it, throw bottled sauce on it, and make passing strangers pay for it." They paid and went out the door leaving the greasy meat, canned beans, and gelatinous cole slaw sinking in the paper plates. In later years, they laughed as they passed by. Steward Junction became their code term for bad food, a private joke, the kind a lot of married people had. They had a number of them, but he couldn't put his mind on one more at the moment. He kept drifting off like a weak radio signal to return to a single question: Was she all right?

There, swinging in beside him, Poke's truck.

Both of them got out at the same time. Poke met him at the tailgate of the pickup and handed him the note wordlessly as if it were an ordinary transaction, as if he were handing him a bill for feed of a list of calves just sold.

Nodding as he took it, Cliff returned to his car.

Dear Cliff, I'm all right. I had to leave. I'm sorry to hurt you. There doesn't seem to be a way out of that. I'll call you later. Love,

Annie

He reread, trying to make sense of the words that wriggled together under the car's interior yellow light. Poke was waiting, leaning against his pickup's door. He appeared to be merely watching the road. Cliff folded the note precisely in the same places Annie had and put it back in the envelope. For a moment he stared blankly out the windshield. A moth bumped against the window. He switched the light off. He'd known it was possible, had known before they married, and put it out of mind.

"Poke."

"Yep."

"It's just as well I didn't call the police. She's . . . she's all right."

Poke studied the asphalt as if he were looking for a map in it. "Guess I'll be getting on back then."

"Thanks for coming."

"Sure."

He stood by the car while Poke turned his pickup around. Funny. Neither of them mentioned it, yet both of them knew Annie had left with Bern Alvarez. Maybe he was the only one she'd ever really loved. How could . . . ? No. It couldn't be so. They had two children, twenty years together, a lot of life. Maybe she had loved them both. And how much was merely circumstance? If her father hadn't been so foolish, hadn't tried to break up an adolescent romance between his daughter and a Mexican boy, would Annie be home right now? What if he and Bern hadn't been friends? What if he hadn't helped him? For a year, the year Annie was sixteen, he'd picked her up at the ranch, gone after her in his own car, then delivered her to Bern. And fallen in love with her himself. He'd had to wait all that time. Had to wait for all of them to grow up. Had to wait until he was finished with law school and Annie came back from Mexico free at last of Bern . . . or said she was.

* * *

"Annie, he will guess you're with me.

"Certainly." Why do we have to go on talking about Cliff? Do we take him with us this way? Is that what he wants to do, to make Cliff an accomplice once more?

"I've chosen to live with you. You wanted me to make the choice."

"Sometimes I feel a little guilty. That's all."

Sometimes he seemed too interested in Cliff's responses, too curious about another man's opinion.

"Look how blue—the ocean and the sky. They're almost one."

"Yes. A blue bowl. We'll be flying over Yucatán soon. See, we're above land again."

From the plane it looked like there were only two or three roads on the whole peninsula. Odd. She supposed there wasn't much to go to and from. Mérida and what else? The islands . . . Cozumel, Cancun. But she couldn't see Mérida. There would be roads to and from the ruins, to Chichén Itzá, and Uxmal surely. Bern was concentrating. Long flight . . . one country to another, one man to another. She'd known only two, loved just two. Why? Other women, some of her friends, the ones she grew up with, fell in and out of love all the time while she'd continually been the point of a triangle. She knew Cliff too well . . . they'd had everything in common. And Bern? She'd never truly known him. When they were growing up, she thought she did. They were strangers now. What had she done? Run away, of course. Anyone could see that. She could have been more discreet if she hadn't been sick of discretion.

Cliff started the motor and pulled out on the highway blinking his eyes at the rapidly moving traffic. Highway 183, where Annie's parents were killed eight years ago. If they were alive would Annie be home now? No. She would have gone even if they were, if she wanted to, if she was ready to. Damn that truck. Why was it weaving in and out of lanes? Why hadn't he been noticing? Lulled. He'd let himself be lulled by normality. Someone would have to write and tell the children. Dear Matthew, Your mother has run off with one of my old friends. Dear Katie, Your mother has gone to live in Mexico with

Bern Alvarez whom she prefers to me. Oh, no. Annie, you must explain it to them. It's not my job. I'm paid to straighten out other people's messes, not yours.

Bern's hand was on her shoulder. Annie looked around at the airport. Lots of glass, lots of polished onyx. The floors were covered with it like the airport at Oaxaca, only at Oaxaca you could see the mountains in the distance and here it was tropical . . . hibiscus, crotan, jasmine, bougainvillea, banana trees, and the smell . . . always it smelled the same. Cheap tobacco, and something they mopped the floors with, something chemical, and dust.

"I decided to bring you to Cancun instead of to Mexico because I was afraid you'd want to leave me immediately if we went to the city."

"Why should I—?"

"You haven't really been to Mexico for almost twenty years. You took the train from the border to San Miguel, flew to Mexico and changed planes to go everywhere else. For twenty years you've only seen the airport. The city has become a different place."

"Overcrowding, pollution—I've read about it."

"Yes. So I had to bring you here first. If you don't like the condo . . . if you don't like the way it's decorated, you can change it to suit you."

As she had thought. Anita's ghost to deal with. Well she would deal with it in time.

"I don't quite understand where we are, Bern. How far from the airport is the island?"

"We're already on the island. We have to drive a few miles before you can see the water again."

For too long he'd looked forward to too little. Cliff recognized his middle-aged complaint. Had Annie felt it too? Had she run off in search of change? What was that over there? A new supermarket? Yes. More traffic to pull in and out of the road, and there were too many access lanes already, too many possibilities for catastrophe. He'd never learned to keep alert enough to see his own approaching. Matter of lack of imagination or will? Or both? Well, he couldn't go looking for disaster every morning, he had to live beside it, unknowing. He should

have known, should have guessed something when Bern
lost Anita. Freakish. What had an earthquake in Mexico
City to do with us? Everything. How was it she died? A
collapsing balcony? Flowerpots falling off a balcony?
Annie would remember. She's not home, you fool! She's
somewhere in Mexico with my childhood friend Bernado
Alvarez whose wife was murdered by a falling flowerpot.
The chain of circumstance is so long . . . stretching from
Mexico to me. And old . . . running through generations
of Alvarezes, Mullins and Sawyers. And there's something more than circumstance . . . something else entirely
. . . Turn. The place to turn. Almost forgot, after years
of making it. All my life spent defining, analyzing,
arguing, what is the one word I want? What is it she
finds in Bern she's never found in me? Passion? No. I
felt it, and so did she. Intensity? Perhaps it's his intensity.
He has enough to match her own. That's why she married me twenty years ago, to let me shelter her from
Bern. She came to me for calm. Annie and I . . . most
of the time we were peaceful together. Turn again. The
last turn. The house will be empty. Children gone. She,
wait? Yes, she waited till they were in college. Used to
tease her when Bern's letters came. We sent condolences
after Anita was killed. He sent back love letters. In every
one he spoke of unhappiness. Misery covered pages.
Women love to comfort.

"He'll be up here after you." I warned her when I
should have warned myself.

"Ah, Cliff. He's only lonely. He'll find another wife
in Mexico I'm sure."

Was she dissembling? Not at first. Later? Perhaps.
Better not to know. Is that why Poke didn't say anything.
He knew? Ignorance, my wonderful shield. All the lights
are on. What can I do now? Why can't I be angry? It
would help if I could be angry.

Cliff went inside and turned the lights off all over the
house. When he reached their bedroom, he lay down on
the bed completely clothed waiting for the shock to wear
thin, waiting for the first wave of grief to hit.

"Bern, I must. I said I would."
"We've just gotten here."

"I was supposed to be home this morning. He's probably frantic even if he did get my note."

"Cliff? He's never been frantic in his life."

"You don't know. You haven't been living with him." She walked to a window and looked out at the sun dipping into the sea. "Either I do what I feel must be done, or nothing will work out. Right now . . . whatever I have to do, I don't want to argue about it."

He put his hands lightly on her shoulders. "All right. Of course."

"Could you send a wire for me? Here, I've written it out. Fill in the number, please." She handed him a slip of paper with a blank left for the telephone number. "I said I'd call, but nothing will be accomplished that way. If he wants, he can call. I owe him that."

"And you will write?"

"Yes. Now."

He nodded.

Somehow she had to be outside to write. She chose a small balcony overlooking the ocean. On one side, a white sand beach curved away to an infinite point and on the other, the beach curved toward her. Afterglow pinked the clouds, turned the water dark blue. *Dear Cliff, I'm on Cancun, an island off the coast of Quintana Roo on the Yucatán Peninsula north of Cozumel. This place wasn't even on the map where we were growing up.* Did it matter? The names of islands, their exact geographic locations? She'd always thought so, had wanted to know them, a habit she couldn't change though she'd changed everything else in her life. Cliff would want to know. He was an exact man. *Bern has a condominium here.*

I know I said I would call, however, I thought it best to write, and easier, I will confess. I regret leaving as I did. I don't, but it won't help to say so. It was the only way I would go.

Of course you want a divorce. Of course I am the one who needs it. *Do you want to file there, or would it be better for me to get one here?* He's the injured one. Best to let him decide.

I will write to the children, and I hope you will also. Let us try not to use them. Katie is twenty, and Matt is nineteen. They are both old enough to lead their own lives

even if they fail to understand mine. It was really too
much to ask, she was sure. What child ever knew it's
mother's true personality? To them, she was Mother,
slightly scandalous now but still Mother. Their lives had
been so different from hers. They were city children.
They took music lessons, went to swim meets, riding
classes, dances, painting classes, summer camp, winter
vacations at ski resorts, summers in the mountains and
on the beaches of Mexico, and when they were home the
house swarmed with children. She grew up in the solitude
her mother had grown accustomed to. She'd learned how
to shoot, to ride and to swim so awkwardly she had to
have lessons when she was sixteen. Except for Poke and
Evelyn and her parents, there were a few aunts and
uncles, some friends, not many until high school. Then
there were Bern and Cliff. After them no one else, no
other man was interesting. She had never known another
person like Bern. He was both a part of her past and
foreign to it. And Cliff had linked them and she . . .

She held the unfinished letter in one hand and looked
out at the little waves lapping against the shore.

GENARO GONZALEZ

❧ ❧ ❧

Genaro Gonzalez was born in 1949 in McAllen, Texas, on the Texas-Mexican border across from Reynosa, Tamaulipas. The son of migrant workers, Gonzalez grew up following his parents as they traveled from farm to farm as far north as Michigan looking for work. Like other migrant children, he attended school when and where he could. In 1968, Gonzalez entered what is now the University of Texas at Pan American on a honors program scholarship, and published his first short story in the campus literary magazine. A rewritten and expanded version of that story later appeared as "Un Hijo del Sol" in the anthology The Chicano: From Caricature to Self-Portrait *(1971). He transferred in 1970 to Pomona College in Claremont, California, where he earned a BA in psychology in 1973, and in 1982 he received a PhD in psychology from the University of California at Santa Cruz. Gonzales taught at several universities before returning to the University of Texas at Pan American in 1989.*

Throughout his career as an academic, he has published fiction in little magazines across the country and in university journals such as the Denver Quarterly, *which first published "Too Much His Father's Son"—included in this anthology—in its Fall 1981 issue. In 1988, Arte Publico Press published Gonzalez's first novel,* Rainbow's End, *a work that follows three generations of a Mexican-American family who live on the Texas-Mexican border. Nominated for the American Book Award for best novel,* Rainbow's End *was also a Critics' Choice selection in the* Los Angeles Times Book Review, *which praised the novel for capturing the ambience of a borderland household.* Newsday *remarked that* Rainbow's End *"uses events in the lives of three generations in the family of Heraclio Cavazos to portray the cultural evolution*

380

*of the region since World War II. It describes a society
in which breath-taking beauty and deep sensitivity exist
alongside violence, drug smuggling and an illicit trade
in human beings." In 1990, the University of Texas at
Austin and the Texas Institute of Letters awarded Gonzalez the Dobie Paisano fellowship, providing him the
opportunity to spend a six-month period in 1991 in residence on the ranch retreat of J. Frank Dobie, the late
southwestern folklorist, working on another novel and
several short stories.*

Too Much His Father's Son

In the whorl of the argument, without warning, Arturo's
mother confronted her husband point-blank: "Is it
another woman?"

"For heaven's sake, Carmela, not in front of—"

"Nine is old enough to know. You owe both of us that
much."

Sitting in the room, Arturo could not help but over-
hear. Usually he could dissimulate with little effort—
being a constant chaperon on his cousin Anita's dates
had made him a master at fading into the background.
But at that moment he was struggling hard to control a
discomfort even more trying than those his cousin and
her boyfriends put him through.

The argument had already lasted an hour and, emo-
tionally, his mother had carried its brunt. Trying to keep
her voice in check was taking more out of her than if
she had simply vented her tension.

His father, though, lay fully clothed in bed, shirt half-
buttoned and hands locked under his head. From his
closed eyes and placid breathing, one would have thought
that her frustration was simply lulling him into a more
profound relaxation. Only an occasional gleam from
those perfect white teeth told Arturo he was still listening, and even then with bemused detachment.

"Is it another woman, Raul?"

His father batted open his eyes only to look away, as

though the accusation did not even merit the dignity of
a defense. His gaze caught Arturo and tried to lock him
into the masculine intimacy they often shared, an unspoken complicity between father and son. But at that
instant he simply aggravated Arturo's shame.

"Who is she, Raul?"

His smile made it clear that if there were another
woman, he was not saying. "You tell me. You're the one
who made her up."

Arturo had seen that smile in all its shadings—sometimes with disarming candor, but more often full of arro-
gance. When he wished, those teeth could take on such
a natural luster that whoever saw it felt invigorated. In
those moments his smile became a gift of pearls.

Yet other times, he had but to curl his lips and those
same teeth turned into a sadistic show of strength. Well
aware of his power over others, he seemed indifferent as
to whether the end effect exalted or belittled.

Out of nowhere, perhaps to add to the confusion, he
ordered. "Bring Abuelo's belt, Arturo."

Instead of strapping it on, he pretended to admire what
had once been his own father's gun belt. The holster was
gone, but a bullet that had remained rusted inside a middle clasp added a certain authority. The hand-tooled
leather, a rich dark brown, had delicate etching now too
smooth to decipher. Grandfather Edelmiro had been a
large, mean-looking man in life, and Arturo still remembered the day his father received the belt. He had
strapped it on for only a moment, over his own belt.
Later that day Arturo opened the closet for a closer
inspection and had come upon his father, piercing
another notch for his smaller waist.

His mother continued to confront his father, who idly
looped the belt, grabbed it at opposite ends, and began
whapping it with a solemn force. At first the rhythmic
slaps disconcerted her, until she turned their tension into
punctuations for her own argument. Suddenly the belt
cracked so violently that Arturo thought the ancient cartridge had fired. He startled, as much from the noise as
from the discovery that his father's legendary control had
snapped. For an instant both parents, suddenly realizing
how far things had gone, appeared paralyzed.

No, his father would never strike her, he was sure of

that. But nobody had ever pushed him that far, least of all his mother, whose own strength had always been her patience.

He wondered why his eyes were suddenly brimming. Perhaps trespassing into the unknown terrified him, or perhaps he was ashamed of his father's indifference. That confusion—crying without knowing why—frightened him even more.

"See, Carmela? Now you've got the boy blubbering."

He was hoping to hide his weakness from his father, and the unmasking only added to the disgrace. Desperate to save face, he yelled, "I'm leaving!"

As always, his father turned the threat in his favor. "That's good, son. Wait outside and let me handle this."

"I'm going to Papa Grande's house!"

Arturo had never been that close to his mother's family, and that made his decision all the more surprising. But if his father felt betrayed he did not show it. "Fine, then. You're on your own."

It took him a while to catch his father's sarcasm and his own unthinking blunder: He did not know the way to his grandparents' house. He had walked there only once—last Sunday—and that time his mother had disoriented him with a different route from the one his father took.

But now, standing there facing his father, he had no choice. Rushing out the kitchen door he ran across the back yard, expecting at any moment to be stopped in his tracks. When his arms brushed against a clothesline, he almost tripped as if his father had lassoed him with his belt. Not until he reached the alley did he realize he had been hoping his father would indeed stop him, even with a word.

He crossed the alley into an abandoned lot. There he matted down a patch of grass and weeds reaching his waist and settled in, so as to give his heart time to hush. He sat for a long time, wondering whether to gather his thoughts or let them scramble until nothing mattered.

From Doña Chole's house came the blare of Mexican radio station, every song sandwiched by the frenzied assault of two announcers. Farther away, David's father continued working on his pet project, a coop and flypen for his game cocks: four or five swift whacks into wood . . . silence . . . then another volley. For a while he lost himself in that hammering, which imparted meaning to the day. If he listened closer he could hear the cursing and singing that gave the neighborhood life. Only his own home remained absolutely still.

Soon the sun began to get in his eyes whenever he looked homeward. A cool breeze was blowing at his back, but he hunkered in the weeds a sun-toasted aroma penetrated his corduroy shirt.

Someone was coming up the path, making soft lashing sounds in the weeds; something told him that someone was Fela the *curandera*. His intuition seemed so certain that when he finally dared peek he immediately dove back into his hiding place, wondering whether to congratulate or curse himself.

A part of him scrambled for a rational explanation: Who else could it be? Fela the healer was the only grown-up unconcerned about snakes in the undergrowth. More than anyone else she had cut a swath through the weeds in her daily forages for herbs. Yet, another side of him was forced to side with the barrio lore—that she had special powers, that she appeared and disappeared at will, that she could think your thoughts before they occurred to you.

The brushing got closer, so he lay very still, trying to imitate his father's self-discipline. When the rustling suddenly stopped, he swore the waft of his corduroy shirt had given him away.

A voice called out: "Since when do little boys live in the wild?"

His heart began beating wildly, but her tone carried enough teasing that he half-raised his head.

"You're hiding from someone?"

All at once, he remembered why he was there, not in words but through a clear image of his father sprawled across the bed, amused, almost bored. He answered her question with a nod, afraid that if he spoke his rage might leap out and injure them both.

"You did something bad?"

He managed a hoarse, determined vow: "I'm going to smash my father's teeth."

He expected the violence in his words to stun her, but instead she disarmed him with a kind smile. "Whatever for? He has such nice teeth. Some day yours will look just like his."

For a moment, in place of the familiar habit of his own body, he experienced an undefined numbness, followed by the fascinated terror of someone who had inherited a gleaming crown with awesome responsibilities. He stood speechless, repulsed yet tempted by the corrupting thought of turning into his father.

"Anyway," she added, "before you know it he'll be old and toothless like me."

She picked a row of burrs clinging to her faded dress, then said as she left, "And tell your mother she's in my thoughts and prayers." Watching her walk away, he tried without success to retrace the route he and his mother had taken to her house during their secret visit last Sunday.

That Sunday morning, while his mother talked to her in the living room, he had sat on a wicker chair on Fela's porch, entertained by Cuco, an ancient caged parrot with colored semicircles under his eyes. Arturo was feeding him chili from a nearby plant to make him talk. "Say it," he urged between bribes: *"Chinga tu madre"*—screw your mother. But the chili only agitated Cuco's whistling.

"Come on, you stupid bird. *Chinga tu madre.*"

Suddenly there was a raucous squawk. "Screw your padre instead!"

As he wheeled about and felt the blood rush to his face, Fela was already raising her arms in innocence. "Who says he's stupid? That's an exotic bilingual bird you're talking to."

From there, he and his mother had gone to his grandparents' house. Her route through alleys and unfenced backyards led him to ask, "How do you know all these shortcuts?"

She paused to dry her forehead on her sleeve, and for the first time in days he saw her smile. "I grew up in this barrio. This is where I used to play."

When he tried to imagine her his age, he too smiled.

When they arrived they had to wait until his grandfather Marcelo finished his radlonevela. After hearing where they had been and why, he shook his head. "I knew your marriage would come to this. But going to

Fela was a mistake. If he finds out, he'll claim you're trying to win him back through witchcraft."

"I had to know if he's seeing another woman."

"And what if he is?"

Arturo had never seen her as serene and as serious as when she answered, "Then he's not worth winning back."

"But a *curandera* . . . Why not see a priest?"

Arturo's grandmother took her side. "What for, Marcelo? He'd only give her your advice: Accept him as your cross in life."

"I wouldn't in this case. An unfaithful husband is one thing, an arrogant SOB is another. Still, a priest could say a few prayers in your behalf."

"Fela offered to do that herself."

His grandmother added, "And no doubt offered good advice."

His mother's fist clenched his own. "Yes," she said, and her firmness made it obvious that that was the last word.

His grandfather, deep in thought, held his breath without taking his eyes off him. Then he closed his eyes and exhaled a stale rush of cigarette smoke, as if unclouding his thoughts. "I've always said your father was a prick."

"Now, Marcelo. Don't turn him against his own father."

"Mama's right. None of this is Arturo's fault. He's going through enough as it is."

"True. But I still wouldn't give a kilo of crap for the whole de la O family, starting with Edelmiro."

"May he rest in peace," said his grandmother.

His grandfather stood. "Not if there's a devil down below."

"Marcelo! He was your compadre."

"I had as much choice in the matter as the boy had in being his grandson." He turned to Arturo's mother. "Remember, if there's a falling out, don't ask that family for anything. Your place is here."

His grandmother added, "And of course that includes Arturo. He's as much a part as the rest of us."

His grandfather had simply said, "Let's hope he's not too much his father's son."

By now the late afternoon sun was slanting long, slender shadows his way, but he was determined to spend the night there if need be. He began counting in cycles of hundreds to keep his uncertainty in check.

Suddenly the rear screen door opened and his father leaned against it, his belt slung over his chest and shoulder like a bandoliered and battle-weary warrior.

"Arturo, come inside." Whenever he wanted to conceal something from the neighbors, he used that phrase.

He slowly stood but held his ground, as much from stubbornness as dread.

"It's all right, son." He sounded final yet forgiving, like asking who had put down a castle uprising, regained control, and had decided to pardon the traitors.

Arturo blinked but once, but his pounding heart made even something that small seem a life-and-death concession.

Then his mother appeared alongside his father, and for an instant, framed by the doorway, their pose reminded him of their newlywed portrait in the living room: his hands at his sides, her own clasped in front, both heads slightly tilted as if about to rest on each other's shoulder. In that eye blink of an interval before she stepped outside, he felt like an outsider looking in.

She was halfway between him and the house when his father said, "Your mother's bringing you back."

He could not believe her betrayal. After all that, she had surrendered and was bringing him in as well. He wanted to cry out at her for having put him through so much. But a deeper part understood he shared the blame, for not helping her; for being too much his father's son.

"I forgot the way," he said. Although she was quite close he could not tell whether she heard—much less accepted—his timid apology. He managed his first step homeward when she blocked his path, gently took his hand, and guided him in the opposite direction.

He heard, or perhaps only imagined, his father: "Come back." He tugged her arm in case she had not heard. She tightened her grasp to show that she had. Then, intuiting his dilemma, she paused, saying nothing but still gazing away from the house. He realized, then and there that the wait was for him alone. Her own decision had already been made.

Unable to walk back or away, he felt like the only

living thing in the open. Then his father called out, "Son," and he knew it was his last call. His spine shivered as though a weapon had been sighted at his back, and he imagined his father removing from his belt the cartridge reserved for the family traitor.

There was no way of telling how long he braced himself for whatever was coming, until he finally realized that the moment of reckoning was already behind him. It was then that he felt his father's defeat in his own blood. With it came the glorious fear of a fugitive burning his bridges into the unknown, or a believer orphaned from a false faith. And in that all-or-nothing instant that took so little doing and needed even less understanding, his all-powerful father evaporated into the myth he had always been.

He felt a flesh-and-blood grasp that both offered and drew strength. He began to walk away, knowing there was no turning back.

CARLOS NICOLÁS FLORES

❧ ❧ ❧

Carlos Nicolás Flores, born in 1944, is a native of El Paso, Texas. He has bachelor's and master's degrees in English literature from the University of Texas at El Paso. His first work of fiction was a collection of short stories that served as his Master's thesis. In 1976, Flores received a fellowship from the National Endowment for the Humanities to participate in a year-long seminar at Dartmouth College. His research project—"A Chicano Looks at a Black: A Comparison and Contrast of Chicano and Black Literature"—inspired him to become more active in the Chicano movement and he began teaching one of the first Chicano and Black literature courses in Laredo. In 1981, Flores founded the Revista Rio Bravo, *a review which received significant critical acclaim during its two years of publication. In 1984, one of his short stories, "Yellow Flowers," appeared in the anthology* Cuentos Chicanos. *Flores's stories have received numerous awards, including first place in fiction in the Sixteenth Chicano Literary Contest sponsored by the University of California at Irvine. "Smeltertown" first appeared in the* Rio Grande Review *in 1984.*

Smeltertown

I.

"Your mother says we won't be able to have the *carne asada*."

"Why not?"

"Your mother had a fight with your sister. Your brothers have gone out with their friends. Your father may not be back until late."

Américo laid the razor on the washbasin's rim, then lowered the toilet seat and sat down.

"I told you there would be no point in having a *carne asada* with my people," he said.

Jovita's gaze fell. The *carne asada* had been her idea, a family cookout like those they had enjoyed so often at home with her family.

"Ni modo," she said, resting her sad face against the doorjamb.

Américo pulled his socks from out of his cowboy boots, crossed his legs, and dusted off the bottom of his foot. He was not accustomed to boots, but he wore them to please Jovita, who had grown up close to the ranch life of South Texas. She enjoyed seeing him dress like the men from Escandon. He did not particularly like the boots although the riding heels did give him a bit of height, and illusion of stature, and another illusion—that he belonged with Jovita, with her relatives, and with the other Mexicans in Escandon who had looked upon him as an outsider. He slipped on his socks, put on his boots, and looked up at Jovita.

"What do you want to do?" he asked.

"We could go eat in Juárez."

"Too much traffic on the bridge. Remember, it's Sunday. Besides, I don't want to touch another drink."

"What about a movie?"

"Chula," he said, wanting to reach for her and hold her tenderly so he wouldn't hurt her, "I didn't drive six

hundred miles to El Paso just to see a movie. Maybe we could go for a ride."

"But where?"

"Anywhere," he said.

They were silent for a moment. Américo thought about the lake. He decided against it when he remembered its muddy waters and gangs of shirtless Mexican men, beer cans in hand. Then he thought about a ride out to his father's acreage down the valley. No, he didn't want to go there either, having been there with his father several times, politely listening to his impractical dream about how one day the whole family might move there, build their homes, and live happily ever after. Instead, the image of a cross atop a peak popped into Américo's mind.

"How about Smeltertown?" he said.

"Smeltretown? What's that? An oil refinery?"

Américo laughed.

"No, *mijita*," he said. "It's where my mother was born. A little Mexican village upriver."

"Is it the place you pointed out when we were coming back from New Mexico on our honeymoon?"

"Did I?"

"Don't you remember. Américo? It was the first time you brought me to El Paso to meet your parents. We drove up to New Mexico and got stuck in the snow."

"I didn't get stuck. The car just skidded all over the place, that's all."

"Well, whatever. When we drove back, you said, 'Look that's where my mother was born,' and then we went to eat at that restaurant nearby."

"La Hacienda."

"Yes."

"Would you like to eat there again?"

"Great."

Américo loved to see Jovita happy, the way her smile revealed a sparkling set of white teeth, the girlish delight in her dark eyes. Though she was twenty-two years old, she looked eighteen and was, to his continuing astonishment, one of the most beautiful women he had ever seen. He felt better now that the *carne asada* was no longer an issue.

Américo got up and kissed her cheek.

"I'll be ready in a minute," he said, stepping to the washbasin.

"Maybe we should stay and talk to your mother before we go."

Américo had forgotten.

"Yes," he said. It was unconvincing.

"It's our last day here," she said. "I don't want to offend her by taking off like the rest of your family."

"You're right, *chula*," he said.

"I'll be in the kitchen."

Américo turned to the mirror and saw a Mexican face the color and shape of a chunk of adobe, his black hair unmanageably aflame. With his fingers he spread the aerosol spurt of white cream against the *tierra-cafe* of his skin. As he shaved, he decided that their three-day visit to El Paso had not been as unpleasant as others in the past. Still he knew that if Jovita had not insisted upon these yearly visits from the beginning of their marriage, he would never have set foot in El Paso again. He cleared the lather, rinsed the razor and his hands, and put the shaving things away. After combing his hair, he slipped on his gold-rimmed, green-tinted glasses. Dressed in dark blue pants and a white *guayabera* embroidered with blue pants and a white *guayabera* embroidered with blue and black pyramids, Americo prepared himself to face his mother in the kitchen.

"Look how handsome my son looks!"

"Good morning," he said.

"Good morning?" responded Señora Izquierdo. "You mean good afternoon?"

"What time is it?"

"There's a clock on the wall."

It was already past 1:00 PM.

"Señora," said Américo, inhaling self-consciously, "I'm on vacation. It's Sunday." Américo never said "Mom."

"At home," Jovita said, her eyes gliding on a smile from Américo to his mother, "he never gets up earlier than twelve on weekends."

"You don't go to church on Sunday?" asked Señora Izquierdo. Her eyes widened with feigned shock at what she had always known to be Américo's indifference towards church. She attended when she could, by herself.

Américo rolled his eyes.

"Too much of this," said Señora Izquierdo, cocking her hand so that her thumb almost touched her lips and her pinky stuck out like an upended bottle.

"Nonsense," said Américo. He smiled. "It's just that Jovita never lets me out of bed in the morning."

"You lie, Américo," said Jovita, embarrassed.

"It's true, Señora," he said. "What else can a man who wakes up with a beautiful woman do except stay in bed?"

"Américo, *te sales*," said Jovita, ready to spring at him and put her hand over his mouth.

"Jovita, why are you so mean with my son?" said Señora Izquierdo, chuckling. "Why don't you let him out of bed in the morning?"

"Señora, it's your son," said Jovita. "The Izquierdo men are terrible."

Señora Izquierdo blinked. "You can say that again." She addressed Jovita. "Jesus Christ, my husband was worse than a bull. Puerto Rican men are like that."

"Is there any coffee?" asked Américo.

Señora Izquierdo's face changed. "*Sí, mijito,*" she said, bundling toward the stove. "Do you want any breakfast?"

"No thanks," said Américo.

He took a chair at the table next to Jovita, who yanked lightly at his hair. Smiling, he pushed her gently away. As his mother poured the coffee into the cup, it steamed. Señora Izquierdo returned the coffeepot to the stove, walked to her place by the kitchen sink, and began peeling potatoes. She had been a maid before she married. Her short, pudgy body was at home in cheap cotton dresses and flat sandals. Her fingers were stubby from housework.

"*Bueno,*" she said, talking seriously now, though with a mischievous sideways grin, her eyes upon the blade sliding beneath the potato's skin, "since both of you have such a difficult time getting out of bed, when, I would like to know, are you going to give me"—she looked up—"a grandson?"

"First, we need to buy a house," said Américo. "We want to travel too, maybe Europe."

"Naw," said Señora Izquierdo irritably, "that'll take too long. I may die before I see my first grandson."

"You're not that old, Señora," said Américo.

"You never know."

"Tonight," said Jovita.

Américo looked at Jovita with a what-are-you-talking-about frown.

"That's better," said Señora Izquierdo. "Did you hear that, Americo?"

"Well," Américo said, an earnest tone in his voice now, "we have been thinking about a child. We just don't know when or how soon."

"It'll be a surprise," said Jovita.

"Can you imagine that?" Señora Izquierdo paused, her eyes filled with sights of the future. "A little Américo walking around. A house without children has no *chiste*."

Américo took out a cigarette. When he looked around for a place to dump the match, his mother found an ashtray hidden in one of the kitchen cabinets. White-edged streams of smoke filled the bright kitchen. Américo knew what she thought about his smoking, but he couldn't put off the cigarette much longer. Besides, his father wasn't home.

"You and Jovita are going to eat here, no?" asked Señora Izquierdo, her eyes on Américo.

"We are going out to dinner," said Américo.

"Ooooooo!" Señora Izquierdo stopped peeling potatoes.

"I want to take Jovita to see Smeltertown."

Señora Izquierdo's face registered dismay.

"Smeltertown? What are you going to do in Smeltertown? There is nothing there."

"Américo wants to show me where you were born," Jovita said.

Señora Izqierdo's eyes flared at Americo.

"Américo," she demanded, one arm akimbo, "when was I born in Smeltertown?"

"I meant to say that you were raised there," Américo apologized.

"Your father put that idea in your head," she said. "He thinks I was born in Mexico. No, señor—I know where I was born. It was not in Mexico. It was not Smeltertown. I was born in Williams, Arizona."

No one in the family knew anything about Williams, Arizona, not even his mother, as far as Américo could tell, but Señora Izquierdo had always made it a point to

say that she had been born there. Not El Paso, not Cd.
Juárez across the river where most of her surviving family
lived in a three-room adobe hovel. Not Smeltertown
where she had been raised from early childhood by *la
abuela* and Tía Rosaura.

"*Ay qué* Américo," sighed Señora Izquierdo, "you
don't even know where your mother was born." Her eyes
flashed upon him again. "Do you know who your mother
is?"

"No, I don't," he said. He loved the banter. It brought
him close to his mother.

"Américo!" Her black hair shook in every direction,
then settled around her bright eyes. "I'm your mother."

Jovita laughed. "Are you sure, Señora Izquierdo?" she
said.

"What?" Señora Izquierdo's eyes flashed at Jovita. A
smile glimmered. "I know my children like the palm of my
hand. I should. I cleaned them enough times with it."

Américo grinned and shook his head.

"I can prove I'm from Williams, Arizona," insisted
Señora Izquierdo. "It's your father I worry about. He's
such a liar I wonder sometimes if he's really where he
says he's from."

But Américo knew better. Señor Izquierdo was not
born in El Paso either. He was from Puerto Rico, a
potato-shaped island in the Caribbean sea. Américo had
visited it once in a disappointing attempt to find out more
about the old man. Señor Izquierdo hated El Paso, an
empty desert surrounded by arid mountains, so unlike
the lush green of Puerto Rico, *la perla del Caribe*. He
sometimes talked of abandoning his family and returning
to his Borinquen *querido*. In that threat and others, he
reminded them that he was no Mexican.

They heard a car in the carport. Its engine died
abruptly, and someone got out. Señora Izquierdo peeped
outside the kitchen door.

"It's Papi," she said, running back to her place. Her
knife whipped around the fresh potato she took from the
kitchen counter, and her face became self-absorbed.

Américo put out his cigarette and sat upright in his
chair. Beneath the table, one of his legs began to pounce
nervously. He raised his eyebrows at Jovita, who reclined
in her chair with her hands together on her lap.

The door cracked open, then slammed shut. Señor Izquierdo wore an Alpine hat on his frizzy head and carried a brown grocery bag in his arms. He was a short man in his sixties. His sharp, restless eyes alighted upon Americo and Jovita. He ignored Señora Izquierdo at the sink.

"Hello, América," he said in a level voice.

"Hello, Pop."

"*Buenas tardes,*" Señor Izquierdo said to Jovita.

"*Buenas tardes.*"

Señor Izquierdo's muscular arms reached, one at a time, inside the grocery bag and retrieved two fistfulls of apples and oranges. "I brought you these," he said to Américo, a boyish smile parting his mustachioed mouth.

"Thanks, Pop."

"Do you want one?"

"No, thank you."

Jovita declined too.

Señor Izquierdo, his eyes momentarily unsettled, put the fruit inside the bag and removed it to the kitchen counter. Without looking at his wife, he strolled to the stove where he poured himself some coffee. His squatty, rural hands were unsteady as he stirred the cream and sugar into it. He wore an old, unfashionable shirt and once dressy pants exhausted by repeated laundering and daily usage. It was part of his refusal to waste his "children's money" on new clothes for himself, though he needed them for his public image as a furniture salesman. He stood in shoes swollen by his vigilance at work.

"I understand you are leaving tomorrow," said Señor Izquierdo.

"Yes, sir," replied Américo.

"Do you need any money?"

"No, sir. Thank you very much."

"You know that you can always count on me if you need anything."

"Yes—I understand."

Señor Izquierdo's eyes wandered towards Jovita, who sat quietly next to Américo. Américo knew she wouldn't speak to his father if she could avoid it, but Señor Izquierdo thought he had gotten her attention.

"My children," he said to her, "come before anything else in the world. They are not like so many children I see in the streets—filthy, hungry, no one to tell them what's wrong or right. My children have a man for a father. As long as I am alive, they have nothing to fear."

Américo hated what his father said and the manner in which he said it, the tone of his voice as impudent as the ridiculous Alpine hat askew on his head.

"Have you eaten?" Señor Izquierdo's attention returned to Américo.

"No sir. We are going out to eat."

"Oh, I see."

"We were going to have a *carne asada*," Américo explained, "but everybody left, and we didn't know when you'd get back."

"You can have *carne asada* without me."

"We want the family together."

"Yes." He sipped his coffee, nodded his head thoughtfully. "A family should always be together, should always work together. A family is a source of strength. Of course," he raised his eyebrows, "it's not easy. There are always people in the family who oppose the family's unity, people who plot against the father, who refuse to serve him a decent meal. . . ."

Américo tensed. His father had flung an insult at his mother. It was an old conflict, this business of the food, and it turned his stomach.

"Have you died of hunger?" shouted Señora Izquierdo. She kept her back towards them.

"Do you know, Américo," he continued, "that half the food in this house is wasted because it is not cooked properly? Do you think that is right?"

Señora Izquierdo turned and glared angrily at the back of the old man's head.

"If you don't eat," she shouted, "it's because you are an old man who cannot eat with your false teeth!"

Américo glanced at Jovita. She swallowed a smile. He focused his eyes on the clock on the wall.

"Américo," his mother said, taking a position at Señor Izquierdo's side, her face drawn and piqued, "ask your father who showed him how to use a bathroom. Ask him who told him he could sit on a toilet bowl, that he didn't have to crouch on it as if he were in some outhouse in Puerto Rico. You should have seen him. For years he perched like a *gallo* on the toilet bowl. When your father arrived in El Paso, he was nothing but a *jibaro* and it was me"—she pointed the knife at herself, "who educated him"—she pointed to her husband.

She remained where she stood, eyes, ears, and mouth alert for whatever else he might say.

"All my life," Señor Izquierdo said to Americo, "I have worked to provide this house with everything it needs. My children have had everything they needed. Your mother has never had to work."

"And who has washed your filthy underwear?" Señora Izquierdo eyed her husband with the tusk-keenness of an embattled *javalina*.

"Yes, this is all I get," said Señor Izquierdo, regarding his wife with contempt. "A filthy mouth, ingratitude, disrespect."

"You are a sick man, Izquierdo," Señora Izquierdo said.

"Shut up," he replied.

"Go to your room and watch television!" she exploded.

Señor Izquierdo shook his head. He turned to Américo and in a confidential tone said, "I'll be in my room. Maybe we can talk in peace before you leave. I am working on some big plans I'd like for you to know about. I am thinking about opening a big store. But I can't discuss these things in the presence of small minds."

He prepared himself another cup of coffee and then disappeared as abruptly as he had arrived, sliding the kitchen door shut behind him.

"Good," said Señora Izquierdo, relaxing by the sink. "He's gone."

Américo's legs stopped bouncing beneath the table, and he felt he could breath at last. Jovita leaned forward, put her arm on the table, and smiled at Américo, though it was a smile contrived out of bewilderment.

"Every day he comes home like that," Señora Izquierdo said, her face engrossed in the knife's slightly erratic movement through the potato in her hand. "I never do anything right. He says he has never been able to eat a decent meal since he left Puerto Rico. There was a time I made Puerto Rican food for him, but I stopped when I saw that he soon found something else

to complain about. Your father is a very hard man to
live with."

"Is it true he's thinking about opening a store?" Américo asked.

"When hasn't your father been up to something that
was going to make him a millionaire? I let him talk about
his big plans; I don't pay attention. What you don't do
when you are young, you won't do when you are old. It
won't be long before both of us are dead."

"*Ay, señora,*" said Jovita, "you are just like my grandmother. Every Christmas she says farewell to everybody
because she thinks she has less than a year to live. She's
been saying that since I was a little girl. Look at her.
She's buried my grandfather and is in her eighties.
You're very young."

Señora Izquierdo's eyes flashed with delight. "Thank
you, thank you." She glanced at Américo. "I've been
told I look like your father's daughter."

Jovita laughed. "*Ay,* Señora Izquierdo."

Américo looked at the clock again. "We have to go,"
he said.

"So soon?" Señora Izquierdo said. "We didn't even
have a chance to talk."

"Why don't you go with us?" asked Jovita.

"Yeah, why don't you come with us?" said Américo
with a smile. "You could give us a guided tour of Smeltertown. After that, you could eat all you wanted at the
Hacienda Restaurant."

Señora Izquierdo liked the idea. She went "Mmmmm"
and then acted as if she were gobbling food. She laughed
loudly and warmly, her white teeth beaming in her round
face, an old and weathered version of Américo's own.
She followed Américo and Jovita to the door.

"No," she said. She whirled her forefinger about her
temple, an allusion to her husband's mental condition.
"I have to stay here and feed the *deschavetado.*"

II

Américo drove up the sloped street away from his parents' white stuccoed house which had been built on the
escarpment at the foot of the Franklin Mountains.

"I'm glad we were able to get away," said Américo, glancing at Jovita, who reclined comfortably in her seat, the elegant contour of her face doused by sunlight. "I can't breathe in that house."

He turned onto the street that would take them downtown.

"Your mother is so funny," said Jovita.

Curious and agitated, he glanced at her. "What do you mean?" he said.

She sat there with a smile, shaking her head at the thought of his mother.

"I don't know," she said. "She's a real character. One minute she's laughing and joking, the next minute she's battling your father, then she is laughing again as if everything had been one big joke."

"Well, it hasn't always been one big joke," said Américo, staring morosely out the window. "There was a time when I had to put up with that nonsense every day. I mean every day. Just to think about those days gives me chills."

Américo stopped at an intersection by a lush green park.

"Let's take the mountain road," said Jovita.

"Okay," he said.

He veered onto Scenic Drive, the popular mountain road that zigzagged across the southernmost extension of the Franklin Mountains. Its curves snaked in and out of the crevasses. As they gained altitude, the vast cityscape spread out below, offering them a breathtaking view of a sophisticated American metropolis glittering in the desert sun of an immense sky. Jovita beheld the sight with wonder.

"El Paso is such a beautiful city," she said. "It is so different from Escandon."

"It is beautiful," Américo agreed, "but I could never live here again."

"My mother came here to visit many years ago. She fell in love with it. She even wanted to come and live here."

"I'm glad she didn't."

"Why?"

"I would never have met you."

They exchanged smiles.

Américo reached the "look-out" area, the highest point on the road. Atop a pole an American flag flapped sporadically. Beyond the urban valley rose the Mexican mountains, dark and remote. In the west appeared the smokestacks. The road curved sharply into the mountain, and the descent to the valley began.

"I used to come this way every day when I was at the university," said Américo. "In the morning it was very beautiful, except for the smog."

"Have people ever driven off the mountain?"

"Rarely. I don't remember anyone having done that, though I once heard of a girl who committed suicide by driving off the mountain."

"What a horrible way to die."

Américo shifted into low gear and stopped riding the brake pedal. He maneuvered through the familiar curves gracefully.

"Your family is strange," said Jovita thoughtfully. "They treat us well. The refrigerator is full of food. Your father brings sacks of fruit and offers you money. Compared to my family, they have everything, but they cannot eat a meal together. Your family seems like a family of strangers."

Américo sighed. "That's the way we were brought up. My father has always said that you don't have any friends but your own family. Yet he has never been a friend to any of us. It's impossible to talk to him. As for my brothers and sisters, I don't know what to talk to them about. I used to think *I* was different, Jovita, but I'm not. At first I thought the problem was my parents' lack of education. I have always seen them as peasants despite the money my father has managed to make. But in Escandon, I've seen families with absolutely nothing, neither money nor education, surviving together successfully. In my family we are all lonely wretches."

"They are good people, Américo."

"People may be good," he looked at her a bit peevishly, "but sick."

She shifted in her seat. He felt her eyes settle on the side of his face. "What I meant to say," she said, "is that they're good people, despite everything. You can't go on hating them all your life."

He kept his eyes on the winding road. "It was here in

El Paso that I learned to live with the assumption that I have no family."

"That's what's so frightening about you sometimes," said Jovita softly. "Sometimes I feel you owe allegiance to nothing, to no one, perhaps not even to me one day."

He looked over at her poignant brown eyes. "Don't say that. I've never loved anybody as much as I love you, and I never will. You're the only valuable thing I've had in my life.

"I would hate to see us become," he added slowly, "what my parents are. But then you never know. This business of living is so tricky. Some families are cursed for generations."

"Still, curses can be lifted, no?" Jovita smiled.

"No," Américo said, returning the smile.

They came off the mountain road. They took the avenue that sloped to the heart of El Paso. Cars glittered like luminous insects in the bright sunlight. They idled past San Jacinto Plaza, once a station on the Spanish King's highway, now the city's main plaza where city buses digorged pedestrians from all parts of the metropolis. Clusters of people, most of them Mexicans, walked in the shadows of the tall buildings enclosing the downtown area. When he reached Paisano Drive, Americo turned west.

"Paisano connects with the old highway at the train depot," said Américo. "I like this route because it runs along the Rio Grande."

"I'd get lost," said Jovita, "if I had to drive here."

"You get used to it."

They drove past the train depot, which resembled a Spanish cathedral, and onto the old highway.

"There's Mexico," said Américo, nodding at the low-lying hills clustered with adobe huts beyond the sandy river bottom. As usual, the stark contrast between the two sides of the river struck him, and it reminded him that his mother and her family were originally from Mexico, despite his mother's denials.

"You can walk across," said Jovita.

"I know. The river isn't very deep here."

"What river?" joked Jovita. "The arroyos in Escandon have more water in them than that."

Américo smiled. Jovita loved to tease him about the

Rio Grande. It was not as large in El Paso as it was in Escandon, but it linked him to her nonetheless. He drove on, passed under a concrete bridge, beyond which appeared the Hacienda Restaurant against a mountain backdrop.

"Look, there's Mount Cristo Rey!" cried Américo, pointing to a small basalt peak in the distance, a tiny cross at its pinnacle. It looked like a small, perfectly shaped volcano set against the enormous Texas sky. "Every time I see Mount Cristo Rey, I feel something special. I feel a tenderness a pilgrim might feel for the Holy Land. It is as I imagine the Holy Land. My mother once told me she and *la abuela* made annual pilgrimages to the top of Mount Cristo Rey. When I lived in El Paso, there were times I felt so desperate and full of hatred that I drove out here, along this highway, just to see all this. It calmed me. There were also times I felt I didn't belong among the gringos, that I didn't belong in El Paso, period. Then I remembered that my mother was part of all this, the river, the mountains, and I felt that I did belong here, no matter what the gringos thought."

They were approaching Smeltertown. To the right of the highway, Américo saw the ASARCO smokestacks—the short one and the two long thin ones.

"Smeltertown is across the highway from the smelter," said Américo. "It should be somewhere around here."

They looked around as they passed a slag-covered ridge beyond which rose the complex of metal buildings overshadowed by smokestacks. They did not see anything. No wooden shacks, no grocery store, no cars or people, no church.

As they drove on, they passed under a black metal bridge where the trains from the smelter crossed over the highway. "Jovita, I'm sure it's not past this bridge. We missed it."

Américo turned back. As they approached the smelter again, they slowed down and pulled off the highway, stopping in front of a bright sign: "For Sale, Coronado Realty 566-3965." They got out of the car.

"The smokestacks are there, so Smeltertown should be here," he said, standing at the edge of an empty field.

"Look, across the field, isn't that a church?"

Seeing the remains—white walls, no roof, debris—he asked, "So this is it?"

"Your mother was right," said Jovita. "There's nothing here."

"She meant something else," said Américo, stopping next to Jovita. "If she had known it had been torn down, she would have told us."

He gazed at the empty field. Though he had driven along this highway several times before he left El Paso and later when he took Jovita to New Mexico on one of their honeymoons, Américo had never paid much attention to Smeltertown. It had merely been the wretched town where his mother had grown up with *la abuela*, his great-grandmother, and Tía Rosaura, his great aunt. When was the last time he had been there? A long time ago as a child, perhaps twenty years.

"I want to look around," said Américo. "Do you mind?"

"No, it's early. I'll join you later. I want to look at the church."

"Okay." He wandered across the field.

There was none of the billowy sand he remembered trudging through every time his mother brought him and his brothers and sisters to visit *la abeula* and Tía Rosaura. The dirt felt compact; severed roots showed that it had been planed recently.

There had been candles burning inside *la abuela*'s wood frame house. Sulfur and incense mingled with the smell of Mexican food. She was a very old woman, short and frail, with a wrinkled face and green eyes. She wore a *chongo* at the back of her head, gold-rimmed glasses, and a black shawl wrapped around her shoulders. He could recall nothing of her temperament. He remembered the other woman, Tía Rosaura, a short Mexican woman with a square head on her neckless shoulders, a woman who seemed to have been smelted from the igenous rock of this land. Their hearts lay buried somewhere in this soil that had poisoned his, and he felt like a ghost crossing an immense desert in search of their blessings.

Not able to find where *la abeula*'s house had been, he attempted to reconstruct the original scene from memory—a picket fence; an outhouse which smelled and whose spiders had scared him; a lanky, yellow-eyed dog in the dirt yard; and a dark wooden house with a corrugated aluminum roof. Once on a visit to Smeltertown, his mother had sent him to the store a block away. It had been a short walk; the store had been on a street facing the highway. If he could locate where the store had been, he might find *la abuela*'s property. To his left Américo spotted a curbstone, a few yards from the highway, where there had once been a street corner. As he walked towards it, he came across a prominent mound of dirt and stopped.

When he stepped onto the mound, the dirt grated beneath his foot. He hit the ground with the heel of his shoe. It sounded hollow. He crouched down. Upon clearing some of the dirt, he found a slab of wood beneath, and when he lifted it, he saw the hole. It had been hastily and incompletely filled in; it looked as if it might have been a cesspool hole. He studied the distance between mound and curbstone and church. If his estimates were correct, he might be standing on top of *la abuela*'s cesspool.

He wanted to tell Jovita about his discovery, but she sat on a wooden beam in the shadow of the church walls. He crossed the field and sat down next to her.

"Did you see where I was standing?"

"Yes."

"There's a mound of dirt there. I think it's a cesspool. Several yards away, there used to be a store on the corner. *La abuela*'s house would have been where that mound of dirt is. I am almost certain it was her cesspool I was standing on."

They sat quietly for a moment.

"Where's the Rio Grande?" asked Jovita.

Américo glanced at the church walls.

"Oh, that's behind the church. We can't see it from here."

"Is Mexico on the other side?"

"I don't think so. Somewhere around here the river turns and ceases to be the Mexican-American border. I don't know exactly where in the river's bend that happens."

"What was *la abuela*'s name?"

"Just *la abuela*."

"Didn't your mother tell you her name?"

Americo paused. He sifted through the assortment of
memories he had about his childhood: Smeltertown, his
mother, the sulfur fumes—all links to *la abuela*—but he
could not remember her name. His mind seemed as
empty as the field at his feet.

He shook his head. "My mother told me her name,
but I cannot remember. It's all jumbled in my mind.
Until *la abuela* died, she lived with Tía Rosaura. Their
last name was Buenaventura. *La abuela* was not really
my grandmother; she was really my mother's grandmother. I never got to know my real grandmother—my
mother's mother. Her name was Guadalupe. Guadalupe
gave my mother to *la abuela* to raise in Smeltertown. I
never understood why. My mother often said she grew
up like an orphan, alone. I suppose she meant she grew
up without her mother and her brothers and sisters. Her
father was murdered, so my mother says, somewhere in
Mexico when she was very young, probably when she
was already living here."

"Did you come to visit *la abuela* and Tía Rosaura
often?"

"Maybe once or twice a year. Some years we didn't
see them at all. Sometimes they came to visit us when
my father wasn't home or when we were at school. My
father objected to our seeing my mother's family. Whenever we came here, my mother would say, 'Shhhh, don't
tell your father we're going to see *la abuela*.' We'd come
on the bus frightened to death my father would find out,
and there would be another fight. But there always was
a fight—even when we didn't come."

"That's very sad," said Jovita. "We grew up with all
of our relatives, and when our grandparents died, they
died at our house. We remained by their side until their
last moments."

"I've always envied that in you. I've always wanted to
have a family like that. To have grown up with aunts and
uncles, with cousins, big family get-togethers and *carne
asadas*. To be able to speak to my father, to respect
him."

"Well, my father isn't a saint. He's never laid a hand
on my mother or any of us, but he's made my mother's
life miserable. At least your father has provided well for
your family. Your mother has never had to work. Com-

pared to your father, my father is incompetent. But just because they're like that doesn't mean that I have to hate them the way you have hated your family."

"Haven't you had other members of your family to turn to, like your aunt and your grandmother? The simple fact that your grandparents died at your parents' home has counted for something, no? Hasn't that been a source of strength?"

"Yes."

"When you talk about your grandmother singing the *Ave María* at church or about walking on Sunday morning to church with your aunt or about how you felt the morning your grandfather died, I feel envious. I feel like a stranger. So when we come to El Paso this is really all I have to show you—this empty field, these beautiful mountains that mean more to you than to me. When people find out I'm from El Paso and they say, 'Oh, El Paso is such a beautiful town. I wish I could live there,' my stomach goes into knots. If we have children," he said slowly, "I don't want them to grow up the way I did, without a solid sense of who they are." He stopped, breathed deeply, picked up a small stick, and drew an "X" in the dirt. "What time is it?"

Jovita looked at her watch. "Three o'clock."

"Are you hungry?"

"Not yet."

Américo looked at the church. He had not been inside a church for years. He wondered if this was where *la abuela* had been brought when she died. He got up and walked to the front of the church's entrance and found a doorless passageway through which he could see the blue walls inside. Piles of smashed wood, brick, and glass blocked his way to the front steps, but he saw a thin path.

"Let's climb inside," he said to Jovita.

'No, it's dangerous."

"I'm going inside," he said. "It won't be long before all of this is torn down."

"Be careful. There are nails all over the place."

Américo took the path and climbed the steps, where he sat on the door sill and stared inside at the blue walls smouldering in sunlight. He pushed himself inside and landed on the dirt floor several feet below. Somehow he had expected to see some vestiges of the original church still intact—a pulpit, an altar, a cross, anything. All he saw were the marks on the walls where the floor had once been and piles of broken wood on the dirt floor. Up front, where the altar must have been, rose a stack of tattered linoleum-like roofing. Set high in the walls was a series of broken windows. Beyond the roofless walls was the sky.

He walked amid the debris to the center of the church floor which was bisected by shadow and sunlight. Finding a wooden box, which he pulled to a clearing, he sat down and lit a cigarette. He imagined two old women leading a young girl down the center aisle for communion and the people in the pews listening to the choir as a priest poised white wafers on the tongues of the communicants. He imagined an old woman lying dead in a coffin.

The images were interrupted by the memory of a story his mother had once told him. During the years of the war, it had been here, in Smeltertown, where his father, a soldier then, had come to look for his mother at *la abuela*'s house. It was one night, months after they had been married and Américo had been conceived. He had come drunk. She would not open the door even after he stopped beating on it and began to thrash about on the ground, crying and threatening to kill himself if she did not return to him. It had been *la abuela* who scolded her, telling her that she was now a woman, not a girl, a wife and mother-to-be, and that unless he abandoned her, she must never leave him, regardless of how unhappy she might be. His mother had opened the door.

Whatever else Américo may have detested in his father, he had always admired his father's capacity for hard work and making money. In a few years his father had moved the family from a decrepit barrio in south El Paso to a nice neighborhood near Five Points and then to the suburb at the foot of the mountains. In his prosperity he thought he could return to Puerto Rico and change everything he had left. The thatched-roof hut he grew up in with his ten brothers and sisters, the poverty and misery of his saintly mother, and tyranny of his tall, red-headed, machete-wielding drunken father. He sent money instead. The times he visited his family in Puerto Rico, he went with his wife's blessing and the knowledge that he didn't have to return. But to the family's relief, he always came back. In his drunken rages he cursed the desert, the mountains, his wife, the Mexicans, and his fate.

Américo could never forgive, then or now, his father's humiliation of his mother and rejection of her family. In his isolation, Américo turned to books. And, when they weren't enough, Mexican cantinas and abandoned women. When his long pent-up desire to leave El Paso forever, to destroy it by his absence, was satisfied by an opportunity to teach in Escandon, he found refuge. He found Jovita.

And every time he returned to El Paso, zipping along the elaborate highway from the south, he felt an immense weight settle upon his shoulders. At first gently. Then it would begin to push down upon him so hard that he felt the mountains were crushing him. At his parents' home and everywhere else he went, everything seemed devastated until Jovita and he escaped to the other side of the Rio Grande, where he drank excessively at the Kentucky Club. That is where they had been the previous night and why he had gotten up so late. It had been a wonderful time, alive with Mexican music, polite waiters in white shirts, and superbly rendered Scotch and sodas. But this time, the Sunday after, he felt unusually weak, as if something that had driven him along all those years was beginning to fail him. The sensation frightened him. Was it Jovita's and his desire to have a child and settle down? Perhaps Jovita's wish to get away from the nightlife whose warmth and charm had sustained him for so long among strangers? Whatever change was afoot, he was certain of one thing though—he would still have to travel a long distance, years, before he could turn around, look at El Paso, and feel free of it.

When he finished his cigarette, Américo stood up and looked around, wondering if he had missed something. No. All of it was dead—Smeltertown, *la abuela*, Tía Rosaura, and even his mother, the little girl who, with *la abuela*, had washed clothes into the Rio Grande and climbed Mount Cristo Rey in the religious processions there. He stood in the graveyard of a past, his Mexican past. Then, as his eyes scaled the church walls, a glint of yellow caught his attention. It was a window, stained blue and yellow, resting high on the church walls, still intact.

He picked up several pieces of brick and tossed them. He missed several times. At last he lobbed a chunk squarely at the base of the window so the pieces cascaded backwards into the church and landed on a pile of wood armed with splinters and nails. The face of a madonna, with drooping eyes and a silver halo around her head, survived in a triangle of glass. Américo got as close as he could. He did not see the nail when he reached for the madonna, just felt it. A thin, rusted nail like a rattlesnake fang curved out of the stick of wood, striking the side of his hand. He cried out, and his feet blundered in the pile of wood, upsetting the madonna. She fell and burst. Was this what he was destined to take back home, to South Texas, a relic of Smeltertown engraved upon his hand?

He heard Jovita's desperate voice, "Américo! Américo!" flying over the church walls.

Without hesitation, he climbed to the sunlight outside. He paused and caught his breath. He turned to run back around to the front of the church. He stopped, gaped. A black man leaned against the church wall, his black arms rigidly outstretched. A smuggler or wetback scorched by the desert sun, poised to assault him? But it wasn't a man at all. It was a cross.

It was unlike any other cross he had seen before, not gold, not silver, not even marble-white like the cross atop Mount Cristo Rey. It was plain, the kind of cross that might have been smelted from the igneous stone of the region, the stone transfixed by iron rods whose protruding ends had rusted.

"Américo!" Jovita called.

"I'm back here," answered Américo.

As Jovita dashed around the corner of the church, she halted, abruptly startled by the sight of cross.

"Wha . . ." she said, awed.

"I just found this cross," Américo said, stepping next to her. "It scared the hell out of me."

"It's so big."

"They probably removed it from inside the church. I wonder what they're going to do with it."

Jovita saw the handkerchief wrapped around his hand.

"What happened to you? I heard a window crash."

"I just wanted something to take home with us. It was a piece of glass with the face of a madonna. It was beautiful, but it broke."

"Your mother would have treasured it."

His eyes embraced the cross. He imagined it hanging inside the church. It was very old; *la abuela* and his mother must have seen it years go. He stepped forward and ran his hand along its upright post. He marvelled. It was so simple yet so strong.

"Do you think we could take it home?" he said.

"What?"

"The cross."

"It's a long way to Escandon. How are we going to carry it? On top of our Volkswagen?"

Américo laughed.

"You're right," he said, running his fingers delicately along the stone's rough surface. "Come on. We'd better go."

Together they crossed the field.

"How does your hand feel?" asked Jovita.

"All right."

"Maybe you should get a shot."

"It'll be too much trouble. I'd have to go to a hospital."

"I'd feel better if you got a shot," she insisted. "Then we could go to eat."

"Okay."

They stopped between their car and the elongated shadow of the real estate sign. Américo looked at everything once more—the ASARCO smelter and its smokestacks across the highway, the curbstone, the empty field, the church walls and Mount Cristo Rey.

"There will be nothing left," he said.

Jovita, who had been gazing thoughtfully at the church walls, turned to Américo and said, "There will be your father and your mother."

DENISE CHÁVEZ

❦ ❦ ❦

*Denise Chávez was born in Las Cruces, New Mexico, in
1948. The desert landscape has always been part of her
interior and exterior worlds. She has noted that she writes
"about the forgotten people of this arid land: the little old
men who philosophize from park benches on the plaza,
the neighborhood handyman with seven children who has
run away from home, an elderly spinster who runs a small
corner grocery store and still dreams of the man whose
offer of marriage she rejected some fifty years ago." Common themes include the interconnected mexcla or mesti-
saje or mixture of humankind, against the backdrop of a
border reality, where Mexico and the United States inter-
sect. For Denise Chávez, "The 'compadres' and 'comrades'
who populate this landscape continue their historical and
cultural dance in an ever-changing world. There is strength
in these characters. These are people who endure. They
exist in a state of natural grace."*

*Chávez began writing as a young girl. She has a BA in
theater from New Mexico State University, an MFA in
theater from Trinity University in San Antonio, and an
MA in creative writing from the University of New Mexico. She is currently an assistant professor of theater at the
University of Houston. Chávez has presented workshops
in theater and writing throughout the United States and
has toured a one-woman show based on her writings entitled,* Woman in the State of Grace. *Chávez has had seventeen of her plays produced throughout the United States
and in Edinburgh, Scotland. A collection of her stories,*
The Last of the Menu Girls, *was published in 1986 by
Arte Publico Press, and a novel will soon be published.*

The McCoy Hotel

Here's your key, Mrs. Chávez. Mrs. Madrid is in 417. The elderly clerk handed the usual key to my mother. Room 415. The McCoy Hotel. El Paso, Texas.

It was a key that signified so much to the women in our family. To my mother this key was a grateful respite from her duties as a third grade teacher, a divorced mother of three children, two of us still at home.

When she had this key there was no rushing to her charges, no small children crowding around, waiting to be soothed. There was no return to feverish midday meals or anxious waits for that long-awaited child-support check, the one that never came.

My mother's everyday worries disappeared on those days at the McCoy Hotel. Her life there was not like her other life, which was always rushed, and filled with disappointment and disillusionment.

My mother's days started with early-morning mass after which she would return home to get us out of bed and make our breakfast. Oatmeal was what we ate every-day, there was never any change. My sister, Margo, and I always left our oatmeal untouched, complaining about its texture. It was always cold, lumpy as well and could literally be lifted out of the saucepan like an unbroken gray mold. Time not having improved its taste, and barely noticing it, mother would eat the oatmeal hours later, sitting in front of the television set during her lunch break from school, her keen ears tuned to the news of the world's ever-altering events.

To my sister and me, both scrawny, underdeveloped, and sensitive teenagers who craved all of life, with its experience, its awakening mystery and passion, the McCoy Hotel meant freedom from the confines of our female-only home, our girls-only school, and our angry, unresponding Father-God dominated religion that clouded and affected every aspect of our lives, which always seemed to be on hold, waiting prayerfully for some better day, some happier time, when the three of us women

413

would know completion, transformation, not of a self-determining kind but one dependent upon someone else, someone who would ease us out from the unspoken prison of our lives, someone decidedly male.

All of our lives tuned ever so delicately upon this unspoken tenet of unshakable faith. To be happy you must be loved by a man. That is what my mother yearned for. That is what she taught us to desire with all our hearts.

What *I* wanted at that time was freedom from that inescapable world where one man, invisible, unresponsible, unpleasant, and selfish as well, ruled our every waking thought, and determined every future action.

When my mother was released from her daily chores or her weekly responsibilities and discovered herself at the McCoy Hotel, her bowed back became at once straightened up. She became another woman, lively, even more beautiful than she was, her long, dark-brown hair in a bun, her intense face, with its burning, deep-set brown eyes, that of another woman, someone I barely knew. This new woman was open to possibility, joyful with hope.

At these times my mother was not the driven, burden-tormented, long-suffering warden of our misery, a divorced mother of two growing, demanding young women who struggled ever inch of the way for individual freedom, she was someone else, almost a stranger.

My mother, having stood so much for so long, now bore the physical and emotional scars of all those years of suffering: a hunched back, bad legs with inflamed, pulsating varicose veins, an inability to sleep throughout the night, an overactive fear of men, all men, who could only hurt and deceive, as well as a sense of overriding anxiety that all her worst fears would come to pass. She worried if my sister and I were too close to the edge of a stairway, if we were too hot, too cold, if we were in the bathroom too long, or not long enough, if our hair was up or down, and if we did go someplace, who we were with, for how long, and why.

Our weekends at the McCoy Hotel, in downtown El Paso, were freedom to the three of us from our life in the small southern New Mexico town of Las Cruces, city of Christian martyrs, ever-present crosses.

The McCoy Hotel was just off the plaza and Mesa Street. A structure of only six stories, it seemed much taller in those days. It was situated south, facing away from the Plaza toward Mexico and the many liquor stores and *Tiendas de Rebajas*, discount used clothing stores that lined the street that became the Old Bridge we used to cross into Juárez at ten cents a car.

The hotel, while old, was quite respectable. The rooms were plain, but unusually clean for all the wildness of the border life outside its walls.

Our room had double beds that faced a moderate-sized mirror on the opposite wall, underneath which was a small basin with an overhead ledge that held two glasses turned upside down. They were wrapped in transparent, shiny, semi-waxy paper and stood next to a small pitcher of lukewarm water, that good "Texas water" my mother always bragged about.

To one side of the mirror was the bathroom door, connecting our room to that of my Tía Chita, my mother's younger sister. She lived in Redford, Texas, a town of around fifty people, where she owned, along with her seldom seen, less often heard husband, a small, but prosperous grocery store.

When we stayed at the McCoy Hotel, we invariably stayed with my aunt, who'd come into town only the night before to see her doctor, or to check up on some insurance policy or other business matter.

The two sisters were always so happy to see each other, sharing between themselves memories and stories of their days on the farm in West Texas, in a town called El Polvo, the Dust.

To my Tía Chita, El Paso was like New York City. For us, it was a new and novel ever-expanding civilization that existed before our time and would be there long after we were gone.

The McCoy Hotel rooms were shared by two sets of sisters, one young, the other much older, both still working on their relationships to each other, always at odds. In the shaded darkness of those rooms, both groups of sisters sought respite from the intense summer heat, the inescapable sun, tormentedly male.

The McCoy Hotel was a meeting ground between family, a place we all came to further knowledge of our separate lives. Here we found out how deeply and irrevocably we had changed because of those secret sins we now confessed to each other. No matter how much we fought, quietly and then with anger, or how much we cried, hard to ourselves and then softly to our other sister half, the McCoy was always for us a place we loved, a place of love, despite our waning youth.

Our room and my aunt's was connected by a white-and-black checkered tile bathroom. It contained an old-fashioned tub with heavy knobby gold splayed feet that lifted the tub high off the floor.

During the daytime, both doors leading to the bathroom remained open, allowing free access to either side of our mutual suite. At night, either side of women closed the door that led to the bathroom. When the bathroom was in use, whichever side which happened to be inside locked the door as well and ran the faucet to muffle any sounds.

I rarely went into my Tía Chita's room, it seemed very far away, despite its close proximity to us, our side, centered by those two familiar double beds, sheets crisp with starch, the blankets, thin but soft.

In all the years we'd stayed at the McCoy, it had never changed. The lobby was always the same, with its red high-backed metal chairs, the paneled reception desk near the elevator, small end tables scattered here and there with months-old magazines. The ancient, still functional elevator, with a creaky metal door you had to swing sideways, to the left, to open, locked into place once it was closed.

EEEEEEKKKKKKKKKRRRRRRR! The metal door slid shut, the tired machine slowly revved up and creakily it ascended, coming to a not uncommon jumpy false stop as the elevator sought the right stoppage point, finally resting midway between floors. Through the firm doors with their ornate black grates could be seen a hallway, indistinguishable from the other five, with its dark carpet, chairs, and ceiling fan.

All those weekends visits to the McCoy Hotel melded into two strong memories. One of them was the magical time of my eagerly sought, never truly won adolescence. I was a child then, still under the rule of my mother, who dictated my life. The other memory is as strong, and defined a period of setting forward into young adulthood, with its time of rebellion. Each of these phases marked a chapter in my life as discovered at the McCoy Hotel.

As a young teenager, I was very agitated by most everything. I felt trapped in a world I could never escape, confined to mediocrity, a pale, thin, overprotected girl to whom imagination was both fearful and a blessing. When we were at the McCoy, I became, like my mother, a new person, startled and then emboldened by my budding maturity, and then challenged by possibility.

One afternoon in summer, when I was thirteen, just learning to assert my growing adulthood, I left our room and wandered down the long, gray hallway. I peered down the mysterious stairs, then ran quickly, breathlessly back to get my sister, who sat in bed reading. My mother was in Tía Chita's room. She lay across her sister's bed, stripped down to her brassiere, wet towels holding her uncomfortably large breasts in place.

There was no air-conditioning, and all the windows were open. The ceiling fan swathed a circular path near the top of the high room, displacing and then correcting the hot air. Tía Chita, as relaxed as she ever became, wore a dark blue cotton robe and slippers, her knee-high hose held up by her soft, pink rubber-covered *ligas*, or garters. The two women talked quietly to themselves, the way people do in extreme heat, slowly, with as little breath as possible, conserving what energy they have.

Eagerly, I begged Margo to join me in my wanderings, and just as enthusiastically she replied that she would.

I liked to sneak around. I loved to be afraid. We both did. We liked to imagine things that would never come to pass. What if the building caught on fire? Who's the man in the far end room? I think he's in love with me. What if the elevator didn't work and stopped between floors and we were trapped in there with the man from the far end room? How many floors are there? Are there really only six? What if there was a secret floor that no one except us knew about? Imagine living in a hotel!

My questions grew bolder and so did my movements. Slithering through the cool, darkened hallway to the stairway, I climbed up on one flight of stairs, then another, urging my little sister forward.

Afterward, we ventured down the elevator to the lobby, controlling the lever manually. Amazement, terror, and joy ruled us as we stared at the open floor moving past us. Fighting to control the lever led to us coming to a bumping and prolonged stop. Landing between floors, Margo jumped out.

More afraid, despite my age, I followed her, a somewhat timid explorer who tiptoed through the silent, tunnel-like hallway to the guest sitting room, where a solitary old man sat staring out into space.

There were no television sets or radios in the sitting rooms, much less in any of the guest rooms; the only form of entertainment was watching other human life. Few children stayed at the hotel with their parents; I never saw anyone near my age. The clientele was older, monosyllabic, long past the fecund time. The lobby clerk and his wife were elderly as well, ever polite to us, in a dry, stiff-smiling, girdle-harnessed, yellow-false-teeth sort of way. We jeered and made fun of them behind their backs, because we didn't know how to react to courtesy and deference from people so much older than ourselves. So, with a cruel and rude cynicism we allowed them to wait on us, little princesses come in from the heat.

In the presence of the older clerk and his wife, I felt mature, comfortable with myself, not just another person, but one younger, more alive, not exhausted and frustrated by a life nearly over, like theirs, or my mother's or aunt's, both passed over in quiet and relentless desperation, living not in the present but in a never-arriving future, with heated nightly dreams of a what-might-have-been past.

I knew I wasn't so well behaved, or so nice, but what I did know was how special I was, if only to myself. I felt my life full of meaning. Surrounded by so many people, so many stories, feelings, I couldn't exactly explain why I felt so different in the body that I wore then, an ill-fitting outer skin that wasn't really me, not the inside of me that was hidden to everyone, even myself: the spirit of the woman I longed to become.

I got off in the lobby. Margo followed. Sitting on a stiff chair, I looked out into the street, half-shaded by a set of merciful blinds, the hot sun boring small holes into my consciousness. Unable to affect longed-for freedom, I returned to our room, to rest from all that longing. It tired me like nothing else ever did. Unable to explain my bad mood to Margo, I said nothing as my mother came out of the bathroom, trying on a new dress.

Pulling it over her head, the bodice stuck halfway and she called frantically to me to help her, she was trapped. Her large, humid breasts were caught in a vise of cloth. Flattened and punched down, at that moment they seemed more of a bother than something to be proud of. I was glad to be myself then, flat-chested, without that burden of softened flesh to drag around, continually subdue.

Extricating Mother from that already zippered dress took some time and was embarrassing to all three of us. Breathy, with tiny beads of sweat near her hairline, Mother was finally freed with one last tug.

My mother's large impressive body was something she could never escape, try as she might, day or night.

Nights she slept in the nude, and it was not uncommon to walk by her room to find her, head facing the window, swaddled like the statue of a carved Greek torso in her thin sheet, her wet towel draped over her prominent chest that heaved and sighed.

Did everyone's mother sleep in the nude? I didn't think so.

In that second phase of the McCoy Hotel, when I was older and had begun to define my individual self, we stayed at the hotel for the last time.

My mother, ever-devoted chaperone, now served as a group mother to eight thespians who earlier had participated in a speech tournament in El Paso. She assigned rooms. My girlfriend, Ellen, and I drew a room connected to my mother's, much to our dismay. Ellen and I slept in one adjoining room, my mother and sister in the other. The six other girls were spread out between two nearby rooms, all interconnecting, with promises to behave.

I wondered: would Mother sleep in the nude this night? I hoped not.

I whispered to Ellen in the darkness, My mother sleeps in the nude.

She does?

Yes. She sleeps with her head at the foot of her bed, her legs facing the headboard, her head near the window, so she can feel the breeze, a fan on the chest of drawers aimed at her head, her long dark hair fanned out on a small, soft pillow like a baby's under head. Like that, nude. And when she's alone, she locks all the doors and does her housework in the nude.

No!

Yes she does. She's told me.

No!!

She says it feels good that way.

Reaaalllly?

In the summer she'll open all the windows and sleep nude with her door open all the way, the fan going all night long, forget the cost!

Really?

She gets up early before anyone gets up and goes to sleep long after anyone.

She sleeps naked?

Does your mother?

No . . . I don't . . . I don't . . . know . . .

Suddenly from the other room came a voice in the darkness. Mother had heard us!

Yes, Ellen, I sleep nude. Want to come see?

Nothing mother said every surprised me. I was used to her loud half-whispers, her scathing but honest asides, her candid and profound announcements: See that woman, she needs a good bra! Look at that girl in the bathing suit, you can see her sex outlined like a man's. *Ese hombre*, that man, he smells! Puuuuuccccccchhhheeee! Excuse me, but your child is very fat, don't you think you should do something to help him?

Can't you. Can't they

do something

about their skin, their hair, their clothes, their bra, their skirts, their pants

Hey, you there!

No one could ruffle her, no hostile salesman or rude saleslady. Mother would turn to them placidly, and with great sweetness say: You don't feel well, do you?

Nothing ever surprised me about my mother, the

woman who lay in the darkness of the McCoy Hotel, a
wet wash rag on her head, a damp towel on her breasts.

She was two people to me: the potentially dangerous
woman who slept nude, who loved to shop, try on
clothes, and hit a good sale; the woman who didn't feel
guilty about tipping, the woman who loved going to the
movies and still yearned for romance. The other woman
was the woman who was my mother, preoccupied with
the person she thought I should be.

The *first woman* I knew was bitter, hard with arthritis,
never really defeated, but in constant pain of one sort or
another. This woman bravely moved through her everyday with actions calibrated to ensure our good, pro-
nouncing by her strict, fearful ways a burden of relationship.
Her Hope or Heaven, her Garden of Eden was centered
by that inescapable tree of life and love, surrounded as
it was by slithering, tempting, always male serpents.

But this tormented woman, and this other life was
always forgotten as we approached the McCoy Hotel.

To the immediate right of the Hotel was the Plaza
Theater, constructed in the luxurious style of those days
gone by. The lobby was just as elegant as the exterior.
When we entered the theater all cares left us, we forgot
the harsh brightness of late-afternoon El Paso.

Inside the Plaza Theater we were transported to a
world of make-believe. The theater had a large screen
that was flanked on either side by a painted facade that
was lit by painted turning silver lights that blinked on
and off. On either side of the screen was a mural. The
one on the left depicted a beautiful Spanish señorita
standing on a balcony, a rose in her hair. The opposite
mural showed her suitor, a handsome, dark-haired man
playing a guitar. There was an aura of yearning, uncon-
summated passion about the scene, as they stood separated by the huge white picture screen. There was a great
and touching sadness as the viewer realized that throughout eternity the lovers would never get any close to each
other, for all in the imminent drama and romance.

We usually sat in the balcony on plush red, very comfortable seats. It was an intimate and special place, as
opposed to the larger lower main floor. In the canver-
nous darkness, I sat next to my mother, who placed herself between Margo and me, "so you won't fight," to

watch double features, and one day, four movies in a row! The movies alternated among the family type, like *The Swiss Family Robinson*, the nature or animal variety like *Ole Yeller*, the relgious like *The Robe*, or were comedies or romances like *Three Coins in the Fountain*, with an occasional back-of-the-hair-raising drama like *Imitation of Life* thrown in.

Mother loved the movies and so did we. Her interests extended to buying all the *Silver Screen* and *Photoplay* magazines she could afford, pouring over them and passing them on to Margo and me. In our room at the McCoy Hotel we read them voraciously, never wanting anything more than to be a part of that world of glamour, intrigue, and veiled intimation.

One block away was El Colón, the Spanish-speaking movie theater, where we went to see comedies with Cantinflas or dramas with Dolores Del Río or Pedro Infante, who was the famous Mexican singer turned movie idol. My mother loved him, and I also came to revere him. Pedro was very handsome with his thin mustache and his serious eyes. He sang to his women beautiful, wrenching songs of undying love, and they were grateful, succumbing always to his emotional, heart-filled fervor that captivated and then overcame them, but never against their wills. While I sometimes missed much of what he was saying, too embarrassed to listen closely, I secretly longed to hear those same desperate, relentless words.

What El Colón gave us was passion, another form of possibility and way of living. Crying with Dolores, or Pedro, laughing with Cantinflas, I embraced my mother and her dreams, as well as those of all my people, the Mexicans and Mexican-Americans of La Frontera, the Border world was my own. When we sat in the darkness, all our faces were familiar, laughing, crying in the same way, and the same language. We were brothers and sisters united in our world away from the Plaza Theater, which is stately red carpets and elegant balustrades, where red-costumed blond ticket-takers greeted you in crisp English and promised you, at least momentarily, the great American dream. Somehow in Spanish, our dreams seemed purer.

At El Colón we made our way alone, no usher to guide

us to the sticky, paper-littered balcony, of course, where we carved out by our insistence a comfortable place with people like us who never had to pretend who they were or how much money they had. The emotions that we experienced at El Colón were more real than those we felt at the Plaza, the stories more familiar, the language rooted in things we had experienced as women, waiting on men, one man, never quite sure if we would ever be truly loved. For an hour and a half, we could be caressed by Pedro Infante himself, who proved to all men and women that it was good to be a man, a state of being that demanded respect, especially from women. I never questioned anything then. That was in the early days of the McCoy Hotel.

In later years, I was to remember Pedro Infante, his untimely death in an airplane with his mistress. Whenever I wanted to run away with someone, this tragedy of his stayed me. I couldn't explain to myself why Pedro's death had permanently touched me. He who struggled so long in celluloid to find true love, who seemed to have found it at last in real life, only to have it snatched away so abruptly and mercilessly by a jealous God who could not condone hard-won happiness, come where it had, lead where it might, an elusive attempt at joy, what others called adultery, was now a tragic character in his own life movie.

Leaving El Colón, I always found myself immensely hungry. I begged Mother to take us down the street to the *chicarrón* place, a take-out restaurant where hot, greasy, dripping sides of pork skin hung from racks to dry. The *chicarrones* were real, not the type with some sort of artificial preservative staining the corners with red or orange dye. They were fat, juicy, the kind I could suck for some time with enthusiasm and then crackle with my teeth. A large greasy bag went a long way. Whole sides of pork skins would be broken up, and holding a treasure dollars worth, we'd walk back to the McCoy. We'd eat them until we could eat no more, drawing the coolest water from the tap and pouring it into our glasses when we got thirsty.

From the hotel, we'd walk down to the plaza to watch the alligators that occasionally lurked outside in the hot Texas sun and then ponderously and painfully crawled back into the tepid wetness of the murky green pond, its flagstone slabs scraping their crusted, dried underbellies. The pond, located in the center of the plaza, was inaccessible to all except these three or four closed-eyed, nearly inert alligators that inhabited that space all seasons, a displaced curiosity.

In later years, this same dusty plaza was transformed at Christmastime by an incredible display of holiday tableaux. In one, cheerful elves cavorted merrily in artificial snow while Rudolph and his cohorts pulled a smiling pale-skinned Santa through the cool desert air. An immense Christmas tree, usually painted silver or white, stood in the middle of the plaza, where once sullen reptiles imagined freedom. Green, yellow, blue, and red alternated blinking on the tree, casting a magical spell, as excited children hovered close to impatient parents, wanting "just one more look" at the brightly colored gift packages and little mechanical gnomes that moved stacatto-like as they played tiny accordions and small tin drums, Christmas carols wafting in the air.

This is the plaza we'd drive forty-two miles to see when we were young, a tradition that in later years had little meaning. Rituals had delighted and sustained us then, like having breakfast at the Oasis restaurant next to the McCoy Hotel, where I'd order pancakes with hash browns or corned beef hash.

Sitting in a booth facing the street, my mother would contemplate her day: I need some comfortable walking shoes, a new brassiere, and my support hose, we'll go to the White House first, and then we'll have lunch at Kress' or Newberry's.

At Kress' Five and and Dime, the majority of my time was spent in front of the makeup or jewelry counters. Mother roamed the store, usually ending up in the bargain basement. She'd have already picked up her supply of hairpins, hair nets, Kapock to stuff pillows, as well as some gum and either candy orange slices or yellow gum drops that made the inside of my mouth rough if I sucked too hard.

Returning to the McCoy Hotel with our purchases, we'd rest a short while and maybe change our clothes. Shyly, and with a muffled voice, Tía Chita would call my Mother from her room, someone having accidentally locked either bathroom door, to see if we were hungry. I always was. Down the creaky elevator we'd descend, my aunt included, to eat dinner at the cafeteria around the corner.

It was at this cafeteria I was first looked at as a woman, or so I imagined. Flirting with a young man over my fried fish filet, I felt him looking at me as well. Burning with embarrassment, I turned away, attempting to ignore him, and when I looked up, he was gone.

Later on, I wondered if I'd really had this exchange or not. I was in my teens, skinny-chested, wild-eyed, with a thick mop of unruly curly hair, straddled on either side by two imposing women, my mother and her sister. Could a look have gotten through?

When we returned to the McCoy, Tía Chita returned to her room. Mother closed the door to the bathroom and emerged in a flowing night gown she'd made, one size fits all. It wasn't long before she was in bed, and the night gown was on the floor, her window open to the noise of late-night El Paso: the metal rattle of trucks, the screech of passing cars on their way to Juárez, and later, the constant, soothing distant lull of that border night life, that coming and going between countries, states of mind.

But before my mother's always troubled sleep, she would ask me to pull her toes. As the older, stronger one, she inevitably asked me to do this favor for her. An arthritic with no circulation in her battered legs, she told me it helped her to relax, just like taking hot baths from which she said she emerged ten years younger.

Taking her fleshy, bruised feet in my hands, her long second toe draped over the rest of her large feet, her Morton's toe that had genetically become part of me as well, I would begin from the toe and work down, pulling and popping as I went, now and then returning to a stubborn digit. Sometimes I was cruel and held my nose as I approached her, lifting her corn-filled calloused feet irreverently as if I were holding a leprous limb.

Tired from my day, I would later join my sister in bed. We sparred awhile, fighting for control of our sleeping space.

My nights were peaceful at the McCoy, dreamless too.
The days were so full, so complete, so full of variety and
stimulation, that my nights were a release from the
never-ending hum of El Paso, La Frontera.

After a sigh of contentment, my aunt's snores from
another part of the suite would cease. I would fall asleep,
under imaginary silver stars, a Spanish señorita serenaded in the moonlight.

The next morning I would wake up Mexican, glad to
be myself, and yet wanting more from myself at that time
than could ever be. I was my mother's vassal, my sister's
companion, my father's faraway, forgotten little girl, no
man's sweetheart.

Sunday morning mass awaited me, my retribution
unholy, complaining thoughts. My mother, sister, and I
visited many El Paso churches, never settling on one.
Each unprecedented visit to an unfamiliar church allowed
me one special prayer. Mother said every time you visited a new church, you could ask God for a new wish.
So, I left my hopes and dreams that way, all over town.

After church we returned to the McCoy, where we left
off our prayer books and gloves, and adjourned to the
Oasis restaurant for more grilled cheese and tunafish
sandwiches. Afterward, Mother drove us home to Las
Cruces, our city of myriad crosses.

Later, when I was older, and in high school, failed
debaters crowded exuberantly, if not exultantly, into our
blue Ford after the speech tournament. To hell with our
defeats! Led by my Mother we prayed the rosary. Mysterious Glory Be's led to stately Our Father's and on to
interminable Hail Mary's.

We arrived forty-two miles later, the rosary completed,
merry but with crippled limbs. Never before had we fit
so many girls into one car. We had set a record.

That was my last visit to the McCoy Hotel.

It's fitting it should have been at a time of celebration
for my emerging adolescent voice, a voice that then was
always prone to laryngitis. I didn't know how to speak
then, what to say. I was untrained, too eager to hear
myself out loud, not caring whether I modulated my
voice or damaged it in my fury to be heard.

To go back to that time is to go into the heart of the
McCoy Hotel; it is to remember those thrilling but small

adventures full of imagined danger. Today they seem as absurd as the overheated alligators in the plaza pond. Poor creatures so far away from home!

After that last stay at the McCoy Hotel, we visited El Paso shortly afterward to see a visiting president, Kennedy, who was staying at the Cortez Hotel, the fancy, removed stepsister of the McCoy Hotel.

In my dreams, my mother sits in our room at the McCoy Hotel brushing her long dark hair in front of an open window. Her head inclines to the shouts of *¡Viva, qué viva!* and there he is, the president! The plaza is filled with people as President Kennedy waves heartily to the crowd. Too soon the echoes fade and my mother's image at the window disappears. President Kennedy's life, as my mother's, had mythical proportions. It was once acted out, now it is only remembered, and always with a struggle.

But I do remember.

I grew in a world of people who were always remembering the past. When you grow up this way, time has a different significance to you than to others.

I can see my mother from my room and yet I cannot get near. I wonder if ever, when I least expect it, she will walk into the room and sit next to me. I will be able to smell her skin the way it was, sweet, smelling of dried flowers, overripe fruit. That is how the dying smell. It does not terrify me.

I breathe in with gratitude and exhale my passing sorrow.

My mother's voice now comes from another room. I see her: proud, naked, dancing. She is not in her seventies as I last knew her, but young, with the beautiful full body I knew she'd always had when she was younger. She wasn't hunchbacked, as she later was, with red, always bruised feet and legs. She wasn't that anxious woman who was always wondering if my father would ever call or write, or maybe even return home. His return to us never seemed a reality. He did in fact return, the year before my mother died, and in a strange way I believe he hastened her death, a process that had begun twenty-eight years before when he left home.

Several years ago I heard the Plaza Theater was to be

destroyed. The local citizenry saved it eventually, calling
it an architectural landmark.

The *chicarrón* place isn't there anymore, or it has
moved, or become one of the many *casas de cambio* that
line the street leading to the bridge that will take your
dollars and convert them into pesos.

The McCoy is now a remodeled office building, a place
I would be afraid to go inside. Call it a phobia. Call it
fear of heights. Call it whatever you like.

If I were to go inside, I would surely meet the ghosts
of that past life, perhaps the solitary old man staring into
space in the guest sitting room, or the phantom clerk
and his wife, both aged specters, with haunting, faraway
voices: Can I help you? Do you need a key?

Yes, the key!

Pedro Infante, dark rebel, but for that tragic flaw, was
everybody's lover. He sings to me, larger than life, on
the huge screen in the timeless darkness of the balcony
of the El Colón Theater. . . .

At the Plaza Theater the Spanish señorita demurely
hides her eyes while her handsome suitor sings and
strums that same sad haunting song on his guitar: *Sola-
mente una vez . . .*

ACKNOWLEDGMENTS

"Fiesta in St. Paul" by Grace Hodgson Flandrau. Copyright © 1943 by Grace Hodgson Flandrau. Reprinted by permission of *The Yale Review.*

"El Hoyo," "Senor Garza," "Cuco Goes to a Party," "Loco Chu," and "Kid Zopilote" by Mario Suarez first appeared in the *Arizona Quarterly* (Summer, 1947). Copyright © 1947 by the *Arizona Quarterly.* Reprinted by permission of the *Arizona Quarterly* and the author.

"Almost a Song" by Willard (Spud) Johnson first appeared in the *Southwest Review* (Summer, 1947). Copyright © 1947 by Spud Johnson. Reprinted by permission of the *Southwest Review.*

"El Zopilote" by Alice Marriot. Copyright © 1947 by Alice Marriot. Reprinted by permission of the *Southwest Review* and the author.

"Over the Waves Is Out" by Americo Paredes. Copyright © 1953 by Americo Paredes. Reprinted by permission of the author.

"Saturday Belongs to the Palomia" by Daniel Garza first appeared in *Harper's Magazine* (July, 1962). Copyright © 1962 by Daniel Garza. Reprinted by permission of the author.

"Maria Tepache" by "Amado Muro" (Chester Seltzer) first appeared in the *Arizona Quarterly* (Winter, 1969). Copyright © 1969 by Mrs. Chester Seltzer. Reprinted by permission of Mrs. Chester Seltzer.

"Cecilia Rosas" by "Amado Muro" (Chester Seltzer) first appeared in the *New Mexico Quarterly* (Winter 1964–65). Copyright © 1964 by Mrs. Chester Seltzer. Reprinted by permission of Mrs. Chester Seltzer.

"Ramon El Conejo" by Natalie Petesch. Copyright © 1974 by the University of Iowa Press. Reprinted from *After the*

First Death There Is No Other by Natalie Petesch by permission of the University of Iowa Press.

"The Judge" by Mary Gray Hughes. Copyright © 1972 by the University of Illinois Press. Reprinted by permission of the University of Illinois Press.

"The Somebody" by "Danny Santiago" (Daniel James). Copyright © 1971 by Danny Santiago. Reprinted by permission of Brandt & Brandt Literary Agents.

"The Circuit" by Francisco Jimenez first appeared in the *Arizona Quarterly* (Autumn, 1973). Copyright © 1973 by Francisco Jimenez. Reprinted by permission of the author.

"In the Pit with Bruno Cano" by Rolando Hinojosa-Smith. Copyright © 1973 by Rolando Hinojosa-Smith. Reprinted from *Estampas del Valle y Otras Obras* by permission of the author.

"The Wetback" by Ron Arias. Copyright © 1975 by Ron Arias. Reprinted by permission of the author.

"Geraldo No Last Name" by Sandra Cisneros. Copyright © 1991 by Sandra Cisneros. Reprinted from *The House on Mango Street* by permission of Susan Bergholz Literary Services.

"Ricardo's War" by Hugo Martinez-Serros. Copyright © 1985 by Arte Publico Press. Reprinted by permission of Arte Publico Press.

"The Pilgrim" by Estela Portilla. Copyright © 1985 by Estela Portilla. Reprinted from *Trini* by permission of the author.

"The Village" by Estella Portillo. Copyright © 1989 by Estela Portillo. Reprinted by permission of the author.

"The Apparition" by Lionel G. Garcia. Copyright © 1988 by Arte Publico Press. Reprinted by permission of Arte Publico Press.

"Vic Damone's Music" by Dagoberto Gilb first appeared in the *Fiction Network Magazine* (Fall–Winter 1987–88). Copyright © 1987 by Dagoberto Gilb. Reprinted by permission of the author.